River Rule

Ameeta Davis

Published by Ameeta Davis. Contact ameetadavis@ameetadavis.com
First published in UK in 2017.

Text Copyright ©Ameeta Davis 2017

The right of Ameeta Davis to be identified as the Author of this Work
has been asserted by her in accordance with the
Copyright,Designs, and Patents Act 1988

ISBN: 978-1-9998928-2-1

Author's website is www.ameetadavis.com

ACKNOWLEDGEMENTS

This book is dedicated to my late father Mr Ram Rup Choudhry.

I would like to thank Miles my husband who used his inheritance from his aunt to pay the bills and therefore gave me three years to write and edit my book. If that was not enough he learnt to typeset and create websites just to propel my dream forward. Without his help, I would never have given up my fulltime employment and dared to dream. (I'm reserving you for the next life too!) This book would not be possible without my editor and new friend Shirley Khan who has provided the finished product and my dearest friend Chris Jones who did the edit for the first and second draft of the book by hand! Both of them believed in me and any my story and have given me the courage to publish my book.

I am indebted to Amanda Carroll of Studio Beam for her generosity to create the beautiful cover and map as a priceless gift. She even helped me realise that my first choice of book title 'Firstborn' would not jump off the shelf in a bookshop and in her free time educated me on the importance of a book cover. I am so thankful and proud of Natasha for drawing the concept art for River Rule and for catching the website reader's imagination.

I am grateful for the feedback I received from my Beta Readers and avid supporters Jill Jones, Michele Blackwood, Jyotsna Sindhi, Deepa Bhartia, Chetna Sultania, Sangita Jaiswal, and Matthew Reddlich. Thank you Shiven Khanna from Doon School for making me rethink the book from a teenager's point of view and realise the importance of a map. Shiven's critique was mature and I believe he will develop into a great author - he is already a published writer at seventeen. I would also like to thank the Doon School teacher, house mistress and friend Stuti Kuthiala for giving 'River Rule' to her class to read and critique in its infancy and especially for introducing me to Shiven.

I would like to thank my unspoken champion, Sonali Sangwan who generously after just meeting me a couple of times supported me with facebook advertising. The following of my fan page is all down to her.

From the bottom of my heart I would like to thank my parents, Mr Ram Rup Choudhry and Sumitra Choudhry for enriching my life by sending me and my sister to India and for encouraging me in this venture. I would like to thank my sister Rekha Balwada, my brother-in-law Russell Davis, and my children Ashley and Natasha for all the pep talks and encouragement they have given. Rekha keep those forecasts going! I would also like to thank my brother, Ranjeev Choudhry for believing in my writing skills enough to write a self-development book with me. A big thank you, to my Welham Girls High School batch '86 friends, who cheered me on to write since I was eleven years old. This is for you girls! We did it!

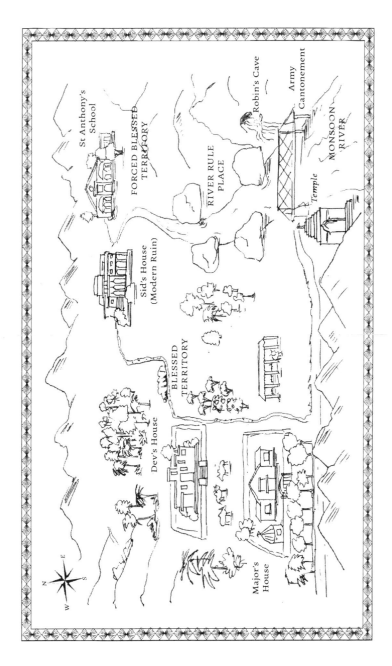

Chapter 1

On the Road from Delhi to Khamosh Valley.

Hanging precariously out of the taxi, with her bottom resting on the rolled down window and her arms folded on the roof, Una was slapped, back and forth, with new senses of extremes. Her endorphin levels ran high as she spun on her hair-raising ride, on the jam-packed merry-go-round called India.

She had barely finished pulling faces in the reflective windows of a tall glass showroom, that starkly sat between crumbling single-storey buildings, when her sixth sense dragged her back. She'd narrowly missed being smacked in the face by a pair of buxom breasts that belonged to a Bollywood star on a ten-foot billboard, promoting the latest swimwear – no, she was selling juice.

Miles and miles of static, squatted human forms, with no obvious purpose, littered the roads and puzzled Una. Why were there no police to move them on? Back in Manchester, the police always honed in on stationary groups of youths. That's pretty much why she was on this journey. Dad hadn't been pleased when she and her two friends, Luke and Charlotte, 'Charlie', were 'cajoled' into a police van for a short ride to meet the rest of the constabulary at the 'Nick'. Apparently, there had been repeated reports of them standing 'aimlessly' outside some empty warehouses along the Manchester Canal. Luckily, nothing had been found on them.

Una perused the traffic. Her taxi, a Toyota Land Cruiser, shared the carousel with a spectrum of bewildering vehicles. For the last hour, they'd been following a gaudy-painted truck that cheekily advised other drivers to expect a spray of black fumes if they dared to sound their horns in frustration – the driver had road hogging tendencies. Una was tempted, but the sullen expression on the taxi driver's face put her off. Swinging her attention back to the traffic, she swore out loud, "Oh, f***!" as a rickshaw carrying an unusual cargo ... a Samsung fridge ... careered towards her. Una squirmed, swung her body back onto her seat behind the driver, and closed her eyes. She didn't have time to withdraw her arm, which was left hovering over the rim of her open window. The moment passed without incident; nonetheless, she retracted her precariously placed appendage and folded her arms. Body parts weren't safe out there. Three-wheeler scooters dangerously passed in all directions, even diagonally, to make a point.

And then the taxi came to a grinding halt.

"Holy cow!" Una screamed.

"Una, what did I say about swearing in company other than your friends?"

"No seriously, Dad, holy cow." Una pointed to a cow with the longest horns, standing amidst the traffic. Travel shows on TV had prepared her for this. Yet, it really was awesomely absurd to come across an indifferent cow, with a big red vermillion powdered 'U' on its forehead. Una pressed her palms together and bowed to it.

The cow wasn't the only animal on the road. Stray dogs and rhesus monkeys hovered along the edges of the traffic, feasting on the edible franchise of the Indian sweet hawker, who was too busy gawping at her face. His attention was interrupted when mayhem broke out in the group. The monkeys had begun to rumble and screech loudly. A flying, white and black furry-faced langur, with a three-lined scar across one of its cheeks, had pounced in the middle of their group with the largest whoop. Una expected a fight, but no, the rhesus monkey troop dropped their food and scarpered! Stunned, Una watched on. Successful in its mission, the langur paused. Instead of picking and eating the Indian sweets, it turned around, gazed at her for a while, then bounded ahead; her own progress impeded by traffic.

"Not much difference between the hawker and the langur then," Una commented. Her Dad didn't acknowledge her. Una wished her Mum had been with her instead. She would've rejoiced in the spectacle of the 'fairground'. Her Mum really loved fairgrounds and candy. Una laughed. Perhaps her Mum was lucky. There were no whiffs of candy at this fairground – instead, wafting spices, fried sugar, open fires, and kerosene, with a hint of manure, thickened the cold air and clogged her nostrils.

Mum would have loved the fair music, too. Amidst the constant honking of horns and people calling out, Mum's guilty pleasure – Guns N' Roses, Paradise City – rocked hard against the latest Bollywood hit number with 'Grass is green and the girls are pretty'. Una giggled, "Mum would have been in heaven ..."

The mention of Mum got his attention.

"Una, for Pete's sake, roll up your window and sit back. What IS the point of paying so much for air conditioning and comfort?"

Glancing away from the window, Una fell back on the cushioned seat backrest and focused on the dull cream interior that surrounded her. Black and white after-images danced off the interior, the after-effect of staring at the sharp lights and bright colours outside. Clamping her eyes shut, she sighed, "Thought you wanted me to experience the real India on my first holiday here? I can't see much through the tinted blue glass, and the drone of that elevator music is driving me crazy. How about a bit of Bollywood to get into the funk of India?" she moaned.

"What about the grime and foul smells drifting in?" Dad rebuked, turning up his nose in disdain.

Grime and foul smells? This from the man who had been born and bred in India. Una wondered whether thirty years of living in Manchester had sanitised all his fond memories. She turned to confront him on his hypocrisy, when she caught the taxi driver staring daggers at her through the rear-view mirror, as though she had broken some contractual rule of 'keeping India' outside the car.

Two against one! Una opened her mouth to protest, but was stumped. Lost in her thoughts about her Mum and Dad, she hadn't realised the taxi was moving again. It had forked off the road and was no longer sitting in traffic, or even in the previous town.

Brr! Una was suddenly freezing. Her t-shirt was poor protection against the cold air rushing through the window as the taxi accelerated up the winding road, away from civilisation.

"Fine ... Okay!" Una glared at the taxi driver, who gave her a triumphant smile in return.

Smug bastard, she thought. Smiling inwardly, she deliberately, and intermittently, pressed her finger on the window control button. The window rolled up painfully slow. Once it was shut, she peered innocently at the driver, expecting him to be furious. Instead, he just leered back and centred his attention somewhere on her body, just below her chin. Her t-shirt was stuck to her. Una glowered. Registering her contempt, he sniggered and returned his roving eye back on her chest.

"Dirty Bugger," she spat out.

Dad threw down the magazine he was reading, flung Una's leather jacket at her, then hurled a tirade of furious Hindi words at the taxi driver. The driver didn't hold back either. He threw back insults; his attention alternating between the road and Dad. Una didn't have to know the language to understand what was being exchanged. The gesticulations towards her body parts were crude enough. What was wrong with the guy? She was wearing her favourite, faded Jimmie Hendrix t-shirt, Levis, and now her worn biker's leather jacket ... How could he see that as provocative? Dad was livid. He tried to unbuckle his seatbelt. Meanwhile, the taxi driver had shifted sideways to reach the glove compartment. His left hand frantically skirted the compartment, looking for something, whilst his right hand remained on the steering wheel. A short gasp left Una's mouth when his fingers settled on an oblong object. He sprung around to face her Dad ... Una sprung forward to grab him ... He elbowed her, flinging her back into her seat ... Distracted, he accidentally shifted his left foot off the brake pedal, whilst pressing down hard on the accelerator with the other.

Una's eyes shot to the windscreen. The taxi was heading for air! Just as her mouth and larynx were working out the mechanism for a scream, a langur, with a distinctive scar across its cheek, appeared from nowhere. He defiantly stood in their vehicle's path, on his hind legs with his leathery palms facing them in a 'stop' gesture. His tail looped forward, above his head. The taxi continued its forward momentum. With a loud cry, the langur extended his long, slender tail vertically and propelled his silver, furry body towards the taxi. His limbs were bent to one side ... ready to deflect the fast-approaching mass!

"Look out!" Una screamed too late.

The driver's attention darted away from her Dad to the windscreen. "HANUMAN!" was the last word she heard him shout out before he swerved the car and hit the scrawny trunk of a pine tree growing on the edge of the cliff. The impact jolted the front of the car, bringing it to a standstill whilst lifting the rear end, before it came back down with a grunt.

The metal grill of the Land Cruiser collapsed and welded itself deep into the tree trunk. Its shiny, silver bonnet rose and crumpled; the windscreen shattered into thousands of crystals. The driver's body was thrown forward at the car's travelling speed. Above the clamour of crumbling metal and the boom of shattered glass, Una distinctly heard the driver's kneecaps snap. In less than ten seconds, from the moment of impact with the tree, it was all over. The sound waves from the continuous beeping of the horn crashed and echoed between the peaks of the cliffs.

Una's own body was leaned forward, her forehead glued to the leather headrest of the driver's seat. Luckily, she had kept her seatbelt fastened, despite the taxi driver repeatedly pointing out the back ones were not yet compulsory in India. Luckily for Dad, he hadn't found the release catch underneath all the newspapers in time.

Unlucky taxi driver.

"Are you alive?"

Una stirred from her shocked state and opened her eyes. When did her father ever speak to her with a thick Indian accent?

"Yes," she replied.

Una glanced over to Dad. His eyes were closed.

"And the person sitting next to you?" asked the male voice from somewhere outside the car.

Una lifted her head awkwardly, unbuckled herself and sidled closer to her father, dreading what she would find. Tentatively, she placed two fingers on his philtrum. Relief flooded in.

"Yes, he's alive."

"What about the driver?"

Una, looked over to the driver's cropped, black head that was slumped forward at an angle on the inflated airbag that pressed down on the horn. His facial muscles were contorted in a primary flaccidity expression of shock. The steering column had impaled his chest; thick, congealed blood trickled from his mouth. Death has its own smell of emptiness and rot. Una was well acquainted with it. Bile rose to her mouth.

"He's dead."

"Sure?"

"Yes."

His lifeless body amplified the chorus of the living around her: her racing heartbeat, her father's faint one, and the heartbeat coming from somewhere close to base of the tree ...

"Where are you?"

"Behind the driver ... where are you?" Una asked warily.

"I'm nearby, but the thing is, I can't get to you. The doors are locked from the inside and the position of the car is precarious. You will have to get yourself and your father out, and quickly, *bacha*."

Frantic seeking between the windows and shattered windscreen did not reveal the position of the man. Instead, it made her feel sick with anger, aggravating her headache.

"Don't waste time looking out the windows for me," the voice reprimanded her. "Just listen carefully."

Una sat with her head between her knees.

The voice carried on. "Just do everything I say, and nothing more. Is that clear?"

"Okay."

"Una, open your father's door, climb over him and get out of the car. Be quick. I don't think the tree is going to hold much longer."

How did he know her name, and that the other passenger was her father? Not even her friends had realised they were related ... she looked Irish, like her Mum, and didn't share any of his Indian features. Rattled, Una unlocked her door. Instantly, gravity pulled half her body over the cliff's edge.

Her upper body hung out precariously as she held on to the chrome handle of the open door, suspended in thin air.

Gulping ... she peered down and gawped at the sheer drop that lay just a foot away from the frame of the taxi. Cool air gushed forward, plastering her arm forcibly to the door panel.

"Slowly and gently shut the door, Una," the voice commanded in a deadly tone.

"I ... c-c-can't."

"Close your eyes. Imagine your right hand holding the handle firmly. Now, pull that hand and the door firmly towards you," the voice spoke authoritatively.

With her heart in her mouth, Una closed her eyes. For the first time in a long time, she followed instructions and concentrated on the feel of the metal handle in her palm. A while later, she heard the clunk of the door as it slammed shut. Only then did she prise her fingers off the metal, one at a time. When all fingers were free, she drew her arms in and cradled her whole body, tightly clasping her upper arms, and tucked her head into her chest. She just about managed to resist rocking.

The voice remained silent.

Una concentrated on her breaths and slowed her heart rate to a normal pace.

"Now, climb over your father, open HIS door and climb out."

She nodded and shuffled her bottom closer to Dad's slumped, unconscious form. Leaning over him, Una unlocked his door and lifted herself over him. Her left foot landed on the floor space between his knees and connected with a metal object. She kicked it under the seat in revulsion. Unlike the first time, Una carefully released his door handle and quickly climbed out of the car.

"What happened?" said Dad, regaining consciousness and clearly alarmed.

"We were in a car accident ... I'll explain later. Right now, we have to get you carefully out of the car, without rocking it."

"What do I do?" For the first time, Dad was asking her for guidance.

"Just put your hands in mine, then gently rotate your lower body sideways and step out."

Dad falteringly placed his hands in her outstretched one. Feet slightly apart where she stood, she pulled him out slowly and gently, staggering slightly under his weight.

The body of the taxi creaked and groaned as they stumbled to the safety of the cliff face, well away from the precipitous edge.

Moments passed in stilled suspense. Both expected the taxi to tip over the cliff at any moment. The wind picked up, as did the sporadic creaking. It was only a matter of time before it would fall. As she leaned back into the limestone wall, the evening's cold wind slashed against Una's cheek and forced the sharp ends of her hair into her eyes, making them water and blink. Holding her midriff against the icy wind, Una studied the perimeter of the car, especially the place where she thought she'd heard a heartbeat earlier.

She found it ... not a heart, but a tail flexing under the taxi's chassis. Ducking down, her eyes travelled from the tail to a furry body, and then to a head turned on its side. Large brown irises stared back at her, with darting red and blue globules.

Chapter 2

How had she missed the blaring sirens and flashing red and blue lights? Had her brain switched off most of her senses so she could cope with escaping death, twice? It was a shame they weren't switched off now. Unsympathetically, the extrasensory commotion had pushed the already excruciating pain in her head several notches higher.

"Stand back with your hands over your heads!" a loudspeaker boomed.

Una complied.

"Sir, put your hands over your head."

Una nervously glanced down to where her Dad was sat. His body was shaking hard, and his arms were stuck to his sides.

"We repeat, put your hands on your head."

Keeping one of her hands on her own head, Una bent down and lifted his hands onto his head. Both his hands shook badly. Una was scared. Not of the sirens, they had stopped as soon as Dad's arms had gone up, but of the imposter standing next to her. Where was her imposing Dad?

The unmarked police car was parked just behind the taxi. Una was struck by how identical the cars were, in terms of colour, model and year. The only thing that differed was the temporary police lights. The two policemen climbing out of the unmarked cars also puzzled Una – both were under twenty-five. Two rookies would never have been paired together back home.

One of the policemen proceeded towards the taxi; the other approached them, halting directly in front of Una – in her personal space. Dad said nothing. Una wanted to, but found it very hard to tear her eyes from his. They were strange. His amber eyes seemed unnatural for someone of Indian descent; they looked unnatural for a human for that matter.

His eyebrow raised and a smile pushed the ends of his mouth upwards. Una looked away, uneasy now. Could he have read her thoughts?

"You can both put your hands down, and perhaps you should sit down, too," he said softly, before turning away and shouting, "Blankets."

Una huddled up with her father against the rock face. The amber-eyed policeman knelt down in front of them and took out a notebook.

"My name is Inspector Rao, and the other fellow is Subridar Mehra. What are your good names?"

Dad barely registered that someone was talking to him, so Una answered on his behalf.

"Una and Vivek Dev."

"Your father has a bruise and cut on his forehead. He must have been hit by something during the accident, which probably explains his concussed state. What about you? Besides being in shock, and the cut on your mouth, are you hurt anywhere else?"

"My head throbs."

"You were lucky if that's all you have ... Ah! The blankets are here."

Not just blankets, but pillows and a flask of hot, spiced tea had arrived, too.

The other policeman muttered, "*Mur Chuka hai* – he's dead."

The inspector nodded.

"We will take your statements at the station. For now, we just need your titles, full names, address and the name of the deceased person in the car."

"Okay. I am Miss Una Dev and this is my father, Mr Vivek

Dev. We are visiting my grandparents at 2 Khamosh Valley. The guy in the front was our taxi driver. His name is ... was ... I'm not sure what it was, but you will find it on his badge." Her voice rattled with nerves.

"Fine, that will do for now. Stay here while we check the car and the driver's ID."

Una was nervous, something was not quite right about the policemen, but she didn't know enough about Indian police to be able to pinpoint what it was. Who became an inspector in their early twenties? He looked to be about the same age as the Subridar, whatever rank that was. Worse than that, she began to fear what they'd think when they found the object under the seat Dad had sat on.

What if they suspected foul play ... by them?

What if they were taken to prison?

Was a sixteen-year-old considered a minor in India?

Una shuddered. She nudged closer to her Dad and grasped his hand – it was limp. Desperately, she rubbed his hand between hers, hoping to stir him out of his dazed state, while all time keeping a beady eye on Inspector Rao and his Subridar, too. They were collecting rocks from the side of the road and placing them in front of the wheels of the taxi. She guessed they were making the car more secure so they could open and enter it.

 Inspector Rao tried to open the passenger's front door, but it was locked. Subridar Mehra opened the rear door where Dad had been sitting and leaned across to release the lock. He carefully opened the door for his superior and then exclaimed, pointing at the open glove compartment.

"What is it?" Una nervously asked.

They must not have heard her. Instead, they huddled over the glove compartment, whispering for some time. Without removing anything from the compartment, they moved on to check the taxi driver's ID badge that was hanging nearby.

They ignored the taxi driver's body. Something was askew.

Even from where she sat, Una could tell that they hadn't given him more than a precursory glance. Infuriatingly, they left his body pressed against the horn, allowing it to carry on honking incessantly. Fine, they couldn't move him, but surely they could have cut off the electrics. Even she knew how to do that. Weirdly, they were quite thorough when searching the passenger seats, windows and the doors, inside and out. They removed all of Una and Dad's belongings from the taxi and arranged them on the ground in a meticulous manner. Then they began searching under the seats.

She was right – they suspected foul play. Any minute now, they were going to find the gun.

Beads of sweat formed on her forehead. Inspector Rao looked over at her, and focused on her hands. She was vigorously rubbing her father's hand – possibly hurting him.

The inspection was over and they moved away from the taxi.

Una's eyes were glued to the handcuffs dangling from Inspector Rao's belt as he strode over to her. She hurriedly released Dad's hand, clasped her wrists together and raised them voluntarily.

"We won't be a moment, Miss Dev. We just need to seal off the area, and then we will be on our way."

Dazed, Una watched him walk past her to his car, and take out cleaning materials.

Una was confused. So much was wrong with what she was seeing. Worrying thoughts competed in her head. Dread seeped through her pores.

Cleaning aside, where was the offensive object? Why hadn't they found it? Or did they have it, and weren't telling her? Was this a trap? Una's headache was worsening with all the questions.

The driver's belongings were left in situ. Yet, their belongings: two suitcases, iPhones, newspapers and other personal parapher-nalia were placed in the unmarked police car in the exact position they had been in the taxi before the crash. Wariness and unease crept through Una. *Who were Inspector Rao and Subridar Mehra? And how did they know where to position every single item? The impact would have tossed the objects from wherever they'd been before the crash.*

Goosebumps prickled over her arms, but she didn't rub them down – she didn't want to draw attention to her edginess.

"We've radioed ahead. The road will be closed until the medical officer examines the body, and forensics examine the car and its contents, and until they move the taxi."

Una nodded. But they won't find anything, will they?

Darkness swarmed Inspector Rao's eyes. "Did you say something, Miss Dev?"

Una shook her head. He studied Una for a moment and watched her squirm where she sat.

Smiling at her, "Let's go then. Before we set off, though, check that we have all of your belongings."

The belongings were all accounted for, but she had forgotten something …

"Wait, there's a monkey – a langur, I think, stuck between the front wheels of the taxi!" As she spoke, she darted to where she'd seen the furry body.

Subridar Mehra ducked down to look. "There's nothing here."

"What?"

Una swung her head below and found … nothing.

Rising, she clocked the policemen searching for something along the horizon. They must have found it because they were both zeroed in on a certain point. Instead of relief, Inspector Rao's lips curled. Interesting. Una quickly ducked down under the car again, not wanting them to know she was watching them closely. They faked interest in the area surrounding the car. Una wasn't fooled. They were hiding something. While they appeared distracted, she squinted in the direction they'd been staring at, and spotted a shadowed body in the distance. Nestled in a cliff, on the other side of the ravine, sat a tiny white temple with an orange flag flying on its spire. She could just about make out the outline of a primate with a very long tail, perched on the spire.

"No monkey here, but there is a large rock and the back wheels have been punctured," Inspector Rao remarked. Una didn't say anything. There was no point.

Instead, she sat in the car and accepted two spiced teas, for Dad and herself.

※※※

Ouch! Una awoke with an excruciating pain in her right elbow. Her vision was filled with a Samsung fridge that was moving away after obviously careering into her taxi door. Her window was rolled down.

"Una, for Pete's sake, how many times do I have to repeat myself? Roll up your window and sit back. What IS the point of paying so much money for air conditioning and comfort?"

Déjà vu? Una was sure he had uttered those very lines a little earlier? Try as hard as she could, she couldn't be certain.

Glancing away from the whirling Indian merry-go-round, Una fell back on the cushioned seat backrest and focused on the dull cream interior surrounding her.

She sighed, "Thought you wanted me to experience the real India on my first holiday here? I can't see much through this tinted blue glass, and the drone of that elevator music is driving me crazy. How about a bit of Bollywood to get into the funk of India?" she moaned.

"What about the grime and foul smells drifting in?" Dad rebuked, turning up his nose in disdain.

Grime and foul smells? And this from the man who'd been born here. Had thirty years of living in Manchester sanitised all his memories? Una turned to confront him on his hypocrisy, but stopped.

Hadn't she just had this conversation with him?

Una was aware of being watched. She caught the taxi driver smiling, knowingly, through the rear-view mirror, as if he had witnessed many a father and daughter squabble. Just like that, her annoyance dissipated. The taxi driver's smile might have disarmed her, but she wondered if he was the same driver. It was a silly notion, but surely she would have picked up on his intriguing amber eyes before.

Staring into driver's eyes, or fiddling with fingers, wasn't going to make the time pass any quicker, so Una reluctantly reached over to read Dad's deconstructed newspaper. Only, it wasn't deconstructed. For some reason, Dad hadn't read the newspaper ... It lay between them, neatly folded, rather than in its expected pulled-out state.

But Dad always read the newspaper first?

Not this time, it seemed. He was immersed in his magazine instead. Una half-heartedly perused the newspaper's front page. The caption 'Teens and why they delve in witchcraft', above the front page main headline, caught her attention. Flipping the page, she turned to page three to read the article, expecting it to be abreast on the page, but found it wasn't. Casting her eyes to the page number, she realised she was on page 11 instead. Una quickly flicked through the other page numbers – the spreads were jumbled. That could only mean her Dad had read the newspaper, then put it back together neatly to fool her? Una doubted it; he had lost his sense of humour when his wife had left them both. She wasn't going to think about Mum, so instead, she peered out of her window, then through her Dad's.

Hadn't she seen this view before?

The scrawny pine tree jutting from the cliff's side seemed familiar.

How was that possible?

She hadn't stepped outside of England before now.

"Should I change the elevator music to some Bollywood, Madam?" the taxi driver asked helpfully. He must have been studying her and mistook her confusion for boredom. Embarrassed, she nodded in response. Rather than Bollywood music, the car stereo blared out the news. She was going to ask him to switch it off, when Khamosh Valley was mentioned.

"Turn it up, please ..."

"Are you sure, madam, it's quite distressing news."

"Yes, turn it up ..."

"Yesterday, around 4 p.m., following an anonymous tip-off,

Khamosh Valley police found a taxi, a Land Cruiser, that had crashed into a tree on the side of a cliff. The coroner's report stated that the driver had died on impact. Luckily, the taxi had not been carrying a fare, so there were no other casualties. The officers at the scene found the glove compartment wide open. Hoping to find a mobile, or other means of contacting the driver's family, they searched through the compartment. Amongst the various paraphernalia, they found duct tape, a box of bullets and several newspaper clippings of murders and rapes that had been committed along the Delhi to Khamosh Valley route. Aware of the severity of their findings, the officers called in forensics, who recovered a gun with the taxi driver's fingerprints on it. The police believe it may have fallen out of the glove compartment when the car hit the tree. More disturbing was the discovery of the signature florescent pink rope, with the rare florescent green stripe running through it, which they found hidden under a blanket in the boot. It matched the description of the rope used in the murders the newspaper clippings covered. So far, forensics have succeeded in matching the rope threads to the ones found around the victims' necks. DNA samples have been taken from the taxi driver's body and will be run against the samples found under some of the victims' nails."

Una turned green. She was desperate to retch, but couldn't help listening to the rest of the story. It went on to report that the deceased driver was now a key suspect in the investigation into the serial killer who, for the last year, had driven unsuspecting tourists to Khamosh Valley from Delhi, on the very same route they were now travelling on. His tactic had been to rob them first, then immobilise them by shooting them several times in the legs, following which, he strangled them. In one case, a young teenage girl had been raped before her ordeal had ended. The killer had disclosed the location of the bodies to the police, through anonymous phone calls. He'd disposed of the bodies in the Yamuna River, except for the last murder, where he'd thrown the girl's body over a cliff. Una looked up at the mirror and caught the driver watching her, waiting for her reaction. "Madam, the villain is dead. You just heard so on the news. I think I will switch it off now."

Una once again nodded in agreement. The suspect was dead and he was not driving her right now ... absolutely nothing was going to happen to her on her way to Grandma's.

"Perhaps Madam would like to finish the spicy Indian tea in the complimentary flask?" Una mouthed a thank you and thought it apt that the golden, sweet syrup-like tea matched the flask owner's eyes.

Chapter 3

Khamosh Valley

"Oh no you don't, Missy. This fake Sleeping Beauty slumber to get me to carry you just won't work – you're over sixteen and a gigantic five feet ten inches tall. You should have stopped growing if you wanted to be carried. Una, get up!"

Una's body remained limp, but Dad wasn't buying it.

"We certainly haven't got time for your shenanigans. So just wake up and get ready." Dad looked at his phone. It was dead. It was a shame that he was too vain to wear glasses, or even ask the taxi driver to tell him the time from the digital clock on the dashboard.

He poked Una instead. In response, she finally shuffled, but then, to his frustration, she curled up tighter.

"Una, for heaven sake, we are only a couple of moments away!"

Una wasn't faking it this time. She really was sleeping ... she was ... she thought she was ... and that was the same thing, right? She was in that place where, if her Dad would just stop shoving ... she would instantly fall asleep; a deep sleep ... snoring, in fact. She knew she was too tall to be carried, but she didn't want to face the dogged feeling that something was amiss with her memory or the surroundings. Somewhere, niggling in her foggy mind, was the idea that if she woke up properly she would no longer feel protected, not even by her Dad!

"Do you want me to help, Sir?"

Una's eyes shot open. It was pitch black everywhere. The taxi driver was driving on the winding cliff road, with just the beam from the taxi's headlights to guide him – there was no other source of light. Even the moon was absent. If that wasn't scary enough, he suddenly steered the car left. The next thing Una knew, they were stumbling down a very steep inclination! Jerking about and almost bouncing off their seats once or twice, Una and her Dad grabbed the edges of their seats' leather upholstery for dear life as the suspension hiccupped over the uneven surface under the wheels.

The rubble better not puncture the wheels of the car again, was her main thought.

Why again?

When had they punctured the taxi's wheels before?

Her mind was playing tricks again ...

The driver pressed on the brakes hard as the taxi rattled down the slope, but all that did was reduce the speed of their free fall.

Slam! The taxi's wheels finally hit the flat surface at the bottom of the valley. Both Una and her Dad let out breaths they didn't realise they were holding. The Land Cruiser trundled on for a few yards before it stopped just outside high walls and double gates. They had arrived at the correct address – Number 2, Khamosh Valley – alive.

Both Una and her Dad yanked their doors open in unison, not wishing to remain in the car any longer. Side-by-side, they stood in front of a fortress. In the light thrown by the Land Cruiser's headlights, the outlined towering walls and double gates, with their intricate grill framework and large crescent latch, seemed formidable. The taxi driver forcibly coughed. Dad took the hint and reached for the latch at the top of the gates. The gates rattled, but remained firmly closed. Helpfully, using his torch, the taxi driver reached over the gates to discover they were padlocked on the other side.

"There must be an intercom?"

They couldn't find one. Exasperated, Dad rattled the gates

hard, hoping to attract the household's attention. Although the lights in the house did not turn on, he'd certainly managed to get attention. Pounding feet raced over the gravel towards them. Snap! Jaws of a canine. Razor sharp teeth snapped shut just millimetres from Dad's hastily retrieved fingers. Undeterred by the metal gate, the aggressor attempted to press his mongrel head between the grills repeatedly, baring his teeth while growling and snarling alternately. The mutt's frustration mounted when the unwanted visitors refused to leave. To encourage them, he jumped high and lobbed his body repeatedly at the gate, while barking ferociously without breath or pause. Finally, in all the commotion, a single flickering light emerged in a window, an inner door opened and a shadow appeared. The outer meshed door remained close.

"*Jo bhi ho! Jao! Kal Aana!* – Whoever you are, go away! Come back tomorrow, if you must," a gravelly voice barked.

"*Pitah Ji, Vivek hai!* – It's Vivek," Dad shouted over the barking of both man and dog.

"Vivek? Tommy, QUIET!" Suddenly the barking came to an abrupt end.

Relieved her Grandad recognised Dad, Una began to take her suitcase out of the taxi's boot.

"You were meant to be here a day ago," her Grandad yelled.

A day ago! Una thought.

"Pitah Ji, I was meant to arrive here now. Just open the gate – I've got Una here with me, too. Come on, Pitah Ji, it's been a long day. First a nine-hour flight from London and then a six-hour car journey here. We are tired and we are here, so let us in."

Una lugged her suitcase to the gate and noticed Tommy, the dog, staring at her, not aggressively but kindly.

"No, Vivek, we can't do that ... We explained why ... These gates CANNOT be opened before dawn tomorrow."

"But, Father, you requested our visit, and we are here now," Dad stressed his last words.

"We told you to come in the hours before twilight ... yesterday."

"Dad, how can he think we should have been here yesterday?

We rang him from the airport this morning, didn't we? Forget the day, according to the news, the serial killer was in these parts until recently. Surely, Grandad can't be serious about keeping us out here?"

"Ssh, Una, you are not helping!" Dad uttered between gritted teeth.

"Pitah Ji, this is not the time to play your games ..." Dad shouted, deeply frustrated.

"Games?" her Grandfather scorned. "Games? ... The jungle behind you is not a game, and nor is the curfew. We are not protected at night, and we certainly don't open gates and break pacts. Then there's the W ... Go and come back tomorrow."

THE JUNGLE BEHIND ... NOT PROTECTED! Una spun her head around and stared into the blackness of the night that lay beyond the little pool of torchlight. Nothing was distinguishable except for the taxi driver's pupils that shone like light globules.

Una shivered. It had to be her imagination. Only certain animals had night vision ...

"But surely if we close and lock it as soon as we are in ...?" Dad pleaded.

"You are not listening ... even opening it an inch is dangerous. Anyhow, I can't stay up all night arguing with you. I see you have not changed. You're just as stubborn as you were before. You didn't listen then when you married that Feranghi, and you don't seem to want to listen now about what's good for you ..."

That Feranghi? Who was he calling Feranghi? Una was about to shout out, but Dad grabbed her hand tight. She stalled.

"Vivek, if you want to come in, then you are going to have to climb over the gates. If you have any sense, you will take heed and stay overnight at a hotel in the town. The choice is yours."

Was Grandad soft in the head, as well as a bastard? Of course, he had to open the gates – the spikes at the top would rip their skins if they tried to climb over.

Una nervously contemplated climbing the walls. They were no better. If anything, they were too steep and were headed with spikes, too.

Dad turned to the taxi driver, "Do you think you could drive us to a hotel at this time of night? I'll pay you double ..."

The taxi driver emphatically shook his head, opened the boot and removed their luggage from the taxi. "There will be no hotels free. The old man will be knowing this, for sure."

"Why?" asked her Dad.

"You see, the boarding schools open tomorrow and the boarders' parents, without fail, book all the hotels. It's so bad, Sir, the schools here. They have to stagger their opening and closing dates due to the shortage of hotels."

"Pitah Ji, the driver says ..."

"Are you going to climb the gate, or can I go back to sleep?" interrupted the bad-tempered old man, shouting from the safety of his house.

Una was gobsmacked. She had to hear it to believe it. No one in Manchester would believe her if she told them about the great welcome they'd received so far.

Dad turned to the taxi driver to plea one last time, but he just shook his head and made his way to the taxi. Dad darted ahead of him, obstructed the driver's door with his body and grabbed the taxi driver's arm with both hands in a desperate gesture.

"Please, just get us over the gate, and then I will give you the money and you can go."

The taxi driver remained silent.

"Look, you don't have to do much – just keep the headlights on so we can see," Una pleaded.

The taxi driver looked over at Una, then brushed Dad's arm off and made his way to the gate. Una sighed gratefully.

"What are you going to do about the dog?" the driver asked Dad tersely. Dad didn't respond.

All this time, the dog had been quiet, but that didn't mean it wasn't ready to pounce once their legs were dangling on the other side.

"Pitah Ji, we are going to climb the gate, call off your dog," shouted Dad.

"Tommy, come! Tommy, come!" Her grandfather shouted, with no conviction whatsoever. Tommy, unsurprisingly, remained put.

"Sorry, Vivek, Tommy's new and doesn't heed all commands yet. Come back tomorrow morning, this gate is not opening until then."

"Father, just open the gate ..." Dad's words tapered off as his old man slammed the wooden door and the candlelight disappeared.

"Dad, don't say anything, just be very quiet while I try something."

Dad turned to her, ready to protest but stopped. Una was close to the dog by the gate's grills, and was whispering, "Good boy, Tommy, good boy."

Much to Dad's surprise, Tommy whimpered softly.

Una didn't have a dog, but she took that to be a good sign. Nervously, she crouched closer to the gate. Tommy scuffled closer towards her. Once he was nearby, Una patted her leg. He came even closer and reached his paw through the gate's grill and placed it on her lap.

Una didn't flinch.

"Handshake? Hmm," whispered Una in a very calm voice as she daringly picked up his paw and shook it lightly. Tommy nosed closer, holding his ears back slightly and his tail slightly off the ground, then made a wide sweeping wag. Next, he tried to put his snout through the grill, but failed. Dad took a deep sigh – prematurely. Una recklessly put her hand through the grill. Tommy moved in for the kill and licked her. Una didn't think it was possible for him to get closer, yet he managed. He shifted on his bottom until he was comfortable, whilst maintaining eye contact with her. Una ventured her hand further, much further, until she could reach under his ears and neck and stroke him. Tommy beat his tail against the gravel on the other side.

The taxi driver cleared his throat again. Una nodded. Tommy

growled. She gave Tommy one last pat, stood up and, without a word, began to climb the gate.

Just as she placed her foot onto the grill, Tommy intuitively gave her space by moving back a few paces. Unperturbed by her progress up the gate, he lay on his tummy, placed his head on his front paws and gave a little whine.

Lucky for Una, the grill apertures were large enough for her to get a foothold on. Once she was at the pen-ultimate grill, her luck ran out. The spikes were lethal and would most certainly lance her skin through her favourite jeans or, even worse, do serious damage if she miscalculated the height of the spike while raising her crotch over it. Dad was too unfit to climb over.

Oh, he so owed her ...

Silently thanking the taxi driver as he shone his torch precisely over the spear heads, in slow motion, she lifted her leg over the spikes and brought it down the other side. Levis intact, she nimbly slid down the other side to the padlocks. Halfway down the gate she whispered, "Headlights off, please."

The taxi driver handed the torch to Dad and went over to the taxi to switch off the lights. In the torchlight, Una could tell Dad was totally flummoxed.

"Someone pass the suitcases and the rest of the stuff."

The taxi driver complied by lifting them high and over the gate. She used her head to help balance as she lowered them down. Cocking an ear, Tommy wandered over to smell the suit-cases. Disappointed, he moved back to his sitting position and rested his head over his forelegs once again.

"Now, Dad, I am going to unlock the padlock, and you are going to unlatch the gate from the top, quietly. First, I need someone to shine a light over the padlock."

Dad's face registered several emotions – none of them good. This was the first time he would witness her 'break and entry' skills, and he clearly wasn't happy about that. His eyes were glued on her. Una nimbly stepped down onto the ground and released one of the larger hairpins holding up her hair, snapped it in two at the bend, bent one straight end at ninety degrees, then bent it again two-thirds of the way down for leverage. Cheekily winking at Dad, she pulled a smaller and thinner pin from the back of her head, snapped it in half and put the straight half in her mouth. Dad's frown looked fixed on his face. Tools a-ready, Una positioned the larger bent pin in the bottom part of the lock and applied some pressure. Under her father's gaze, she coolly took the thinner one out of her mouth, placed it in the top hole and wiggled it about.

Dad's thunderous expression spurred her to voice what she was doing. "Just a little more tension on the bottom and ..."

CLICK!

Dad gawped at her. "That explains the missing bottles of vodka and gin?"

"Pick up your jaw from the ground, Dad, and pass me the torch."

Without a single word, he complied and unlatched the gate. After slinking through the open gates, he brought them back together and reapplied the latch. Una, in turn, snapped the padlock to locked position, passed the torch back to Dad and walked quickly over to Tommy.

All this time, Tommy had been quiet. However, as soon as her Dad started walking towards the house, he rose quickly and began to make low growling sounds, whist baring his gnashes at Dad again.

"Hey, Tommy, this is my Dad. He's your owner's son." She was kneeling by his side again and carried on quietly talking to him as she stroked him under the collar. Dad made his way to his father's veranda and then stopped abruptly, "Wait! I've got to return the torch and pay the driver."

They both turned to face the gate. The taxi and its driver had vanished.

"How is it that we didn't hear the car door, the engine starting, or even the wheels reversing on the gravel?" Una asked incredulously.

She didn't expect a reply, and wasn't given one.

Tommy began to bark; Una also sensed a presence at the gate but couldn't see anything. Tommy moved closer to the gate, cocked his ears and then lifted his canine head. Like his ancestors of old, he let out a mournful howl. A huskier and longer howl resonated in answer through the chilly evening air, forcefully parting the clouds away from the moon. Bewitched, Una stared up at the moon. When she brought her gaze down to where she thought she'd heard the mysterious howl, two glowing eyes met hers.

"Get in, both of you! Quick ... before it thinks of joining us!" an outraged voice growled from behind them. Una hurried up the steps and, for the first time in her life, stood face to face with her Grandad, separated only by a screen door. He stepped back and allowed them in.

Tommy sniffed at the gate. Using his paw, he dragged an object from under it – the taxi driver's ID badge.

Chapter 4

"It is a shame that this year will be remembered for the series of murders committed in and around Khamosh Valley. It's going to take forever, if ever, to forget the atrocities." Avi half sat up from his lying position. "Shit, man, how lucky was Dev's son to travel a day later than he was supposed to from Delhi, In fact, how lucky are you that they ignored your booking the day earlier. It was on the radio just now that the killer worked for the same taxi firm as the one you booked on behalf of Dev."

Meeru put out her cheap tobacco rollup to the side of the bed, on the marble floor.

"Seriously, Meeru, don't fowl your mouth with that junk when you can equip it with Benson & Hedges, the top-notch cigarettes!" Meeru pointed her chin upwards, raised her eyebrows, making her eyes appear larger, and gesticulated towards Avi. "What Benson & Hedges cigarettes? What are you talking about?"

"You know we're going to Dev's house later, right?"

"Yeah?" Meeru shuffled on the bed to make herself more comfortable.

"Well," Avi propped himself up, "I bet the snobby London NRI, like all Newly Recreated Idiots, will come loaded with glittering golden boxes of Benson & Hedges jewels. They'll pretend to take pity on us poor tobacco smokers by giving us a few fags." The last few words were muttered as Avi distractedly bent over the bed's edge to pick something up.

Before he could even put it in his mouth, Meeru flicked it from between his fingers. "Brat! How is it that the rollup is still good enough for you, huh? And what's this 'us' business, anyway?"

Avi smiled sheepishly.

"Don't think YOU can smoke this shit just because I sometimes deem your room fit for my bad habit."

"What, Auntie dearest! You've been smoking since you were 15 and I'm nearly 18 – a little too late to lecture, hmm!" Avi pretended to be upset, but couldn't stop his tell-tale dimples from appearing.

Meeru shrugged her shoulders and stretched out her arms to her sides. Feathering her fingers lightly over the corner of his pillow, she stole it from behind him, deliberately fussing and puffing it up before laying it back on the bed. Dramatically sighing, she said, "Ah ... actually, I was eleven when I began smoking AND, whilst I now admit it's a stupid habit, one that started off as two fingers up to the establishment at home, it's pretty neat to think that I'm in my early twenties and still not been caught." Meeru hammed up her statement by doing the typical sassy, slow snake-like nodding that R&B singers seemed to favour.

Nonplussed, Avi folded his arms behind his head and leaned back.

"God, you're irksome!" Meeru muttered under her breath. She had expected him to retaliate. Suddenly she jerked forward and spurted, "And another thing – STOP CALLING ME AUNTIE DEAREST!"

"Knew you would react!" Avi chuckled and, with gecko-like speed, quickly retrieved the pillow and placed it behind him, before retorting innocently, "But you are my aunty."

He deserved a punch for that and he got one.

"You only get to call me Auntie because of my annoying oldest brother – your Papa, because he wanted to get laid without constantly getting into trouble with his parents. To achieve this, he joined the army. Then, after all of ... TWO MINUTES, he dramatically announced that he was posted somewhere dangerous and might not come back from the war."

"Which war?" Avi liked hearing about his mostly absent father.

"I was barely five, how would I know ...? Anyhow, my parents bought his soppy story. Mostly because they couldn't pass up the opportunity of another heir, even though they had five spare sons in the wings."

"But he could have been posted somewhere dangerous, and there was the possibility that he might not return?"

"Yeah, and your point is?"

"You said he was posted somewhere dangerous ... So, why would he want to leave a widow behind? Dadi should have stopped him, knowing how widows are treated, and being a woman and all that."

"What? No. If their precious son died, they still had an ideal scapegoat and a readymade servant, plus Dadi would have the chance to scream ..." Meeru put her hands up to the ceiling and mimicked her mother's voice, "This devil of a girl brought bad luck to her husband, my son. She cast an evil spell on him ..."

Meeru grabbed hold of Avi's cheeks, pinched them and cooed, "But all that pain would be worth it, they would have a cute grandson ..."

"As if!" interrupted Avi, slapping her hands away.

"Okay, not cute then. Let me finish the story ... So, days before your Papa's posting, a temporary structure, draped with marigold flowers, was strutted. Literally, the first available girl of age was tied to him as he took seven rounds of the fire. A splattering of sickly ROMANCE during his leave periods and a year later, Wham Bam, Thank You, Ma'am! You and your twin, Gag, were born!"

Holding both palms upwards, wearing an exaggerated face of anguish, Meeru woefully wailed, "I was made an aunt at six! Not once, but twice over! Gross! Double Gross."

"Ha, ha ... very droll," laughed Avi. "You had it easy, I tell you."

"And how did you work that out?"

"Quite easily. If we were born girls, what do you think would have happened then? Ma and Papa would have kept trying for a boy, and ten children later they still might not have succeeded. Count your lucky stars you were spared the extra-sugary sweet romancing for trying for a second child or a third, fourth, fifth ..."

The colour drained from Meeru's face.

"It just wouldn't happen in this family," Meeru spoke softly.

Avi looked bewildered at the change of tempo in his aunt's usually feisty stance.

"Meeru, you were born a girl. Whilst most might doubt it in this house, as you are just as feisty and mean as the rest of us, you're definitely a girl according to all the guys at PTI College. Have you forgotten?"

She smirked and brightened up, looking more like her usual self.

"Poor guys regretted not knowing about the six brothers who came before you. Jay alleges that one of the guys is still learning how to walk again."

"Yeah, and whose fault is that?" Meeru asked accusingly.

"Mine?" Avi quizzed meekly. It had been Avi's fault, and he knew it. In all innocence, he had asked the younger of his twin uncles what 'a sick chick' was? When they asked Avi why he wanted to know, he let slip that his best friend, Jay, who happened to be visiting that day, said his brother thought Meeru was the most desirable sick chick. Uh Oh! What an idiot! Moments later, he and Jay were whisked over to PTI College by his uncles. Under duress and much heavy handling, Jay pointed out his brother and his entourage, who were practising in the outdoor basketball courts, and then ... WHAM! Avi's uncles wrestled the players to the ground, leaving a cloud of dust with mangled bodies amidst it. They looked askance at Jay. Avi wanted to save his friend, but at the same time, he couldn't be seen to be doing nothing. With some compunction, he grabbed hold of Jay, winked at him and then punched him in the stomach. Jay had many layers of fat in comparison to his aggressor, who was lean. However, familiar with the drill, Jay keeled over and seemingly rolled about in pure agony, keeping well away from the uncles' feet. Avi remembered how relieved he was that his mate had been so convincing. Any suspicions that he was play-acting, and Avi would have been used as a human punch bag for real when he got home. Avi's uncles hated weakness and, to put it mildly, were always looking for an excuse to rough him up.

Both aunt and nephew pondered over the incident in their heads.

"Have you ever wondered why all your cousins are male?" Meeru asked, coming out of her daydream state first. The sadness in her voice made Avi stare at his aunt again.

"No? Why would I? They're a bunch of losers, and that includes my own twin brother."

Meeru tutted.

"THEY REALLY ARE! If they were of any worth, they would be able to hack it at school like me, without terrorising the other pupils. Luckily for the school, they're hardly ever there."

"Never mind. Because of your nerdy gene pool, we get to meet the English dignitaries." Meeru ruffled Avi's head.

"Yes, AUNTIE DEAR!"

A pillow was demolished in response. Between the feathers, Avi wondered what Meeru meant by English dignitaries. Surely only one came from England. His thoughts were interrupted by Dada, his grandfather, as he hollered for the two of them to present themselves to him. Even in retirement, Dada retained his Major army role.

Chapter 5

They were too late. The Benson & Hedges boxes had been placed behind locked glass doors, in an otherwise bare wall cabinet in the drawing room, for all to see.

But, as it happened, no one noticed them on that day. For when Avi opened the tall gates of Dev's property, he came to an abrupt stop. Major, who was walking behind him, stumbled against him, and Meeru paused in time to prevent a pile up.

"*Bavekoof!* – Idiot! Buffoon! Why have you stopped? Get in, boy; no one is going to eat you." Major tried to look past his grandson, but Avi was too tall and the gate had not yet opened properly. Major began to push Avi aside when he remembered Tommy – Dev's vicious dog.

"Is the dog, Tommy, there? Is that it?" Major whispered in Avi's left ear, gently prodding his grandson's left shoulder forward, which just rebounded. Avi remained silent, his gaze fixed on a point ahead of him.

Unfortunately for all, Tommy's ears pricked up with the mention of his name and prematurely woke him up from his afternoon slumber on Dev's roof. Much to Major's horror, a snout and paws appeared on the roof's low wall, and Tommy's famous continuous barking loop began. Dev popped up from behind Tommy and held him by the scruff of his neck. Without looking down, he shouted, "Come in, Major. I've tied Tommy upstairs. Don't worry."

"Lock the roof door this time!" bellowed Major.

When Dev appeared on his veranda a few moments later, he glanced at the empty cane chairs and was surprised to find all three of his visitors still at the gate. Following Avi's gaze, he zoomed in on his granddaughter, who in turn was sitting on the veranda's marble steps, glaring at the vagrant.

"At least she has taste, if not manners," he muttered.

"Major, I see you have spotted my granddaughter, Una."

Dev enjoyed the stunned expressions of his neighbours. "Don't hang around at the gate, please do come in, but be forewarned ..." Pointing at the girl, he emphasised, "... this one can be more ferocious than Tommy, our dog!"

Una was offended. "In that case, Grandad, I ought to go and join him." And just like that, in front of his guests, she leapt from the side of the veranda, ignoring the steps, and charged to the back of the house.

Spell broken, Avi stumbled back into his grandfather, who grunted in displeasure and walked past him to go and sit with Dev on the veranda.

Meeru chuckled. "A little love-struck, aren't we?"

"Love-struck? No, I just wasn't expecting a girl to be sitting on Dev's step."

"Figures, but you were gawking at her in a pitiful and desperate way."

"How would you know? You were behind me."

Of course, Meeru was right ... He'd taken one step into Dev's property when his attention was pulled to her; her gaze had held him to the spot. His chest had risen and fallen with each gasping breath, until the girl dropped her eyes from his and did the unthinkable, at least for an Indian girl – she'd slowly looked him up and down, studying him like his friends at high school would have checked out a girl. His breathing became ragged, and wild fire spread through his body. Her slow perusal tightened the body area between his jeans-clad thighs, especially when she hesitated momentarily on his lips, before travelling and settling back on his eyes.

"*What's up, pretty boy?*" He didn't see her mouth moving, but knew for sure the words were hers.

Stupidly, he smiled – dimples and all. Big mistake. Rather than having the expected response of a corresponding smile, she glared at him with total loathing, as if he was SATAN! Her unexpected response completely floored him.

"Let's go and find her. She might improve her mind and English temperament when she gets to know us." When he still didn't move, Meeru sniggered, "Come on, lover boy!"

Grabbing his hand, she set off to the back of the house to find the rude girl. An English accent from the roof indicated she was there with the wretched dog.

Already halfway up the stairs, just inside the back entrance of the house, Meeru did a double take. Avi noticed it, too. Mrs Dev's usually-locked fridge was wide open. Before Avi could protest, Meeru sneaked back down again and motioned for him to stand behind her. Dev's grumpy wife was shouting at her servant for something innocuous, giving Meeru ample opportunity to extend her arms once, twice, even three times, back and forth between the fridge and Avi's grasp. She took three coke bottles from the open fridge, unnoticed. All the while, Dev's wife held the fridge door agape with her own big hand, aiding and abetting her own loss. Mission accomplished, the thieves tiptoed up the stairs and didn't breathe until they were on the other side of the roof door.

"Anyone who can get anything from that witch downstairs is a genius," said Una, poking her head from behind the water tank.

Meeru smiled conspiratorially. "It's a bit early for you to have figured that out – how did you find out?"

"I asked her for some hairpins earlier, and she got then from a locked safe."

Meeru laughed. "You know she will expect you to return them after you've used them."

"She's welcome to them, but they won't be in one piece by the time I've finished unlocking the safe she got them from," thought Una

Unlocking the safe? Avi's hand stilled as he held a coke bottle against the roof door. He felt Una's eyes on him and quickly relaxed his grip.

"What's wrong, pretty boy, can't open a bottle?" Avi turned to meet Una's quizzical eyes. Pretty boy? Oh man, she had used that brat terminology earlier when she was giving him the once over. He had been too shocked by her behaviour to notice that she hadn't actually spoken those words. But now, he heard her thoughts again. Avi felt sick. Is this another change? If so, why can no one else hear her? And then only some of her thoughts? Staring at her, Avi addressed his next thought to her. Can you hear my thoughts, Miss English?

There was no reaction.

Shaken, Avi returned his attention to using the leverage of the heavy teak roof door to pop the bottles open. Just as he handed two of them to Meeru, they both picked up on a movement behind the tank. Meeru and Avi peeked around. Tommy was squirming with joy on his back while Una tickled his tummy!

"He lets you do that?" asked Meeru nervously as she approached the domestic scene.

"Hmm ... yeah ... he doesn't respond to my grandparents, his owners, but he lets the house servant, Johnnie Walker, and I do it. Bizarre right? I've only been here for a day."

"Yeah ... strange." Meeru was lost in her thoughts.

"It's a relief to meet people who speak English fluently. The dragon downstairs just roars inaudible stuff, or scowls and gesticulates madly at me." Una paused and pointed to Avi whilst looking at Meeru. "I am right in assuming that that thing standing next to you speaks English, too?"

Avi's lips curved into a small smirk. He was in deep trouble. Una's acerbic tongue was just too delicious. She didn't hold back when offering her opinion about her nearest and dearest, or complete strangers for that matter. She sure was worth getting to know, but how? He didn't have much experience with girls, and this one was not any girl.

Meeru handed Una a bottle of coke, then sat cross-legged at a slight distance, watching Tommy all the time. Avi stood where he was, noisily swigging his coke, looking every which way but not at what he wanted to look at, just in case SHE set the dog on him.

"That dragon?" Meeru was still stuck on the term. She glanced at Avi for help, he pointed downstairs, "Ah! You mean your grandmother."

"Yeah her, she just scowls and nods her head in answer to anything I say. I don't get the feeling she likes me at all."

"I can't imagine why ..." muttered Avi under his breath.

Meeru kicked his foot.

"She's your grandmother. Of course she likes you."

Una didn't respond. She was fascinated by Meeru's method of drinking coke. She held the mouth of the bottle a distance from her mouth, avoiding the rim of the bottle, and let the drink pour in. Una watched in fascination at her accuracy, as did Tommy, who would have preferred her to miss.

"If you're sleeping in the house, she likes you," said Meeru wiping her mouth.

Una turned to Meeru, confused. "Meaning?"

"Meaning, you would be sleeping in the servants' quarters if she didn't like you. She makes her own brother stay there when-ever he comes to visit, because he empties the fridge of its goodies too readily."

"If they have servant quarters why doesn't Johnnie Walker sleep in the garage?"

"The servants' quarters are deemed too good for servants."

"Really? She's that bad? ... So how come she let you empty her fridge of cokes ..." Meeru raised a single eyebrow. "Oh, you stole them!" Una began to laugh.

Avi and Meeru exchanged conspiring glances.

"That figures! Whenever I ask the dragon for coke, she drags me into the dining room, points to the clock and says 'no Coca Cola'. If I ask why, she just replies in very loud decibels, 'NO

COCA!' It's as if you can only drink coke at a certain time, but what that time is, who knows!"

Avi decided it was time to join the group and squatted on the roof floor.

Tommy growled.

Meeru laughed. "Avi, he's got the measure of you."

Avi poured some of his coke on the floor near him. Tommy happily noticed and, within a split second, made a move. He did a quick roll onto his tummy and pawed forward, commando style, until he was noisily lapping up the coke, all the while keeping an eye on Avi. When he finished slurping up the last drops, he shuffled forward on his paws and placed his head on Avi's lap, and whined for some more.

"Friends, huh?" said Avi stroking the dog's head. "Please to meet you, Tommy. My name is Avi and that is Meeru or Auntie Dearest to you." Both Meeru and Una rolled their eyes. Una was no fool; she'd guessed who the civilities were aimed at. Still, with a nothing ventured, nothing gained, attitude, Avi put his hand forward towards Una and boldly asked, "Your name is?"

Una crossed her arms. "Grandad already introduced us, but you were gormlessly gawking like an idiot at me, which, incidentally, is damn right rude," retorted Una.

Meeru burst into laughter, which resulted in Avi playfully jabbing her in the ribs. Although Una's words were acidic, she was smiling ... smiling at him! If he didn't know it already, he was in deep trouble.

"My name is Una ..." she said and then stopped when, to both Meeru's and his surprise, she accepted Avi's hand. Avi held it longer than was expected and Una let him, despite her initial minute jerk when their fingers made first contact. Avi's chest tightened as he noticed her rising blush. Her eyes bore into him ... She was appraising him anew.

He must be several inches over six feet ...

Avi knew she couldn't hear his thoughts, but was compelled

to comment, "*No big deal in my family, except for Gag, all of us are over six feet.*"

Avi smiled as she continued with her thoughts.

Lighter skinned than Major, but not dark, more tanned. Grey eyes! I'm mixed so I've got green eyes, but do Indians have light eyes, too?

Black hair and so much of it!

Avi dragged his hand through his hair and caught his aunt staring at him, too. Her original bemusement at the silence between the teenagers disappeared, and was replaced with a wistful glance at his hair. They both knew his hair was ready for the shears. His heavy hair was flopping over his forehead and grew past his ears to just above his shoulders. Meeru called it his mane. The rest of the men in the household had army regulation hair. He didn't keep his hair long by choice, it just grew fast. Many a pair of scissors had broken while cutting his hair ... he had even tried hacking at it with a sickle.

Avi signalled to Meeru to break the awkward atmosphere, but she pretended not to understand and looked away. He had to do it himself before he upset Una and gave her a once over, too.

"We knew Uncle Dev's London returned son was meant to come for a visit, but we weren't expecting you," said Avi, hoping it wasn't too lame a conversation.

"London returned?" Una quizzed frowning. "But, we're from Manchester!"

"It's just a term we use, not everyone knows where Manchester is? For instance, this idiot probably thinks England is in London!" Meeru added.

"There's no love lost between you two siblings, is there?" Una chuckled.

Avi would have set her right if she hadn't continued talking. "My father was fed up with my new antics of climbing to high points in abandoned warehouses and factories, and using hairpins in an inventive way. Especially when I caught the attention of the pigs ... sorry the Greater Manchester police. He thought spending time with him and his family, who I had never met before, would help. I think Dad forgot about his mother. She blatantly hates me, and worse still, I think she hates Dad – her only child. Talking about my Dad, I wonder where ..."

Una's words were drowned by an ear-piercing cry. In shock, she grabbed the nearest thing to her – which happened to be Avi. Face turned to one side, she twitched against his chest as she frantically searched for the epicentre of the howl. Avi was confused by her actions, especially as she sounded so tough. *If this was going to scare her, then how was she going to survive?* Thinking about survival ... he was finding it hard to breathe. Her vanilla essence was not helping. Embarrassed, Avi wondered if she could feel his heart beating wildly under hers? Disgusted with his train of thought, considering she was vulnerable, Avi loosened her grip on him and removed her arms from around him. The adults would have removed them from each other's company if they'd seen them.

She gripped him again after the next howl.

"It's just the lone wolf; we have one in these parts," he whispered.

Una raised her head. Her pupils were dilated, forcing her green irises to narrow rings. "Are you sure it isn't a human cry? What about the serial killer taxi driver from yesterday?"

Meeru answered this time. "He's dead ... Wait, how do you rememb ... know about him?"

"It was on the radio in the taxi."

Meeru nodded her head.

Still looking up at Avi, Una asked, "Wolves don't hurt humans, do they? That only happens in fairy tales, right?"

"Right," whispered Avi, trying hard not to unravel with her proximity. Hesitantly, he brushed her hair away from her eyes and ran his hand down her arm and then ...

The Earth and the sky reverberated with a tumultuous uproar.

From the opposite direction of the wolf's howls, from the other side of the jungle, a tremendous commotion erupted. Monkey troops, bears and other beasts filled the air with their cries. Una shuddered and held onto Avi tightly, burrowing deeper into his chest. Avi was disorientated by the human contact. He couldn't help himself. Other than a punch from his uncles or Meeru's administrations when he was ill, he'd never held anyone, let alone stroke their arms to calm them down. Still, he had to focus, and quick. Something was wrong in the jungle ... just like five years ago. His eyes darted to Meeru.

Meeru was frantically scouring the perimeter of the roof, until she leaned into the wall close to the water tank to look out in the distance ... to their backyard.

Avi tensed and shifted. Una broke out of her trance. He was looking for words to reassure her that fear wasn't a weakness in this situation, but he was too late. Her fear had turned into mortification and she violently jerked away. Avi's body reacted as if part of it had been ripped off. A great sense of loss overtook him. *How could such little contact feel so immense, and so much?*

His sense of loss was soon filled with one of dread. Over the barks and whoops from both sides of the jungle, Avi picked up the beginnings of a familiar blood curdling holler. Seconds later, Tommy let out a painful yowl. Una rushed to hold Tommy. One moment she was stroking his head, the next she was rotating her body to face the direction in which Tommy's ears were cocked, to where Meeru had been standing. *God, she was clever.* Admiration for Una's perception was laced with relief – Meeru had already stepped away from there.

Tommy violently shook Una off and positioned himself between Avi and Meeru. Madly wagging his tail, he barked at Avi in short barks and whines, almost as if he was telling him something important. Avi knelt down, which Tommy didn't want. He grabbed onto Avi's blazer sleeve with his jaw, and pulled.

"*Chor kuta!* – Dog! Let go of my sleeve ..."

The canine paid no heed and kept pulling.

Rip! Tommy dropped the sleeve, but did not give up. He head-butted Avi's body towards the direction of the door. The human cries became louder, evoking a reaction from the wolf and the rest of the jungle.

"What does he want?" Una cried.

Avi didn't answer.

"Meeru come down! We are going!" Dada's voice boomed up the stairwell.

Picking up the bottles, Meeru scuttled quickly to the roof door.

"Don't forget to bring your nephew down, too," Dada added.

"What nephew ... surely he doesn't mean Avi? I thought you were joking in your introductions?" said Una, glad to be distracted.

"Sick, na? Una, this is the third world, where a mother, daughter and daughter-in-law can all have babies at the same time, let alone a few years apart," said Meeru as she draped her arms around Una and almost forced her to join her at the stairwell door. "Come, your grandparents will be expecting you downstairs. The curfew has begun."

Tommy's furious scraping at the door hindered Avi's ability to unbolt the roof door. Avi had barely opened it when Tommy flew past him, down the stairs and out the mesh door at the back entrance.

"Stupid *kuta*," Meeru pushed Avi aside and ran down shouting, "*PUKARO!* Someone catch Tommy!" Johnnie Walker came forward, caught Tommy and brought him back in.

"Come on! We need to get down," urged Avi as he captured Una's hand in his own and hurried her down the stairs before she asked more questions. The hitch in her throat let him know that she felt their pounding heartbeats pulsing through their clasped hands, too. On the bottom step, both let go at the same time.

Chapter 6

Avi's body was abuzz, and this time it wasn't due to the screams. At least, he didn't think so. Still, he had to get back to his house quickly, before the sky ... Too late, it had already begun. Like a flick of a switch, the sky turned from sunset to bleak darkness. Clocks meant nothing in the jungle. Avi groaned. Wolf's early howl had cost dusk its turn, and his household trio their self-imposed curfew and safe passage home.

Disquiet slit the throat of his protection, and finally, the bawling anguish once more clutched his senses. This time it was useful and a blessing. The position of the nearing jungle beasts was apparent to him. Their heartbeats were faint, which meant they were still on the other side of the path. If the three of them rushed, they could still use the path safely and make their way to the inside perimeter of their property.

"We don't want your relatives."

Avi tried to block his mind. It wasn't just Una's thoughts, then.

"We just want you!"

Avi hurried to catch up with Dada and Meeru at the gate. In the kerosene beam, Avi locked eyes with Tommy, who was whining and scrapping at the mesh door. Unlike his household dogs, Tommy was not joining in the discordance of the night.

Avi took one step on the path, which coincided with the crescendos of the human wail. Meeru gave him a pitiful look. Dada missed it; he was too busy arranging Avi's and his body so they flanked Meeru on both sides. With one arm looped with Meeru's, Dada walked backwards. Meeru held onto Avi's waist as he faced the jungle boundary and sidled the path. Meeru navigated them ahead, holding the kerosene oil lamp high. Shadow heads projected from the jungle onto the path, but nothing stepped across. Perhaps the shadow created by their linked bodies kept them away. Perhaps not. In the to-ing and fro-ing of the kerosene lamp light, Avi caught sight of the different pairs of nocturnal eyes at varied heights, watching from the foliage. Still, they left them alone. The trio made it to their own gated property unscathed.

Avi's heart was racing fast. The wild animals in the jungle were a worry, but his nemesis was close, too close. This was the first time he was out in the open, in such close proximity to the spine-chilling wails of the creature cooped up in the outbuilding.

His body shuddered violently, trying hard to resist the stronger draw of its cries. His delicate flesh could not protect itself from the pulsations it cased, with his blood close to boiling, leaving him feeling sick and faint. He wasn't the only one who knew the effect they had on him. Meeru had found him on the ground in a feverish and fitful state two months ago. She'd forced him under a cold shower, despite the cold weather, and made him promise he wouldn't share what was happening to him with the others. He could see her point; his fits were like epileptic fits. Epilepsy sufferers were 'possessed', according to his Dadi and uncles' wives. They genuinely believed that beating an epileptic sufferer with a shoe, or asking a tantric sadhu to exorcise them, was the only way to rid the sufferer of their demons.

Avi really needed to get to his room before the others realised his secret.

The screeching was relentless, borne of supernatural ability. Then it suddenly stopped. Released from the cry's control, he quickly sprinted towards the door. Just then, demonic squeals from just a few feet away from him, tore his senses apart, sending his body into paralysis. The creature was out in the open ... a breath away. Dada and Meeru held their hands over their ears.

Unable to move, Avi witnessed the howls amplifying, moving closer to where he stood. They were becoming clearer. The creature was repeatedly calling out ... 'Tar'? The word unlocked his terror. Relieved, he blurted out, "Dada, listen, she's calling out something in particular."

Major yelled, "Avi, stop talking and move!" Avi's body was too clumsy to comply. Misunderstanding Avi's stance, Major bodily shoved Avi against the front door of their house.

"But, Dada, it was an understandable word ..." Avi protested before he felt the knuckles of his grandfather's fist nestle and push him closer into the wood grain.

Major uttered something under his breath, then bellowed, "*Darwaza Kholo!* – Open Up! AgggggHHHH!"

Major leaned into his grandson and daughter's backs, covering them with his body as he continued to yell and knock harder on the door. "OPEN THE DOOR!"

Nothing happened. "Come on, imbeciles! What are you waiting for? Open it before ..."

Pinned to the door, Avi could finally feel the bolt moving on the other side. He yelped when the thud of the falling bolt reverberated through the wood, making him jump. Mysteriously, Avi sensed someone else to his side jump at the same time, someone whose breath he could feel brushing past the hair under his left ear, not the side Meeru was on, but the other. It couldn't be his grandfather because he was pushing his back. With dilated pupils, Avi nervously peeked sideways, then past Major's shoulder.

"Dada, did you feel that?"

Any possible answer was interrupted by the heavy teak door falling open and Chaz's hands pulling him in backwards by his scuff.

"BARRICADE THE DOORS!" Major roared at his sons as he lunged into the house.

The uncles frantically secured the various bolts. Grunting and cursing, they dragged the wooden almirah that stood proud in the hall, across the door – just in case.

Baffled, Avi watched in wonder. How strong did they think the Crazy was?

Two hours later, not a single syllable was uttered around the dinner table. Avi pushed his food around his plate. When he looked up to find everyone's eyes on him, he just shoved the plate away. His uncles' wives cleared the table, and every one retired to their rooms.

Meeru followed him to his room and grabbed his wrist in time to stop him from locking her out.

"Ouch!"

His skin was boiling. Meeru stood back as he yanked his one-sleeved blazer off. This time, the remaining sleeve tore and remained on his arms. Cautiously, this time, Meeru ventured forward and helped remove his sleeve, shirt and jeans. Leaving him lying on his bed for a few minutes, with his legs dangling to the floor, she went to fetch the now familiar basin of ice cold water and sponge.

In his feverish state, questions in his head collided with each other, giving him a throbbing headache. *How did the Crazy get out? Did someone let her out? Who could that be?* More questions were generated: *Will anyone come investigating tomorrow? Dev and his wife didn't normally bat an eyelid, and they were closest, but what about Una and her Dad? What about Una?*

Magically, his fever broke.

Una's defiant face loomed large just above his head. He tried to touch her mirage, but it disappeared then reappeared out of his reach. Frustrated, his temper rose. *Why do I care what you think?* He had lots of things to worry about, like, would he be in a better shape to make it off the bed tomorrow? Would he get worse? Or was the Crazy going to get in? Yet, here he was fantasising about a girl he'd met two minutes ago! His head was floating. Even if he had a clear head, why should he care about what she thought? Avi tried to dismiss her, but his hormones were greedily devouring images of the evening only the mind could conjure. From the first encounter, he hadn't been able to take his eyes off her, until she physically fled from the veranda! Yet, he couldn't forget her boldness when she appraised him, and then the hypocrisy when she scorned at him. *Were all girls from England like that?* His body flushed further, if that was possible, when he remembered how his body reacted to her body innocuously coming into contact with his.

Avi's aunt was interrupting his memories by forcing him to drink milk. It tasted weird, as it had done for the past eleven months. Drugged, drained and emotionally exhausted from the day, he finally fell into slumber. Sometime later, he felt his pillow shift. Meeru must have fallen asleep; the weight of her hand removed the damp facecloth that had been propped on Avi's forehead.

***

Una tossed around in her bed, holding her pillow tightly over her head, hoping to muffle the continuous howls. Her thoughts were not taken up by Avi per se, but by the abrupt ending of his and Meeru's visit. Grandad's refusal to open the gate the previous night now made sense. However, his belief of being safe within his walls confounded her. They weren't protected by electric fencing or barbed wire ... surely scaling the walls in their current state wouldn't deter leopards or bears? The flimsy padlock was absurd. Una mulled over her other curiosity – Grandad's rifle in his room. Why hadn't he trained that on the jungle when she and Dad were 'letting' themselves in? Thinking of guns, she thought it was extraordinary that the retired Major didn't carry one when he came to visit?

Una's belly interrupted her thoughts. She hadn't eaten since breakfast, which consisted of two hard boiled eggs. At lunch, she had insisted on waiting for Dad to come home from wherever he was. How was she to know that dinner would be completely forgotten by the whole household? Barricading themselves after their neighbours had hastily departed was all they'd cared about. It took ages to lock down. There were far too many exterior doors and, instead of plain walls, the exterior walls were ceiling to floor grilled windows, each with its own screen and glass shutters, and individual bolts. If that wasn't enough of a distraction, Johnnie Walker, the servant had become excitable and refused to leave the main house. In the end, he won. Grandma finally lamented and guarded the back door for as long as it took Johnnie Walker to carry a pillow, blanket and a string bed on his head from the garage. So pleased was he to be indoors, he willingly placed his bed and bedding under the stairwell, so as to not to encroach on the family's space. There he clasped his hands in prayer and chanted. Strangely, Tommy, who was desperate to go out, wasn't allowed. He was their guard dog and, from what she could tell, he normally slept outside.

Una removed the pillow from her head. Most of the animals had tired, and the human-like wailing had softened. Grandad had assured her earlier that the human-like howls were the cries of a female jackal. Perhaps he was right – the city vixen that lived in her back garden at home sounded banshee-like when mating with her fox. Comforted by the memory of the annoying foxes in Manchester, Una began to drift off, but then sat bolt upright. *Dad …?*

In the morning, she had risen to find Dad missing. Grandad just told her that her Dad had gone to town. Predictably, Grandma didn't say anything, unless Una counted her utterance of 'Englessh bad' after she pinged open Una's Mum's locket that hung around her neck.

Una tried to ring Dad but there was no reception in the house. She rushed from the ground floor, up the stairs and barged through the door, expecting more rooms atop and a better mobile reception. Instead, she was blinded by brilliant sunshine and an expanse of green. She couldn't believe it. Her grandfather's house was just one of two houses and both were dwarfed by an expansive evergreen jungle encircled by purple mountains, with very little vegetation and no mobile mast and signal.

"AWWWW, Unnn na!"

Una's bottom flew off her bed and she landed on the floor. Tugging the end of the quilt towards her, she shook with the possibility that the loud mournful howler was human.

Chapter 7

"Wake up, Grandad ... Dad's not back yet." Una tugged at his quilt. "Grandad, did you hear me? Your son, my Dad, is not back?" Grandad carried on sleeping. "Oh, Grandad, please, just ... just WAKE UP!" He didn't even grunt. She moved closer to him and repeated her request, which had no impact either. Exasperated, she shook his bony shoulders as he slept on his side, "How can you possibly sleep through the screams and howls coming from outside, and the racket I'm making?"

Quite simply, it seemed. Big, white fluffy clouds of cotton were poking out of his ear canals, which tickled her nose as she leaned into him. Not only that ... the stench of strong, fermented sugar oozed from his pores. Ugh! He must have consumed a lot of his famous army supplied rum before going to bed.

Una covered her nose and mouth with her pyjama sleeve. Grandad was completely out of it. Una knew that unblocking his ears wouldn't wake him. She'd been through all of this with Dad in the first three months when the household just became the two of them. The fright Social Services gave him when they'd called around their house to discuss her absenteeism from school, in the middle of the day on a week day, sobered him up permanently.

Defeated, she glanced away from Grandad's sleeping form to the interlocking door leading to Grandma's room. Would Grandma help, or even care, that her son was not home? Una thought not, she shrugged her shoulders and despondently retreated to her room.

Truth be told, she was a little scared of Grandma. The dragon – she'd unwittingly named her earlier when talking to Meeru and Avi – was probably, at this very moment, sleeping, with one eye open in her den. Una half-heartedly scolded herself. She shouldn't be so judgemental of her darling Grandma yet, but no amount of positive thinking would shake Una's instincts, which were founded on the day she had spent in the valley. No, she was quite sure Grandma would most certainly hinder her efforts of looking for her missing Dad, rather than prove helpful. Back in Manchester, her Dad had led her to believe that Grandma's desperation to meet and bond with her only grandchild, was a likely story. Yesterday evening, when they'd arrived, instead of the expected boisterous warm first welcome, Grandma took an instant dislike to her. Far more shocking than that was Grandma's unexplainable loathing for her own son. She bristled every time he spoke, or came into her view. Animosity aside, she'd be of no use now as Una didn't speak Hindi and her Grandma didn't speak English. Una's decision was made – she would have to find, and possibly rescue, Dad herself.

She'd barely begun to plan her next steps, when her ears pricked and cut off her thoughts. Just over the animal and human cries, she could distinguish the faint rumbling of a vehicle ... it was coming from ... the east facing window in her room, where the curtains were partly drawn.

Una scrambled to the window's ledge, which was at floor height, and stepped up on it. Now that she knew where the sound was coming from, it was easily identifiable and became progressively louder. The vehicle was heading towards them. All day she had watched out for Dad, and not a single car had arrived at her Grandad's house. Johnnie Walker, who checked on her several times while she was on the roof, used his hands to mimic a steering wheel and a sideways head shake to suggest it was unlikely she'd see a car. During the day, no one except for Major's household drove on the path. Subsequently, there was more than a remote chance that the engine sound heading towards the house would be Dad's taxi. Relief washed over Una. How silly she'd been – all that fuss for nothing. She'd have to help Dad with the gate. Thankfully, Tommy was locked indoors this time.

Una parted the curtains all the way back and squinted. Two pinheads of light were moving in the far distance, from the narrow road on the cliff. They were approaching the fork to its left and then ... drove straight on ... past the dirt track that led to her Grandfather's house, and was soon rattling over a metal grid on the bridge in the distance, before disappearing out of sight. Una stepped off the ledge – it hadn't even been a car – it was a heavy army truck.

Dilapidated, she sat back on her bed and listened out for anything, anything at all. Except, the engine had quietened the jungle. The human cries had ceased. Surely 'things' only went quiet when a kill was made successfully?

Una had to find out. With quiet resolve, she threw on her dressing gown, tightly pulled the belt ends together to induce courage, and took a step to the door that led to the front veranda.

Achoo! Was Grandad awake? Una padded towards the gallery passage to investigate. In the dim light of the lantern, she discovered Grandad was still asleep and Grandma's door was still closed. Achoo! The sneeze came from the shadows of her Grandad's coat stand. Someone was definitely hiding amongst the coats.

Una concentrated on the spot and bravely said, "I see you, so there's no point in hiding." Cornered, the movement halted in the shadows and then ... a whine!

"Tommy?" whispered Una.

The poor dog emerged sheepishly and walked into the light, visibly shivering as he did so. Through all her worry, Una hadn't realised the house was freezing cold. Poor Tommy! Kneeling, Una rubbed him hard but still he shook vigorously. Not to be defeated, Una rummaged through the coats until she found her Grandfather's new tartan scarf, gifted to him by her Dad. Surely he wouldn't mind? She dislodged it from its hook and wrapped it tightly around Tommy's belly to warm him up. She thought about muzzling his snout, too, but then thought better of it. Then, she slipped on her florescent pink, Michelin-tyre styled, long jacket over her dressing gown. Mum had bought the ghastly thing as a joke. She hadn't expected Una to wear it, but Una did, initially to tease her, and later because ... well, she just did.

Una retraced her steps back to her room and realised she was still wearing her slippers. As she knelt down to change her shoes, Tommy brushed past her and noisily began to scrape at her veranda door with his paws. She hadn't thought of taking Tommy with her, but all things considered, he was a welcome companion. He might dissuade any unwelcome animals or other creatures from approaching her, that is, if he didn't give her away first, of course. Una shushed him with a warning stare. Immediately, Tommy took in a large gulp of air and became very still. With her right forefinger clamped to her lips, she cautiously opened the inner wooden door and the mesh outer door. She let Tommy out while she quickly retrieved the barely lit kerosene lamp her Grandfather had left on her bedside table, to help her see where she was going when she required the toilet. Inexplicably, the valley's electricity was cut off in the evenings, just when it was most required. Out in the fresh air, Tommy didn't scamper to the gate as she'd expected. Instead, he stood stationary at the top step of the veranda. Perishing darkness engulfed them as they stood huddled together at the precipice of the wilderness.

"Come on, Tommy," Una muttered bravely and pulled him along with her as she walked down the steps, adjusting the lantern's knob to increase the flame's brightness. She dealt with the lock as before, but the tall gate's crescent locking device was difficult to open and close during the day, let alone while holding a lantern. Clank! Finally, the gates swung apart. Before Una could decide which direction to take, Tommy sniffed around and ran ahead. He was on the trail of something – could it be her Dad?

Stumbling away from the dirt track she followed Tommy and

crossed into the neighbouring plot of land. Fragrant cow dung suffocated her nostrils and flooded through her slightly open mouth. Back and forth her lantern swung, shedding enough light to allow careful placement of her feet. Fresh cowpat was a dank hazard best avoided. She scuttled sideways to avoid a high pile, and fell into a thorny shrub.

"Ouch!" Una pulled away from the prickles, but didn't get far. Her coat was stuck in the shrubbery. Tugging at it just entangled it more.

"DAMN, DAMN!" Trying to avoid pricking her fingers, she took in a big gulp and knelt close to the cow dung pile, slowly untangling the fabric of her coat from the criss-cross of thorns. Tommy pawed her from behind, making her twitch and flick her hand in his direction, thus grazing her index finger against a thorn. "Ow, see what you made me do ..." Una went to suck her injured finger but thought better of it. Instead, she raised her hand to remove his paw from her right shoulder.

Instead of a paw, she felt narrow fingers with curled, long nails. They dug into the fabric of her florescent pink sleeve, tore it, then scratched her exposed skin, forming three long scratches.

Una yelped out loud and frantically tried to free herself of the hand, but it gripped her harder, deepening the scratches into furrows. Una's body slackened in pain. A cold sweat swathed Una as a warm breath tickled the nape of her neck. Una wasn't giving up, she surveyed the ground for a stick or small rock, when her eyes fell on the lantern. Still bearing the weight of the hand, Una slowly raised the lantern and rotated her head.

"*Nahi! Nahi!*" A hoarse voice shrieked from behind her. The creature's hand slipped off her body completely. Something, other than the two of them, moved in the shrubbery. The creature went down. From the faint light of the lantern, Una was relieved to see Tommy, scarf-less, poised on the creature's stomach.

Una's relief was short lived. Tommy was wagging his tail madly as he licked the creature in a frenzy. Tommy knew the creature! Warily, Una shone the lantern slowly, up and down the fallen body. Tommy wasn't randomly licking the creature's body; he was licking welted skin and removing dried blood. The creature was a human ... a woman in a dirty sari. Una concentrated the lantern's glow on her face. Bewildered eyes peeked up between gnarled, long-nailed fingers. Una moved forward. The woman screamed. Paradoxically, Una was relieved – the human screams were not Dad's.

"It's alright, I won't hurt you. I'm Una – what's your name?" said Una moving away.

"Una, Burfani ..."

The exchange didn't soothe her. Instead, it sent the woman into a frenzy. "Don't press my neck! Please don't put your fingers around my throat. I beg you!"

Una stepped back on her heels, the words 'Don't press my neck' rolling in her head. She held her own neck with the free hand and realised the true meaning of the words, "Don't strangle me."

Una shuffled back two more steps, landing straight into the dung she had laboriously tried to avoid. At the same time, the bedraggled woman rose onto her feet, in a hunched posture, and scuttled towards the Major's boundary wall, with Tommy right behind her.

No longer worried about the dung, Una wanted to follow Burfani, but she just disappeared into the night's mist. Turning the knob on the kerosene lamp proved ineffective. The flame was starting to fade.

Forlorn, Una turned back to her grandparent's home, leaving Tommy behind. How was she going to explain where Tommy was? She decided not to tell them. That meant she couldn't discuss the strange woman, either. In the mist, she missed her Grandad's tartan scarf trapped in the shrubbery.

Sitting on the bottom step leading up to the veranda, Una studied the soles of her shoes. They were caked with cow dung and stank. Sighing, she prised them off her feet and carried them to the side of the house, placing them just outside her shared bathroom's external door. She would sort them out tomorrow.

✳✳✳

Her right shoulder was throbbing. Still half asleep, she touched the angry ridges. It wasn't just her shoulder; her face was burning, too, and then ... A foul smelling wet sponge swiped diagonally across her forehead and down her nose.

"What the ..." Una sprang off her pillow and sat on her heels. From her elevated position, she looked down to see mischievous Labrador eyes focused on her, the dog's tail thumping the marble floor. Una hesitantly grabbed the hem of her pyjama top and vigorously rubbed the dog saliva off.

"Aggh! Tommy! How did you get in here! Did someone ..." Una turned to check the bolt on her door; it was still in a locked position, "... let you in just now?" Una turned to look at her watch on the bedside cabinet. It was six a.m., and the household was still asleep.

Una poked her head under her bed to locate her slippers, and found her – shoes. How did the inanimate pair walk their way indoors? Nervously, she examined the soles and found they were spotless. She even dared to smell them – all she could smell was rubber and dust. "How ... is this possible? No way did I dream the whole expedition last night."

She flung the shoes down as if they were possessed and held her face in her hands.

"Ugh! Tommy!"

Her face was still damp with dog slobber. Disgusted, Una used her t-shirt to clean her face properly. "Now I smell of dog's breath, too!"

She roughly removed the offending t-shirt and realised her right shoulder didn't hurt when she moved it. She checked her shoulder for the deep scratches and found nothing but slobber. Confused, she grabbed another t-shirt and opened her door to wash herself in the bathroom, and walked straight into something.

"Larki, this is not how you walk around. You'll give the servant ideas," her Grandfather said, stepping backwards and covering his eyes with his arm.

Una threw on her t-shirt hastily. "Great, now I've ruined two t-shirts ..."

Una was lost for words. Grandad was wearing his tartan scarf, firmly tied around his neck and reaching up to his lower lip. He pulled it away from his mouth, "Remember to wrap up warm. The temperature has dropped drastically since yesterday. The snow must have fallen higher up on the mountains."

Oblivious to his words, Una uttered, "Where did you find the scarf?"

"On the coat stand, where you put it after your father gifted it to me."

Hanging on the stand! That could only mean she dreamt the whole of last night's expedition.

"It's too early for this. First the nakedness, and now the silly questions," Dev grumbled whilst pulling up his scarf. "Ouch!" Deftly, he unwound the scarf from his neck and chin to reveal a nasty scratch. Una watched, confused, as a lone prickly leaf fell to the ground.

Chapter 8

A deep frown settled on Major's face as he inspected his outhouse building. He'd expected to find the door torn off its hinges, and the creature to have absconded. To his amazement, though, the door was intact and the occupant in deep sleep. Not believing his eyes, Major carefully examined the door, expecting it to be scuppered. It was in perfect working order. Like it or not, it pointed to a traitor, or traitors, within his household. Someone other than Avi, Meeru and himself must have unlocked the door. Major pondered on who would have been bold enough to go against his wishes. He ruled out his sons and their wives, who were too superstitious to let the 'thing' near themselves or their children, in case it cursed them with the same affliction. The only person who could open the door, besides himself, was Avi's mother, but she was away visiting her parents.

Still, the 'thing' had sensibly returned. The reasoning for her return, unlike the door, was not a conundrum.

✳✳✳

In the main house, Avi was stirring awake. He'd uncharacteristically slept longer than the rest of the household and could hear them going about their business.

"Wake up, Avi, breakfast is ready!" shouted Meeru, walking through the corridor outside his room.

He groaned, lifted his head and then fell back. His body was heavy and unnaturally stiff. Avi flexed his arms outward and knocked the glass tumbler off his bedside cabinet. He waited for the clink, but it didn't come. Instead, his attention was drawn to his heartbeat, pulsating hard in the palm of his hand, which was wrapped tightly around the glass tumbler. Spooked, Avi released the tumbler. This time it clinked and smashed into smithereens on the marble floor. In disbelief, Avi turned his palms upwards. They were larger than usual. He had new, protruding veins snaking up from his wrist. Avi roughly pushed up his kurta's sleeves and discovered muscles that hadn't been there before. Avi gawked at his arms and then his legs. They were a little longer, as he had come to expect after each scream, but this time, he had a sprinter's calf muscles. Avi's night kurta also felt tighter. He pulled the neck of his night kurta forward, trying to loosen it, but only managed to tear it. Ducking his head through the widened neckline, Avi clocked his lean torso. It had morphed and was now tapered and more compact. "Increasing in height is one thing, but this is another," he exclaimed, stabbing his chest with his fingers.

"It's just puberty ... your uncles went through it, too," Meeru said in a soft tone as she walked in with a bundle of ironed clothing in her arms.

Avi straightened his torn kurta.

"Puberty has nothing to do with this body," he said, taking of his kurta.

Meeru hesitated for a moment, noticeably working through an explanation. With a flourish of her arm she said, "It's natural, but what isn't natural is what you're feeling yourself."

"Natural? So, my twin, Gag, will be going through this, too, at Nani's house?" quizzed Avi, unconvinced.

"I doubt it," replied Meeru as she threw him one of his uncle's kurta from her ironed pile. "Quit admiring your body and dress quickly for breakfast before your chachas turn up – you know how they like to leave you with nothing."

Meeru was right – his uncles' appetites were infinite, and unfortunately, Dadi's kitchen produced a finite amount of food and worked on the principle of 'first come, first served'. Admiring his new pecs, he wondered if he was truly going to have any trouble this time. Eager to find out, Avi rushed out of bed, only to stumble and fall.

Meeru rushed over to check his limbs and ribs for any break-ages. Preoccupied, she helped him up. Avi was sure she mumbled something like, "It's happening too fast."

Before Avi could question what she meant, Meeru walked out of the room, calling as she went, "Come on, Bambi! Let's get you some breakfast."

Chapter 9

Una heard a loud grunt from inside her Dad's room as she approached it. She quickened her pace and pushed his door open. God, was she pleased that he was back.

Crash!

She ducked, lost her balance and fell into the room as a foot swung towards her. She just missed the bamboo ladder on the floor with Dad's suitcase trapped underneath it. Johnnie Walker's body was suspended in the air, above the doorway's storage hatch.

"What are you doing on the floor?" cried Grandad as he closed the door and propped the ladder up against it. He must have been in the room with Johnnie Walker.

"Looking for Dad," answered Una, her eyes glued on Johnnie Walker as he scuttled down the ladder and nervously moved around with her Dad's suitcase, not knowing where to put it until Grandad indicated the small table in the room.

"Your Dad?" Grandad looked thoughtful. "He's ... he's out."

Una perused the room. None of her Dad's usual paraphernalia was out. That was a little weird. Dad had a habit of spreading himself around. Bile infiltrated her mouth. What was her Grandad not telling her? She wanted to ask, but instead, she asked, "Out since yesterday morning?"

"Yes ... why not? From all the stories I've heard, you are quite capable of doing that, too. Never mind that, have you taken it upon yourself to walk into people and scare them out of their wits and cause injury?" Una refused to respond. "We will talk later. For now, I suggest you remain in your room till your Grandmother brings you your breakfast." Her Grandfather waited for her to challenge him.

She was going to protest, but then she thought, talk was good; talk meant she'd find out her Dad's whereabouts. Una relented and left the room.

"We will talk later about you sneaking up on people," said Grandad before shutting and locking her Dad's door.

What? Talk about her behaviour, but not about Dad's whereabouts? Forget that, she was going out to find him, again. First, she had to remove the bitterness in her mouth and drink something. She couldn't go to the kitchen to get a drink, but last night's tea was still on the bedside cabinet. The local tea was delicious, even when it was stone cold.

Quenched, Una slipped out of her room's external door and was at the gate in no time. Before she could even release the latch on the gate, from nowhere, a fleshy torpedo arrived, knocked her down and then sat on her. Grandma had literally rugby tackled her to the ground. Huffing and puffing, Una tried to move from under her, unsuccessfully. From her lowered position, she spotted Grandad's trousered legs hurriedly appear, then ... move to the boundary wall. Instead of rescuing her, he chose to holler something in Hindi. Una thought she was going to pass out, but then a familiar pair of jeans and shoes appeared – Avi. Still no rescue. Instead, her grandparents and Major were involved in heated whispers. Una's breathing sharpened and her back succumbed. Feet shuffled around her and, not a moment too soon. Grandma rose, but not before applying downward pressure on Una, pretending to lose her balance.

Grandad waited for Una to stand, with Avi's help, before he spoke. "What are you up to? This is the third incident this morning. Do you know that leaving the premises without telling anyone is dangerous and irresponsible when you live in a jungle?"

"What do you expect?" Una scowled. "I was looking for Dad.

None of you seem to know where he is and, worst of all, you don't care. I'm sure I heard human screams amongst that jungle noise last night. They could have been his screams!" cried Una.

Worried looks were exchanged between Major and Grandad.

"No one walks off the premises without telling anyone. Is that clear?" Grandad repeated, ignoring her words.

Before Una could say anything more, Avi grabbed her hand and herded her out of the gate. She should have felt indignation towards him for not letting her speak her mind. Instead, the simple gesture of holding hands distracted and stirred something ... something she didn't want to acknowledge or explore. Instead, she recalled the previous time she'd left the gate. She didn't believe it was a dream, even if the morning's evidence proved otherwise. In her mind, she wondered:

If so much drama occurred with her opening the gate in daylight, what would they have made of her escapade the night before, when she'd left the compound, unaccompanied ... unless Tommy was considered responsible company?

Avi's clasp tightened. Surprised, she looked up. He ignored her enquiring expression and, unrelenting, dragged her on as if she was a child being taken to school by an older sibling.

"Where are you taking me? Are you taking me to Dad?"

"To your dad?" Avi came to an abrupt stop, jolting her body against his.

Vertigo hit. Her head didn't feel right. She could see Avi's lips moving. She knew he was saying something about her father. "Just tell me, is it to do with Dad?"

Avi released his grip. "Of course not! Haven't they told you?"

"What?"

"He's back in England ... Uncle Dev just said that back there ... in Hindi."

Avi carried on walking.

"Back in England?" Una clenched her fists against her sides. "You've misunderstood or you're lying! My Dad wouldn't leave without me."

"He wouldn't ..." Her own mouth was spouting out a jumble of words, but her brain was not in charge. The last time Una remembered her head feeling like this was when she emptied her father's drinks cabinet of its contents, on her Mum's anniversary. That night, she kept falling, blanking out and finding herself in different places, before she landed in the bathroom, heaving over the toilet bowl.

She wasn't drunk, but perhaps she was woozy from missing another meal. *Forget me. Where did Avi go?* She spotted him walking ahead without her. Peeved and without inhibition, she ran up and jumped Avi from behind, bringing him down in one fell swoop. With a self-defence movement, she flipped him on to his back.

Hoping for a menacing look, she straddled him. "If we're not looking for Dad, where are we going?"

"You are on a tour of the jungle to learn about the ..." Avi stopped as he raked over her with wide open eyes. He was having problems with his breathing. Several uncomfortable moments passed, and then, in a voice that seem to come from a distance, Avi continued from where he'd left off. "... to learn about the rules of the valley." A quick manoeuvre later and he had them both on their feet. "You must learn the layout of the valley. Teenagers aren't permitted to move freely in all the areas of the jungle." She'd barely registered Avi's spiel on the dos and don'ts and the layout of the jungle surrounding the valley, when Avi abruptly stopped talking and hauled them through an opening in the jungle that she hadn't noticed before. Until now, she had thought the jungle boundary was a continuous wall of tall trees, with knitted branches and dense foliage. Surprisingly, the opening he used was wide enough for the two of them to walk through, side-by-side, between two trees. The third, middle tree, which gave the illusion of a continuous wall, was several metres behind the other two. *Had nature intended to create a secret gateway?* The temperature dropped a few degrees. She hadn't expected to see familiar fruit and temperate trees of various heights growing together, with respectable ground and sky spaces for them to flourish. While many of the bows interlinked, the jungle canopy wasn't continuous, even if it looked that way from Grandad's roof. Large blue patches of the sky brought in dappled light between the trees. The jungle floor was mostly dust with rhododendron bushes. She was a little disappointed; she loved the emerald bracken carpets of the woods found in England. Here, she could see the ground clearly. *Perhaps not so clearly … was it moving?*

In response, Avi threw a stick not too far from her feet – the scales of dust writhed away. Una shuddered; her legs were shaking. How could she be so stupid and forget about the wild animals? Her body didn't have any in-built alerts. Perhaps she should have paid better attention to Avi.

"It's not just me, everyone walks carefree through woods in England," she said hoarsely, not quite sure if she was explaining her naïvety to herself or Avi.

"How lucky you are to have done that. I've lived in sight of the jungle since I was born, but only dared to venture into it when I was a teenager; then only to find out that most areas are difficult to enter, or forbidden by the forestry commission. The adults, despite choosing to build houses here, are terrified by the jungle, hence the curfew. But this is not the place to talk about fear, for it will engulf you. Instead, if we remain silent, I promise you will find the jungle more beautiful and wondrous than your woods."

Una was too dizzy to do anything else. A few moments passed, and then it happened – a baby rhesus negative monkey appeared, hanging upside down, as its mother, who was mostly hidden, walked on a branch just over Una's head.

Una swung her head around to see if Avi had spotted the wonder. He had. It was written all over his smiling face. He mouthed the words 'Bandar – monkey'. Although he was still watchful, his face and body were noticeably free from his wary tension – his usual trademark.

Lifted by his mood, she whispered, "You love it here."

Avi's face lit up and he gave her a heart melting smile. "Is it obvious that I love it here?"

Una nodded.

"I feel connected to this space, more alive, truer. Do you think that's strange?" quizzed Avi, cocking his eyebrow up at Una.

Una knew how he felt, that's why the warehouses were such a pull, but she didn't let on.

"I'll let you into a secret. Sometimes I take risks and cut through the jungle, from just in front of your grandfather's house."

"But you just said that area is prohibited."

Avi shrugged, "Occasionally, your grandfather sees me, but he's never said anything to Dada, Meeru or Ma."

"So, what's your problem?" Una said, walking into a low-hanging root. Awestruck, Una traced the root to a mass of tentacle-like roots that hung down a vast ancient tree of cathedral proportions.

"It's a banyan tree," Avi explained. Slightly irritated, he continued, "About your question, don't you think it's a problem that I'm invisible to the adults?"

Still distracted by the tree, Una answered, "Perhaps. So, do you cut across the prohibited area because you might get caught?"

"What? Why would anyone want to do that?" asked Avi, clearly offended by her suggestion. "It bothers me because, to your grandfather, clearly I'm not significant enough to worry about."

"Obviously not." Una had no idea what he was talking about, but she knew the happy mood in the jungle was broken. Why did he have to go and be so pissy?

Bristling, Avi decided it was time to leave the jungle, and more or less marched her on to the path just beyond Major's house. The sharp rise in temperature winded Una.

"Can we go home now?" asked Una, holding her head. Avi stalled and peered back at the gate she'd left through earlier, and then shook his head.

"Sorry, you'll need to learn about the River Rule to survive the jungle – our grandparents expected me to do that after we'd left."

Una protested, but Avi was on a mission. He pushed her off the path and into a cowshed.

"As I said, we teenagers can't walk everywhere as we please. The river on the other side of this path is mostly out of bounds for us."

"River? What river? Why can't I hear the sound of flowing water nearby?"

"Are you going to question everything?"

Una shrugged.

"Fine then, showing you the River Rule will be quicker and easier to explain. But first you will have to trust my motives and follow whatever I say to survive."

Keeping eye contact with her, he wound and secured the loose end of a rope around her waist which was already tied firmly around a post concreted to the floor in the cowshed. Then grabbing her shoulders from behind, he pushed her forward as far as he could across an expanse of pebbles and rocks.

Dust flurried from under her feet as she tried to skid to a stop. She opened her mouth to scream but nothing came out.

"Una, you're now standing in the river!" Avi called out.

Shocked, Una took a three-sixty degrees peruse of the terrain, dusted her clothes down and incredulously uttered, "What the *hell* ... This can't be the river?"

"It is!" Avi shouted. "Don't be fooled by the quiet solitude. Una – it's dangerous. Stay between the four boulders to keep safe!" Una looked carefully at Avi's right index finger, which pointed, in turn, to four boulders placed in a quadrant.

Avi continued. "And it's only safe during the time between when the sun has completely risen and the first sign of sunset."

"I expected the River Rule to be based on fast currents, deep waters infested with crocodiles," exclaimed Una coming out of her trance.

"Alligators," Avi muttered.

"Seriously, you're going to correct me on type of reptile?"

This time Avi shrugged.

Una stood akimbo. "There isn't a rule is there? You are having me on!"

"No, Una! It's not what it seems – the river is dangerous," Avi said tersely as he picked a section of the rope between her and the cow post.

"How is it dangerous?" she giggled. Her laughter echoing against the boulders resting on the cliffs on one side of the river. "There isn't a real river here. There isn't even a drop of water to dip my toes in." Una lifted her foot and rotated her booted ankle. "It's not like I'm going to drown."

"If you don't believe me then walk beyond the four river boulders and see what happens to you."

Una shouted, "Okay!"

"No! Una, no! I didn't mean that! Come back right now!" he shouted and then jerked his head up to study the sky. She did, too. Not a wing or call could be seen or heard. Yet something had spooked Avi. Using his feet, he dragged the pebbles about, obviously surveying the ground around him.

Una huffed. "There is nothing to hear!" she shouted to Avi with her arms stretched outwards.

"Precisely!" Avi shouted back.

"Precisely what, Avi? Oh this is silly," she spouted and galloped backwards, while still facing him. "Oh look, I've found ..." She paused and then laughed with mirth, "... nothing so far!"

Avi lost all colour as he frantically checked the invisible vertical lines between each boulder in turn, all the time looping the slack in the rope around his hand.

"Forget this ..." Avi moved towards Una.

"Walk back to me, Una. It's not safe!" he yelled – the desperation in his voice clear and loud.

Una cupped her hand near her right ear. "I can't hear you."

"Una, stop walking backwards and don't tug the rope!" hollered Avi, as she tugged hard on the rope and brought her closer to him.

She countered him, which he had not expected, by pulling the rope back towards her, and called out, "Jesus, Avi. There's nothing here, so chill." Barely had she spoken the words when a chilling cry ripped through her throat as her body was pulled by something very powerful behind her. Frenetically, she tried to free herself, but to no avail. She swung her head around to see what was holding her back and found ... nothing. Petrified, the whites of her eyeballs protruded out, triggering her traumatised mind to pull a blanket over her already drugged head. One moment she felt the momentum of flying into Avi, and the next, she blacked out.

❊❊❊

Una awoke in her bed at noon, sore and exhausted. Her bones and organs ached, as if they had been rearranged. She tried to remember walking back with Avi, but she had no recollection of it. All she knew was that Avi had saved her from something related to the River Rule. Oddly, she couldn't remember seeing a river either. Una made up her mind, it was time to leave. Except, where was her Dad? Avi had said something to her at the beginning of the Valley Rules excursion – something about her Dad not being missing. If he wasn't missing, then where was he? He wouldn't leave her, would he? ... no, of course he wouldn't.

Chapter 10

She was wrong, so wrong – the realisation that she hadn't known her father at all was enormous. Just as enormous as the trunk she now sat on. She was still confused as to how she'd missed the metallic 'white elephant' in her room when she went to the restroom – it only hogged most of the free floor space in the bedroom.

One hand over her mouth, Una scrutinised the single, hand-written word on the sealed envelope that had been placed flat on the trunk beside her.

'SORRY.'

She didn't have to open it to know what it was going to say – the aluminium trunk, embossed with her name and destination, gave the game away. What a coward!

How could he have disappeared without a spoken word, leaving her with guardians who, at best, tolerated her. How could he separate her from her friends when they provided the only affection she'd had after Mum? Surely, he knew who the bad influence was in their group?

Her passport was no longer in her wardrobe – had he had taken it? She could ring the British Embassy, but how? Her phone wasn't working and Grandad didn't have one.

Her father's betrayal, and the consequential treatment, was overwhelming. It was too much to bear. Streams of hot tears soaked her cheeks unashamedly. Did he not realise he would induce a monumental chasm between them?

When her tears subsided, she was left with one thought in her head: She was never going to forgive him. He was as good as dead to her. Defiantly, she scrunched up the unopened envelope, threw it on the floor and then climbed onto her bed, fully clothed and with her shoes on.

Grandma came in and found Una lying in the foetal position, staring at the ceiling. She could have hugged and cradled her granddaughter, wiped her tears even, but she didn't. Instead, a cold smile swept across her face as she picked up the scrunched letter. She carefully rubbed the creases with her hands and straightened the envelope. Taking the letter, she left Una to herself.

✻✻✻

Avi: The next afternoon.

"No doubt our grandparents have assigned you to the task of watching over me."

Avi held his tongue. She had guessed correctly, but she was wrong about his sentiment – he had wanted to come.

"Thought so. I'm sure you covered all the rules yesterday, even though I don't actually remember the day clearly."

She can't remember? How was that possible when she'd been so petrified yesterday? How do you forget that? How do you forget nearly being 'taken'?

Avi frowned.

He had to admit, she had seemed out of sorts yesterday. He'd thought she was suffering from jet-lag. Even so, the river incident had been life threatening and could not be easily forgotten. He thought to question her further, but her eyes flashed green, accusing and hostile. His own eyes dropped from her gaze and wandered over her dried tears and the strands of hair that stuck against her high cheekbones. Avi wasn't equipped for this. Meeru was the only other girl he knew, and he couldn't remember seeing her cry – her brothers had seen to that.

"I'll leave you to it, you obviously need to be alone." His voice audibly softened as he withdrew and walked back to the stairwell. At the door, he hesitated, "For the record," he paused to check he had her attention, "it was my choice to come today, and yesterday afternoon."

"Yesterday afternoon?"

"I came back again after dropping you off, but you were fast asleep." Confusion over Una's new vulnerability affected his voice.

Hesitant to leave, he studied Una as she used the heels of her palms to rub her cheeks.

"Thanks for coming then," whispered Una, imploring him to stay with her eyes.

Avi was torn.

"Please, Avi, don't go!"

Avi sighed and returned to where she sat. Tommy, who, until that moment, had been snoozing at Una's feet, woke and ambushed him with jumps and licks. Avi's laughter died when he caught her eyes on his knees.

She'd noticed his unnatural growth. He didn't need to read her mind to know that. He pulled his rucksack off his back and took out the lotion Meeru used on him to soothe his muscles during changes.

"I came yesterday because I was worried about the scratches on your arms and the muscular pain you must have been experiencing ..."

"We just went for a walk, Avi!" Una spat out in a whisper. "Why would I feel pain? I don't think I have any scratches." Una removed her denim jacket. Avi stared. He saw three red lines across her shoulder and involuntarily bent down to touch them.

"Don't touch me!" she shrieked, shifting away from him.

"I didn't mean to," he blushed, confused by his wayward impulses. "I was concerned ... I was checking to see if the deep claw marks had healed."

"Claw marks? How did you see them? ... they'd disappeared ... if it happened at all." Una shifted and pulled her shirt away to look carefully.

"It ... it was there!" Avi was confused. Had he imagined the angry markings?

Una looked carefully, but there was nothing there. Nor were they any scratches.

Avi placed the lotion down, pulled out a Coke and sat down. He opened the Coke with a bottle opener and passed it to Una. He tried to, at least. Instead, Tommy jumped between them and went for the bottle. All three of them collapsed on top of each other in absolute chaos. Winded, with hearts beating fast, they self-consciously disentangled themselves. For a while, they stared at each other while Tommy tried to lick them, before settling where the Coke had formed a puddle. Their earlier awkwardness disappeared and they settled into a silent camaraderie as they sat against the roof wall.

Fidgeting with the button on her denim jacket, out of the blue, Una blurted, "My Dad is dead to me!"

Avi didn't react. He knew she expected him to contest her words and say she was stupid, and that she should 'grow up'.

Instead, for the first time ever, he voiced his thoughts. "My father could be dead."

"Oh, sorry. I didn't know." Her cheeks were flaming red as she nervously asked, "Is he on the Kashmir frontline?"

Her diffident self appealed to him, as much as her feisty one. It distracted him momentarily before he answered, "No." Avi paused as he watched relief spread across Una's face. "For as long as I can remember, he has only taken a day or two's leave from wherever he is posted in the country."

Una sat up taller and turned her body towards him.

"He's no longer on the frontline and could easily be posted here, in Khamosh Valley. It's the best cantonment. But I'm sure he requests to be posted elsewhere. In the past, when I asked why, the adults in my house, without any real explanation, implied it was my fault! My twin, unlike me, doesn't mind his absence."

"Twin? You have a twin?" asked Una in surprise. "How come

I haven't seen him?" Avi opened his mouth to reply, but Una shot out another question, "So there are two of you with crazy hair?" Una stretched over to touch the hair that arched over the side of his head.

Avi wasn't sure if he unravelled because he was finally able to talk to someone, or because that someone was Una. Avi removed her hand from his hair and held it. Eyes on her mouth, he said, "Take a breather between questions so I can answer them."

Embarrassed, Una retracted her hand.

"Yes, I have a twin, and no, his hair is cut short like the rest of the men in my family." After a pause, he continued, looking at a point ahead of him, "We can't stand each other and the reason you haven't seen him is because he has gone with my mother to my maternal grandparents, my Nana and Nani."

"Does he have your eyes though?" Una forgot her earlier embarrassment and leaned in closer. He turned his head and just missed her nose with his.

"What is this ... are you flirting with me?" Avi asked lightly to diffuse the awkwardness.

Her eyes pierced through his. "Absolutely not! It's just that I thought your eye colour would be quite rare in the valley. I expect most people have brown or black irises."

Her face was too close. Avi was feeling a new kind of nervousness – one that compelled him to stay sitting, when he desperately wanted to flee.

Unaffected by his discomfort, her eyes darted between his. "They're almost mercurial grey."

"Can we talk about something else."

"Something else? Oh, okay. I met a lady in the field between the two houses. I thought it could be your mum. She spoke in English, like you and Meeru."

"*Kya*? I mean ... what?" Avi was baffled and stood up. No other female relative spoke English.

"When did you see her?"

"The evening I first met you, after the screaming. I was out looking for my Dad ..."

Avi's jaw dropped. "What the hell! It was a curfew!"

"Don't worry, I took Tommy and searched the neighbouring field," Una guiltily explained.

He pictured all the men in his house hiding from the Crazy indoors, and this girl, the reckless '*jaan baaz*', was breaking curfew at that very same moment, breaking her home's protection while the Crazy was on the loose and wailing! She put her life at risk to look for her Dad, who wasn't even in the country.

"Wait a moment, you were all over the place the next day. Are you sure you didn't dream all this?" asked Avi.

"Initially, I thought I had. When I woke up in the morning, everything was in order, and it shouldn't have been. But, now you've seen the exact spot where the lady scratched me ..."

Crazy harmed Una? Avi thought.

Avi blinked at Una. "Why don't you tell me what you think you saw."

Avi listened carefully, without giving much away as Una explained the confusing episode, including the squeaky-clean shoes after stepping in the cow dung. She finished with Tommy reappearing in her room whilst it was still bolted from inside.

It should have put Avi's mind at ease because it all sounded like a fantasy, but he couldn't get past Una's description of the field between their houses. It was a perfect description, down to the geography surrounding the shrubs the cows loved best as it was the sunniest spot. Could she have seen all that from the roof? He peered over. In his gut, Avi knew Una was talking about Crazy. Una said her name began with a B, and sounded like Murphy. It didn't ring any bells. Una had to be telling the truth; she had seen welts on the lady's body. She was definitely talking about the creature in the outbuilding – Ma's elderly, crazy relative. Yet the creature speaking in English didn't fit. Ma couldn't speak English, so why would her elderly relative?

"Una, was it a *Budiya* ... sorry, I mean an elderly lady?"

Una shook her head, "Not unless you consider a mid-thirties to forty-year-old as being old."

Mid-thirties to forty-year-old? He slumped back against the wall and, without really thinking, traced around her fingers as her palm lay face down on the ground beside him. Speaking softly, he said, "Whoever you saw, it could not be my Ma because she's at her parents' home – a day's travel from here. On top of that, besides Meeru, there are no other females in the family who speak English. The scratch marks aren't there, so they're not real. It's official ... you dreamt the whole thing up." He was humouring her; he'd seen the scratch marks himself.

He expected Una to react to his words, but she was distracted by his fingers tracing the join between her index finger and thumb. Perhaps she could feel the tingling heat, too. She hadn't removed her hand, so was it something she liked, perhaps. Una's gentler, more vulnerable demeanour left him confused. He wasn't sure what to do next.

"I've got to push off now – remember the curfew means staying indoors?" He removed his hand and raked his fingers through the back of his hair as he stood up.

He had to leave before she asked more searching questions about his family, and for other reasons he preferred not to admit. Disappointed, Una nodded and quietly followed him down the stairs to the front door.

"Do you think you will come tomorrow?" Una asked in a quiet voice.

"Sorry."

"Oh, you don't have to ... just forget it." Una nervously tucked her hair behind her ear and fiddled.

"I'm not apologising to you. I'm merely reading the note in the cabinet."

Una glanced over her shoulder. A creased, unopened letter was propped against the much-coveted Benson & Hedges cigarettes in the walled glass cabinet that stood in the drawing room.

"Why would she do that?" Tears welled in Una's eyes. "That's my Dad's letter, which I haven't read."

He moved forward and, with his forehead touching hers, he used his thumbs to wipe her tears. "Why don't you want to read it?"

Girls just didn't make sense to him, especially not at this proximity. He moved back quickly.

"I just didn't," her lower lip trembled. A strange impulse to still it with his lips swept over him, but he held back. He knew he was already crossing lines, according to his customs.

"Budhi probably wanted to make a point." He lifted her chin. "Una, don't feel sad, feel the opposite. Every time you pass the cabinet, do a salute. That will show the budiya." He then went on to salute the cabinet and lifted her hand to do the same.

She followed suit and chuckled.

Avi smiled as he heard a snort from the kitchen hatch. Avi's gaze returned to Una, who was scowling at a Windsor School blazer draped across the sofa's back.

"Is this the school you are going to go to?" he said as he lifted the garment up.

"Yeah, although I won't be going there straight away. They are waiting to see if one of the boarders returns after an illness. The principal has given her a few weeks' grace. Even so, I haven't agreed to going to that school."

"Really? Have you any idea how lucky you are?"

Una looked at him curiously, and then at the blazer.

Avi picked it up and helped Una into it. Her lifted her hair and noticed the little hairs tremble on her exposed neck. Sucking in a breath, he gruffly said, "Hey, I know it's bad that your father left without telling you, but seriously, Windsor School is a school the locals can only dream of going to. Only the very privileged manage it."

He stood back from her and saluted her.

Una smiled and bowed.

"Your Dad is not as bad as you think. He could have placed you in a mediocre school – instead, he chose one of the best, if not the best, in the country."

"Oh! Do you go to the school?" Una asked.

Avi jumped over the sofa's back and onto the cushions, where he rolled about, laughing.

"No, Una – it's a girls' school."

Una dragged him off the sofa, at least he allowed her to, and pushed him to the door. "Out you go!" He knew how to handle *this* Una.

He looked over his shoulder and asked cheekily, "Why?"

"Curfew." Una tried to look serious, but merriment was back in her eyes.

"You are a quick learner," Avi laughed, letting himself out, but not before he glimpsed the dragon moving quickly away from the kitchen hatch.

Chapter 11

Una

The monsoon river was an expanse of pebbles, with an iron cattle bridge over it. The very same bridge the army truck had driven over the second night she had arrived.

"Where's the water?" asked Una.

Avi sighed out loud, "I told you the other day ..."

"The day, I already told you, I don't remember."

The same stony expression appeared on his face; the facial expression he wore when she'd first admitted that she didn't remember much of that day, when they were on the roof a few days ago. He sighed out loud, again. "This is a monsoon river. It's floods during heavy rains, and I know you won't believe it but, it can be mighty ferocious. It floods and destroys the nearby vegetation and tribal homes. At a minimum, it stores enough water underneath these stones and rocks for the roots of nearby vegetation."

"A ferocious river, hmm," Una wasn't convinced. "When do I get to see this miracle?"

"End of June, July and August, sometimes September."

"Ah! That's a pity! I won't be here." She was going to explain how she planned to find a way back to Manchester for her seventeenth birthday, when an iridescent pebble twinkled between her shoes. Una couldn't resist and picked it up. Avi looked at her strangely. *Had he thought she would stay just because he thought Windsor School was a privileged school?*

"They're like precious stones, aren't they?" Avi broke his gaze and took the pebble from her hand. After a quick examination, he said, "Thought so."

"Thought what?" Una quizzed, looking at the stone in his palm.

"You picked up the stone because it called out to you."

"Whatever gave you that idea?" Was Avi trying to tempt her into staying with a stone?

Preoccupied with writing something on it with a sharp stone, Avi muttered, "Well, that's obvious – it has a streak of jade that matches the evil glint in your eye when you're angry or being stubborn."

"Let me see," asked Una. Avi smiled as he gently placed the pebble in her palm. She twirled it around and paused to read the neatly etched 'UNA'. Fixing her eyes intently on his, she returned his smile and threw the pebble into the forbidden area of the riverbed.

"If it's mine, it will make its way back to the part of the river through which I am able to walk before I leave."

An awkward silence followed.

Rather than deal with the angry energy arching between them, Una walked away and continued her own exploration of the area between the boulders. Earlier in the day, Avi had expected a fight from her when he'd explained that it was unsafe to go beyond the boulders, but she believed him ... For some unknown reason, they gave her the heebie-jeebies. *Since when did she follow rules without questioning them?*

Una lost her footing as she stumbled over the uneven drift-wood. Avi appeared behind her and roughly dragged her up, as if she was a sack of potatoes.

Luke will be jealous when I turn up at school with this for an art prop, she thought.

"Luke is a boy's name, isn't it?" Avi asked curtly.

"Yes, and?" She must have thought out loud, as usual. She seemed to be doing that a great deal around Avi.

"But I've already told you, Windsor School is a girls' school," he arched a dark eyebrow.

"Yes, and he won't be joining Windsor School, silly! Were you not listening to me earlier when I said I will NOT be here for the monsoons because I'll have gone home to Manchester?"

"Really? Then you'd better tell your grandfather that. Just yesterday, he told Dada that your three weeks of waiting for a place at Windsor School was over. He said something about your Dad having already paid for you to start in two weeks, when the spring term starts." Avi's voice was cold and sharp.

Una was shocked. Why would Grandad tell Major and not her? She thought he was giving her time to make up her own mind about joining. For some reason, even after the trunk had arrived, they hadn't discussed the school.

"Everyone thinks you've given up on going home, especially since you haven't opened your Dad's letter, and the fact you have willingly joined me on these jungle excursions."

How dare they think that she'd stopped thinking about going home, just because she'd been enraptured by the occasional animal footprints or glimpse.

"I thought, we all thought, you had given up on going ..."

"We? Who's we?" spat Una, "OH MY GOD! All this time you were distracting me with that *cold fish*, so I would forget about leaving? How could you be so devious?" Una kicked the driftwood and ran, skirting the edge of the jungle, looking for an opening to the path – Avi was blocking the way to the cowshed.

What came next happened so fast. The jungle leaves parted along the edge of the forbidden bank of the river. Just then, Avi ran into her and threw her down with his weight, urgently whispering in her ear, "Play dead." Winded, Una complied, but twisted her head slightly and opened one eye for a fraction of a second to witness Avi throw himself at an angry sloth bear on its hind legs. Avi was unarmed.

In slow motion, she watched as the bear pushed Avi back and mauled at his torso. His t-shirt was slashed. Avi staggered backwards and fell. Una's breath hitched as the bear loomed over Avi. Instead of a final blow, the bear blew and clacked its teeth, then licked Avi's wounded torso, before backing down and bounding back into the jungle. Its behaviour seemed familiar, but Una couldn't place it.

Avi sat up. Dust-greyed hair flopped over his face, but didn't manage to hide his grey, shimmering angry eyes. Frustrated, he pulled off his shredded t-shirt to check on his injury. A deep gash cut across his packed muscles.

Una gasped. Instead of bleeding, a thin scab had already formed across the width and the length of the gash. From her own parkour injuries, she knew he should have been bleeding profusely by now, requiring stitches. She'd had stitches for much more superficial gashes than his.

"How?"

Avi stared at her from where he sat. With his knee up, he dragged a hand from behind him, touched his shoulder and pointed to her shoulder. Una involuntarily touched her shoulder. It didn't make sense. His healing didn't counter the guilt of her stupidity, which nearly cost them their lives.

"I'm ..."

Avi raised his hand to stop her and, with a voice full of vehemence, said, "Una, just go home ... go home to Manchester ... because, I hereby resign from the role of saving you from your own stupidity."

Chapter 12

Avi

Crazy was screaming again. Her ear-splitting screeches resounded against the walls in his room. Pressing his pillow over his head and ears was not good enough – the screams still penetrated through. The only one who could have quietened her was on her annual holiday, with her chosen son, Gag, at her parents' house. Chosen one? No, it was more that. He was the rejected one. Avi groaned and turned onto his stomach, still holding the pillow over him. He was almost eighteen, but had still not met his maternal grandparents. In the early years, Ma used the – now lame – excuse of not being able to cope with more than one child on a long journey. His grandparents, Nana and Nani, could have visited, but they didn't. Their excuse was that traditional Indian household customs didn't allow for them to even take a sip of water at their children's in-laws. Of course, he could now travel on his own to see them, but he no longer cared about visiting them. A scream at the dreaded decibel arrowed straight through his eardrum, causing his body temperature to rocket sky high, throwing his body into violent convulsions. With each consecutive scream, his blood clamoured hard against his organs. His blood, a body of iron filings, was drawn to the screaming magnet – Crazy. The gash he'd got earlier in the day, courtesy of Una, felt no more than a thorn scratch in comparison. He knew that at the time, but Una's stare reminded him of these moments, when he was his turning into a freak. It was best to send her away.

Avi could hear several pairs of feet running in the passageway outside his room. *Thank God! Someone's going to deal with Crazy*, he thought.

The runners stopped just outside his door. The next thing he knew was that his door had been flung wide open. Riki pulled the pillow away from his head, while Chaz aimed a brightly lit lantern in his eyes. The person to stop her screams had been chosen, and that person was him.

His uncles grabbed him by his armpits and dragged him backwards through the gravel to the unkempt building, built at the furthest point from the house. The ice particles in the night atmosphere were wincingly cold against his bare torso and loose fitting pyjama bottoms. His pleading merged with the high-pitched shrieks emanating from the outbuilding.

"*Chup* – Shut up! You're making the Crazy worse. You don't want her to break out again, do you?" asked Riki.

Words didn't come easy to Chaz so, unlike Riki, he did what came naturally to him and elbowed Avi in the side of his head repeatedly, until he was forcibly silenced and his body fell limp in their hold. Avi barely registered the moment they stood him up to unlock the door and shoved him into the outbuilding. Chaz hurriedly placed the lit kerosene lantern on the dirt floor near Avi's feet and, despite his fears of being in there, kicked Avi hard on his right side, before jamming the door shut behind him. Avi elbow crawled himself along the earth floor to the door. Once there, he beat his arms futilely against it.

The clatter of the external bolt grinding through the slot, and the clang of the lock, registered with him this time. As did the receding jingle of the keys, until they were no longer audible. His hands slid down the door. Left in semi-darkness, his physical senses heightened, amplifying his heartbeat to form a continuous boom in his ears. His nostrils picked up the stench of faeces and mouldy straw. When he stretched out a leg, it hit an object that sounded hollow and felt like a long, dry bone, possibly a femur. Avi sat up, alert now. *Why would there be bones in the hut? Did Crazy eat raw meat?* His ears picked up the nightly sounds outside, his own heartbeat and open-mouthed breathing, nothing else. *Where was she?* Making the smallest of movements, Avi adjusted the lantern's beam and balked. Enlarged, red eyeballs and a ringed nose were just millimetres away from his face. Avi scuttled backwards. That didn't hinder the being in front of him. She placed her hands on his shoulders and pulled him forward, as if his lean, but more muscular, six foot two body weighed nothing. He tried to resist her by applying downward pressure on his flat hands and pulling away, but her super-strength won and he found himself pressed hard against her torso. When he struggled, she just pinned his arms close to his sides in a hug, almost crushing his ribcage as her claws lightly dug into his back. Claws? Could he really feel claws? Slowly, he turned his face upwards, expecting to see an old and wrinkly woman's neck. Only, the neck belonged to a much younger person, younger than Ma. It was tattooed all over with faint rosettes, like those you found on a leopard. A soft, padded hand tapped his head as she held him with the other. She was singing a melody, it was familiar ... His eyes began to droop and after the smallest of inner fights to stay alert, his head fell forward on her shoulder and the world around him dissolved.

Hours later, Avi's nightmare felt 'real'. His body was a dog's ragged ball, kicked, rolled and then shoved and dragged across an unlevelled floor. His head flew against a wall before the rest of his body felt the stone bricks. Back on the floor, he mustered some strength to raise his knees to impede his aggressor, instead they connected with a wooden object – a tall stool, which came crashing over his ribs, breaking several in the process. Pinned in place, he became a new target for sidekicks, then his face became a punch bag. Fists connected with his high cheek bones, his nose, and finally, the space between his eyes. Thwack!

Blurred streaks of yellow-grey pushed through his swollen eye slits, waking him up. It was the next day, and he was in his very own bed. His aunt, Meeru, was gently sponging his face; he knew it was her because of her Ponds talcum powder scent and her now familiar matron-style administrations. Besides, no one else would have bothered with his swollen face. The others would have liked it to be scarred, and sometimes he wished it, too.

"How did you come to be in the outbuilding?"

Avi opened his mouth to speak but winced loudly and placed his hand over the side of his jaw.

"Oh, so sorry! You don't have to answer that. It's pretty obvious. With your mother away and Dada out for the night at his Old Veteran's yearly dinner and drinks and me ... I ... they saw their chance ... I didn't think they had the guts though ... the cowards."

Avi stared past her. He was still catching up with the fact that he was in his own room and on his own bed. He pulled the neck of his kurta and smelt it. It was clean, but seemed to be inside out. He looked enquiringly at Meeru.

"You were shivering, when they brought you in. I had to put that on you in the dark with the shutters closed and lights off." Avi could see why – Meeru was still in yesterday's clothes. She must have just sneaked back into the house, in the early hours.

"What were they thinking of when they put you in there?" Meeru dabbed close to his bruised eye. Avi winced.

Meeru shook her head in disbelief. "I really can't imagine the lady doing this?"

Why couldn't Meeru imagine her doing it? Just the other day, he saw how terrified she and his Grandfather had been.

"Meeru, give me a mirror, I want to see what you can't believe."

"You don't need a mirror." Meeru raised his hand to his face.

Avi winced as he followed the contours of his face with his fingers; it was far worse than what Chaz had done to the side of his head. His face had been remodelled with sharp, gauging tools – claws.

Barely opening his lips, he said, "Meeru, it was the *lady* ... Meeru why do you never call her the Crazy, because that's what she is."

Meeru swore under her breath whilst cleaning his forehead.

With vehemence, she said, "Perhaps you are right." Meeru examined his ravaged flesh closely. "Brute force has been used. Tell me, was she wearing rings?"

"Rings ... no ... but she did have claws," he said, still disorientated.

"Claws ...?" Meeru hesitated and then examined the cuts carefully. It was the way she said 'claws' that drew Avi's attention. She should have been surprised, yet she wasn't – not enough.

Meeru seemed nervous as his eyes widened as he studied her quietly. "What an imagination you have. These are ..." she raised his chin up gently to look carefully at the marks again, "these are circular marks."

"Perfect circles or circles with a break like a rosette?" Avi enquired. It was quite possible for the Crazy to have tattooed the same patterns on him as she had on her neck.

"Rosettes ... What?" Again, there was that fleeting comprehension. Avi's suspicions about Meeru hiding something was deepening, but he said nothing. Instead, he fixed his eyes on her, which unsettled her further.

"I've cleaned the blood, but I'm afraid your face is going to get worse before it gets better," she said, ringing the bloodied cloth out in the basin on the side cabinet.

"Sit up so I can see where else you've been hurt." Avi obliged and pressed against his right side as he gingerly sat up. Meeru pulled up the edge of his kurta to look. "Oh my God! You ... you are completely blue! Whoever gave you these bruises, didn't want you to rise from your bed for some time."

✳✳✳

Avi dozed fitfully. He kept his eyes shut when his uncles sneakily entered.

Riki came in first and gently slapped his face. When Avi didn't stir, Riki breathed aloud, "Oh man!"

"See, I told you he's out for the count," Chaz proudly blurted.

"*Ulu, kisne kaha iska bharta banao?* – Idiot, who told you to beat him to a pulp? We didn't say we'd hospitalise him!" Riki spoke in disbelief.

"*Chup, dhirai bolo* – Shh, keep your voice down. Whilst it's unlikely he might hear us, our sis most definitely will," Niki interjected, carefully making sure nobody was in the passageway before closing the door behind him.

"Oh, shit man. What has she done to him?" Niki obviously hadn't heard the earlier conversation properly.

All three brothers stood around Avi's bed.

"She didn't hurt him at all," Riki whispered to his twin, Niki.

"Yeah! I'm the one who gave him the pretty face," Chaz boasted loudly.

"Yeah, and because of your stupid signature rings, he might work out who did it," Riki offered in a quieter voice, hoping Chaz would take the hint and stop speaking loudly.

"*To kya hua* – What's wrong with that?" Chaz asked stupidly.

"What's wrong with that?" Riki gave up and turned to his twin. "Bhai, you explain it to him."

Niki pushed off the wall he was leaning against and grabbed Chaz by his t-shirt, just under his chin.

Riki grabbed the rings off Chaz's fingers and pocketed them.

"The problem is, *ulu*, Avi is a cunning sod. If he wasn't in a comatose state, he would have worked out that the crazy hag would never hit or harm him. This isn't good for us."

"Bhaiya, put me down! You'd have done the same thing in my situation. Instead of being tortured in there, when I went to fetch him, he looked a little too comfortable. His head was resting on her lap. A bit like in the beginning of Tarzan's movie, where baby Tarzan is cocooned in his Mummy Ape's lap," Chaz chirped.

Niki released Chaz from his hoisted position and the twins fell about laughing. "Sorry, bro, you do crack us up. If it weren't for you, there would be no laughter."

Jollied on by their approval, Chaz decided to have another crack at making them laugh. "We should call Avi the human dummy. Soon as the Crazy laid her eyes on him, she instantly stopped the frantic wailing. Just like that. Even Gag's Ma can't do that. Next time she screams, we'll just pop the human dummy in her room ..."

"Remember, Chaz, Papa should never find out what we did, or he'll probably feed us to her. *Bap rai!* Oh God! He will be furious if he finds out that she had contact with him."

The brother's jostled Chaz between them and out of the room, through the passageway. A little later, a jeep pulled away with the twin's signature horn salute.

Avi winced as he turned over and spoke softly to himself, "So the Crazy didn't hurt me ..."

Deep inside, Avi already knew that.

Chapter 13

Una

It really sucked ... First her Dad, and now Avi, had abandoned her. Squatting on the water tank on the roof, as she had done for two weeks, Una hopelessly stared out towards Major's property. She'd initially thought Avi's absence had something to do with his last words, especially when Major told her Avi didn't want to see her. But now she didn't believe that. She'd clocked several tall, crew cut men enter and leave Avi's house. Avi, on the other hand, did not appear once. Not unless he'd cut his hair ... Una rejected the thought. Avi's shoulder length mop was his trademark; she could never imagine him doing that. An ugly thought entered her mind: *what if the gash hadn't healed?*

Aggh! She was frustrated. If only she had her Mum's binoculars. Mum's binoculars ...

Her face broke into a little smile. She could picture Mum, propped up on cushions, sitting in her armchair near her bedroom window, while Una sat close by, holding Mum's binoculars up to her nose. She was too frail to hold them up for any length of time herself.

Impatiently, Una swiped at her uninvited tears. Days before Mum died, when the pain became too much, she passed on the dreadful task of identifying the garden birds to Una. Of course, she wrongly identified all the birds, except for the pesky magpies.

Memories of Mum's fragmented laughter floated in her memory.

Laughter was an alien emotion amongst the residents of Khamosh Valley. Without Avi, the day was unbearably quiet. Sparse human speech and muted human activity amplified the rustling and twitching movements of leaves, grass and bushes in the surroundings. Just a day or so ago, she watched something slither up and down the lower branches of a lychee tree for nine long minutes. In the tenth moment, her patience broke. Using a fallen branch, she'd parted the leaves and thorns on the lower branches of the tree to reveal a mostly intact cobra skin. Mum would have been proud of her patience.

Back in the present, Una looked over to the orchards gleaming in the winter sun and sighed. "This is all wasted on me, Mum. You would have loved it, but I crave my sort of garden – Piccadilly Gardens' bus station and the noise of buses pulling out of their bays. I would do anything to be messing around with Luke and Charlie on the top deck of a number 86."

Dejected, Una moved off the tank and slumbered in the space between it and the corner of the roof walls, where she found her phone. Perhaps this time, if she pressed hard on her iPhone's top button, it would miraculously switch on. She pressed several times. It was hopeless. The phone was dead. Disgusted, she flung it onto the blanket she kept nearby.

"HUMM MMA. MA."

What was that?

Una grabbed her iPhone again and placed it to her ear.

It was still dead.

Thud!

Large, dark wings and claws landed on her head and paused. Una stilled, her body the way her Mum had taught her to be when they'd fed the birds. She didn't want to have her eyes gauged out. A little time passed before the claws lifted. The wings started to beat and it flew away. Una cranked her head upwards. A crow hovered above her, before flying in the direction from which the lone wolf howled each evening.

Head still upturned, Una spotted a speck ominously growing and moving from the opposite end of the jungle canopy. It was making its way to her. Her watery eyes blinked and opened wide as an emerald feather fell past her vision. She caught it and held it out to examine, when she noticed a green curtain fall all around her. The feathery verdant fringe of long-tailed, rose-ring parakeets soundlessly stood along the walls of the roof, with their red, closed beaks and circular eyes eerily trained on her. Una fled down the stairs, pausing to frantically remove the doorstop so the door would shut behind her.

"HUMMA HUM HUMMA ..."

The hypnotic hum was coming from somewhere outside, from the front of the house, not from the roof. Peering out of the drawing room windows, Una hunted for the source. At first, she couldn't see anything, then waves of dust began to blow up from under the main gate. Tommy was at the gate sniffing the ground. Strangely, he wasn't barking. *Why wasn't he picking up the danger? Damn, she would have to bring him in.* Without thinking about her own safety, Una thrust open the doors of the drawing room and was immediately struck between her eyes by the sharp beak of a severed cockerel's head. She shrieked and swung her head back. Blood – her own, or perhaps the cockerel's, dripped down her nose and parted lips. The cockerel's head, its claws and intestines swung on a string across the door. From their frayed edges, a vertical curtain of slow moving blood beads pooled around the door's threshold. Una's reflex gagged. Tears filled the edge of her whites as she held her mouth and stomach. From nowhere, her Grandad's bony arm appeared behind her and locked the doors.

"Don't talk! They mustn't hear your voice." Una nodded, her hand still on her mouth, as he unearthed a key from beneath his vest. With it still around his neck, he used it to unlock the bureau resting under the infamous glass cabinet. Her hand fell away as he reached inside and took out a big, 1950s black Bakelite phone. Mesmerised, she watched as he pulled the old finger dial mechanism four times. Four clicks and two long shrill rings later, someone picked up the receiver on the other end. Grandad took a short intake of breath and whispered into the handset, "Major, they're coming."

The line went dead.

Grandad slammed the handset down, grabbed Una's shoulder and frogmarched her to her bedroom. In the room, he poured her a glass of water from the jug on her bedside table and gave it to her, then placed his hands on her shoulders.

"Drink." He waited for her to drink the water, then snatched the glass back and put it on the bedside cabinet. "Now sit, and don't move until I am back. I have to make sure the rest of the family are in."

She nodded, not really listening to what he said. She couldn't believe there'd been a phone all this time! She could've rung her father, her friends ... the British Embassy.

HUH HUM HHMM MA, HUH HUM HHMM MA HUHHA HMMA AHMM HUH HUM HH ... the repetitive, never-ending drone was unnervingly loud. It was similar to the buzz of the honey bees in her Mum's man-made beehive in their garden in Manchester, only magnified a thousand-fold. Worse still, the buzz was no longer external, it was within her, too. The hum was under her skin, strumming her nerves relentlessly.

"Move away from the window, Una!" her Grandfather boomed as he burst into her room. He proceeded to draw seven pairs of heavy brocade curtains and bolted both the wooden and mesh exterior doors. She hadn't realised that she was no longer sitting on the bed.

"Sit back down on your bed. NOW!"

She did so and, for the first time, was intimidated by her Grandad as he cowered over her.

"Not a squeak from you, madam. They mustn't see or hear you."

"Who mustn't see or hear me? Wait! Are you implying the door hanging was meant for me?"

"Yes."

"But, I've only been here for three weeks and it's my first visit! Are you sure ...?"

Grandad's hand shot up. "I SAID, stop talking now!"

A gasp left Una's mouth.

Grandad's complexion turned to chalk as he registered the position of his hand. "Don't be the first to make me hit a girl," he said as he quickly lowered it.

Major was on the premises and frantically shouting out for her grandfather. He must have come from behind the orchard, via the hill at the back, which linked both properties.

"I mean it, Una! Don't even try to peek out."

Una nodded, again. Grandad stared down at her for a short while, checked the curtained windows again and left the room.

As soon as he disappeared, Una stood up, locked the bedroom door and scurried to the window facing the gate. She lifted the curtain from its hem and poked her head under it ... and gasped.

From the gap along the bottom of the gate, several bare feet rhythmically pounded the ground. Higher up, between the grills, three horizontal lines of green, red and cream swayed. She couldn't see faces, but long poles with menacing spearheads loomed above the gates, making the gate's speared top look harmless. Coincidentally, the humming was soon joined by the clanging of metal spears against the metal gate in rhythm as she twitched the curtains. Unable to tear herself away, Una listened to the clamour reach a crescendo, then jumped back when the gates flung open and a throng of tattooed men, wearing fierce expressions, pushed through, all the while keeping the rhythm of their stomping feet and thumping long spears in sync with the mysterious humming flowing from their lips.

Chapter 14

Menacing, oversized headdresses, with yellow-billed horned beaks, long black and white feathers and cowrie shells stood erect above the tribesmen heads. Rigid rings and amulets, made from strands of the same material, hung from their necks. They wore black lengths of cloth wrapped diagonally across their gleaming bare torsos. Around their waists, they wore short black kilts with bright geometric patterns in red, green and cream, displaying their bulging calves and knives.

Major and Dev nervously approached and embraced three of the tribesmen. Una chortled in surprise as they then walked backwards to the steps with their hands in a 'Namaste' clasp. The three representatives of the tribe ventured forward, the rest stayed just inside the gate, forming a straight line across the width of Dev's property. Scraping of chairs on the veranda followed. Reluctantly, Una left the window and sat with her ear against the bolted wooden veranda door instead.

"Good Major ... so we come for ... land."

Una could barely hear what was being said. Quickly, she retrieved her glass tumbler and placed the wide opening against the door, and pressed the bottom of the tumbler to her ears, just in time to hear Major speak.

"Payment? We paid a fair price for the land, much more than the army were ever going to give when they proposed to buy the land for the Gorkha's accommodation," said Major, levelly.

"It was not theirs to sell. We don't want money; we never have. We want proper payment – we want ..."

Major was angry, "You want? You don't actually own the land you live on. You have no deeds. Sharman, where is the paperwork?"

No reply.

Major continued. "You would have nothing if it wasn't for the forestry interfering and giving you the title of indigenous tribe. They've made sure the land you live on is safeguarded, *for now*."

Sharman piped up. "We want payment from each member of your family, or you leave the land."

Dev, her Grandad, finally joined in. "We paid good money to your *rishtedar*, relative, and if you had a problem, you should have split monies with them. They are now *shaheris*, town dwellers, like the rest of us."

Sharman retorted, "Not rishtedar! Not since they turned traitorous and gave up our ancient ways and us, their kin folk, to become Christians. It is strange that they think us to be devil worshippers when the devil only materialises in their Christian beliefs, not in ours."

Una wasn't really following the conversation. Land ... Christians ... payment ... that wasn't money and devil worshippers?

"Too much talk, we want payment, give us the teenagers – the girl and the boy, and our leader. Time is nearly up for the boy and leader," said another tribesman.

Dev snapped, "You can't expect us to take your payment threats seriously. We live on the right side of the path. We are not a threat to you, yet you hassle us while Sid Rao lives on your side."

Who was Sid Rao? wondered Una.

"Yes, Dev, you are quite right. Sid Rao lives with his wife and two daughters on the wrong side, your side. Yet, Sharman, how is it that you have not exacted payment from them?" asked Major

"He paid," replied Sharman.

"How, Sharman? His firstborn, the eldest daughter, still lives with them. She is twenty now. Yet, when they first moved here four years ago, she was a teenager. She's still living on the wrong side of the path, in your territory, which means Rao has definitely not paid your tribe in kind," Dev refuted.

"Wrong side of the path?" Una whispered to herself, totally confused.

If the oldest teens were payment, and they wanted one from Major and Grandad's household, that meant the boy would come from the Major's family, as they didn't have any teen girls. And the girl would be herself – Una.

But then, if she and Avi were the girl and boy, then who was the leader?

"Whose fault is it, Dev, that we live on the wrong side?" A mature male voice spoke between Tommy's barks.

Oh, great, now he barks! She had forgotten about Tommy. He should have barked before now.

Dev grunted, "Even if what you say is true, Sharman, I can't help you. I don't have a teen girl or boy. I only have a son who is in his forties and he lives abroad."

"Yet, you have a teen girl," the tribe's spokesman shouted. "We have seen her."

Una's heart stilled. How did they know she was here? She'd rarely been out.

Chapter 15

Una leaned against the wooden door, her arms crossed as she held herself tightly. Her temples rested on her raised knees.

"For the first time ever, I'm really scared, and there is no one to help."

"I'm here."

"Avi?"

Una frantically looked around her room for Avi, but he wasn't there. His voice was strong and warm, though, and resonated from her core ... her core.

"Avi? Where are you?" Una whispered.

No reply. Had she heard Avi's voice, or did she think and imagine it?

"Avi, are you here?"

"Not bodily." A pause followed before Avi said, "I'm in my room, but I can hear your thoughts."

"What? ... my thoughts but not my spoken voice?"

"Una, calm down. I can hear your voice, but only faintly. You must be whispering. Normally, I can hear your voice clearly."

"How are you doing this?"

"I don't know, but I've been listening to you for two weeks, hoping you could hear my thoughts, too."

For two weeks! Una blushed. He knows how many times I thought about him. Worse still, he knows how I feel about him. Una felt violated and snapped, "Avi, answer me truthfully ... have you heard all my thoughts?"

"*YES.*" His voice was laden with guilt. She could feel his guilt, something else and ... pain ... an all-encompassing pain. Una began to shake. *The thoughts were enough, but experiencing his current feelings sent her off the rails.* Una's body felt hot and cold at the same, thrilled and broken.

"Why can I only hear some of your thoughts?"

A long pause followed, and then the answer came, "You can only hear the ones that are associated with intense feelings of pain, anger, hate, fear and ..."

I get it! Una felt even worse.

"In my defence, I tried to share mine equally. I tried to send messages to you, but you weren't ready. This is the first time you have heard me ..."

Avi halted mid-sentence. "*What's that?*"

Una felt a large ripple in the surrounding air. It was knocking at her temples.

"IS THAT YOU, AVI?"

"NO, Una! I think somebody else is trying to listen in. The vibrations are coming from somewhere near you."

"The tribesmen?"

"No, the intruder has only just arrived."

Una shuffled to the window, pulled the curtain back slightly and gasped. Gasped at what? There was nothing there. In her mind, before she'd peeked through the curtain, she'd seen the image of a wolf's face pressed up against the glass window, behind the grill. It had stared directly at her, then creased its face in a smile, as if to say – Gotcha!

There was nothing by the window, but her eyes were diverted to the fifteen ropes lassoing the spikes on the property's side wall, and the fifteen male youths clambering down them. Una watched, wide-eyed. In unison, the fifteen youths approached the tribesmen. The tribesmen's stoic faces dissolved in outrage and anger. Their feet remained stationary but their spear hammering began again – the beat was less ceremonial and more combative.

Feral eyed, the youths responded, stare for stare. They exuded confidence and controlled discipline. Una had narrowly escaped street gangs on a couple of occasions when she had explored the back of the Victorian warehouses that loomed over the dark canals, but they looked tame in comparisons to the fifteen individuals in combat clothing. These boys were organised to a breath, and were akin to militia recruits, except for their tattoos. Both groups "facing-off" had similar abstract tattoos on their faces.

Under a silent command, Una watched as the urban youths deftly converged to a V shape, dead opposite the tribesmen's line. Una opened and closed her mouth like a fish – their formation was a textbook Roman wedge. Like attacking Roman legionaries, the boys had formed a triangle with one of them placed at the tip, thus allowing the youth's cohort to thrust well into the tribesmen and then expand. They'd forced restricted mobility for the tribesmen's. Una was trembling; her panic was rising. *Why are they all here? Has such a gathering ever happened before?*

"No, not as far as I can remember."

They've come for me, haven't they? Her thoughts became scrambled as panic rose in her.

"Una, calm down, nothing is going to happen to you today, the army are on the way. I heard Dada call them. Look, I can't help you if you don't think clearly."

"Wh-what army?"

"Never mind the army, Una, tell me what you see so I can picture it and help you calm down."

Una trained her eyes on the youth gang's leader and explained what she could see, and then stopped.

"What is it?"

"The boy ... the boy at the tip isn't a boy. He's a man, in his twenties. He doesn't have the normal dark Indian hair, either. His hair is tawny brown in colour and razored in a jagged pattern on the sides."

"Repeat that."

When she did, she felt Avi's shock.

"What's wrong, Avi?"

"Una, focus on his eyes and tell me if they are unusually golden?"

"Golden?" Una leaned forward and managed not to flinch when the youth leader simultaneously turned his face towards her hiding place. Una gulped and answered, "I've never seen amber gold eyes like his before, Avi. Who is he?"

"I don't know his actual name, but he sounds like the knife thrower from the circus that came to town last month, a few weeks before you arrived. I went to see him specifically, because he was going to perform 'The Veiled Wheel of Death'. In the act, a lady was strapped onto a wooden wheel as it spun around. A large sheet of paper then hid the wheel from the thrower, so he couldn't see where the lady was when he threw twelve steel knives in her direction. Apparently, only a handful of people in the world have tried this. Strangely, I thought the lady looked remarkably like our Meeru. I can't remember the man's name, but he had tawny hair and eyes."

How many tawny guys could there be in India? Una looked for evidence of a knife on the frontman's person and spotted one in his right hand. It was a combat knife, similar in size to the short legionary *gladius* the Romans would have carried. Held low, it was a deadly, thrusting weapon used in combat where spears would be difficult to wield. Una ran her eyes down the V shape. Each boy had a combat knife. Travelling down their faces this time, she realised that their facial tattoos were different from the ones the tribesmen had. Bizarrely, they were abstract Celtic-styled wild animals. Celtic abstracts? ... In India? Tawny had the most distinctive tattoo. It took up the whole left side of his face; it was a Celtic wolf howling. *The tawny man's tattoo looked EXACTLY like the wolf image I thought I had imagined!*

"Una, are you sure? Because that means ..."

"Avi, what does that mean?"

"... Oh God, they really exist ... he's a Blessed. Una, if you can see his tattoos, then you are in trouble ..."

"Avi, you are scaring me. What's a Blessed, and why can I see one?" Una's mind began to collapse on her.

Suddenly an ocean of calm wrapped around her. "Una, I'll explain later. He is the one who is trying to listen in. For a little while, I don't want you to think at all. Let your mind go blank. Go and listen at the door again. I'm going to try something else."

Una knew he had evaded the question, but she didn't want the Blessed tawny guy in her head either, so she filled it with a particular shade of grey.

She crawled to the door and lifted the glass tumbler to listen in on the heated meeting going on outside, and then abandoned it – they were so loud, she didn't need it.

"Thank you, Rao, for bringing your martial art students from St. Anthony's School to hold off the tribe till the army arrive. I'm just surprised that you taught them how to use knives. How does that work with the school curriculum?" snickered Major.

"Major, I don't want my two girls picked off any more than you do. When nothing happened when Agnes turned eighteen, I thought their story was a hoax. But now, I know it isn't," Rao replied. Una noticed that he avoided Major's question. The combat knives were real, not like the wooden fencing sword she'd practiced with at her school in Manchester.

"So how did you find out?" her grandfather asked suspiciously.

"A little crow told me."

"Crow!"

"Una, stop!"

Una checked herself, and thought hard of the colour grey.

Major cleared his throat and, in a serious voice, said, "Sharman, why don't you tell the army and the forestry what you are doing here when they arrive – I've phoned both."

The Sharman's voice showed surprise and hurt. "Why do you make it so difficult? We just want what we are due. We do not wish to talk to anyone else." His voice then hardened, "The boy is nearly eighteen, so he is ready to come with the leader to our side now; we can wait for the girl."

A tense silence fell over the veranda.

Una sat frozen to the spot. Her mouth hung open and her eyes were wide. She could barely think the words she thought next.

"Avi, is your eighteenth birthday soon?"

"*In a few days.*" The terseness in his voice wanted her to drop the line of thought.

"*Oh God, Avi … that means …*" Horrified, she stumbled for words.

Una closed her mouth and shut her eyes tight. Instead of the calm grey she wanted, she glimpsed tormented grey eyes with strange purple and yellow rings above dark eyebrows. Una flinched. *How was she able to see him? Was it something he was doing?* Una focused on the hazy projection of his face lying on a pillow. His hair was plastered to his sweat drenched face; pain contorted his face. "*The bear didn't do this, Avi. So, who did, and why didn't you tell me, instead of trying to keep me calm, Avi?*"

"Shhh, Una! There's lots of movement near you, so concentrate." Avi's voice was deceptively flat. His words dispelled her vision of him. With it, the knocking against her temples decreased, too. Una didn't need to check the window to know that Rao's Tawny man and boys had left. Her core relaxed, relieved they were gone. Unable to resist checking if she was right, Una crawled back to the window facing the main road on the cliff and carefully parted the curtains a little. The sound of iron rattling drew Una's attention to the Cantonment Bridge that stood over the dry river bed. Her gaze skimmed over the army convoy that was tentatively making its way down the dirt track.

"Wimps!" uttered Una. Just three weeks ago, Una's taxi had free-wheeled most of the way down due to the dodgy brakes – in pitch black. The memory left her with an unsettled sensation. The image of Tawny's eyes in the rear view mirror of the taxi formed in her mind. Tawny was the taxi driver! She couldn't be sure, of course, as the taxi driver's cap had overshadowed his face for most of the journey, and it had been dark when she had got out of the car. She was sure the driver didn't have a wolf tattoo like

Tawny, though.

"You are getting distracted."

Una bristled.

The army convoy stood motionless outside the house, whilst a minibus, with National Forestry Research Institute printed in gold and black letters in a wreath formation, beeped its way down the hillside until it came to a screeching halt behind the last army truck.

Seconds later, countless boots thudded across the gravel path. Soldiers carrying rifles, wearing metal combat helmets, barged through the gates, scattering tribesmen to either side of it. Unperturbed, the tribesmen realigned themselves, like ants, into a feet-stamping line again. Una puzzled over why the tribesmen seemed more nervous and hostile towards the youths. Open-mouthed, Una watched the soldiers take up every spare square inch of her Grandfather's driveway, garden, and even the stairs that led up to the veranda. Each soldier marked a tribesman with their rifle.

When everyone was positioned, officials wearing forest green blazers nervously acknowledged both the tribesmen and the soldiers as they entered. Una assumed they were the peace keepers.

Quickly, she slumped against the door again and placed her ear against it. Her hands shot up over her ears, hoping to drown out the horrendous scraping of the chairs.

"Una, move your hands. I think someone is talking."

Una submitted to his order, but her frustration with him grew. She desperately wanted to sneak out and see him in person and ... *and what?*

"Please, Una, stop getting distracted. We need more information about what our grandparents agree to. Una, please!" Una relented, he was right, yet again.

"Major, it seems we are all here now, but we don't really know what this is all about?" an authoritative female voice prompted.

Major cleared his throat. "Madam, there has been a great deal of unrest in the evenings. We've got to the point where the sun barely drops between the mountain peaks before the animal kingdom becomes restless. We can't even walk in our compounds due to the terrible cries that come from across the path. We are worried the animals will cross over and unleash their terror on us and our families. We need you, the Forestry Office, to venture over to the other side and perhaps kerb the animals."

"What? That wasn't what was discussed earlier – why isn't Major telling them about the threats the tribesman made?"

"I don't know."

Two knocks interrupted their thought-talk. A clipped voice spoke, "Our Shaman says that Major and Dev are cheats. They have stolen the land from the animal and tree spirits and, if that wasn't enough, they want more."

"Please, speak slowly. I have to take notes of this meeting," an officious male voice interrupted.

The tribesman complied.

"Animal spirit? Where did that come from? Avi, weren't they talking about payment earlier?"

"Both sides are covering up!"

"There are no disturbances. You just wish for more land. Yet, you have not yet paid the right price for it," accused the tribesman, interrupting again.

"*Bakwas!* – Absolute rubbish!" said the female voice. "Sherman, *Tumko theek paisa milai* – I know you paid them fair and square. *Mai thi jab exchange hua* – I was officially present when the money was transferred to the people who live here."

Major replied, "*Bilkul* – My point exactly. We agreed the price with these people. Madam, you, the Forestry, negotiated the exchange. Even the army, who originally wanted to buy the land for the retired Gorkhas, were present."

Una wondered why they were going over old ground, and why the Sharman chose not to speak at all.

"Sharman says *zameen* – land, cannot be held by any tribe of people. It was an illegal sale. Together, we all cleared the trees on this land to grow rice, but it did not grow. So, we left the area intentionally, to allow the jungle to grow back. We did not think the infidel Christian converts would sell what does not belong to us. You can no more sell land than the air above it." The tribesman was angry. His raised voice triggered an increase in the volume of the stamping, and the tribesmen began to hum again.

Someone rustled papers, possibly the female Forestry official, who impatiently spoke, "The land on both sides of the path up to the river technically belongs to Major and Mr Dev. Their buildings are restricted to this side of the path because the river floods in the monsoons, making it unsafe. Based on the reports I have read, Major and Mr Dev, in accordance with their agreement, have not hunted or killed any wild animals. I also know they have not restricted you, the tribesmen, from eating the produce of trees on both sides of the path, if you so wish. Now, Sharman, explain what is disturbing the animals in the jungle and what can we do to stop this?"

Una heard a large paper being folded up. A map perhaps?

No one spoke.

The Forestry official broke the silence. "Perhaps there is a lot of big cat activity? We could always send a team of experts to stakeout the jungle and investigate for you?"

"No!" Sharman shouted.

Una's concentration was withering. Her forehead and the left side of her face and jaw felt raw, and throbbed hard.

"Una? Concentrate!"

"I can't. My face hurts and my brain wants to shut down. Please, Avi, they're just making up stories. We aren't going to hear anything we can use to help us ..."

"Oh, Una, I'm sorry. I didn't realise how I could affect you. We must close the channel. Rest now."

"Avi, this pain is unbearable. Oh, Avi, is this why I haven't seen you? Who did this to you? The bear didn't touch your face."

The thoughts in her mind were just hers. Avi was gone.

Drained and exhausted, Una picked up her glass tumbler and rose from the floor. She unlocked her bedroom door and lay on her bed. As soon as she was rested, she would go and see Avi, somehow.

Half an hour later, Grandad entered Una's room and found her feathered fringe blowing with her outward breath as she slept.

In the curtained darkness, Dev missed the shadowed ring indentations on her forehead and the slightly swollen left side of her face and jaw. If he had covered her trembling body with a blanket, his touch would have revealed her high temperature, but he noticed nothing. Until now, he had been careful not to encourage any physical contact. Any form of attachment to his son's firstborn child would just lead to heartbreak, if the tribe's prophecy was true.

Chapter 16

Avi's fevered and scabbed flesh lay lifeless, but his self remained connected ... connected to everything. He deliberately silenced his thoughts after Una's last shared thought, hoping her pain disappeared as she slept. A gentle, cool breeze undulated beneath his epidermis, rapidly cooling him. He knew it was Una; her vanilla essence gave her away. His elation only lasted a moment, though. Her cool breath stilled and her essence evaporated with the breaking of his fever, leaving him momentarily bereft, until he felt the faint tug of an energy tendril demanding his full attention. It wasn't Una – she'd slipped into slumber.

Astonished and curious, Avi gently spoke to the presence, "Who are you. I know you're there." The tug increased in strength. He waited for an image to appear as he pondered over their undefined connection. There's a possibility that it had always been there, and he'd just been unaware of it. The same was true for Una. Avi had become accustomed to Una's face slipping behind his fevered eyelids, especially when he picked up on her loneliness, yet she had been completely unaware of him and their connection for two whole weeks.

A surge of energy brought Avi's attention back to a ... a large pink tongue ... it leapt forward and licked him. *How was it possible for a projection to feel so real?* Avi tracked the tongue as it darted in and out from a fuzzy creamy form. He swiped his hand over his face and felt dampness – his forehead and the bruised side of his face was wet. Only when the tongue stayed put in the dark mouth did his eyes avert from the tongue to study the fuzzy form surrounding it. It was patterned with rosettes, like those on Crazy's neck. Perplexed, Avi reached out his hand to stroke them, but found his fingers caressing air. His hand dropped to his side.

His own voice boomed in his head. Remember, you told Meeru that Crazy had rosettes and held you with claws.

Avi doubted his sanity. Crazy was a distant relative – a human relative. Not a big cat.

His poor neurones could not cope with the conflicting messages and severed the connection between him and the hazy rosette face. Involuntarily, his attention moved to his heart's rhythmic motion: expansion, depletion, and expansion again … until it was no longer outside him. His self rushed back into his physical body, which joyfully jerked forward to meet it.

His rusty eyelid shutters pushed awake. His brain, woozy and disorientated, moaned and took its sweet time in reclaiming the weight of his body. With great concentration, he coaxed his body to roll from his back onto his uninjured side. He had anticipated pain, tenderness and some trembling. Instead, his body spun easily, without a smidgeon of pain. In shock, he stupidly sprung up to a sitting position on the edge of the bed. He felt nothing. Repeatedly, he twisted his midriff, expecting blinding pain from his cracked ribs, but he felt no discomfort. He drew his kurta hem up and was speechless. His skin was smooth and unblemished. Avi ran his thumb across his ribs. They were all intact. Unhooked, he lightly roamed his fingers over his face. His touch spurred his skin into action, smoothing itself swiftly, and healing his swollen face. Unsure of what was happening to him, he closed his eyelids, only to be rewarded by visions of his skin knitting itself quickly under the scabs. One moment he was observing his skin as it healed, then, in the next, he became the taut skin under the healing scabs, pushing the redundant crispy heads upwards and away. Baffled, and with eyes still shut, Avi pressed his fingers hard over the area where the scabs should have been. They had vanished.

The wonder disappeared as quickly as it came. Was he turning into something ... Hadn't the Sherman said he was ready? *Was Una changing, too?* It was quite possible that Una had triggered his healing. No, it had to be the fuzzy cat's tongue cleansing ministrations. *Was it possible that Una suffered from unfounded feverish nights and growth spurts, too? She'd already told him she suffered grogginess the way he did, and she was tall. But he'd only begun experiencing this in recent months, whereas Una had just arrived a few weeks back and was still sixteen. Was he the source of her change, and was he responsible for the channel between them?* Nothing made sense. Worse still, *how did the Crazy fit into the grand scheme of things? He had to visit Crazy again, before his birthday, which was in two days.* Instead of the learnt trepidation he felt towards Crazy, a rush of adrenaline rose from his gut. He knew his life had been leading up to this moment.

Meeru stood in the shadows behind Avi's door. She'd entered his room earlier, expecting him to be asleep. Instead she'd found him examining his unscarred body, totally unaware of the hues of white and orange light that emanated and arched from his body. Captivated, Meeru put her hand out to touch a bending stream.

SMACK!

Her whole body had jolted backwards, battering her head against the wall behind the door. Clenching her teeth tightly, she stifled her cry of pain, hoping she hadn't given herself away.

With his back to the door, Avi stood tall and alert. He glanced over his shoulder and smiled. He knew she was there. If she wanted to spy on him, that was her business. He had to get dressed and meet the Crazy, then go to Una. He didn't think the jungle was going to wait for her to turn eighteen. He sprinted across to his cupboard and rifled through his clothes. Most of his limited wardrobe was too small for him now, and lay, wasted, on the ground. Frantically, he pulled on his black jeans, which were just short of the new skin over his pelvic bone. Avi's hands paused. He couldn't address the relative in the outbuilding as Crazy; she must have a real name, but what was it? He'd never heard anyone else refer to her as anything but Crazy, but then he remembered that Meeru never called her that. *Was it possible that she knew her name?*

Hooking his belt through the jeans loops, he spoke pointedly at the door. "She's not crazy, is she?"

Avi took her silence as a 'No'.

His face scrunched in revulsion as he buckled his belt. The buckle reminded him of Dada's army regulation belt, the one he used to tame the Cr ... lady in the outbuilding.

"If she isn't, why do they treat her like an animal? Why whip her?" He fed the buckled belt through the double loops.

Not a sound came from behind the door. Avi furrowed his eyebrows and sifted through the discarded t-shirts that lay on the floor. He chose the darkest one – running away with Una might be the only way of escaping their fates. Perhaps the nameless person in the outbuilding might have an idea; he knew she had compassion. *Compassion.* The word soaked in and set off shock waves in his brain, spurring it into rewiring itself. Slowly, intense rays of compassion filled her image with more form and shape, morphing the deranged googly eyes and long-haired monster's portrait in his head. By the time he began to pull his fleece hoodie over his head, her wiry outline had morphed into a strong, tall woman with familiar features.

"Meeru, tell me truthfully, who is the lady in the outbuilding?" Avi asked. "Una thought she was related to me."

A loud gasp came from behind the door. "Una said that?"

Avi expected Meeru to reveal herself, but she stubbornly remained behind the door frame, and out of sight. *Was she scared of him?* Avi wondered.

"It's not possible for Una to have met her! You only chanced upon her because of those idiot brothers of mine. You were never meant to meet her. We weren't even meant to know her name. This changes everything. I'll ... I'll have to let him know." Meeru finally pushed at the door and revealed herself.

"Let who know?" Avi's muffled voice came through the fleece. Meeru's hand slipped off the knob. She hesitantly replied,

"Papa, of course."

Avi had expected 'Papa' to be the answer, but her tone did not ring true. She was lying! Avi was drowning in cryptic images and questions. Frustrated, he grabbed the tight neck opening of the hoodie and forcefully pulled it down, ripping it at the hem. Meeru gasped loudly.

"Tell me her *real* name. Meeru, if you ever loved me, you will tell me her name, because I know you know it."

"Rosetta."

"Rosetta?" Of course, it would be. Surprised, Avi looked up from tying his trainer laces to face Meeru, who was clinging onto the door knob; he hadn't expected blackmail to work.

"*That's my name,*" a stranger's soft voice spoke in his head.

"Rosetta." Avi stared on at Meeru, who stared back, mouth agape.

"Say it again and again."

"Rosetta ... Rosetta ... Rosetta." Slowly, Avi's voice broke with emotion. Voicing 'Rosetta' repeatedly had unlocked the hippocampus in his brain, freeing fuzzy early memories associated with her name, which in turn sparked changes in the electromagnetic patterns of the emotional control centre of his brain. Removing the name Crazy from his vocabulary had triggered the prefrontal cortex to decimate the emotion of anxiety and crippling fear associated with the Crazy tag. Instantaneously, the truth settled around his heart – Rosetta had never posed a threat to him. In fact, it was quite the opposite.

"Thank you for setting me free from my bondage."

Anger consumed Avi. Barely holding it in check, he asked, "Meeru, why ... why didn't you tell me her name before?"

"I haven't always known."

Avi shook his head in disbelief.

"You have to believe me, Avi, I didn't. When I found out her name, I was warned not to use it. I was told that her name connected her to you, and, to keep you safe, it was important that no one used it."

Avi's hands balled into fists along the side of his body. "How can her name be a threat? Meeru, you fool, her name has triggered an emotion, but it's not a threatening one. You were the only one I trusted, but now ... never mind, I get it wasn't sincere. Just tell me what you're hiding?"

Tears fell from Meeru's eyes as she shook her head.

Avi shot to the door and banged it shut – almost busting its frame.

"All these years I thought you were my best, and only, ally. The only one who cared ..."

His fierce, no nonsense aunt was trembling ... because of him. Avi backed away, clenching his fists open and closed to calm himself. Yes, he was stronger now, but he wasn't a bully. Affronted that she thought he was capable of hurting her, he opened the door and left the room. Meeru didn't follow.

Chapter 17

Twenty steps away from the courtyard, Avi hovered at the gated post. Surprisingly, it had been left open. When he was seven, he had once tried to sneak in. Ma had forgotten to lock the gate behind her when she'd taken lunch in for the lady in the outbuilding. Unfortunately, his uncles caught him sneaking around and beat him up as their father watched. Since that day, Dada never said a word to stop them, and they continued whenever they chose to, just for a bit of sport. Incensed by the memory, he rocked the cemented post on the other side of the open gate, forwards and backwards, until it slipped out from the cement base. Not questioning the ease with which he pulled it out, with one mighty grunt, he hauled it over the boundary wall. A surprised *moo* came from beyond the wall. Avi continued up the path to the outbuilding, until he saw a familiar figure sitting on a charpoy. Avi quickly stepped into the shadows of the surrounding trees. A frown crossed Avi's forehead – since when did Chaz have the courage to sit near the outbuilding?

Suspicious, Avi raked his eyes over his uncle and found the reason behind his bravery; he had a couple of rifles and a box of bullets beside him. He was also scouring the area. Chaz was not guarding the family from the lady, he was guarding her instead! Avi was furious. *How come they weren't guarding his door? Surely, he was the one who would be taken away as a form of repayment?* As soon as he thought it, he knew the answer. *She was the tribesmen's leader – a bargaining chip for more land, and he was the expendable pawn.*

It was time to play dumb. He pulled his hoodie over his face to cover his bruise-free face, then walked over to Chaz. Chaz raised his gun and shot a bullet close to his feet. "Stop. You aren't allowed here."

Avi stopped in his tracks. "Chacha, I'm happy not to be here, but Dada has put me on the rota. He insisted I got over my fear of *that thing*, and ordered me to guard while you have a break. Believe me, I have no intention of going inside after what she did to me last time."

Chaz couldn't hide his smirk. "Hmm, I think you are lying. After all these years, and the fury Papa showed when he found out we brought you here a couple of weeks ago, I would have thought you were the last person Papa would send."

"I questioned Dada on the same thing, but he said things have changed since his meeting with tribesmen this morning."

Avi saw the shift in Chaz. He looked more hesitant. "Meeting? *Tujhai bata diya? Phir jo tu khai raha hai sach hee hoga* – If he told you about the meeting, then what you are saying is true, but *mun nahi manta* – My head doesn't believe it."

Today, Chacha, is not the day to have brains, Avi thought.

"*Chacha, mai to kilo meel ki doori par rahna chata hu* – I'd rather be miles away from her, but Dada thinks I should punish the one who left me in this state, if she tries to escape. You are to leave your rifles here for me. However, if you don't want a break, I'll just go back and let Dada know you're fine." Avi turned to go, faking pain in his recovered ribs.

"*Itna bhi kya jaldi hai* – Not so fast, sunny boy, you need a rest ... out here." Chaz rose and pushed Avi down into the charpoy, purposely making him stumble sideways onto his injured side. "You might as well make yourself comfortable. Hot tea and shit breaks take a long time."

Laughing, he poked Avi in the ribs with the butt of a rifle and said, "Here, catch," then left.

Just as Avi's hand hovered over the outbuilding keys on the

charpoy, Chaz reappeared and grabbed them. He smiled contemptuously at Avi, then jogged backwards to the house. Moments later, Avi heard a distant groan and then a shout, "Where did this hole come from? *Shukar hai kisi nai dekha nahi* – Thank God no one saw that."

Avi smiled.

With no time to waste, he began the task of looking for another way into the outbuilding. Making sure no one was nearby, or watching him, he searched around the walls of the outbuilding until he found a grilled vent the size of four bricks. Even with his growth spurts, the vent was too high. Avi cast around for something to aid him and found an empty, overturned oil drum, which he quickly rolled to position, just under the vent. Once on top of it, he pressed his face against the grilled vent. The overcast sky made it difficult to see into the building. Undeterred, Avi slid a hand through the grills and was rewarded with a scuttle.

"Rosetta, please don't be scared. It's me, Avi. Remember?"

He paused for a reply, but nothing came.

"I just ..."

I just what? Avi thought. I just wanted to know whether you were crazy?

"I should be, but please go back. This will only get you in more trouble."

"I just wanted to know who you are."

"You still don't know?"

"Why should I ... how come you speak in English and not Hindi?"

"Because I haven't spoken it for a long time, and you talk to her in English. Shh! Since you are here, let me see you in daylight, and then you must go before they catch you."

Knock ... knock ... knock! Avi hurriedly withdrew his hand from the window to check whether his uncle had returned. The knocking was coming from inside the outbuilding. Avi gripped the grills tighter and pushed his nose between them, hoping his face would extend further into the room. It worked. He could just about make out shapes easily. It was unfortunate, however, that he could smell the stench, too. Narrowing his eyes, Avi focused on the limited square footage, and found a *dari*, a cloth mattress, with a shawl or blanket heaped in the corner. A splinter of sun light broke through the clouds above him, lifting the darkness for a few precious seconds. He glimpsed the three legs of a stool and, resting on them, were two big toes peeking out from under a dirty grey shroud.

Knock ... Knock ... Avi's gaze travelled up to the shrouded body, which was slowly elongating from its squatting position, using the bare brick wall for support.

"Ow!"

Avi could see that the material draped around her body was trapped on a nail. The same nail must have scraped her exposed midriff, too. He helplessly watched her tug hard on the material, making the uneven leg tilt backwards.

"Watch out!"

He was too late. The unstable stool gave way and she toppled backwards, hitting her head against the wall before falling flat on her face in the dirt.

"Can you get up?"

She cocked her head sideways and brought her upper body to a sitting position. Through her entangled hair, her piercing grey gaze punched him low in his gut. Her mercurial eyes were identical to the ones he saw in the mirror every time he looked at one. Una was right.

A slow stream of drool trickled from Rosetta's mouth as she mouthed something at him – but he couldn't work out what it was. Frantically, she swung her gaze to the door and then back at him several times.

Avi sadly shook his head and said, "No keys."

Hurriedly, she rose and noisily dragged the fallen stool to the wall beneath the window he stood by.

The expected rocking noise began again.

"Careful, Rosetta," Avi took a deep breath in and held it. Any moment now he would get the chance to see her close up.

Just then, a rock nicked him in the neck.

"Get down from there! What do you think you're doing?" Riki shouted,

"The bastard lied to me. Just as well I noticed the post was missing," Chaz said.

Riki grabbed Avi's legs and tried to knock him off the oil drum. At the same moment, he felt something sharp touch the flesh of his slipping fingertips. Barely holding on, Avi's eyes darted to her gnarled, yellow fingernails that gripped his fingers, which were barely wrapped around the grills. His hands rapidly heated up, causing circular bubbles to appear under his fingertips. He gasped in shock as claw-like appendages pushed through his fingertips, before retracting. He lost his grip on the grills and fell on his uncles, winding them. His body landed on the butt of a rifle and he blacked out.

✳✳✳

The light was hazy in Avi's bedroom, and everything seemed out of focus. Meeru was saluting Major's imposing, uniformed portrait that hung over the bed she sometimes used. She kissed Dada's painted cheek in the portrait and sighed, "Sorry, Papa, your time is up."

"What do you mean, Meeru?" Avi anxiously asked.

Meeru looked around. "Avi where are you?" She couldn't see him. At first, he was shocked, but when Meeru turned her attention to the painting again, he stood shoulder-to-shoulder with her. Furrowing her eyebrows, she tilted the portrait forwards and rested the heavy frame on her forearm before swiping her free hand hastily up and down the length of the back. He could see her upper arm was barely holding the bulk of the frame as it pinched the hair on her arm. He also knew that Meeru would be unable to remove the portrait completely from the wall, due to its colossal size and weight; Dada's ego and pride had dictated its grandeur proportions. Finally, she yanked her hand from underneath the frame after retrieving a narrow, short box between her fingers, which she quickly dropped onto her pillow. Hurriedly, she opened the flap and tilted the contents onto her palm. Then, she raised the object to her lips after saying a quick prayer, and blew the soundless whistle.

Nausea took over Avi.

＊＊＊

Avi's uncles moved from under his weight, bringing him back to consciousness. "Let's get him into the house before Papa sees him," Niki grunted.

Avi had struggled to free himself from their grasp, so he changed his tactic. He let his body go limp, thus making himself heavier, as they began to drag him to the house. This impeded their progress, giving him some time to think of his next move.

"How is it possible for him to be heavier than the last time we dragged him to the Crazy? He was incapacitated for the last two weeks?" Riki groaned.

"The Crazy probably did some black magic on him," Niki answered.

"Don't call her that!" Avi retorted.

"What's that, dickhead, don't what ..." Niki asked, punching Avi with his free arm.

"He said, don't call her that," Chaz said unhelpfully. He was at the front of the procession, carrying Avi's legs, while the other two were at Avi's side, carrying him by his arms.

"CRAZY! CRAZY!" Chaz chanted.

Furious, Avi contracted his torso and thigh muscles then brought his knees to his chest and kicked out violently, knocking Chaz to the ground and loosening the twins' grip on his arms. He was free.

"You will call her Rosetta."

A gunshot stopped all movement on the compound, unnerving the parakeets that must have not left Dev's rooftop since the time

118

he'd seen them through Una's eyes. Panicked, they flew toward the jungle, squawking, "The trigger has been released."

Since when did he understand birds?

Chapter 18

Una

Was that a gunshot?

Bleary eyed, Una awoke from her long slumber with a residual headache. The talking through thought had exhausted her body, leaving it drained. The unbearable pressure on her frontal lobes was only surpassed by the shrieking screams in her head. She placed her hands over her ears, knowing it to be an ineffective remedy. But it worked this time! The screaming was coming from outside her head – outside the building. It wasn't screaming, but squawking.

Squawking? It was the parakeets! They must have stayed on the roof all this time.

With her vertigo head, Una moved as quickly as she could to the veranda, just in time to see the winged cloud scud across the evening sky.

Poomb! A second gunshot. Una turned to face Major's property. Unnerved, Una didn't know what to do. At home, she would have called the police, but here ... Perhaps she should start by securing her own safety first. She returned to her room. The curtains were already drawn shut from earlier, as were the windows, which just left locking the doors and keeping low. Sitting alert on the edge of her bed, palms pressed into the mattress, her brain turned to who could be firing the gunshots. Perhaps the tribesmen attacked Major's house and one of them, or one of Major's family members, fired the shots. Una felt as though she was tightly wound up on a yoyo's axle.

Could the tribesmen, or any other intruder, be in her house, too?

She had to find out. Taking one of Grandad's walking sticks from his coat and umbrella stand, she quietly searched the house. Nothing was out of place, but the usual suspects, her grandparents and the servant, were nowhere to be found. Initially, she thought they might be outside but that thought dissipated quickly. Both main entrances were bolted from the inside. The only place they could be was on the roof. Una stealthily approached the open roof door and, despite her indifference towards her grandparents, was relieved to see them unharmed and on their own.

"You're here, but where's Tommy and Johnnie Walker?"

"The servant and Tommy are on their evening constitution – nature's call."

A third gunshot ricocheted across the valley. Una dropped to the ground and flattened herself as much as she could. She noticed her grandparents had remained standing, with their eyes fixed on Major's compound. Meaning, *they* weren't under fire or in any danger.

Confused, Una stood up and dusted herself off before joining her grandparents. Following their gaze, she could just make out Major's profile as he stepped out from underneath the roof over-hang of his property, with a rifle.

"Was he shooting at the parakeets earlier?"

"It's not the parakeets he's after," Dev answered solemnly.

"What then?" Una asked, turning to him.

Dev silently stared on. Una shifted her gaze by a few metres. She could make out four people, including Major, pointing rifles at a person, no two people; one was Meeru. Una's jaw dropped as she saw Meeru being hauled away by two of the gunmen – Major's relatives. She'd spied on them long enough to recognise their familiar profiles. The person tied to the poles seemed familiar, too. The hair ...

"It's Avi!" she exclaimed in disbelief, slamming her palms

against her open mouth.

The colour drained from Una's face and she hurried to Dev. "Is that some sort of soldier game they're playing? Is that why you aren't you worried?"

Dev ignored her and carried on observing.

They weren't playing ... Una tugged on her grandfather's arm. "Major wouldn't really shoot his own grandson, would he?"

Dev took in a sharp breath. "Shoot his grandson? Of course, he would. But he mustn't ... not now. Not after waiting for so long ... There are only two more days left."

Una backed away from Dev, her heart in her mouth. It wasn't that Grandad believed Major could shoot his own grandson, but the fact that he thought the timing was wrong!

Una stuttered, "You're not making sense ... it's not normal to shoot your own grandchild."

He looked at her with pity.

Una changed tact. "What's going to happen in two days?"

Dev muttered something to his wife in Hindi and left the rooftop hastily. Grandma in turn grabbed Una's hand and made for the stairs.

Una had had enough, she wasn't helpless. Applying speed and force, she made a fist of the hand her grandmother was holding, rotated her arm in the opposite direction to where Grandma's thumb was pointing, and broke her grip. This unbalanced her Grandma, making her stumbled forwards, and indoors. Una simultaneously stepped back. Grandma took a moment too long to compose herself and Una quickly locked the roof door from the outside. Grandma protested and banged against the door. When that failed she indignantly slung the bolt on the other side of the door, huffed and made as much noise as she could as she took heavy steps all the way down the stairs. Fine! Una didn't want to go down – down the stairs, that is. Breathing hard, Una ran to the wall to look for Avi and screamed in shock. The Major was whipping him.

"Oh my God!" She had to act before they finished him off.

Narrowing her eyes, she assessed her Grandad's boundary wall. Could she jump it? Luckily, Grandad's house was only a single storey. She didn't have the momentum of an accomplished jumper, but there was enough building scope to help propel her body forward. Her optimism faded when her eyes strayed onto the familiar spikes. It couldn't be helped, she would have to vault over the roof ledges, somersault and clear the wall.

Una didn't have time to figure out where she would land. Completely absorbed in her strategy and the distance to the wall, she took a running jump. She hadn't thought about how she would save or protect Avi from the four guns and the whip.

Chapter 19 – Avi

Half an hour earlier

"Get up, Chaz! The boy only kicked you once. Stop writhing on the ground like a whore!" Major commanded.

Chaz instantly stopped moving and raised his hand to be helped up. Major side-stepped him and signalled to his other two sons to help instead.

From beneath his hood, Avi smiled – the roles had been reversed. Not long ago, it was he who was writhing on the ground.

"It's his fault, Papa, he tricked me ... he told me that you had sent him ... Meeru told us you hadn't ..." Chaz pleaded as his older twin brothers helped him up. "But don't worry, Papa. Nothing happened, we managed to stop him before he could do anything."

Major fired his gun for the second time, ending Chaz's rant.

"Just a few days ago, I took you to task for putting him in the building with the very thing we were trying to keep him from. What is wrong with you boys? How could you be taken in by Avi so easily? I reminded you that no one was to step past the post in the ground." Major pointed in the direction of where the post used to be and wondered where it had disappeared to. He caught Avi glancing over his shoulders but carried on talking to his sons.

"This time, I even gave you army guns to keep people away!"

The three brothers made their lame excuses and blamed each other, but Major was not listening. Instead, he reduced the distance between himself and Avi. Avi eyeballed the twin barrel of

Major's rifle, aimed at his head. Despite his quickened heartbeat, he kept his composure and pushed the rifle down. Major bristled. Avi had called his bluff. He knew his Dada couldn't shoot his own. Besides, how would he explain the mess the short-range fire would make of his skull as being accidental?

"Pull your hood down and show some respect."

Avi didn't stir.

Something snapped in Major.

Avi's behaviour confounded the onlookers, but he knew what he was doing. He would no longer let others enforce their power over him, even if it was his own Dada.

Major was rattled. "Seems you have grown some false confidence to challenge me like this. Do you know what happens to that crazed creature when she defies me?"

Avi thought ... she got whipped. Dada is bluffing; he couldn't possibly use the belt on a family member, any more than he could shoot one. Or could he?

Avi stood defiantly in silence as his grandfather waited for an answer.

Not knowing how to break the impasse, Major snapped, "Why couldn't you have stayed away?"

"I just wanted to see her properly, to make up my own mind up about her." Avi was surprised by the nakedness of his own words. They were devoid of pleas and excuses, and while he thought his clarity showed his honesty, Major and the others took it differently.

Avi had gone too far.

Out of control, Major barked at Riki, "Go and fetch my belt. Perhaps the rules of the outbuilding need to be engraved on his body."

Riki responded quickly and returned with the belt, with Meeru close on his heels.

Major snorted. "I was wondering when you would turn up, Meeru. How, I wonder, is the guardian angel going to stop his lashes?"

Meeru put herself in front of Avi's body. "Avi, apologise to your Dada, and he won't whip you."

"Don't make promises on my behalf. He will be whipped now, but maybe his apology will reduce the number of lashes."

Wide-eyed, Avi surveyed Major, puzzled. There was no contempt in his eyes.

"Dada, will you whip me just because I went to the outbuilding? ... I didn't even get in."

Major blanked him.

"According to Chaz, Chacha, she didn't hurt me. Which must mean she's not as dangerous as you think."

"Please, Avi, stop!" Meeru pleaded.

Avi ignored her. "Dada, what exactly did Rosetta aunty do for you to lock her up?"

Meeru hands shot to her mouth in shock.

As soon as Rosetta's name left his lips, Avi registered his mistake. Major's facial expressions turned from grave to murderous in an instant.

"He used her name ... how does he know it?" Major cried out, eyeing each of his children, one by one. They all stared back blankly. His eyes darted back to Avi, who's stance hadn't changed. His arms hung loosely by his side, as if he really didn't understand the significance of what he'd just done. Major wouldn't be fooled.

"Who is the traitor ... who gave you her name? Tell Me! Who was it?" Major was foaming at the mouth.

"What is the big deal about her name?" Avi asked. He knew the lashes were a certainty, but if he got more answers, then maybe it was worth it.

Major savagely grabbed hold of Avi's shoulders and hunted for something in his face. "Her name is a big deal. It is a powerful catalyst. By uttering her name aloud, you have unleashed her dark magic on yourself, as well as on all my sons' firstborns."

Dark magic! Avi didn't know what Dada was talking about, nor did he know what Dada was looking for when he scrutinised his face. Tentatively, Major raised Avi's hood a little, then promptly backed away from him. Avi intuited the familial threads between them break, and panicked. He needed his Dada – even contempt was better than withdrawal.

"Papa, what did you find?" Chaz asked. "Is he deformed like her?"

"This is what I found ..." Using the butt of his rifle, Major tipped Avi's hood off, "... I found nothing."

His uncles came forward to look and stared in disbelief.

"Where are your bruises, and the rings on your forehead, Avi?" Niki asked.

"They healed naturally, Dada," Avi said evenly, choosing to address his answer to Major rather than his uncles.

He knew they would think he was lying, but his body had healed itself. Even modern day surgeons believed the body could do so in some circumstances.

Major shoved Meeru aside.

"Tie him up, boys, before he completely turns. Once he gains too much strength, we won't be able to beat the devil out of him. We were too late with the other one."

Niki and Chaz approached Avi as if he were a malevolent creature rather than their nephew. Nervously, yet with unnecessary brute force, they held him tight by the arms and began to drag him to the poles where Rosetta was usually tied for her beatings. Avi showed no resistance. In any case, he was distracted. His eyes were pinned on the infamous belt. Riki placed it with great care in Major's hands. Clocking Avi's interest, Major fed his belt lovingly through his fisted hands several times before cracking it against the concrete floor of the compound. Ker chack!

Sucking in his breath, Avi toughened and tightened his body muscles as his uncles tied his wrists and legs to the pole. He knew he had the strength to overcome his uncles. However, he would accept his Dada's punishment as everything else from him had been withdrawn. It's not like he had a choice though, Riki had his rifle aimed at him.

Avi tugged at the ropes and wrapped the slack tight round

his fists. His Dada had never whipped his grandchildren or sons before. The thought brought moisture to Avi's eyes. The drops dampened the tongues of his shoes – his final token of compassion for his Dada.

"Crying already?" Major mocked.

"Don't fool yourself, Dada. This will hurt you as much as it will me – more perhaps," grunted Avi.

Ker chack! Major hit the ground.

Meeru once again flung herself in front of Avi, covering him with her body and wrapping her arms around him.

Major picked up his gun and shot it in the air for a third time.

"Niki, you have my permission to shoot Avi in the head if Meeru does not step aside." Meeru winced – Niki was a great marksman. She knew he wouldn't miss his target so she turned around to face Avi and, with the saddest of eyes, kissed his cheek and stepped aside. Relieved he didn't have to shoot his sister, Niki signalled to Riki and they both seized her roughly by the arms and moved her to the side.

Avi snarled at them.

They didn't need to hold her like that. Meeru had the capacity to stand like a statue if she knew that the slightest movement would harm her nephew. Her brothers knew that, too. They had tested her resolve on more than one occasion in the past.

Major positioned himself a few strides behind Avi. Avi waited and wondered: how had trying to see Rosetta and stating her name turned him into a pariah?

Ker chack! Ker chack!

Aggh! I've got to concentrate on something, something innocuous.

He pictured the leather belt as a toy in his Dada's hand, from when Dada had pretended to scare seven-year-old Avi and Gag, and their cousins. He used to crack his belt in exactly the same way, harmlessly, against the concrete floor in his bedroom when they played the sneaking up game – the game that always ended with Dada giving out sweets.

Ker chack! Ker chack!

Despite his own advice and efforts, Avi couldn't think of the belt as something innocent.

The belt held pride of place on a peg on Dada's bedroom wall. At some point in the past, they'd allegedly held Dada's army regulation trousers up, but that was a long time ago. Now it remained in the house for one purpose only – to keep Rosetta in line. Avi had never witnessed the beatings. However, everyone in the house was familiar with her blood curling screams during the sessions.

Ker chack! Ker chack!

Until now, he'd thought she must have deserved it because it had never been used on anyone else. Now he knew better.

Ker chack! Ker chack!

Avi grimaced. He was no longer standing straight.

Ker chack! Ker chack!

Meeru let out a cry, followed by a louder yelp. Chaz's elbow had connected with her mouth and cheekbone. Her teeth cut her bottom lip and drew blood.

Avi's eyes stung with a mixture of fury and sorrow.

Ker chack! Ker chack!

Avi realised the layers of clothes on his back were protecting his skin from breaking. The welts would only leave some discolouration, even if he didn't have the capacity to heal.

Ker chack! Ker chack!

After twenty lashes, Major stopped and passed the belt to Chaz. Avi's brain was slowly shutting down. His vision was distorted and arranged Meeru's facial contours into reflections, similar to those made by fairground mirrors. Her split lip and bruised cheekbone grew monstrously larger than the rest of her face.

"Avi, leave your body, you have done it before."

He didn't know how to do it, but even if he did, he wouldn't do it. The physical pain would at least nullify his family's betrayal.

Ker chack! Ker chack!

Meeru's sniffles seemed too loud as the lashes continued.

"Stop, Meeru, stop faking love. This is just physical pain. You keeping things from me hurt me more," Avi forced out in a flat voice. He thought they would leave her alone, but he was wrong.

Chaz stopped at fifty lashes and walked around to face Avi. With his brothers' and father watching, he turned and swung the belt wide and hit Meeru, knocking the last sob out of her.

A bubbling volcano erupted in Avi and spurted out of his mouth with an almighty roar. The ferocity of his anger stoked his strength. With two short tugs of the rope he held in his fists, he brought the poles crashing down.

Instantly, the twins dropped their hold on their sister and picked up their rifles again.

Avi was free of all his restraints but he didn't flee – there was no point.

"Meeru, get back in the house!" he bellowed.

Meeru ran, but in the opposite direction. She charged up the hill at the back of the compound and disappeared from sight.

"I can outrun Meeru," Chaz spoke, relishing the hunt.

Major shouted, "No ... not you. I need all three of you here. We will deal with her later."

Chaz looked disappointed.

Meeru's departure plugged the vent of his volcano. Avi took a long, deep breath and hoped she didn't come back. If she did, siding with him would cost her dearly.

Occupied with thoughts of Meeru, Avi missed the insidious glances between Major and his uncles, who now surrounded him like four compass points, with their guns pointed at him.

The brutal beatings had taken their toll on Major's nerves, yet they had failed to break Avi.

Major took a cursory stroll around Avi, looking for weaknesses in his stance and posture. "Still standing? Very impressive, but don't you see it proves you are not my grandson, Avi."

Avi faltered. Major smiled. He'd made a chink in Avi's armour.

"Are you saying I'm not your grandson because I showed bravery, or because I didn't apologise like I've always done?

Which one is it, Dada?" Avi asked in disbelief, lifting his head to get a better look at Major.

"Fifty lashes wouldn't kill a man, especially a clothed one, but how is it you are not unconscious. You are still standing relatively well. The strength you used to bring down the poles is not human. For heaven's sake, they were set in concrete!" Major's loud voice held some admiration, but mostly abhorrence.

"Are you saying I'm not human?" Avi asked in disbelief. He scoured the ground where he had uprooted the poles. A pneumatic drill couldn't have broken the concrete as well as he had.

"Please have some decency and tell me what you think I am?" Avi was overwhelmed by his own strength. It gave Major some hope that the old Avi was still here.

Major quietened his voice. "You are in a limbo, somewhat. From what I remember, you are not yet Blessed, but no longer human either. From memory, you can only be Blessed once you are initiated by a Blessed, and have set foot onto the other side of the path, in the jungle."

"From your memory ..." Avi repeated the words not as a question, but really as a reflection. "Rosetta ... she's a Blessed and she's the tribesmen leader, isn't she?"

Major nodded.

Avi finally made the connection. "Was she meant to take me across?"

Major moved closer over to Avi. Using the butt of his gun he traced Avi's face. "Meeru was meant to keep a very close eye on you. She was to report any changes, yet it is quite obvious she hasn't."

Avi didn't flinch but he puzzled about that, too. Meeru looked after him most evenings when his temperature rose. Earlier, she implied that she reported to someone. If it wasn't to Dada, whom he had suspected, then who did she report to?

Major continued. "Chaz's stupidity has enabled the creature in this outbuilding to connect with you, and impact you, even when you were stuck in your room. Did she tell you her name while healing you?"

Avi pressed his lips together tightly and stared ahead.

"Answer me, dammit! If she spoke to you, then she broke the pact." Major shifted the barrel from Avi's forehead and aimed it at the outbuilding.

Avi held the gun. "No! It wasn't her."

"If it wasn't her, then who? ... Was it any of you?" Major turned on his sons.

"How could we, we've only found out her name this evening," Riki appealed. "We were young when she first came. If she had a different name, we don't remember it."

"She's always been 'Crazy' to us," Niki protested.

Chaz had had enough of being in trouble with Major. "Papa, all we knew was that we weren't to ask about her real name so Avi would be safeguarded from her."

Avi interrupted, "And why was that, Uncle Chaz?" Although Avi asked Chaz the question, his gaze was upon Major.

"Because you are the bastard child of Crazy and my oldest brother."

A guttural growl came from Avi as he rushed at Chaz.

A fourth bullet rippled through the air, but this time it hit its target. It tore through Avi's jeans, entering his left thigh from behind, and exited the front. Avi fell onto one knee on the ground. As he tried to stand, Niki shot a fifth bullet, which buried itself in the wounded thigh. Avi rolled onto his side in agony. Niki reloaded his rifle.

Blood spurted continuously from the back and front of his left thigh, soaking through his jeans. Avi expected an outcry from his Dada, but none came.

"Is this ... human ... enough for you, Dada?" Avi managed to ask as his body buckled and squirmed.

Major's face was that of a dead man – devoid of expression.

Avi turned away from his Dada in disgust.

"You are my first grandson, and a legitimate one, too."

Chaz began to protest then stopped.

"Chaz is confused. Rosetta was your father's first wife, but the cold truth of the matter is ... and I don't want you to forget this, Avi," Major took a few seconds to deliver the blow, "the moment I saw her transform and I realised what you would become, I was ready to kill you, even though you were a defenceless two-year-old."

Somewhere deep inside, Avi knew his Dada was telling the truth.

"Why didn't you then?" Avi spat out, trying to keep his eyes open. Niki's bullets had nicked a major artery and he was losing blood fast. His body temperature was plummeting and his brain was shutting down. The battle to live had begun to fade as his heart slowed. His ears faintly picked up on the sound of someone running on the concrete. Someone was shouting. It sounded as though he was under water. His last thought was:

In action movies, the cop always shoots the leg and the villain lives, but the reality is – I'm dying.

Avi managed to turn his face in the direction of the shouting.

"MAJOR! STOP! Stop before you kill him!" Dev appeared from nowhere.

Major looked down at the puddle of blood under Avi's body, and then at Niki's countenance. Numb with horror, he slipped to the ground and dropped his rifle.

Niki was furious. "He was meant to heal himself; I thought he would heal himself!"

Dev bent down and tried to find a pulse. "I think I feel a pulse, but I'm not sure."

He untied his tartan scarf and deftly wrapped it around Avi's leg. "Major, you are two days from removing the curse, but you need him alive. Riki, call Dr Verma. Perhaps he can come over as he doesn't live far. The army ambulance won't come now, it's nearly curfew. Even if they could, it will be too late for Avi. Major, only the Crazy can help now."

Niki snapped out of his 'rabbit in a headlight' state and wobbled. "No, you mustn't call anyone. I'll be arrested for shooting him."

Dev grabbed hold of Niki. "Dr Verma will not ask any questions if Riki says Major has called him. If he does, I'll tell him that Avi accidentally set off his gun while it was on his lap. He'll recognise Avi's name, and knows to be discreet."

Riki came back. "No one is answering. We will have to take the car out and bring the doctor ourselves." He started back to the house, and then stopped. "Papa, your outbuilding keys are missing. They weren't in their usual place near the telephone."

"Never mind the keys, Riki. Go quickly with Dev, now! Chaz take your gun and see if Rosetta is still there."

Chaz obeyed but was soon running back. "It's open and she's not there!"

Major frantically scanned the compound. "She could be in the shadows, anywhere, waiting for the curfew ... Go, boys, lock yourselves indoors. It's me she'll want when she finds out what happened to Avi."

Niki and Chaz didn't protest or wait around to help their father. They ran in and locked the house.

Major gingerly lowered himself to the ground and lifted Avi's sweat-streaked head onto his lap and broke down.

Chapter 20

Observing from aloft, Avi watched as his sobbing Dada tried to rub his dying body warm as it rapidly cooled. Avi was distracted by a voice approaching them.

"You couldn't help yourself from having feelings for him, could you?"

Major hurriedly wiped his face with his kurta's sleeve and turned to face the person with the ragged tone as she asked, "Was it because he is like you in many ways?"

"How did you get out ..." he stopped the query when he spotted Meeru behind the humped Rosetta. "I should have guessed." Resigned, he redirected his attention to Rosetta's face. "It doesn't matter now. Just save him, he's your ..."

"... Son." Rosetta intently gazed at Avi's ethereal form with sorrow and longing as she squatted by Avi's legs, just opposite Major.

Avi's spirit wavered, causing his injured leg to jerk violently. Rosetta reacted instantly. She caught his legs between her hands and placed them gently on an overturned bucket, which lay nearby. She then tied his elevated legs to the bucket with a strip torn from her saree. Dada might have taken everything from Rosetta but, Avi noticed, her wide, quicksilver eyes shone intelligent and unbreakable. Major noticed, too. His own eyes reflected wonder and contempt before he squirmed and looked away. "I suppose you want me to regret this and ask for forgiveness, but

I ask for none. I would do it again if I thought it would save him from the same fate," Major said.

"I know," Rosetta's voice was soft. "I need something to tie around his wound, this material s soaked through." *NO!* Avi desperately wanted her to leave. He feared she would save him, and would live the remainder of his life as an abomination. A fate worse than death.

"PLEASE, ROSETTA, LET ME SLIP AWAY."

She pretended not to hear him. Thinking fast, Meeru snatched two dupattas that were drying in the compound and handed them to Rosetta. Rosetta tore them into strips and went about tightly wrapping them around his injured thigh as she spoke to Major. "Papa, the time to regret or even talk has gone. Our suffering will soon be over." Avi wondered if she aimed those words at him. Rosetta nodded.

"Soon be over? But you can save him, yes? You have the power to save him?" Major grabbed her hands.

"Papa, it's up to him," Rosetta sighed. "If only your hatred for me had not blinded you to your love for him. He desperately wanted your affection and approval."

"She's right, Papa. Do you remember how desperate he was to be like you? Remember that time when he cut his unruly hair with a sickle and ended up cutting himself badly? The poor guy had to have his head shaven, in winter, of all seasons," Meeru reminisced.

Major's sobs made Avi's body shake dangerously.

"Papa! Stop! Keep Avi still," Rosetta screamed. "Please leave, Papa."

"No," Major shook his head.

"You've got to go so I can try and work on him. Please go before he dies! Please!"

Major stopped sobbing abruptly and nodded.

Rosetta's voice calmed. "Go indoors, close your curtains and keep the rest in, too. Don't let anyone out." Then, holding her deformed back, she stood up from where she'd squatted and sat knee-to-knee with Major. She slowly transferred her son's head to her own lap from Major's.

Tearing up, Meeru quietly said, "Papa, don't wait for Dev and Riki tonight. They will have to spend the night at the doctor's because the army has blocked the roads over the pass. A senior government dignitary is arriving this evening – it could even be the Prime Minister."

Major nodded. It was a common enough occurrence since the government had created the new state of Uttarkand, in which the valley sat. He looked despondently at Meeru. He clearly didn't understand her relationship with Rosetta and was hurt by her betrayal. He shook his head and, in a voice deep with hurt and resignation, spoke softly, "It was you who revealed Rosetta's name to Avi. What I don't understand is, who told you and what else do you know?"

"The answer to the first question is: I told him her name today because the changes had already happened. The answer to the second question is: I know all of it."

"All?"

"Yes, Papa. I learnt of her name. I also learnt that she was Avi's mother and his father's first wife. I also know that Rosetta saved me from drowning."

"All of it ..." Major repeated, alarmed.

Dejected, Major moved to get up but couldn't, he had no energy left. Meeru came forward to help him. He clasped her wrist and, with tears in his eyes, said, "I didn't want him to die."

Avi believed him.

As soon as Major left, Meeru took out a whistle from her shawl and blew on it. The same silent whistle he had seen earlier. Rosetta held her ears momentarily, then swung around to Meeru. "You've just called the person who gave away all our secrets, haven't you?"

"Yes. They are Blessed and can help us save him. Rosetta, it's too exposed here. It will be better for Avi if we wait for them in your outhouse."

"Do you think me a fool to allow your friends to corner and kill us?"

Meeru gently kissed Avi's sickly forehead and then let rip. "How dare you! You might be his biological mother, but I have cared for him forever, even before I learnt how you saved my life. Your track record for safeguarding your own children is poor, or have you forgotten you were unable to foresee and stop the death of your daughter – Avi's sister?"

Sister? Avi's body gasped noisily.

"Stop Meeru! He can hear you. Your words are killing him! He's lost too much blood and his body can't heal fast enough. He's fighting my healing because he wants to go, and your words are speeding him on."

It was true. Avi was soaring higher. Relief and serenity buoyed him further away from his earthly body.

Meeru took no heed and continued to rant. "Don't you dare blame me! It's your fault that he's in this situation in the first place. You're a coward. You could have run away anytime, I'm sure your tribe would have helped. Even now. My friend tried to help you, but you refused. He told me how the death of your daughter, after you turned eighteen, somehow triggered your Blessed guise. My parents were all for killing you, but Ma's occult guru advised the family to keep you prisoner in the outbuilding instead, away from Avi. How could you bear it? Why didn't you leave?"

Angry tears rolled down Rosetta's cheeks. "I had to stay, to make sure my son stayed safe until he turned eighteen. While they had me, the tribe did not retaliate, and the lands remained in Papa and Dev's hands."

Avi's lips were turning blue. Rosetta clasped her hands together. "Meeru, I beg of you to be quiet."

For a short while Meeru was quiet, immobilised by Rosetta's extended arm and hand movements over Avi's body. It was as if she was working with invisible strings. First untangling them and then pulling on one as if it were attached to a soaring kite. Avi's spirit tugged hard in the opposite direction, forcibly breaking the last thread of attachment to his life. The momentum lifted him towards a comforting warmth, away from the coldness below. Through the fuzzy warm thermals, Avi could hear faint sobs. Away in the distance, he could see Meeru slapping his lifeless cheeks.

"Avi! Avi, don't you dare die, come back! You have to live. You won't be on your own for long. I promise! I helped bring Una over from England so you wouldn't be on your own in the jungle. Avi, you like her don't you?"

She what? Avi pulled away from the warmth. A smile broke out on Rosetta's face. She placed her ear to his chest. "Are you responsible for putting Alice's girl's life at risk?"

"Yes! Didn't you just hear me say that? What do you care, just bring him back. Do something! Are you going to let another one of your children die?"

The distance between Avi and his body halved.

Rosetta pushed further. "So, you and your friend ruined an innocent soul's life, a life that had once been saved, so that my son would not be lonely in the jungle?"

"You crazy woman, your son is dying. Save him instead of ..." Meeru stopped when Avi's torso jerked violently

Avi was back in his body. Meeru shoved Rosetta's head off Avi's chest. A short while later, Meeru stood up.

"Will he heal now?"

"It's up to him."

"I've got to tell the others that he is barely breathing, and that we need to move fast to the jungle."

Rosetta did nothing to stop Meeru leaving.

Chapter 21

Time of Curfew

Scarlet ink bled into the indigo ones and turned the sky dark and moody; it was time for the curfew to begin. Una covered her ears in anticipation, but nothing happened ... The lone wolf, for the first time since she'd been there, missed his cue. Unperturbed, the flying fox bat that was suspended upside down at eye level, stirred. She wasn't normally squeamish, but its huge, piercing brown saucer eyes were held captive on an uncomfortable spot on the mango tree. The bat's large, furry body and long pointed ears hung from the tip of the branch just metres above her head. Una had always thought bats in the wild fled from human proximity, but this bat remained silent and still, even when her thigh twitched with unexplained pain. This was probably the reason she hadn't noticed it when she climbed onto the tree earlier. Teasingly slow, the bat finally unfurled its wings from over its furry body and flew off with its family members in tow. Una shuddered. She dare not look up, even though she knew there were probably more bats there.

Relieved to be on her own, she glanced down between the branches and groaned. The evening light had completely faded. Earlier, when she'd jumped off the roof ledge, there was good enough visibility. The short cut she'd taken turned out to be a longer route up the hill behind the properties. It would have been shorter had it not been for the triple barbed wiring surrounding Major's land. Major and her grandfather obviously knew a better route, or used an opening she'd missed. By the time she'd climbed onto the overhanging mango tree to get into Major's property, she could just about make out Major's outline, and another person lying with their head on Major's lap. Not able to bear her weight on her thigh, she had been held captive in the high boughs of the tree, too high up to hear the conversations below. Not that she knew any Hindi, and she couldn't imagine Major talking to his family in English.

Just as unexplainably as it came, the pain in her thigh subsided. Released from its grip, Una carefully moved through the branches, negotiating the lower branches until her hands were firmly on the lowest branch. She dangled her legs, ready to make the jump to the ground, but froze just in time to miss Meeru's head by centimetres as she passed under the tree and climbed up the hill behind. Una gulped hard.

Why was Meeru breaking curfew and heading towards the jungle behind the house? Meeru's sure-footedness in the dark, without the aid of a lamp or any light source, reinforced the possibility that Meeru had ventured out many times during nightfall, and curfew hours. Meeru's departure stumped Una. From her grandfather's roof, Una had watched Meeru shield her nephew with her own body, and now she was leaving him in an injured state – heading away.

✳✳✳

"Ah, a difficult conundrum, isn't it?"

The voice was at once strange and familiar.

"Why didn't you ask her?" the voice queried.

Her hiding place no longer a secret, Una rotated on the branch she sat on and swung her head upside down. Just like the bat, she eyeballed the alert face that belonged to the very woman whose existence Avi had denied.

Una's nose screwed in revulsion, killing any words she held in her mouth. The stench of body odour, blood and something much darker, forced Una's gaze down to Avi's broken body that now rested at an awkward angle on the strange woman's lap. Una straightened herself and prepared to leap down from the tree. Her shoulders dropped when her gaze fell upon Avi's damaged leg. It was covered with a bloodied gauzy material and was suspended over a puddle of deep crimson.

Both hands flew to her face to hold back a cry of anguish as she slipped off the branch and tumbled forwards. She had waited two long weeks to see him, and now, perhaps, she was too late. Heartbroken, she registered the twitches and jerks of his body. It would be over soon. Memories of standing over her own mother's writhing body, before her painful and raspy breaths ceased, flooded her mind.

"Oh Avi," she whimpered, jerking her hand out towards him.

"*RUKO.* Una! Stop!" The stranger tightly clasped Una's raised wrist in mid-air. "Don't you dare touch him with those *deadly* thoughts. He's only just come from the brink."

Stung, Una immediately drew back on her haunches, quickly retracting her hand on its release.

"How? How can you read my thoughts?"

Rosetta gave her a wry smile. Una knew how, she'd learnt how just this morning. Una rubbed the nail marks on her wrist.

"I've been listening to them from the day I met you in the field."

Her words, like the cold air, left her raw and exposed. Una stilled her hand over her wrist and focused her whole attention on Rosetta. Despite her intentions to remain calm, her voice shook. "I thought I dreamt you up. Avi said you didn't exist."

"I'm Rosetta."

Una scrunched her forehead as she repeated the name slowly. "Rosetta? I thought it was something else, something beginning with 'B'?"

The bucket rattled loudly beneath Avi's injured leg as it jerked spasmodically. Una rushed to still the bucket, bringing her to a kneeling stance within touching distance of Avi. Meanwhile, Rosetta held Avi's arm down. Una was struck with the way she held him. "Why did Avi lie to me and deny your existence?"

"He didn't lie, he doesn't *remember* me."

She had to be lying. Rosetta had fled to Major's house with Tommy, towards the trees and the hill on Major's property. Una snapped her head around to the cluster of trees that were shrouded in darkness behind her. As she thought, a tiny flame from a lantern burned, throwing shadows into an entrance to a small outbuilding that was hidden between them.

"You *do* remember the evening well." Una swivelled her attention back to Rosetta. She was busy arranging a *dupatta* over Avi's injured leg. The simple action somehow stilled his leg, and Una's heart. The slight rise and fall of his shoulder restarted hers again.

"I seem to remember you were looking for your father." Rosetta's words were a whisper.

Una's eyes flew up to hers, confused. "I don't remember saying that."

"You didn't."

Aloud, she asked, "Don't you remember? You fell in the cowpat you tried so hard to avoid."

Una's whole body jolted. "What else do you know about that night?"

"I know everything."

Then you know how Tommy and the shoes came to be in my room the next morning.

"That's simple. Tommy bought the shoes to me and I cleaned them. Getting in the room was easy for him. He entered via the skylight that's concealed behind the fitted cupboard doors."

My room has a skylight?

"Stop invading my mind, Rosetta."

"You let Avi do it. I wonder why that is?"

Una felt her cheeks and neck prickle in embarrassment. "Because ... I can't answer that. It's strange; as strange as Avi being beaten and shot by his own family!"

With a saddened expression, Rosetta murmured, "You must have learnt more from Major and Meeru's conversation?"

"I was too high up. Besides, if they were speaking in Hindi, I wouldn't have understood."

"They weren't speaking in Hindi, and even if they did, you should have understood. Alice, your mother, promised mine that she would teach you. Never mind, it won't matter. Soon you'll be able to speak and understand more than English and Hindi."

Una's eyes widened and shone like brilliant cut emeralds. "You knew my Mum ... How is that even possible?"

"I knew her well. We were friends when your mother lived in India."

Una shook her head in disbelief. "It can't be true, she would have told me if she'd ever been to India."

"But, Alice Didi was here. She was employed by the Forestry Commission. You were conceived here ... she promised ... she promised she would prepare you," Rosetta excitedly retorted.

Una made to stand up, and fell back down as short electrical spikes jolted up and down her left leg.

"Calm down, Una! It's not happening in your leg. It's happening to Avi, just calm down."

Rosetta was right. Her leg was fine, but Avi's had begun to shake again.

"You are intuitively and emotionally bonded to him, Una. You are feeling what he feels, and he likewise. Una calm down, you have to remain calm. If not ..."

"If not?"

"You could kill him."

As Rosetta uttered the words, Una knew them to be true. Alarm and embarrassment spread through her.

"Careful, Una!" warned Rosetta.

"Why do you care when you never let him know of your existence, even though you were nearby?"

"I lived in that outbuilding as an outcast; kept away from most of the family."

Una wasn't convinced – curiosity would have grabbed any child to explore the outbuilding. Especially for someone like Avi, who was happy to break jungle rules, which were far more serious.

"I know what you are thinking, remember. Avi, and most of the family, were taught to fear the 'Crazy' in the outbuilding. His Dada made them believe I was mad, dangerous and out of control. I let him do that. It was the only condition placed by Major to keep Avi alive. Avi was young when he was taken from me, and soon enough believed his stepmother to be his birth mother."

Una held her face in her hands while horrific images of possible brutality and evil danced through her mind. She yelled, "How can that be true?"

Rosetta removed a creased photograph from inside her blouse and offered it to Una.

Hesitantly, Una shuffled forward and accepted it. All the while, her heart thudded hard in her chest. Between aged creases, a young Rosetta stood in a doorway, holding a toddler on her hip. Their laughing eyes, smiles and dimples matched as they gazed at each other. The mass of black hair that flopped over the toddler's forehead was uniquely Avi's.

Una returned the photograph with a shaky hand as tears flowed freely down her cheeks. Una rasped, trying to hold back her sobs. "All this time you were only metres away."

Rosetta returned the photograph to its safe place and motioned for Una to sit next to her. "Come and sit close to him." Shaking, Una stood up and sat cross-legged in front of Rosetta.

"Avi learnt the truth this evening."

"How is that possible? He's been unconscious all this time," whispered Una as she leaned forward and stroked Avi's high cheekbone lightly with her fingertips. She couldn't help herself but was so glad she did. His skin was warm, not cold like her Mum's had been, which meant he was alive. Gently, she rested her cold palm on his heated cheek, whilst gently running her fingers lightly across his skin. Avi's skin leapt in answer to her touch. Electrical sparks flew down her fingers, wrist and arm. His eyeballs whipped around. Scared, she lifted her hand, only for Rosetta to grab it and push it firmly back down. Relief stormed through Una. She wanted to be as close as possible, to *protect* him. She wanted him back with her.

"Only *you* can do that!"

"Why?" Una's voice was barely audible.

"Una, he's choosing to wake up ... for you. I was only able to do so much, but he fought me. I couldn't stop him from slipping away because he was fighting to speed his death."

"Why?"

"He preferred to die than face the betrayal and complete abandonment of his family. Your bond, however, made you risk coming here. Your presence is compelling him to stay and fight."

Una sat in stunned silence then, with a large sob, uttered words that her own heart rejected. "I can't, he barely knows me. How can I force him to live a doomed life and hate me for bringing him back? *Who am I* to do that?"

"Una ... he needs you. He MUST wake up and face his destiny."

Una shook her head violently.

"Fine, then all is lost. I should have killed him myself when he was young, instead of putting the jungle and my tribe at stake." To Una's dismay and shock, Rosetta lifted her son's head to move away. Her body, with a treacherous will of its own, sprung forward to cushion him on her lap. Overwhelmed by her own need to be so close, she held back. Instead, with light fingers, she parted and smoothed Avi's mop so she could see his face clearly again. Despite his predicament, he was beautiful.

"This was how I last saw him, when he was just two ..." Her words were interrupted by the late call of the wolf.

Rosetta and Una's heads jerked towards the hill behind Major's house. "Time is running out, Una. In this half-state, Avi is most vulnerable. I need you to talk him into awakening so I can save his life. Please help him!"

Half-state? Rosetta made no sense, but she knew she couldn't let him go. Praying she was doing the right thing, she bent her head towards his face and whispered, "Avi, it's me, Una. Please open your eyes." He didn't. She repeated her words several times, but still nothing happened. Una coaxed, "Please, Avi, just open your eyes." Desperation infiltrated her voice as she begged, "Please, please wake up, Avi. I'll even stay in this wretched valley for you, just wake up."

Nothing.

Her despair rapidly turned into anger. "Don't you dare sneak away and leave me in this mess. You have to wake up, even if it's just for me." To reinforce her words, she vigorously patted his face several times. "Come back, Avi. Please. I promise to listen carefully to whatever you ask for. I'll even go to Windsor School. Just ... wake ... up!" Nothing. Her tears dripped down his face. *Please, Avi.* The realisation of her true feelings for Avi left her speechless.

✳✳✳

"Why do you feel so real?"

"Because I'm here with you."

Avi's eyelids snapped open. Bewildered, he waved his hand through her hair. This time, his hands made contact with real, long strands of hair, instead of the thin wisps of air when she'd appeared in his thoughts.

Mesmerised, and with the faintest of smiles, Avi gazed into her shiny wet eyes and wound her hair around his finger. Una simply gazed back.

Avi blink, don't torture yourself.

He complied and replied. This is not torture, this is heaven.

A wolf howl broke his concentration. Avi's face paled further, if that was even possible.

"Una, leave now before Meeru gets here."

"Meeru? But she tried to save you from your grandfather and uncles."

"She will harm you."

He turned his face away, too weak to explain. He wanted her to leave, to run. He wasn't in a position to protect her if they chose to take her, too. His mind could hear voices. Whoever Meeru had summoned, they were coming for him now. He lifted his head an inch, then let it drop back onto Una's lap. A moan half left his mouth before it was captured by the gentle caress of lips. Una's hair cascaded around their faces, trapping his frozen expression like a willow would a still lake. The gentle movement of her lips stoked the desperate need he'd kept at bay after each meeting they'd had, forcing his lips open to swallow her weak protest and devour her mouth. He felt such hunger. Their heartbeats were loud and merged, their breathing shallow. Avi tried to adjust himself so they could breathe, but she moved away. Guilt and concern replaced the soft vulnerable expression she had earlier. As she straightened herself, dark shadows and jungle noises rushed in to fill the gap between their bodies, jerking Avi back to reality. His euphoria dissipated with the realisation that Una had dragged him from his death, only to drive him into a living hell, which, thanks to his changes, he knew to be quite close.

He inhaled slowly. There was no point fighting it, but he could make sure Una was safe. "Una, you have to go. I don't want you to be here when it happens."

"Avi, nothing is going to happen. You're not going to die ... I brought you back!" Una's words quivered.

"You promised you would listen." Avi's tired voice took on a desperate tone as he lifted off her and steadied himself into a sitting position.

Una shifted to face him and pleaded, "I can't."

"Una, it's too late for me, you've got to go," Avi let out a frustrated grunt. "If you stay, I won't be able to save ..." He was about to say 'save her from him' but she never let him finish.

She sprung up from where she sat and planted her feet firmly on the ground in front of him. "Save me? Look!" She thrust her hands, palm up, in his face. "To get here, I jumped off the roof when I saw you cornered and heard the gunshots, because the dragon locked the roof door to keep me from coming." Concern and admiration flooded Avi's body. "No one else dared to come to your aid, not Meeru, not anyone. I did. I was ready to stand up before YOUR family and would have got here earlier if I hadn't got lost between the barbed boundaries." The enormity of her actions punched him hard in his solar plexus. She barely knew him, yet she had risked her life for his. The stupid girl could have broken her neck or got caught in the crossfire? In his heart, he knew he was duty bound to honour the life she'd misguidedly given him. Even though, with every fibre in his body, he wished he was dead. The only comfort he could take to live was that he could use his ill-fated destiny to save her from her own. Avi grabbed her grazed palms and used them as leverage to help him stagger to a standing position.

He didn't think he could hide the sorrow from her shocked eyes, so he grabbed her sides and pulled her body into his. She swayed into him, nearly knocking him over.

Thankfully, she let him move so his back was against a pillar, providing him with extra support. Stable, he brought their bodies tightly together by placing her arms around his neck and, for the last time before he sent her off, kissed her savagely. Just when he thought it would never stop, a metal object fell at his feet, just under the excessive bandaging around his wounded leg. Alarmed, they both moved apart, staring at a bloodied bullet. Still weak, Avi leaned back on the pillar and winced internally. Una picked up the bullet and held it between her fingers. For the first time, Avi could see she was petrified – petrified of him. Caught off-guard by his first kiss and hunger, Avi had missed the swift healing of the gunshot wound and the earlier whippings. It was humanly impossible and she knew that. Desolate, he waited for the words she barely let escape. "Your injuries were life threatening. How did you get up so easily?"

He stalled for a better explanation, but none came to mind, so he just told her the truth.

"I don't know how I managed to do that. It happened to me once before, this very morning actually, after we thought talked."

For a fleeting moment, he could tell she wanted to trust him but, as expected, she backed away in fear and closed her heart to him.

"Think thought? Oh God ... you, you bewitched me!" Una shrieked.

Avi shook his head in denial.

"Rosetta did the same. Whatever she tried to do to bring you back didn't work so she *convinced me* to call you back. Maybe I didn't have a choice in jumping off the roof either. Wait, where did Rosetta go?" Ashen faced, Una glanced around and fixed her eyes on the faint outline of the outbuilding. The lantern was missing.

"Rosetta is some sort of witch, *isn't* she? That's probably why she was locked up!" Near hyperventilating, she bent over and drew in deep breaths until Avi moved off the pillar to be closer to her and calm her shaking body. Arms wound around herself, she drew up when she spotted his feet near her. She took several uneasy steps back. "Una! Slow down! Remember, it's me, Avi. Look, you can cope with this. Remember, I can hear what you are thinking, and you me. So, it stands to reason that, if I'm bewitched, then so are you. You heard what they said this morning. My birthday is in two days ... Self-healing could just be one of the changes. You must have noticed some changes in yourself, other than being able to 'thought talk'?"

"She has a couple more years before she turns eighteen." Una and Avi's gaze swung to the outbuilding from where Rosetta's voice came. Their jaws slackened when they laid eyes on a snow leopard standing in the doorway.

Avi recovered first. "Your howling in the night was barely human ... it inflicted such painful growths and high temperatures." He now understood why his grandfather had protected him from his own mother. It made absolute sense.

Rosetta squirmed; she didn't like his accusing tone or thoughts.

"I did bring on your Blessed changes. But once you turned eighteen, your body instigated the greater change. Thinking of my name, then saying it aloud, released a block I could not overcome myself."

"But. I'm not yet ..."

Rosetta ignored Avi and carried on talking. "Avi, greater changes are yet to come and they will come furious and fast, because you are soon going to be a day over eighteen. That's why we must leave this place quickly and enter the jungle on the other side of the path, to complete your transformation."

Una gasped. "Blessed!"

Avi shot a hesitant look at Una and then snapped at Rosetta. "You are wrong, Rosetta, I'm not eighteen yet! My birthday is in two days."

"No! Your stepbrother, Gagan's, birthday is in two days. Yours is today."

Avi staggered back against the pillar. The differences and mutual dislike between himself and Gag made sense now. Even their official birthday wasn't shared.

Avi, self-pity is not the virtue of a Blessed. Una, you have to go quickly, before they take you before your time. Meeru and many Forced Blesseds are coming for you. We have to get out of here.

Una let out a scream.

Avi moved towards Una. "Una, nothing is going to happen to you, I promise. But you have to let me take you back before I change, and Meeru comes back with her friends."

Una backed away from him, all the while talking to herself. All those growth spurts, I should have guessed they were out of the ordinary. I kissed him – what if I change because of that? What if I change into something before I turn eighteen?

Rosetta interrupted her thoughts. "Una, it's not his fault, just as it's not yours. It's your destiny; you will no more be able to change your destiny than he can."

Avi groaned.

Una's jumpiness increased and she quickened her backward steps until she stumbled on a crack in the concrete. Avi leapt forward to help her.

Una threw her arms forward. "Stop! Don't come near me.

Don't you dare touch me!" She shuffled backwards on her bottom. "I've got to get away from here. Away from *you*, away from that creature, this valley and this country before I turn into some sort of freak like you."

Avi ground to a halt, stricken as she flayed her hands about on the ground and found Niki's discarded rifle. With shaky hands, she grabbed the rifle and slowly stood up, all the time keeping her eyes fixed on him.

Avi and Rosetta, from opposite sides, stepped towards her.

Una bounced glances between them and shouted, "Get away from me or I'll shoot." Avi took several steps closer to her, sending her finger onto the trigger.

Swinging the rifle in their direction, she shouted out, "Don't move, because I will really shoot!"

"Calm down. It's alright, Una. I won't touch you, and I won't come after you." He held his hands up. "Just go – no tricks."

Avi wanted to hate Una for her behaviour, but he couldn't.

Why can't he just listen? thought Una. Her arms were shaking as Avi crept even closer. In slow motion, he saw her pull the trigger. Her shoulders rebound and bullet six flew towards him. He sidestepped it. His ear stung as the bullet passed and fell somewhere behind him.

Did she mean to kill him?

Tears of anger made his vision hazy as a trickle of blood slid down his earlobe. Twice he had saved her and yet she believed him capable of hurting her? Was it just bravery and duty that had recklessly brought her to save him? Or would she have risked her life for any human? The thought of being human stuck in his mind. He no longer qualified. He reduced the distance between them quickly. When he was close enough, he stretched out and flung the gun from her hands, as if she'd been holding a snake. Picking her up over his shoulder, he propped her atop the boundary wall. Una didn't retaliate, but looked away from him.

"The least you can do is look at me." Reluctantly, she did.

"Get out of here, away from freaks like me. Make sure you leave Khamosh Valley before your eighteenth birthday, or I might be the freak coming back for you. Most importantly, don't trust anyone, least of all Meeru." With that, he turned and walked away.

He clocked a whimper before she disappeared over the wall.

Chapter 22

"Now why did you have to go and say that? Hmm? It's going to be so much harder for Meeru to deliver on her promises." A familiar voice said from behind Avi, making him turn. His grey eyes locked on amber ones, confirming what he suspected. His knife thrower, and Una's Tawny was the same person. Avi checked to see if Rosetta recognised Tawny, but he couldn't tell – it was difficult to read a snow leopard's eyes. Besides, he was distracted by the two youths who were kneeling and flanking Rosetta's animal body. They were dressed in combat outfits and held rifles. Their rifles were pressed hard into her fur, presumably to prevent her from jerking her head about to use her canine teeth to get a grip on them. A third youth pulled a sack over her feline head, muting her attempts to set herself free.

"Get off her!" Avi's indignation was interrupted by his own yelp as his hair was yanked back and held, forcing his chin up to jut up unnaturally. Avi was swift to attack the hand holding him. He spun around to face his assailant. Using both hands, he applied brute force on his assailant's shoulders and propelled him backwards.

"Call your boys off, Tawny," growled Avi, standing in a fighter's pose as two other combat youths came forward.

Raising his hand, Tawny halted their progress.

"Tawny? Did Mummy forget to tell you my name?" questioned the leader.

Rosetta swung her head violently.

"Well, it looks like I'm going to have to introduce myself. No wait ... I've changed my mind, I actually like Tawny. It matches my eyes. How *cute*? Meeru didn't tell me I was going to be dealing with a 'sensitive' boy." Avi grunted. Tawny's expressions hardened. "By the end of the night, I guarantee you will learn and respect my actual name."

"Don't count on it," Avi hissed.

Tawny just smiled.

Irked, Avi changed the subject. "Earlier, you said Meeru wouldn't be able to keep her promises. Why would she make promises to you?"

"I wanted to join the Forced Blessed," answered Meeru as she slipped out of the shadows and stopped next to Tawny. Kissing him lightly on the cheek, she muttered, "You promised you wouldn't play with him."

Avi stared blankly at Meeru. She was in combat uniform, identical to the one in the knife throwing act. At the time, he had thought the assistant resembled Meeru, but he couldn't credit Meeru with such recklessness. Avi stared at the two of them, his body gathering tension and rage. He flew at Tawny, but two of Tawny's boys grabbed him. "You bastard, how did you get her to risk her life like that on the spinning wheel."

"Ah, Meeru, it turns out your nephew saw you on your initiation night."

Meeru barely nodded, but said nothing.

Stunned, Avi faltered. "He could have killed you, Meeru ... how could you be so dumb?"

"It was all part of her training." Tawny pulled Meeru closer to his side. "She wasn't being dumb. She was showing complete faith in my excellent marksmanship."

To make the point, he threw his knife over Avi's head. A sleeping fox bat fell to the ground, squirming, the knife lodged in its belly. Releasing Meeru, Tawny wandered over to the small victim, crouched over the body, and pushed the knife in deeper, killing the bat quickly. In a matter of fact tone, he said, "Meeru didn't flinch and that's why she's alive and still standing. It's a necessary skill in the jungle, and part of the training." Ensuring the mammal was dead, he freed his knife from its body and wiped the blood against his knee. "Of course, should a knife have found her vital organs, I would've finished the job just as cleanly as I have today."

"You bastard ..." Avi tried to lunge forward, but the youths were much stronger than his uncles.

"Avi, stop! It was just one night!" Meeru protested. He twisted his head towards her and glared at her in cold anger, making her wince and quickly glance away.

Avi spat on the ground and directed another question at Tawny. "Training for what exactly?"

"Well, that would be telling, but let's just say her training will be useful when we take you with us to help you on your way to becoming a Forced Blessed." Tawny assessed the blade of his knife.

Avi's attention swung back to Meeru in horror. *Meeru wanted him to be Blessed? Why?* It didn't make sense. *How could she wish it for him, someone whom she professed to love?* His body faltered and relaxed in the arms of the youths, who, on Tawny's signal, let him stand free.

"What do you want with Avi?" Rosetta's muffled voice came through the sack on her head.

"Oh, sorry! Did I leave you out of the conversation?" asked Tawny, sarcastically. He signalled for the bag to be removed. When she was free of it, he remarked, "I thought you would jump into the conversation a little earlier, Mummy dearest."

The word 'mummy' rankled Avi. He couldn't get over the fact that he had finally reconnected with his mother, only to find out she was a Blessed snow leopard, and he would be one soon.

Bemused by Avi's dislike of the word 'mummy', he used it again. "Mummy, here, tricked everyone for all those years. Just imagine the surprise I felt when Meeru reported that you had begun self-healing this very afternoon, two whole days before your official birthday.

"Healing yourself is one of the first signs of becoming a Blessed on your eighteenth birthday. By healing yourself this afternoon, you practically sent out a message that was as clear as hanging up birthday balloons and serving cake with eighteen birthday candles."

Avi was seething with anger and a new-found emotion for Meeru ... hatred.

Meeru realised this and squirmed. "Don't look at me like that; you were going to be transformed regardless of my involvement. I've paved it for you, to be in W ... Tawny's cohort. If you are permitted to live in the jungle with your mother, you will be under her jurisdiction. Rosetta, as leader, will continue to let Papa and Dev destroy the Khamosh Valley. We can't allow that."

Alarm bells were ringing in Avi's head. Until today, Avi had been very fond of Meeru, but he wasn't deluded enough to think she was of the selfless kind. Also, Meeru was alluding to the possible demise of Rosetta, his mother. The role of a leader usually only ended with death. Avi's chest tightened. "Did you use me to get his attention?"

Tawny chuckled. Meeru and Avi swung around to face him.

"Meeru, your nephew knows you well."

Humiliated, Meeru stepped away from Tawny and gave Avi a look of hurt and disappointment. Avi momentarily relented. If Meeru had been completely selfless, she wouldn't have survived in the Major's household. Slowly, he made his way to her and gently grasped her hand. "Why would you side with Tawny, who is obviously against your own father? Tell me you're not in love with him."

Meeru jerked her hand from Avi's grasp. Then, full of scorn, she angrily spouted, "Think back to the day Una arrived and the conversation we had in your room. Do you remember me telling you that our family would never accept a female as their eldest grandchild? Well, it's true. All the female babies were murdered by Ma."

"But, if that's true, how come you exist?" asked Avi.

"I was born after six males, so my odds of surviving were better. Although, I would have died if it weren't for Rosetta, who saved me from drowning."

"Did HE tell you that? You know he's lying Meeru," scoffed Avi.

"No, I told him about it, three years ago, after my last high school examination. I found out when I rushed home on my moped to get ready for the last combined social at my school with the St Anthony boys and my date. Anyhow, Ma was bragging about how she dealt with unwanted babies to Dev's wife and how she'd wanted to kill me from the moment I was born, but only got her a chance to nearly drown me when I was five."

Avi balked.

He knew there was more to come from Meeru. He braced himself for her punch line.

"I had always believed it was an accident. Ma didn't stop with her own girls either, she killed your sister." Avi shook his head in disbelief. "Your twin sister," clarified Meeru.

Avi backed away from her. His sister was his twin; he'd shared his mother's womb with another. *Was that why he always felt at a loss and incomplete?*

"Avi, I tried to tell you before, several times. I even tried to get you to think about why there were no more girls in the family, but neither you, nor the other men, were interested in following up on it."

Avi thought back to the day Una arrived, and the banter he and Meeru had shared. He vividly remembered the moment Meeru had gone quiet and serious. She had said that two girls could never be born. What she'd really meant was that firstborn girls were murdered. His sister hadn't been allowed to survive. His hand flew forward to stop Meeru from stepping in to comfort him.

"Instead of a thank you for looking after you and keeping you safe, you still don't trust me?" Meeru was deeply hurt.

"She's right, Avi. She didn't have to care for you. At first, she looked after you because I saved her, but then she genuinely became very protective of you. She is the only one in the household who cared," Rosetta murmured.

"Dada did." Avi wasn't sure if he was right about that.

"Your Dada would have killed you sooner, when he realised I was a Blessed. However, he was advised by your Dadi's occult guru to keep you alive. If you've received any affection from him, it's because Meeru softened his attitude towards you. If it wasn't for her, and Gagan's mother to some extent, you would have been neglected, like me."

Avi looked up at Rosetta. "For what reason did he keep me alive?"

Rosetta couldn't bring herself to tell him, so Meeru did. "He was hoping you would kill Rosetta when you turned eighteen. I overheard Papa explaining it to your Ma, sorry stepmother. Your stepmother felt some sympathy towards you and couldn't face your end. That's why she and Gagan are still at her parents. They're waiting for confirmation of the deed from your Dada."

That made sense. Avi had wondered why Gag hadn't come back in time for the start of term.

Meeru continued, "Your Dada's plan was simple. On your supposed eighteenth birthday, my brothers were to leave the outbuilding unlocked, rough you up to provoke Rosetta, who, predictably, would come to rescue you. Anger would transform her from human to snow leopard."

Avi worked out the rest for himself. "I would see her as a vicious, big cat attacking my family and I would instantly kill her to protect them. The only question I have is, why wait till I was eighteen to kill her?"

Tawny was getting impatient. "Killing a Blessed is a sin, but to kill a snow leopard is much worse. If you kill a snow leopard you become one. As Rosetta's firstborn son, there is a good chance you are destined to become a snow leopard anyway. Once she was dead, they would show false compassion to you. The tribe, at the same time, would make you their leader. You would feel compelled, just as your mother had before you, to allow Major to continue his fraudulent behaviour, just so you could remain a family member ..."

Avi now understood Tawny's involvement. "And you don't want Dada and Dev to manipulate the tribe through me. You want to control me, but I'm not clear about your purpose."

Tawny did not like being interrupted. "Your Dada and Dev are responsible for making us Forced Blesseds."

"Forced Blessed?"

Meeru spoke up this time. "Dada and Dev have sold plots to unsuspecting buyers. They're aware of the rule that children born on both sides are to be given up to become Blessed, whether they are from a tribe family or not. Rosetta knew all this, but, even as leader, she couldn't stop Papa or let anyone else kill him. You see, Papa used her son, you, as leverage."

"But why hasn't Agnes, Uncle Sid's daughter been turned in to a Blessed?"

Meeru twitched. "Uncle Sid built the house after Agnes turned nineteen; Grace is the younger sister."

Tawny stepped forward. "Enough talking now, we need to leave." He signalled to Meeru by curling his fingers and blowing threw them. She nodded and quickly pulled a whistle from her pocket and blew through it, making no sound. Promptly, ten more tattooed-faced youths in combat clothes emerged from the shadows.

"They can't be Forced Blessed, too? Only Sid's house is on the land!" Avi challenged.

"That isn't quite true," Meeru replied. "Your school's land tapers down the hill to the jungle where Sid built a dormitory for martial art students. Remember, Papa sold it to St Anthony's."

Avi's eyes frantically darted between the youths' faces. His heart sunk as he recognised them from the photographs he'd seen pinned on the 'Wall of Fame' in his school. One or two were from the batch that had just left, some were from his current batch, and the others were a year younger. They were all high achievers, and were expected to become the next generation of lawyers, surgeons and politicians. Avi jolted his attention back to Tawny. He had to be a past student, too. Tawny smiled. He knew what Avi was thinking and didn't deny it. If anything, he raised his eyebrow, as though challenging Avi to place him. Avi wondered why he was resisting the group. Technically, they were his band of brothers and they were right, Rosetta's weaknesses hadn't protected them. Avi stood up to Rosetta. "Why didn't you do anything to save them?"

"This man is lying. The land belonged to the Forestry before the school founder bought and built on it, before your grandparents were even born. No conversions were had before because no one resided on that part of the land until the new building was built recently. Dada, not Dev, was involved, as you can see."

Rosetta turned her furry head in Tawny's direction. "These Blessed conversions are linked to you – aren't they?" Tawny's lips curled into a snarl. Rosetta continued, unperturbed, "You've used Meeru's anger against the rest of her family purely for your own means. If you really cared, you would have reported her to the police, but you didn't."

Tawny stomped off, pulling Meeru with him. Soon all the Forced Blesseds were huddled around him.

Rosetta seized the opportunity and thought talked with Avi.

"Avi, you must stop Tawny from killing me and capturing you. If we work together and communicate through thought talk, we can fool them."

"I assume all Blessed can thought talk, so how can we stop them from hearing us?"

"To block our thought talk we have to imagine we are in a sound-proof bubble. When you want to hear other Blesseds' thoughts, other than ours, you just step out of it. Right now, Tawny has walled himself in one, so I can't hear his thoughts. Try it, Avi!"

Avi imagined a bubble. Suddenly he could hear her amplified thoughts.

Today's shooting nearly cost you your life. Now, we have to get past them quickly. The Forced Blessed might be young and new to being Blessed but they are more organised and mercenary. A by-product of hatred brought on by the union of your father and me. So, stay alert, Avi. Tawny's plans will be more revengeful than Meeru thinks. Avi cleared his throat to signal the breakup of the Forced Blessed huddle. On prompt, Rosetta shouted, "Meeru, I hope you know this man is lying when he says he is saving Avi and me."

Meeru blanked Rosetta.

Rosetta rattled on. "You are aware that he has been to see me in his Blessed guise, and tried to barter and scheme with me. Did you know that he only went to you because he had no other chance? You don't really believe that he has feelings for you, do you?"

"Avi, we are making our way through the jungle, but not across the river. We are going to go through the forbidden area just opposite Dev's house. Tommy has spotted you entering the jungle from there. You must have subconsciously known that you wouldn't come to harm as you are a Blessed's child."

Avi listened and just about managed not to physically nod.

In the meantime, Rosetta held Meeru's full attention. "If I'd joined up with him, then you would have been fodder for his revenge. He probably told you that Papa married your brother to me, knowing I was a Blesseds' daughter, and that if I remained on the tribe's side of the river, I would definitely become a Blessed after my eighteenth birthday. Your father said his son was happy to take the risk."

Meeru flared up. "But he lied and sent you away the day after you got married."

Rosetta scouted the region. "Wow, he really has told you everything. The morning after my wedding day, Papa asked if he could use the land on the forbidden side of the path. In the capacity of Sherman and protector of the jungle, my father refused to sanction his wishes. Furious, Papa retaliated and encouraged Ma to send me back to my parents after my wedding night. Only the birth of their first grandson persuaded them to let me come back."

"Avi, I will tell you about all this later. Please concentrate on the task. When I say 'run', sprint to the entrance we discussed and hide in the foliage. Whatever you do, don't enter the jungle without me. Wait for me. I promise I'll be there as soon as I lose Tawny and his troop."

Unaware Rosetta was making a reconnaissance of the area to make a quick exit, Meeru engaged with Avi. "From you own mother's lips, you have heard of your Dada's treachery and her helplessness. You have to trust me over her. I've always protected you, haven't I?"

Before Avi could reply, he heard the word: **Run!**

Chapter 23

Avi vaulted over Major's boundary wall and ran harder than he thought was humanly possible. Dashing across the field, he had a fleeting awareness of not being followed by anyone – neither Rosetta nor Tawny's troop. It puzzled him, but he didn't pause. Instead, he ran blindly with his eyes momentarily shut, scouting for Rosetta through his thoughts. Her thought voice was muffled behind a translucent elliptical wall in his mind. Somehow, he had broken the shared thought connection and found himself outside of the bubble. He tried to imagine a new bubble with Rosetta in it, but it didn't work. Concentrating hard, he rammed the barrier, which resulted in an explosion of white light behind his closed eyelids.

Suddenly, he found himself escaping in two directions simultaneously. His body was physically running towards the jungle but, through Rosetta's mind, he was clambering up the mango tree in the yard. Seeing through her eyes, and hearing and feeling what she could, he was almost becoming her, while fully alert in his own body. The phenomenon astonished and elated him all at once. It was different from the passive connection he had with Una earlier that morning, as he lay on his bed. His adrenalin shot to dangerous levels to cope with the double jeopardy. Was it possible, he wondered, for him to inflict his own will on another via this connection?

"Firstly, your impolite way of pushing in only worked because

I let you in. Next time, just think up a request. Secondly, don't fill my mind with useless ponderings."

Sheepishly, Avi obeyed and passively concentrated on Rosetta's peripheral vision and thoughts. Her mind was briskly going over the details of their routes. Her heart was booming loud as she propelled herself higher up the mango tree and across a bridge formed by the entanglement of leaning branches from a fig tree. Soon, she was beyond Major's property. Rosetta's fear for their lives charged Avi's speed as he ran in bounds, agilely missing the short thorny bushes and heaps of cow dung, before leaping straight over the path – almost off-shooting the spot where he was meant to wait for her. Just in time, he put his brakes on and fell into the shrubbery on the jungle side of the path, just opposite Dev's house.

Crouched between the prickly arms of a shrub, thankful for his hoodie, he kept his attention on the path and puzzled over where the Forced Blesseds were. Could they all be with Rosetta?

On cue, Rosetta glanced down from her leafy, lofty walkway and, to her dismay, found that her agility, and the height at which she'd progressed, had not shaken off Tawny, the next fastest pack runner. Somehow, they had kept pace. She had to get out of the trees. Strapped to Rosetta's mind, Avi involuntarily ducked and dived as Rosetta tore through a mass of evergreen leaves and needles until she cleared the trees and leapt onto grass. She sprinted up the hill behind his house, easily outrunning Tawny and his gang, but then came to a sudden standstill, forcibly breaking Avi's link.

Sweat ran down Avi's face and his front lobe throbbed. Massaging his forehead, he reconnoitred the path. Somehow, he was able to see in the gathering darkness. *Night vision? Was he going to be all animal before the night was over?* He shook his head. He didn't have time to dwell on it. Instead, he had to work out where the rest of Tawny's gang were.

"They're all here with me, Avi. Don't thought talk now. Listen and stay vigilant. The Forced Blesseds miscalculated your exit.

They obviously relied on Meeru's feedback, and she underestimated your risk taking. You must have kept your 'little adventures' in the forbidden regions to yourself."

Avi was desperate to speak but he knew she was right and gave in. Instead, he concentrated on quietening his mind by picturing the word 'RELEASE'; a technique which kept him calm through his rough encounters with his uncles when they drank too much. He felt the curve of a smile from Rosetta and instantly knew she had something to do with him learning the technique. Slowly, his thoughts dissolved and the hazy elliptical frame reappeared between his closed eyes, letting him once again open up to Rosetta's senses and thoughts.

She was completely trapped. Despite her earlier smile, she was agitated and pacing backwards and forwards to find a gap between the ring of armed Forced Blesseds. Her restless oscillating movement brought on something akin to motion sickness for him. Avi pleaded with her to focus on something. Straight away, she zeroed in on a monstrosity of a weapon, something he had never seen before. It was constructed out of a green translucent alloy, with several menacing rotatory appendages, which were gyrating even though the weapon was not in use.

Rosetta's breathing quickened, which increased her oxygen intake and accelerated her heartbeat. Dancing strobe lights filled her head and she screamed in his mind:

"They're not going to let either of us live. They intend to butcher us mercilessly so we can't heal ourselves."

A cold dampness rose off Avi's pores.

The encircling Forced Blesseds encroached closer and closer.

"Stand down, boys," Tawny commanded from behind Rosetta.

She turned to see both Tawny and his running companion appear at the crest of the hill, completely out of breath.

"Luckily for Meeru, she got one thing right," Tawny said between breaths, straightening himself. "She thought you would take this route, but that was the only thing she got right so far. In our animal forms, we could have kept up with a snow leopard, but Meeru insisted you were in human form when she left you. In any case, we needed our ..."

Rosetta interrupted. "Weapons?"

"Very perceptive, Rosetta."

Avi wondered how long it would take Tawny to be just as *perceptive*. He didn't have to wait long.

"Where is Avi? He's not at the river, as Meeru ..."

"... Expected?" Rosetta finished Tawny's sentence again.

Tawny regarded Rosetta carefully. She shifted under his scrutiny, causing his frown to change into a smirk.

"Although you have tricked us, he must still be vulnerable. His DNA is unstable and you need him to safely cross through the four boulders on the river bed. He isn't there because you want him to become a snow leopard, too, and he can only be there if you take him. You can't have sent him to the jungle because you can't risk someone else blessing him and transforming him into another form of animal. So, if he's not on the river or in the jungle, that can only mean he's hiding and waiting for you in the peripheral edges of the jungle bordering the path."

Rosetta's fur bristled. For just a blip of a second, the walls safeguarding their communications came down. For the second time that day, Avi shared another's mind space with an intruder. The intruder's thought signature was identical to the one he had felt when he'd talked to Una, during the tribesmen's visit. Avi heard Tawny send a message to a small group of Forced Blesseds, telling them to head down the hill towards the path.

"You were never going to let Avi or myself live, were you?" Rosetta murmured.

"Now, why would you think that?" Tawny asked, resting on a tree stump just in front of her.

'The fact that you've assembled your entire troop up here on the hill, instead of standing ready beyond the boulders in the river, as is customary when a Blessed is brought over from this side of the path. The presence of the ancient weapons in some of your followers' hands also suggest you intend to finish us off completely, so we can't reconstruct."

"I think you can tell I'm terrible at remembering to follow the River Rule and the creation of Blesseds." He pointed to his team.

"That's going to change for you."

"Really?" Tawny questioned, unworried. He borrowed one of the ancient weapons and began to meticulously inspect it.

"I imagine you think you can kill Avi and I with your sophisticated weapons and intimidate the tribe to cower, allowing you to rule the jungle."

"Correct," Tawny replied. Rosetta was nicely framed in the viewer of the monstrosity he held.

Rosetta's voice wavered. "But you can't, only a ..."

This time Tawny finished her sentence. "... Snow leopard can rule? I know. It's amazing what you can find out from a few dusty books buried deep in the library from the days it belonged to the Forestry. In fact, it was your son, the school library monitor, who found the relevant book in the library. No doubt, if Avi was here, he would explain my solution." Tawny raised an eyebrow. He knew Avi was listening.

Rosetta groaned as Avi's mind cast a memory of himself studying the book 'Myths and Mythology of the Himalayan Tribes', which he'd found in a locked, 'Reference only', glass cabinet. According to the author, before the 1900s and the 'Big Game' hunts the British loved so much, it was traditional for the tribe's bravest youth to keep the wildlife numbers from diminishing by volunteering to safeguard the jungle, through turning into Blesseds themselves. The devastating depletion of wildlife, due to excessive hunting practices, forced the tribe's elders to make it mandatory for all firstborns of the land to become Blesseds.

"Rosetta, according to the book, if Tawny has found a volunteer tribesman, he doesn't need either of us because, when you die, the tribesman will take on your spirit, and will thus be transformed into a snow leopard."

Rosetta already knew the facts, and was frantically looking for the volunteer.

"You don't have a volunteer or a Sharman to do the conversion."

Tawny faked a look of concern. "Don't I?"

Rosetta wasn't fooled. "Everyone here is tattooed, which means your Forced Blessed faction have animal spirits entwined with their human ones already."

Tawny looked past Rosetta and pointed.

Rosetta snapped her head around and followed the direction of his finger until she spotted a body moving up the slope of the hill.

Would he? Oh God, surely not!

Avi stood up in his hiding place. Rosetta's thought had shaken him. Tawny didn't think it was a possibility.

Tawny chose that moment to 'thought talk' to Rosetta, easily pushing past her barriers in her weakened state.

"You are very perceptive, Rosetta."

"But ... but, Meeru is not from the tribe. She can't volunteer, and she's the last of seven children?" Rosetta blurted, pushing hard at Tawny in her head.

"Ah, but I don't intend her to become a Forced Blessed. She can't, as you said. But she can ..."

"Be possessed by my soul once you kill my body, as it has nowhere else to go." The blood drained out of Rosetta's body, turning it cold, as if the deed had already been done.

Avi recognised Meeru's unhurried gait and, despite himself, he thought shouted, "*SHE DOESN'T KNOW!*"

Tawny's gaze shot from Meeru to Rosetta.

To distract his attention from Meeru, Rosetta blurted out loud, "Meeru might love you, Tawny, and, perhaps, she has convinced herself that you love her, too. Even so, remember, she's not as self-sacrificing as you might think she is."

"We will see," uttered Tawny as an out of breath Meeru stumbled up to him. In between panting, she asked, "Where is Avi? He wasn't at the river so I thought he must be here."

Tawny glared at Meeru. "He isn't. Perhaps you have tricked us into thinking you are helping us. You said Rosetta was in human form, but here she is in her snow leopard embodiment. You haven't deliberately misled us, have you, Meeru?"

Meeru startled at his accusation. "What? No!" She began to panic. "Rosetta's done something. If he's not here or at the river, then ... Oh God! He's already in the jungle!"

Meeru drew up in front of Rosetta. "You were meant to enter the jungle together. How could you be so stupid? You of all creatures should know the risks."

Tawny placed his hands over Meeru's shoulders, gave her a kiss on the cheek and smugly directed all his attention to Rosetta. "Let's hope your son hasn't entered the jungle without you, Rosetta."

Avi couldn't help himself and he shouted in Rosetta's head. "TELL MEERU THE TRUTH!"

The shout pushed against the bubble walls and tore Rosetta's thought protections.

"Ah, Avi! I thought I heard a shout earlier, but didn't think it was you. Budge a little, Avi. Let me join the party in your mother's mind."

Rosetta squirmed inwardly.

"Rosetta, you were never part of my plan to rule the jungle, and I was right to think Avi would be difficult to control. Meeru didn't know he could thought talk, and he shouldn't have been able to so early on, anyway." Tawny paused before continuing, "Never mind! The silly fool has broadcasted his presence. Now, through your channel, I know where to send my scouts to find him." Rosetta shook her head about, trying to dislodge him. Tawny shouted a thought command for her to stop. Rosetta shook her head even harder. Angry, Tawny retaliated and, with all his mental might, tried to push through Rosetta's channel all the way to Avi's mind.

The pressure was far too much for Rosetta. A throbbing pain rushed from the back of her neck to the rest of her body, throwing it into violent convulsions. A high-pitched scream forcibly followed, hurling Tawny off his axis, thus breaking his connection. Avi held on with invisible suction pads despite her desperate motions to retract from him, too.

Avi was resolute. Instead of running away from Tawny, he intended to rescue Rosetta. Thinking so, he stepped back from the edge of the jungle, into the open, and onto the path.

"Don't be stupid, Avi! Tawny wasn't lying. A third of his troop left when Tawny discovered you weren't here. Why are you so bent on giving up your life so easily? First, you gave your location away, and now you have made yourself a visible target. Tawny is right. You have an untrained mind, and a lack of regard for others. Otherwise, why would you make a mockery of my sacrifices to keep you alive?"

Avi stepped back into the foliage.

"Good decision. NOW RUN! Run into the jungle and aim for the temple. You can go around the perimeter of the four rocks this time, now that you are on the cusp of becoming a Blessed."

The gravity of the meaning of her instruction hit him. He was no longer human. He peered down at his body. It still looked human.

"Now is not the time for self-inspection, Avi. Please, let go of my mind ... your connection is draining me."

Avi hesitated, not wanting to leave Rosetta behind.

"Go, but remember this, I have always loved you and nothing is going to stop me from reuniting properly with you. Hurry on and wait for me in the temple. I will be there soon."

With eyes and jaws closed, Rosetta dug her claws in the soil and applied all her unused feline kinetic energy to her mind. She pushed Avi out and stopped Tawny, who was in the process of latching on again. Connections severed, her body shut itself down, and crumbled in a heap.

***

Reluctant to leave Meeru and Rosetta to their fate, Avi hesitated for a few moments, even though he knew he would never make it to them. The only option he had was to outsmart or outrun the Forced Blesseds in their territory – the jungle.

With great trepidation, Avi took hurried steps into the forbidden dark jungle – the jungle he had always been drawn to from a very young age. It had called to his heart and soul and compelled him to visit, again and again through the years, in the daylight. Now he knew why. Barely twenty paces into the jungle, the air swished over Avi's head. First, a harpoon fell at his feet with a thud, then two running steps further, a metal object with rotating blades hit a trunk close to his shoulders. Both objects came from the same direction, just beyond the path where he'd been stood earlier.

Avi turned around to face the path and roared, "You've found me. Now, come and get me!" Avi angrily repeated himself. With his arms splayed outward in defiance, he faced the trees and the hiding foe. They had weapons but he had one, too. He bet that Tawny thought his greatest weapon against Avi was Avi's fear of death. Little did he know that Avi had the antidote to fear – indifference. In just one day, he'd lost a family. Most likely, he would lose Rosetta as well. So, what did it matter if they killed him or not? He'd only run into the jungle to honour Rosetta's sacrifice, that's all. Despite him calling out, no one appeared.

"What are you waiting for?" he bellowed.

"Nothing," a high-pitched voice replied, before a collective human wail of "charge!" broke out.

Instead of making a run for it, Avi crouched down and deliberately untied his laces then looped them again. He arched his back and imagined his school's sports pistol going off: 3 ... 2 ... 1. He exploded from the imaginary starting blocks, accelerating from nought to twenty mph in just a few seconds. He carried no excess weight and his almost-Blessed enhanced aerodynamic legs soared through the thicket of the jungle. His spine flexed and extended, enabling him to hit top speed. He increased his stride to maximum capacity. His genetics were altered and enhanced to match his matriarchal genes. One foot on the ground at a time, he swiftly advanced forward. His gaze forever remained resolutely locked on the temple, sitting on a precipice with a hundred and eight steps leading to it.

The jungle flew past in a blur. Roots tripped him but he was quick to steady himself using trees trunks or by throwing his arms out. Thorns and branches tried to ensnare him. Some ripped his clothes, but they could not impede him. His hood was no longer on his head. Instead, the pouch it formed, along with his mop of hair, collected twigs, leaves and other jungle bounty.

Avi was pursued keenly. Feet pounded along the jungle floor, while overhanging low tree branches were savagely snapped in their wake. His foe were several metres behind him when suddenly, the tree tops came alive with monkey frenzied howls as the monkeys flew over him from branch to branch. He had no time to wonder if the monkeys were foe or friend, so he ignored them. Nor did he have time to ponder over why the Forced Blesseds hadn't used more of their weapons. Nearly all at once, Avi was at the edge of the jungle and on the stony river bed. A shudder ran through him as he diagonally ran through the quadrant, between the boulders, and beyond.

Behind him, numerous feet clanked against the pebbles as they rushed towards him, shifting and dragging the gravel, bringing a rushing clamour to his ears. With concentrated ferocity for the last bout, Avi summoned his reserved energy and sprinted towards the steps before leaping onto the first step up to the temple.

"Slow down! Slow down, boy!" a hoarse voice boomed. He gave no heed to the words as he flew up the steps, almost depleting his energy levels. The burning sensation in his legs slowed him down completely before they violently shook and gave out beneath him. He landed halfway up the steps, clutching his sore legs in agony. Through tightly closed eyes, tears of pain streamed down his face.

Chapter 24

Avi?

Avi flayed his hands across the surface where he lay. The granite step was cold and bare – exactly what his body craved. The hard surface absorbed the pain seeping through his body, but left him exhausted.

"Have I lost you?"

"*No.*" He paused. "*I'm alive.*" He was alive, but how? Bewildered, Avi elbowed himself to a sitting position. They should have caught up with him on the steps where he lay squirming. They'd been so close. So, why hadn't they? He was puzzled. They were still there. He could hear them down below.

Too tired to give Rosetta any further reassurances, he closed his eyes and cruised down the channel Rosetta had opened between their minds. He needed to know how she was faring.

He recoiled.

Tawny was on his haunches, prising one of Rosetta's eyes open with his fingers. Rosetta did not miss her chance. She jerked her head forward, hissed and opened her mouth wide to bite down on his hand. But before her jaw shut, Tawny rocked backwards on his heels.

"About time you woke up from your earlier meltdown," he said nonchalantly, dusting his hands against his bent knees, before standing up.

The arrogance! Avi's mounting hatred for Tawny made it

difficult for him to stay calm. Nonetheless, he kept quiet.

"Get up, Rosetta, we have to find Avi before the other Blesseds do," Meeru's voice was harsh.

Avi groaned. Meeru was still none the wiser.

"I really can't believe you're stalling, Rosetta," accused Meeru as she stood akimbo, towering over Rosetta. She was clearly frustrated and angry by the delay. "Running away in different directions didn't help. Now, we have to hope Avi hasn't been blessed by a lesser creature."

Rosetta stretched out her paws. "Meeru, Avi is out of harm's way. There is no rush."

Her nonchalance stiffened Tawny's demeanour.

"You really need to check, Rosetta. I think you will find he is surrounded."

"Maybe, but I won't. You are not entering his mind through me."

Tawny shook his head. "Rosetta, your reluctance to cooperate with us leaves me no other choice."

Before Rosetta could ask him what he meant, Tawny withdrew his arm from Meeru's shoulder and roughly held her in a neck brace. Surprised and shocked, Meeru's initial disbelief transformed into alarm as she thrashed about attempting to free herself from Tawny's clutches. She aimed her legs and elbows at the vulnerable parts on his body, to no avail. Instead, to contain her, he raised the side of her combat outfit. Exposing her waist, he pressed the tip of his knife deep into her flesh and drew a trickle of blood. Meeru let out a cry as he maliciously screwed the knife once and then twice, lodging it deeper into her skin.

"Warwick, let me go. Please ... this wasn't our plan. I don't understand." Teary and wild-eyed, Meeru begged on, "I'll help you find Avi, just let me go."

"Find him? Meeru you are so naïve. I have him surrounded." Tawny looked at Rosetta as he finished his sentence, "And he'll soon be dead."

"But you need him!" Meeru protested. Her voice broke further.

Tawny smiled and jolted her head backwards, still holding her by the neck. "Sweetness, I lied. I just want Rosetta to help you on your way to becoming a snow leopard."

Meeru screamed and tried to pull away, but all she did was send the knife deeper.

"How can she help me? I'm not a firstborn. It's not possible for me to become a Blessed," she sobbed.

Tawny stared at Meeru intently.

"You know how."

Meeru jerked her head from side to side.

"Really, Meeru, you must improve your memory recollection," Tawny said unhelpfully. "Especially as it was you who informed me of Avi's discovery in his school's reference library."

Tawny's smile grew as the truth slowly dawned on Meeru.

"*Meeru, how could you be so stupid.*" Avi was enraged by her betrayal. He hit his fist on the marble step, stirring snarls and hisses from somewhere below him. He'd forgotten about them. He hollered, "What are you guys waiting for? Just finish me off!" He wished they would do just that. He didn't even care how they did it. Nothing could be worse than watching the demonic act Tawny threatened to perform on Meeru.

"Tawny let her go, just take me. You can spare Meeru and Avi if I agree to do your bidding willingly," Rosetta pleaded.

"I could, but I much prefer a younger and more malleable leader. It's too late for Avi. If you channel back to him, you'll find he's not got long, if he isn't already dead."

Rosetta's posture faltered.

"You know he's lying. I'm fine and I'm in the temple."

"Rosetta, I hope you can cram yourself into narrow places because you're going to be a little squashed between Meeru's organs and her slender body," taunted Tawny. He was enjoying himself far too much.

Avi's insides felt as wretched as Meeru's looked.

Tawny's lips curled and he kissed the top of Meeru's head. "Don't be scared, Meeru. Look at the positives. We'll be together, forever, just like you wanted."

Meeru protested, "I didn't want to be with you like this ... I thought ... I thought you loved me, but all this time I was just a pawn in your revenge strategy."

"Oh! Don't be so tough on yourself, Meeru. I do like you, and I did have a crush on you, but you're right about the scheming. If I had confided my true plans to you, you wouldn't have helped me trap Rosetta and your nephew, Avi." Tawny paused, then winked at Rosetta. "Particularly, as the plan always involved killing Avi, straight away."

Meeru let out a howl. One of the youths cleared his throat and pointed to the lightening sky.

He wasn't the only one who looked nervous. The whole cohort was restless. It was clear they wished to end their mission before dawn. Tawny relented. Keeping hold of Meeru, he moved away to brief his cohort on their next moves.

"Rosetta, you've got to stop the bastard and save yourself, and Meeru."

Tawny's arm froze mid-instruction and, seemingly, stared straight at Avi through Rosetta's eyes. Rosetta didn't flinch. Keeping an eye on her, Tawny ordered his cohort to herd her down the hill, towards the field between Major and Dev's house. He prodded Meeru, his knife still lodged in her side, in the same direction. As they passed Major's boundary wall, he raised his voice so Rosetta would not miss the words, "Meeru, scream as loud as you can when Rosetta possesses your body, so your Papa can hear." Then, for good measure, he added, "Avi's body will soon be dumped here for them to find the next morning."

Rosetta stalled.

Tawny sneered, "It's a shame we need his body. He would have made an excellent meal for the other animals of the jungle."

Meeru's voice rose in desperation, "No! You can't mean it. Warwick, please, you promised you wouldn't harm Avi." She motioned to Rosetta. "Kill her and make me a snow leopard, but leave Avi alone. You, yourself, said he couldn't transform into a snow leopard without her. If he can't be a snow leopard, then he can't be a threat to you."

Avi felt sad and relieved at the same time. Meeru's affection for him had truly been genuine.

Rosetta said nothing. Instead she busied herself scouting for another mind. She must have found one because she was back to masking her thoughts with spoken words, to deflect any listeners. Avi couldn't understand how she let him hear her thoughts, but kept Tawny out.

"Avi will be waiting for me, Meeru, so don't worry about him. Nothing is going to happen to you. Have faith." And then, under her spoken speech, she fast thought talked.

"Are you on guard duty?"

Avi was stumped. Rosetta was thought talking, but not to him.

Aloud, she talked about relatively mundane things with Meeru. "Is Warwick the boy you were desperate to dance with at your last social?" Avi mulled over Tawny's real name. He was sure he had read the name Warwick before, in a newspaper or somewhere else, but he couldn't remember.

"Tommy, they're planning to kill me and force my spirit to join with Meeru's. The only way she can escape is if you distract them ... Don't worry about me ... I'll make it to the jungle today ..."

Avi gulped, Rosetta was talking to Major's dog as if he was human. Was he a Blessed, too?

Not realising she was being used as a decoy, Meeru answered Rosetta's question. "It must be quite obvious that Warwick is the boy I was meant to meet at our last socials."

"So, what happened?" Rosetta enquired, and then gave Tommy instructions to attack.

"I ... I already ..." Meeru stopped mid-sentence.

Avi was relieved when Meeru began to speak again. He was sure she knew Rosetta was diverting Tawny's attention.

"After the socials, he came to check on me because he knew something was wrong if I missed the event. Not fancying the long walk through the roads via the army cantonment, he took a short cut through the jungle. He was confident of his route because he'd visited the jungle a couple of times with his parents when they were looking for land to build a house. Warwick was drunk that night and hadn't considered the dangers of meeting wildlife, let alone Blesseds."

"Rosetta, don't put yourself at risk. Let me help you get away and save your son. I am the only one who is immune to the enchantment on the wall, so I can leap over and help. I don't know why you didn't let me help sooner. Meeru brought this on herself and she should suffer the consequences."

Avi didn't like what Tommy was saying about Meeru, but he understood where his loyalties lay. It was startling to think Tommy the dog could speak.

"Tommy, stop the whining! Position yourself close to Dev's boundary wall and when I shout 'now', create a diversion." A few seconds later she thought shouted: "NOW!"

Tommy flew over Dev's wall and fell on Warwick causing bedlam as the rest of the cohort went to their leader's rescue. Meeru was pushed to the side in the commotion. Rosetta saw her chance and quickly herded Meeru to the wall. "Get on my back and get over Dev's wall. You're not Blessed so you can cross it."

Meeru didn't need to be asked twice. Despite the pain in her side she did as she was told and pulled herself up the wall, using the spikes for leverage. The sharp spire tips tore ribbons of flesh from her palms, but she didn't even flinch. Avi's heart rested when she made it over to safety.

In the meantime, the Forced Blesseds successfully freed their leader from Tommy and bludgeoned him to a pulp.

Tears tickled down Rosetta's fur. Avi felt her despair at the sacrifice her friend had made.

With Meeru safely on the other side, Rosetta stepped back and leapt high in the sky, making sure she jumped much higher than the enchanted wall. Dev's roof was not protected against the Blessed so she would be safe. Avi was air sick! His vision blurred.

While she was in flight, he smelt iron. The next thing he sensed was the excruciating pain she felt as her bones crushed against the cement roof floor. Her eyelids close as she thought talked to him. *"Meeru is unchanged and safe in Dev's boundaries."*

Without thinking, he replied, *"Thank you, Ma."* Rosetta's body shuddered and once again Avi was on his own.

❋❋❋

On his own? Not really.

In the dim light of the temple's flickering diya, Avi's eyes travelled slowly down the empty steps. The Forced Blesseds had not taken a single step towards him. Instead, they stood huddled together on the ground with their faces – *their animal faces* – upturned in snarls, facing him.

"I told you to slow down, but you didn't listen. Those things can't come up the steps unless invited." Dumbfounded, Avi turned to the voice coming from the top step just as the diya flame went out.

❋❋❋

The final bullet found its target in the field and a high pitched canine scream erupted across the valley, continuing endlessly. In Una's nightmare, Meeru covered her ears and squeezed her eyes shut as she repeated, "God, what have I done?"

Someone, no several people were kicking Tommy relentlessly, torturing him.

Meeru was shouting, "Warwick, please just put Tommy out of his misery. Please, Warwick, please!"

Una wasn't sure if Meeru's screams made it above the clamour on the other side of the wall. Then she heard a male voice that sounded familiar, but she couldn't place it.

"I suppose you aren't going to give yourself up?"

He must have been leaning against the wall adjacent to Meeru, but on the other side of it.

180

"What! No reply? ... Never mind. For old times' sake, I'll grant you your wish." Una gulped. The speaker was the taxi driver who'd brought her to the valley. A silence fell. Una breathed a sigh of relief as she continued to dream. It would be over soon and she would awake, but she was wrong.

A long, strangling squeal came from over the wall.

"You bastard!" Meeru cried out as she covered her ears.

***

Una shouted out in her sleep, "Tommy, where's Tommy?"

Vaguely lucid, she listened out for him, but then rolled to her side and went back to sleep. She had been in Khamosh Valley long enough not to be disturbed by screams and shrill animal noises.

Unbeknown to her, Tommy lay on the ground with his tongue hanging out to one side, an iron rod shoved down his throat.

Chapter 25

Drat! She must have left the window open in her bedroom. Una pulled the borrowed blanket closely around her, only to accidentally expose her midriff. The cold fingers of morning air gripped her waist and shocked her fully awake. Her neck hurt ... possibly from falling asleep at an odd angle or because her head ... was propped against the corner of a wall ... her usual alcove by the water tank.

Hurried slapping of flip-flops against marble ascended the roof stairwell. "I can't believe you kept her locked up here." For the first time ever, Grandad sounded livid. "The thugs, probably the tribesmen, were just outside our boundary wall last night. They must have come to steal her. You better hope Tommy didn't die in vain and that she's safely tucked away in her usual corner on the roof."

"Dev Ji, you are being optimistic. It's the middle of winter. If she's been on the roof all night, then she's been exposed to the bare elements. There is a good chance she is suffering from hyperthermia or worse."

"We will soon find out, Dr Verma."

Una trained her eyes on the roof door as it opened. She stared blankly as her grandparents and a prune-faced man with a doctor's bag ran towards her.

"She's here and alive, thank God," Dev exclaimed. Prune-face hurriedly placed the back of his hand on her forehead, then put two fingers under her jaw and stalled.

"What is wrong, Dr. Verma? Has she got hyperthermia?" Una was surprised to hear genuine concern for her well-being coming from her grandfather.

"Dev Ji, I don't know what to make of it. Not only does she not have hyperthermia, but she is quite warm and her breathing is normal."

"Normal?" Dev uttered, then kneeled over Una.

"What do you remember about yesterday?" Dev asked Una, holding her lightly by the shoulders.

"Remember? I remember seeing Rosetta ... I'm sure Avi was shot. I saw a snow leopard ... I ran away from Avi ... he was going to change into a ... snow leopard." Una stopped her babble, petrified of her own words. Her rosiness drained away, giving her a ghostly appearance. Dr Verma sighed out loud. He pulled out a hypodermic syringe, filled it with amber liquid from his bag, tapped it, rubbed her arm and, before she could protest, thrust the needle into her skin. All three adults faded into ghostly outlines.

Chapter 26

Almost three months later.

Nana told him to be patient, to concentrate on being human and, most importantly, to remain inconspicuous until his great uncle came back from the Valley of Flowers. Of course, it was easier said than done. To Avi's dismay, days had turned into weeks, and weeks into months. The initial intrigue and curiosity from the tribe and the Blesseds towards the son of Rosetta and the grandson of the Sharman, distorted into distrust and rebuke. Some of the tribe even made threats. Avi didn't care if they finished him off. On most levels, he wished it. However, his nana's and mother's sacrifice compelled him to work hard at suppressing his conflicting animal instincts as much as he could. It was becoming more difficult as each day passed. The fever and bouts of pain he previously experienced on the other side of the path had intensified a hundred-fold, mainly because his mother had died before she could accompany him across the river, making his transformation into a Blessed snow leopard incomplete. In the evenings, his skeletal structure began to metamorphosis into something entirely different. Nana believed a Blessed or Forced Blessed had intervened with him when he ran to the temple on his birthday. The existing Blessed animal hierarchy deterred Avi from sharing his own suspicions. He prayed for his great uncle to come back soon, before the change became irreversible and complete.

His prayers were answered in late spring with his great uncle's appearance at the bottom of the temple steps. Pity, and something more sinister, flitted across his great uncle's face as he made eye contact with him, before averting his attention and making the slow climb to him. Avi's destiny was decided and it didn't look good. Down crest, he pushed past the aged langur at the entrance of the temple and disappeared into its darkest corner. Worried, the Sharman called to his brother in a quivering voice, "*Him tendua ka bacha terai jhole mai hai kya?* – Is the snow leopard cub in your bag?"

"*Nahi jhole mai latai hai* – No, there are only clothes in my bag," yelled the Sharman's younger brother.

An anguished cry left the Sharman's langur body as he slid down the pillar to a crouched position on the first step, where his brother eventually joined him.

"*Kaee him tendua ayai milai par koi bachara nahi mila. Mai hairan hu ki apko baras pahelai Burfani ki atman mili thi* – Although I found a couple of lone snow leopards, I didn't find any offspring. How did you find the spirit of Burfani all those years back?"

The Sharman's head dropped, "*Mainai nahi dhunda, jamidar Major aur Dev kai anai kai bad woh Meray sapnai mai ayee aur usnai mujhai Chamoli bulaya* – I didn't. After the property developers, Major and Dev, arrived she appeared in my dreams and guided me to her in the Valley of Flowers."

His great uncle nodded and gestured to where he thought Avi sat indoors.

"*Bhai apko lagta hai ki yeh apkai baad bachaiga?* – Brother, do you think he will survive after you have gone? *Apko pata hai ki iskai vajai sai humarai dushman ki jeet aur paki ho jay gee* – You know this strengthens the Forced Blesseds' campaign to take over leadership. *Hamai koi aur adhikari banana chaiya* – We must think of another Blessed to take his place as the successor."

Avi moved closer.

The Sharman threw a sharp look at his brother and snapped, "*Aap apnai potai Gopan kai barai mai soch rahai ho?* – Are you thinking of your own grandson, Gopan?"

"*Nahi tho*! – No, of course not!"

Avi was suspicious, mostly of his great uncle, who was squirming on his haunches.

"Chalo acha hai, Tum thakai ho, tou isjkai barai mai baad mai baat karaigai – Good to know. You must be tired, so we will talk about this later."

As Avi watched his great uncle make his way down, he came out and uttered, "It doesn't look good for me, does it?"

The Sharman gave no reply.

"Will my Blessed form stabilise now?"

"Yes, but not in a good way. In time your snow leopard characteristics will be entirely replaced by the other animal form."

That night, Avi tossed and turned on the makeshift bed on the temple floor, waiting for the dark hours to shorten and the morning hours to stretch and push their daylight fingers through the temple door. Questions besieged him and his imagination ran riot, torturing him far more than the physical tyranny of pain. Images of Meeru and Tawny taunted him behind his shut eyes and awoke the spirit of hell in him. He had to stop Tawny before he planned a similar revengeful or worse fate for Una. More sinister than the ones he had planned for Meeru and himself.

Chapter 27

Six months later

Sitting behind Dev on his moped, clutching a small attaché suit-case, Una travelled from her boarding school to Khamosh Valley in under ten minutes. A short journey perhaps, by all standards. Yet, she had only visited her grandparents once over the last six months. After that disastrous visit, both guardian and charge jointly agreed that it was unnecessary for Una to take up the twice-a-month opportunity to come 'home' for weekends during term time. Una was over the moon when she found out there were three terms a year, each four months' long.

Since she had left her grandfather's property, winter had given way to spring, and spring, in turn, to summer. The valley was lush and beautiful, and the barren garden, where the tribesmen and soldiers had once stood, was welcoming and breath-taking. Perhaps she had underestimated her grandparents – truly indiffer-ent people could not have planned such a thing of beauty. Bright marigolds, geraniums, roses and hibiscus bushes, planted at ground level, were offset by hanging baskets of rainforest plants, suspended high from the roof.

Una's gaze travelled admiringly between the roof-hung baskets of ferns and other succulent combinations, until she saw some-thing move between them. Shading her eyes from the sun, Una scrutinised the gaps between the green foliage and caught the flash of a pale body pass between the baskets.

Could it be a ghost?

"Tommy, is that you hiding up on the roof, you silly mutt?" she shouted.

Una dumped her suitcase on the gravel floor and ran through the house, leaving her grandfather to deal with her suitcase and his moped. With her sandals flapping on the steps, she charged up the stairs and pushed hard against the roof door. Instead of opening, a metal object dug into her belly button. Confused, she gazed down and saw the largest, shiniest cylindrical lock she had ever seen, hanging from a new sideways latch on the door.

There were more bolts and locks, but no key in sight.

Besides the key, something else was amiss – the usually polished teak door was dull, dusty and untouched.

"If the door is locked, then Tommy is ..."

She was going to say 'not here' but Dev, who now stood behind her, finished the sentence. "Dead."

She swivelled around and faced his familiar, exasperated, expression.

"Dead?" She'd forgotten. "Of course he is. Tommy is dead." Una slumped down on the top step with her head in her hands. Dev gave her a withering look and left.

Why did she keep forgetting? Perhaps, if she'd seen Tommy's body and buried him, she would not need reminding. By the time she found out about Tommy's strange death, he had already been "dealt with". Those were the words her grandfather had used. Dev had been shocked by her tears and the many questions, which he evaded. He thought her silly and indulgent, and had no time for her emotional outburst over a mere animal. He compared Tommy to a useful object like her hair brush, rather than her constant and friendly companion. Her only companion, other than ... Avi.

Avi ... she had blocked him from her thoughts for other reasons. Doctor Verma had seen to that. For a whole week following Tommy's death, he'd injected her daily after asking her the same question: "What do you remember about the evening before you fell asleep on the roof?"

A week on, she finally learnt to answer the question correctly with "I don't remember."

Her answer had rung true until two months ago. During a gym lesson, she had an accident and broke her arm in two places, a result of her foot slipping off the climbing apparatus. She was operated on straight away. Under anaesthetic, the cloak over her memory was removed and images of the kiss she'd shared with Avi came flooding back, shocking her all over again. She also remembered the trauma she'd experienced when they'd parted. The images were clear, but she could only recall snippets of Avi's conversation. He told her he was changing to a Blessed, which was confusing because he looked no different to her. Although Una believed her memories to be true, they were too weird to share with anyone.

Two weeks after the accident, her arm had healed completely, confounding the hospital doctors. She wasn't surprised at all. While they exclaimed over and discussed her x-rays excitedly amongst themselves, the image of a falling bullet flashed before her eyes. She had to sit down on a nearby chair as her gut turned inside out, responding to the overpowering vehemence she recalled feeling towards Avi.

Before she went to Windsor school, she didn't think she had seen Avi on the evening she was found on the roof. Now, sitting on the stairs, she knew she had. Sighing loudly, Una slowly retraced her steps to the carport to retrieve her abandoned suitcase, which was where she'd left it.

Carrying her attaché into the living room, Una stopped momentarily in front of the glass cabinet. It had a new addition – her mother's wind up Timex watch. Una had worn the watch ever since her Mum's death, until she had left for the new school. The clock hands were stuck on 7:30. It had been found in the neighbouring field, not far from Tommy's body. Initially, Dev had accused her of having something to do with his death! At the time, she was appalled, but now she wasn't sure.

Her English life was frozen behind the glass. With just a

hairpin, she could ring her local school friend and ask for an iPhone charger and revive her previous life. She could wind the watch and remember her Mum. She could read the letter and bring her Dad back, but she no longer wanted to. They had all abandoned her. Perhaps she had been harsh on her English friends but, in truth, she had a new life. Besides the sanctuary provided by Windsor School, nothing mattered.

Una's new friends did not include Avi or Meeru. Meeru put paid to that.

Inconsolable after Tommy's death, Una had run to their house. She'd called out for Avi many times and, when no one answered, she brazenly walked to the back of the property. In the backyard, she found an outbuilding with its doors wide open. Una ventured in. Floral and fresh fragrance permeated the air. A heavy-duty iron and a special ironing table stood in the centre. Nylon clothes lines criss-crossed the room with white sheets and kurtas drying on them. Una was somewhat disorientated. She couldn't say why, but she had expected an animal to be living there. On that day, she believed she had not been on Major's property before, but, of course, she was mistaken.

"He's not here," Meeru had said, appearing in the doorway and startling Una.

If Meeru had not spoken, Una would not have recognised her. The Meeru walking towards her was dull-eyed and sallow, and closely resembled a walking corpse.

"Is there anything you need?" Meeru asked wearily as she placed the back of her hand against her forehead. Before Una could reply, she continued, "No? Then if you don't mind, I've got a lot to do, as you can see."

"You've got a lot to do – in here?" Una had been surprised. "What about your servants and the sisters-in-law who normally do this work for you?"

Meeru just shrugged and irritably replied, "Una I haven't got time for chit chat ..."

"Meeru, I just wanted to know if you or Avi knew about

Tommy's cruel killing last week, and whether you saw something. It's just that I can't understand why somebody would kill Tommy so brutally, and how he came to be on the other side of the wall." Una had hurried through her sentence as a deluge of tears fell down her face.

Unsympathetically, Meeru had unpegged a handkerchief from the washing line and passed it to her. "No." Unable to speak, she'd watched Meeru fidget with her salwar kameez's dupatta. She knew Meeru was hiding something, especially when Meeru protested. "I don't know anything about Tommy, but what in heaven makes you think Avi and I would care about the death of a dog?"

Besides Meeru's constant fidgeting and trembling, there had been something else about her that was quite out of character with the girl she'd met on the roof when she first arrived. After staring hard she wondered how she hadn't noticed it straight away. Meeru's western clothes had been replaced by a mismatched Indian outfit, one an older woman with no sense of fashion would choose to wear. It was so unlike Meeru.

Meeru had shifted uncomfortably under Una's curious scrutiny, and tartly said, "I have lots to do and, quite frankly, I would appreciate it if you left instead of gawking at me, Una."

Hurt, Una had stumbled out of the building.

Not satisfied, Meeru had called out, "By the way, Una, I wouldn't bother coming around anymore. Avi got his calling papers from the army and has begun his training. He would have come around to tell you, but he stupidly got hurt by a dummy bullet when he was horsing around with his uncles."

Una stopped and turned around to face Meeru.

"Oh, so that's what I saw from Grandad's roof – an initiation game of sorts."

Meeru didn't reply. Instead, she had stared at something near Una's feet.

Una had followed her gaze and found a nearly empty pail of white paint and a box containing oddments, such as a white enamel plate and mug with navy trims and a dirty nylon material. The same material she had seen in her dreams, worn by a vagrant while she was looking for her Dad.

Following that awkward meeting with Meeru, Una had returned to her grandfather's house, and, to their astonishment, agreed to become a boarder at Windsor School the very next day.

Chapter 28

Two days into her summer holiday, Una wished she was back at boarding school again. It wasn't a holiday. It was more like boot camp. Meeru's wedding boot camp! Meeru had just finished college and was about to marry an airline pilot who had just got his American Green Card. The way everyone talked about the Green Card, it felt like Meeru was marrying Prince William himself. At first, the news of Meeru's wedding left Una off-balanced. She was jealous of Meeru. It should have been her leaving the valley and country, but, by the second day, she remembered that it had been her own father who had brought and left her in the valley in the first place. She didn't want to go back to where she wasn't wanted. Una was determined to make her new school experience work – it would be like showing her Dad two fingers. No, if Una was miffed now, it was because she just didn't like being drowned by wedding paraphernalia – especially someone else's. It was a pity that Grandad's house was the overspill for the wedding preparations.

Una's latest chore gave her a break from those indoors. She felt a sense of wicked exhilaration in beheading the marigold flower heads in Grandad's garden while they were in their prime. Threading them together with market bought ones to make garlands, however, was quite tedious and she pricked her fingers with the needle endlessly, drawing blood several times. Who knew flowers could inspire the macabre in her. Sid Rao's daughters, Agnes and Grace, giggled the entire time they worked alongside her on the same task. Major's cheapness was the main subject of their mirth. According to them, it was the norm to use wedding organisers to do most of the tasks they'd been set. Still, they expertly threaded the flower heads and made most of the garlands. Una ignored much of their exchange, but was intrigued by their hushed conversation about the change in Meeru from hipster to "bhenji". Apparently, bhenji meant dowdy. Incredibly, Meeru had not met her fiancé yet. The Rao sisters said it was unusual in the millennium, but Meeru was following all the outdated traditions of the family, which she used to ridicule and infringe. Una agreed, something was off. A contrary image of Meeru walking beneath her during the curfew in pitch darkness flashed across Una's mind.

When the last kitsch orange and yellow garland hit the basket, Una volunteered to deliver it to Major's house. Johnnie Walker, the servant, was meant to take it, but no one had seen him since early morning. Una didn't mind, besides, she wanted to meet Meeru once more before she got married. Closing the gate behind her, Una sighed and stepped onto the path with the basket of flowers, only to halt after two steps. Further along, a large lorry was blocking the path. A constant stream of men carrying chairs, tables and other heavy gear blocked the way into Major's drive. While Una wondered if it was wise to navigate her way through the assault course of swinging furniture, something small and hard hit her back.

"Ouch!" Una swivelled around and faced the rhododendron bushes. They were the very same bushes that Avi confessed to using when he entered the forbidden parts of the jungle. Una chuckled over how put out Avi had been by Grandad's indifference to his breaking the rules. Una blushed when she realised how happy it made her feel to think of Avi. Normally, she checked herself; there was no point in doing anything else.

He was gone, but worse still, it reminded her that she was changing, too. This time, however, she indulged herself. From memory, she mimicked his fake indignation.

"Obviously, I wasn't significant enough to worry about."

"Obviously not!" a young male voice chirped. Una froze.

"Who ... who said that?" Una faltered. "And how did you know what I said?" With some trepidation, she stepped closer to the bushes, her hand nervously hovering over them. She was about to part them and step in to see her stalker, when a shower of leaves and something heavier fell on her, before hitting the ground. "Ouch! Why do you keep doing that?" Una exclaimed. Really ticked off, she put the flower basket down, grasped a handful of the gravel freshly laid in honour of the wedding procession and aimed it at the tree branch overhanging the path.

A tribal skirt fringing two knobbly knees and bare legs appeared before her. "Ow, that really hurt. You could have blinded me!"

"Serves you right!" Una called back, expecting the owner of the legs to show himself. When he didn't, she spoke to his knees instead – in Hindi. It was the first time she'd spoken Hindi outside of the school grounds. She didn't want her grandparents to know, especially since they rudely talked about her in Hindi, in her presence.

"*Neechai aao*! *Mai bhi dekhu tum ho kon*? – Come down so I can see you."

"*NAHI* – NO – you're joking. I'm a lookout and I'm not supposed to come down. I never come down on this side of the jungle." Una smirked, the lad spoke some English.

"Lookout? Ah, so you have been spying on me!"

"Yes ... No! Not in the way you think!" he cried out, flustered.

Una couldn't help smiling. "Whatever! If you ask me, you are a pretty lousy lookout if you throw things at people and give yourself away."

"*Bilkul bhi nahi!* – That's not true ... I was asked to deliver a written message to you this time."

Despite the glaring sun, she felt a chill and all the banter in her dissipated. "A message? For me? *Kya?* – What?"

"It was wrapped around the pebble I threw at you." Una looked down confused. "*Tumharai pare ke neechai* – Under your feet."

Una shuffled back on the gravel and spotted a corner of lined paper peeking through it. Her fingers trembled, in complete contrast to her calm and controlled voice, as she removed it from around the pebble. It read:

Your father is coming today. You must leave with him before it's too late.

They know you are READY!

"Who gave you the message?" Una asked nervously.

"*Jawab chaiya to pathar ko dekho* – Study the pebble and you will get your answer."

Una's heart stalled. She shut her eyes and rubbed the pebble between her thumb and finger. Three letters were clearly etched on its surface.

"Did he give it to you?"

"*Haa* – Yes ... he said I wasn't brave enough to get a message to you, but I am!" The boy's gloating turned to nervousness. "You can't tell the Blessed or the OTHERS about the message ... *Kya? Maine usko kya galat bola hai?* – What? What have I told her that is wrong?" Una gasped, the latter part of the boy's conversation was not directed at her, but to someone else. SOMEONE else was watching her!

She stepped back, her eyes fixed on the legs in front of her.

"*Ok, bhai* – brother – I'll speak in English so no one else understands. When did you say don't talk to her? ... OKAY, you did say the pebble would be enough of a message ... Kyo? – Why? I wanted to talk to her because I wanted to know what you liked in her ... OH NO! Do you think they heard?"

Una's insides clenched – the boy was talking to Avi. He was here. She wasn't sure whether she cared for him or loathed him at that moment in time. It was too confusing. The only surety was that Meeru had lied about him joining the Indian Military Institute. Her heart hurt. She couldn't speak. How could they even be friends after she'd accused him of being a freak, and then running away after they had kissed?

"Is Avi here?"

The boy spoke urgently to her. "No, not quite, Una. I'm sorry but you must go now. Go quickly before the Sherman or the Forced Blessed see you."

Una wanted to protest but knew he was right. She tried to turn back to the house but her body stayed put. Something other than herself was blocking the command from her brain to her limbs. It was too late for her. Her heart rate and breathing dramatically slowed, as if they were machines and were switched down by the flick of an unknown hand.

She tried to scream to get the attention of the workers loading the lorry but her tongue was unnaturally stuck to the roof of her mouth, and her eyes were stretched open. The glare of the sun's rays faded to darkness as the sun eclipsed and blackened the sky. Although she could not see them, Una felt the eyes of the working men looking through her to the jungle beyond. All activity had ceased, except for the boy's, who began to turn in jerky movements until he was facing the inner jungle ... a full one-eighty degree turn. With the last click of his foot, an unnatural gust of air snaked past her ankles and moved upwards into the tree, wrapping itself around the boy's legs. Its fangs lashed out and rippled through the jungle canopy as it moved away from the boy to a point beyond her vision. Moments later, a similar ripple made its way from the deep of the jungle towards him.

"Are you ready to join us?" Although the words came from the boy close by, she recognised the voice to be that of the Sharman's. She couldn't answer at first. Suddenly, her tongue was peeled off the roof of her mouth with the same excruciating pain she'd felt when she had licked an icy metal school railing as a dare.

"Let me go!" Una screamed as her tongue loosened itself.

"Have you come to the jungle to join us?"

"What? NO! I'll never be ready. You can't have me ... I'm not eighteen. In fact, I'll only turn seventeen in two more weeks."

"So you were eavesdropping when we visited you." The Sharman sounded amused. "It seems that, in your case, eighteen is not a milestone you need to reach. I suspect you have been ready for quite some time."

"How do you know?" Una asked. Suddenly, the treetops parted and a red-beaked parakeet flew out of the jungle and settled on one of the rhododendron bushes within arm's reach of her. It parted its beak as if it was going to peck her but, instead, it spoke to her in the Sharman's voice. "Girls your age stop growing. Yet, you are still experiencing growth spurts and high temperatures."

Una's mouth opened wide in horror. "How do you know?"

"That's not the only thing I know. I heard you thought talking within weeks of you entering the valley. That is usually one of the last changes that happens close to your eighteenth birthday. Of course, it's quite possible that Avi unlocked something inherent in you, but I wonder. Have you tried to see through someone else's eyes yet?"

The parakeet fluttered away.

"See through someone else's eyes?" Una balked. What devilish invasive skill set was he talking about? Thought talking was barely acceptable to her.

A mongoose poked its tapered snout out the rhododendron bush. Its teeth were too close to its flip-flopped feet. "If you can hear other Blesseds' thoughts, you can also use their sight and feel their emotions and reactions."

"Blessed? Mongoose ... I mean, Sharman, I'm not Blessed. Even when Avi did it, he wasn't a Blessed," blurted out Una, horrified.

The Sharman changed his commanding tone to a gentler one. "Una, it's natural for you to be scared, but there's no point. Trust me, you can already do these things, and more."

Trust him? Una pulled her lips in, refusing to believe it.

"It's time I show you what I mean."

Terrified, Una watched the leaves on the ground whirl around her legs and then up her arms. They lifted her hands one at a time and clamped them tightly against her mouth. If Una's body had been her own she was sure she would have weed herself and shrieked.

"Now, Una, say something."

First a muffled sound came from her mouth, then she spoke quite clearly, despite her palm and fingers locking her mouth shut tight. "I'm not a Blessed." Her ears heard her voice clear as a bell coming from somewhere above, not from her vocal cords.

"How am I doing this?" she asked fearfully.

"You are, as I suspected, an advanced kind of Blessed. You can speak through non-Blesseds, just as I can. At the moment, you are speaking through the bird perched just above you."

Una's gaze was released so she could look up. She startled, it was the first time she had ever seen a flycatcher, her school house bird, in reality.

"Now, speak if you like, and watch his beak." It was more of a command than a request.

Una's mind screamed soundlessly as she watched the flycatcher open its beak in sync with her repeated screams of, "I'm not Blessed!"

The Sharman ignored her outburst and continued, "Una, you are more than ready, but the final part of your transformation can only happen on our side of the path. So, I ask you again – are you ready to come over to where you belong?"

"NO! I don't belong there. I don't belong in the jungle any more than I do on my grandfather's side of the path. My home is in Manchester," she screamed via the flycatcher.

"You are wrong. You belong here. You were conceived here in this valley. If Rosetta's mother hadn't warned Alice to take her unborn child to England, you would never have lived there. We were furious when she left, but, luckily, it seems like no one can change their destiny." The Sharman's voice transferred back to the boy and took on a threatening tone. "You are here now. The balance of the jungle will be maintained. If you had not drunk the amber tea on your journey to the valley, you would have realised that you are already indebted to me. You are only alive because I saved your life *en route* to your grandparents' home."

Indebted ... to him? Nothing happened to her on the journey.

Before her very eyes, a hazy image of a temple with an orange flag and a dark shadow appeared. Still not able to divert her eyes of her own accord, Una watched as the blurred shadow slowly came into focus and transformed into a black face surrounded by white fur.

Confused, Una asked, "Why are you showing me the face of a langur instead of yours? This image has no relevance to me."

"Look at the bottom left corner."

On the bottom left corner, Una recognised the curved edge of her mother's Timex watch, wrapped around a wrist peeping from a leather jacket cuff.

How did this prove that he'd saved her?

In desperation, she shouted, "This doesn't demonstrate how you supposedly saved me. It's just an image of what I saw from my taxi's window. This is just a hallucination you have planted in my head."

The Sharman's voice turned to ice as he delivered his next words slowly, "Believe what you want, Una. Once you are eighteen, you will have no choice. Remember, it is both yours and Avatar's destiny to be Blessed."

Avatar? Did he mean Avi?

"So, you have Avi, and now you want me. Who is the leader you talked about that day you visited Grandad? Do you have him too?"

Sharman softened his tone. "The leader is not with us. She died protecting Avatar – her son."

Una was confused. The leader was Avi's Mum, which was Rosetta?

"Rosetta was your leader!" Una couldn't hide her shock. A vision of Rosetta in a dirty nylon saree arose in her mind. "If she was your leader, why did you let her live the way she did?" she asked disdainfully.

"Never mind that. All you need to know is that you owe her a lot," he impatiently replied. "When Rosetta learnt of the conspiracy to bring you back from England, she tried to stop it. When she couldn't, she placed Tommy in your grandfather's house to protect you from coming to harm. You owe her, Una."

Although fantastical, Una believed him. Tommy had stuck to her like glue, and it explained why she found it hard to visit once she'd joined the school. "How did she die?"

The Sharman's response was strained. "She was killed. Avi was not involved. She died alone on Dev's roof. I'm surprised he didn't tell you."

A lump formed in her throat. Rosetta was obviously someone he had cared about. Una's mind raced back a couple of days and in a soft voice she said, "I think I've seen her ghost." Her words were strange to her because, this time, they came from her vocal cords. Next, her eyelids blinked and tears drenched her eyes. Astonished, she swept away her tears and paused as she watched the sun break through the darkness.

Una fell to the ground, winded. Avi was right – *they knew.* Una pondered over the rest of the message and wondered if it was true.

Out of his trance, the boy spoke quietly in his unbroken voice again. "Avatar says his message is true. He wants me to tell you to stay away from the jungle and to find a way of getting home to Manchester as soon as possible. Staying in the valley is not an option."

"How dare he listen to my thoughts and tell me what to do?"

"I dare to, Una. Now get away from this place before the Sharman changes his mind and returns. Or worse still, the Wolf may work out what the Sharman has. Today, when you see your father, persuade him to leave with you straight away. Save yourself from turning into a freak like me."

Even in thought, his words were bitter. She desperately wanted to tell him to go to hell and motioned to throw the pebble away, again, but this time she couldn't. She knew what it meant.

Conceding her need, she picked it up from the ground where it had fallen when her hands were forced to her mouth, and slipped it into her dungaree pocket.

Una raised her head to see if the boy was still watching, and was relieved to find he had already left. His unbroken voice sounded from a distance.

"*Mai aah raha hu*! *Abhi pahunch jaunga* – I'm coming, I'm nearly back. I'm *fida* – in love. She looks amazing up close – the legs just go on and on, so does her hair. *Itni gori nahi hai jays Tujhai yard hai* – She's not as fair skinned as you remember though. What colour would I say she was? ... You saw her, too. Not as well? Okay then. I think she's the colour of grass seed, no ... the colour of your favourite amber, yes the stuff you like. *Pagal mut bano ... uske ankhia abhi bhi hari hai* – Don't be an idiot ... her eyes are still green. What else would they be? You didn't expect them to be red from crying for you ... Aw! That hurt ... Next time you can go and see her in the flesh ... no, I forgot you can't and won't. *Bhai* ... the legs went on and on ..." His voice faded, but his route visually punctuated the treetops to a faraway pinpoint as he swung between them.

Una's face was flaming red. Glancing down at her legs, she realised, for the first time, just how much she had grown since she'd arrived in India. The dungaree shorts finished high up her thigh. Without thick tights, they were too risqué for Manchester, let alone the valley.

This is how the boy saw me? This is how Avi might have seen me.

Una's whole body turned lobster red.

Her embarrassment broke through her state of trepidation and she felt lighter. Technically, she was safe for more than a year if she trusted the Sharman, which she did because he could have taken her minutes ago by controlling her movements. Avi had been safe until he turned eighteen, even though he'd roamed the forbidden parts of the jungle. The mention of a wolf niggled at her. But, she decided, Avi could be wrong. Anyhow the wolf might have disappeared, his howls hadn't been heard for a long time, according to Grandad.

Una shook her head. At the moment, her immediate concern was the walk back to her grandparent's home, in her short dungarees ... past the male workers unloading the lorry!

Chapter 29

Una regretted her decision to walk back the minute she was brought to a standstill by revving bikers, who had followed her as she entered Major's driveway. They must have come down from the road above at top speed because, minutes ago, she had walked on the path leading off it, in complete isolation and silence – glad that the lorry workers had already left.

One by one, the bikers helped themselves to a garland as they rode past. Open mouthed, she watched the last one rise up into the air, then fall over the head and neck of a dumpy youth sitting on a shiny, red chrome Harley Davidson. He stayed in front of her as the less fancy motorbikes circled them.

"Call off your dog's, Gag, or else."

Una's head snapped to the veranda where Meeru stood.

Instantly, the gravel dragging and revving stopped. Una focussed her attention back on the teen on the Harley Davidson. So, this was Avi's twin. Beneath the black leather and gangster-style thick gold chains and rings, his flesh was tame and flabby. The army crew cut crowned his big skull like a shrunken wig. When he took his dark glasses off, a ripple of revulsion swept through her body. He was scrutinising her in the most lascivious manner. Una clicked her fingers, forcing his roving eye to meet hers.

"You've got my whole attention babe."

Before Una could say anything, he smacked his rubbery lips

and made a sickening, smooching sound. His ignorant friends hooted and cheered him on.

"Gag *hato vaha sai*! – Move from there. Take your filthy disgusting self, and your sycophantic groupies somewhere else and leave her alone."

He pulled a hurt face and pouted at Una. "*Kya* – What, Meeru? I was only showing our new neighbour what a friendly lot we are." He then brought his bike closer to Una and asked, "What say you gorgeous – want to be my buddy?"

"I've got all the friends I need, thank you," Una replied, keeping her eyes steadfast on him.

"Gag, *dubara nahi boloongi, hato vaha sai* – I won't say it again, move away from Una."

"What, Meeru! I was only teasing!" Something in Meeru's stare must have changed his mind because he rode past Una to the gate, his gang in tow. "*Chalo chor diya* – Fine, I'll leave her. Come on, gang, we've got to go and pick someone from the airport, with Johnnie Walker."

"Stop!" Una raised her voice and pushed her basket forward. She desperately wanted to ask if that someone was her Dad but knew he would play with her feelings if she showed interest. "I would like the garlands back, so could you please handle them carefully and arrange them in the basket as you found them?" Una savoured the bikers startled expressions, so added sweetly, "Thank you."

Gag snorted. "How sweetly she asks, *Chalo* – Fine. I think it's only fair that we return the garlands as she asks." Surprisingly, they did exactly that. However, when it came to his turn, he lifted his garland above his head and put it around Una's neck. Una tried not to squirm as his hands lingered on her shoulders.

"*Hoh!* – Oops! By mistake, I've married you according to our Hindu customs. What are you going to do about it, Wifey?" He flicked the garland looped around her neck.

Unperturbed and smiling, Una first put the basket down and then took off the garland. After meticulously arranging it in the basket she cooed, "Oh honey, your ritual is rather tame. By our British customs, we like to seal a marriage with a big kiss."

Gag stared agape before cat calls from his friends brought him back to earth. Gleefully, he jumped off his ride and stood close to Una. "I'm ready for my kiss, Wifey."

"Oh, why so far?" she baited him.

He gulped and shuffled closer to her. *Oh, was he in trouble!* Fluttering her long eyelashes, she tutted and put one of his arms around her. He almost melted when she raised her hands to his face to ready him for a kiss. Whoops and cheers filled the air. Una smiled until she noticed his free hand quivering. It was protecting his groin – he wasn't so stupid after all.

Staring into his eyes, Una placed the heel of her palm on his nose and threw her whole weight into the move, using his arm as leverage – causing maximum impact to his nasal bone. Gag yelped. He tried to shake her off his arm using his free hand. Big mistake – as soon as he did that, he'd exposed his delicate parts. She kneed him hard.

A shrill scream came from Gag and he fell to the ground, rolling from one side to the other around her feet.

Unperturbed, Una stepped over him, picked up the basket and sauntered over to Meeru.

Gag's gang sat on their bikes in stunned silence.

"Bitch ... wait till I get you! Meeru will be gone tomorrow. Who will protect you then, whore?" Gag spluttered as he lay on the ground with his knees up. Una turned around. With the basket on her hip, she kicked him below his knees, making them collapse, and said, "Me, that's who."

Gag's friends collectively jumped off their bikes. Some leapt to his aid, the others moved to block her from walking away.

"Don't touch her, boys! She will pay later. I'll make sure she does."

Una walked up to Meeru and followed her into the house.

"Gag was harmless until you provoked him and made him look foolish in front of his mates. Una, he doesn't forgive easily."

Una knew she had made herself a target for the future and inwardly cursed herself. Everything Meeru said was true. She had done the reverse of what she had been taught in her self-defence classes. Gag had come off his bike only when she'd summoned him with the promise of a kiss. She felt sick inside. The jungle was enough of a threat without her complicating her situation even more. Una looked over to Meeru, who just shook her head and gestured to a passing servant to relieve Una of the garlands of flowers.

"Never mind Gag for now, come with me to my room, I have been waiting patiently for you."

Sheepishly, Una complied with Meeru's wishes and followed her.

Meeru's room was quite dark as the shutters were down to block out the sun. "Lock the door behind you and come sit on the chair facing my bed."

Una hesitantly followed her instructions. Just when she opened her mouth to speak, Meeru waved a pencil at her from where she sat on a stool and began to draw Una on a miniature canvas. Una burst out laughing.

"Seriously, Meeru, you can't possibly be painting a portrait of me hours before you are due to get married?"

Meeru's face was scrunched as she concentrated on Una's face. "Please don't talk. It's not as if you can go out right now with Gag out there. Consider sitting for me as a wedding present."

"But why would you want a portrait of me?"

Meeru ignored her question. Instead, she picked up a well-used wooden palette with dried acrylic dollops of paint. Una sighed and sat quietly, her mind wandering between the morning warnings and the absurd situation she had created in Major's courtyard. She wanted to confide in Meeru, tell her she knew Avi was not in the army, but then remembered that Meeru was getting married and didn't need the worry and tension. It's not like he hadn't changed already. No, she had to remain silent. If Avi was right, she had to get out of the valley herself. Una cleared her head and followed Meeru's quick brush strokes and rapid eye movement as she switched between Una's face and the canvas. She sat very still when Meeru sized her with her hands, with her brush in her mouth. Just then, Una squirmed and some of the black paint smudged the base of Meeru's hennaed palm. Meeru reacted angrily. "Damn you, Una! You've made me extend a short line with your squeal." Una apologised.

"The henna is not important and won't spoil, but the miniature painting will be ruined if you squeal like that and make me lose my concentration. The painting must be perfect."

Una did not dare move again, not even when Meeru's sisters-in-law and college friends knocked on the door.

"Ignore them. In the next hour, they will have my attention. To please them, I will marry a man I have never seen or met. We can't all be lucky like you and Avi."

Me and Avi?

"There is no Avi and me."

Meeru shrugged her shoulders. "Perhaps, but I saw a change in him when you came. In a big family like this, it would be unusual for all members to be equally loved. Avi was a loner and spent his time studying or reading, generally staying out of everyone's way. But when you came along, he began to smile."

"Meeru, it's all irrelevant. He's not coming back and you lied. He has not joined the army."

Meeru's paintbrush stilled in the air.

"Meeru, I know the truth. I spoke to him today."

Meeru's brush dropped to the floor. "You can't have spoken to him, unless ... oh no, it's too soon!" Meeru panicked and looked her up and down. "When did you grow so fast?"

"Meeru, you're not making sense, but it's a shame you couldn't have told me the truth. Never mind, I've got to go." Una rose from her chair.

"Wait, I have a goodbye present for you."

Before Una could get to the door, Meeru pushed a kitten into her arms.

"I don't like cats, I hate them!" Una said and placed the kitten on the floor.

Meeru looked at her in shock and dismay.

People were banging on the door. Before Meeru could accost her again, Una unbolted the door and walked out.

"Una, wait."

She didn't.

Just as she made it to the gate, one of Meeru's sisters-in-law called out to her and handed her a bag. "*Tumarai liyai* – For you ... *wedding shaadi ka kaprai* – Wedding clothes. *Papa ka thank you hai Meeru ki madat karne kay liya* – Dad has thanked you for helping Meeru."

Una could see the lady was struggling to make herself understood and reluctantly took the clothes from her.

She headed for the only sanctuary from the wedding she could find – her grandfather's roof. Una placed the wedding gift bag on the ground as she once again picked the padlock on the door. It took longer because her attention was distracted by the wedding bag – it was moving. Curious, Una unzipped the bag and took a deep breath in. Cursing loudly, Una placed her hand at the back of the creature's neck and picked it up by the loose skin close to its ear to lessen the chances of it struggling, then held it in front of her. Her friend Charlie would have thought it cute with its mottled green saucers for eyes, little rounded ears and furry white face with black markings. But Una wasn't fooled. Cute kittens grew to become vicious cats.

One of the Rao sisters was calling for her. Una put the kitten down and whispered, "If I were you, I would disappear before I come back later. Do that thing of climbing down and roaming the Earth as if you own it ... just don't come back."

Closing the roof door behind her, Una left, missing the piece of paper on the top of the stairs where the bag lay on its side.

Chapter 30

Una crouched between the two trunks covered by Meeru's trousseau. People were calling her name to do different tasks, but when they peered in the room, Meeru and her friends didn't realise she was there. Luckily, Meeru had been in the bathroom when she and the Rao girls had arrived with the wedding lehenga. Agnes and Grace had eagerly left her holding the lehenga so they could join Meeru in the bathroom to have their legs waxed by the visiting beautician.

Una had laid the heavy lehenga on the bed and looked for a hiding place, where she'd fallen asleep. Hours later, when she awoke, the shutters were open and the sun had lost its shape and sharpness.

Una stared at Meeru's reflection in the long mirror, while Agnes and Grace argued with the makeup artist over which shades of eye shadow, lipstick and nail varnish Meeru should wear. Meeru's expression was vacant as she squeezed a Benson & Hedges cigarette packet in her hand. The packet was almost empty.

"Before you squash the life out of the remaining cigarettes, do you mind if we rescue a couple?" Grace asked.

Meeru handed them over to Grace, who lit three cigarettes. Finally free, the beautician matched makeup to the wedding outfit and to Meeru's skin.

"Where did you get the cigarettes from?" Agnes asked after

letting out the smoke in her mouth.

Grace examined the box, "It looks British ... Was it Una? No wait, there's a message: Bedi substitute, all is forgiven."

Meeru grabbed the box back and silently mouthed something, but Agnes's head was in the way and Una couldn't read her lips. Clutching the box, Meeru stood up and walked to the window. Tears rolled down her cheeks.

"Hold that look right there – wedding blues, I think, Meeru." Sid Rao entered the room with his camera around his neck and started to click furiously. Sid framed supposed candid shots of Meeru in the foreground, with her packed trunks and suitcases in the background. He took pictures of the gold and diamond sets, which had been carelessly left on the bed, where the girls were sitting and chatting. Each shot took several minutes to get right. He even took pictures of Meeru's abandoned easel and the paintbrushes that sat in a jar of blackened water, along with the canvases he'd scattered onto the floor. Una looked for her miniature portrait, but it wasn't there.

"Take a picture of us three friends, Papa," Agnes whined. Sid Rao obeyed and arranged them in a pose, then clicked. "Damn, damn, damn. I've filled my memory card, girls, and we haven't even got to the ceremony yet." Sid looked pleadingly at his daughters. "Which one of you will go and fetch my other memory card?"

Both his daughters protested, and tried to volunteer the other to undertake the seemingly tedious task.

"Fine, girls, you can stop squabbling. I've found another volunteer." The girls looked at each other, baffled.

"Come out, Una. I know you're there. Unfortunately for you, the trunks are not wide enough to hide your feet." Una reluctantly rose from her hideout as the rest of the room gawked at her in surprise.

"Fed up with all the wedding stuff already? Well, in that case I don't think you will mind running an errand for me." Una shrugged her shoulders and nodded in resignation.

"I need my memory cards. They're on the dressing table in the spare bedroom at my house. The spare bedroom is the first room you come upon when you enter the house. The front door will be open, even if Sheila, my wife, isn't there."

"Uncle Sid, I don't think it's a good idea to send Una to your house. She might get lost!" Meeru exclaimed.

Sid chuckled. "What nonsense! She just needs to stay on the path until she gets to the house. She can't miss it. Una, just look for an unfinished house."

"I'll be fine, Meeru. It will get me out of the house, and out of other more mundane chores."

Una was already at the door.

"Wait, I wouldn't go out looking like that." Meeru rose from her stool. From her cupboard, she brought out a white kaftan with brown suede ties threaded through silver ringlets at the waist. "This will cover most of you, and keep you cool at the same time. Here, tie up your hair with this hair scarf to finish the look."

As soon as Una was ready, Meeru pushed her in front of the mirror. "Look at how the turquoises and greens in the scarf make your face come alive. You look like a ..."

"Cat?" Agnes interrupted.

Meeru smiled, the first time today. It lit up her face completely and reminded Una of when she'd met Meeru for the first time. "Maybe, but I was going to say retro chic from the sixties."

Chapter 31

It felt good to escape the wedding mayhem, even if it meant walking on the path and past the two rhododendron shrubs. Against her better judgement, Una stood just beyond the bushes and the overhanging trees for a while. Somewhere, within herself, she believed that if she never did it, she would forever be frightened of venturing beyond her grandfather's gate, or anywhere else, on her own. She just had to stay put to the count of thirty, and then she would make her way down the path to Sid Rao's property. As she counted in her head, the gentle evening mountain breeze flapped against the seams of her kaftan and rustled the leaves on the mango trees. Una's nostrils flared and her counting faltered as the wind carried a strong, sweet fragrance and fruity aroma from the plump, pinkish-yellow mangoes. Swayed by the calm, Una took in the dappled light as it softened the edges of the jungle, making it seem so inviting and serene. In a trance, she rose on her tiptoes and stretched out a hand to pluck one of the mangoes. A noisy grunt startled her before her fingers even wrapped around one. It happened so quickly. She lost her balance, and a flip-flop, in the process of falling. Expecting an animal to come at her, she was shocked to find a ripe mango rolling towards her instead. A nervous giggle half escaped her mouth and then stopped as she carefully inspected the mango in her hand. 'NO' was etched into its flesh. Una dropped it and hastily walked in the direction of the 'Modern Ruin'. Something shifted in the jungle foliage behind her. Despite her growing trepidation, Una looked over her shoulder and halted. Open mouthed, she saw a large, black mass with white, thick claws quickly retrieve the mango and scuttle back into the foliage.

Una hurried on.

The path ahead narrowed and the verdant wilderness grew thick around her. Una's nerves were working overtime, heightening her alertness and apprehension. She ran the last few metres to the infamous 'Modern Ruin' that Major and Grandad had laughed about.

The building unsettled her. She had expected it to intrigue her. It was right up the street with the sort of structures she'd explored with Luke and Charlie, before the police had cautioned them and she was sent to the valley. Una glanced away from the building and then looked back at it, in the hope her second impression would be better. The place disturbed her even more. She couldn't explain the emotion. It wasn't fear, it was something else – something indefinable.

Despite her misgivings, Una pressed forward to the veranda. Its beautiful pillars were topped with smooth rectangular slabs, but the roof was missing entirely.

Una knocked on the front door several times before shouting out. "Mrs Rao ... Sheila, it's Una. Are you here?" No one answered. Sid Rao had told her to enter if no one opened, so she opened the screen door and entered the building. As soon as she walked in, the most extraordinary thing happened. She felt light and free, the earlier weight of dread just vanished. It was like she had taken a heavy coat off. Shocked, Una walked out of the door again; the cloak of dread engulfed her again. The house was enchanted. Was it protecting itself from the jungle – making the inhabitants less enticing?

Una ran back into the house. She decided to get the memory card and leave promptly. Yet, when she entered the spare bedroom downstairs, she felt calm and at ease again. It had to be her imagination playing tricks on her. It was the Sharman's fault.

Una found the memory card, exactly where Sid said it would be – on the dressing table. She had no reason to linger. Yet, on her way out, Una realised the urge to explore without permission hadn't quite left her, despite it bringing her to Khamosh Valley.

The house watched in silence as she sneaked around like Goldilocks. She pushed open a door in the hall and walked through a master bedroom with walls covered with photos. She would have liked to have studied them, but was startled by a loud noise. It had come from another part of the house.

Sheila? Una rushed into the adjoining room and found a very basic kitchen, with no cupboard units or counters. It just had planks of wood bolstered on empty drums. Una couldn't believe an educated family would think it was okay to put a gas stove on an upturned, flammable wooden crate! At the far end of the kitchen, a large opening, where double doors should have been, drew her in. The space beyond did not disappoint. It was styled in the proportions of a stately home drawing room, had it been complete. Sadly, the walls were exposed to the elements and 'painted' green by the moss and vines clutching its mortar. The ceiling, once again, was the ever-changing sky. Sighing, she retraced her steps back to the kitchen and left through a back door. Outside the kitchen, an odd staircase hugged the shell of the building. The Rao sisters had described their bedroom as having an umbrella stand and an odd staircase while they'd been threading flowers earlier. Una had let on that she missed her own bedroom in Manchester the most. The umbrella stand outside their door stood on a small, floating wooden platform. Una chuckled and thought, *the Rao girls really did use an umbrella to go to bed when it rained.*

Una couldn't resist the steps and made her way to the bedroom. It was a ridiculous climb. Each weathered brick was randomly placed, like the boulder holds she used on the climbing frame at her local leisure centre in Manchester. Una shook her head. *Running out of money while building a house had a harsh but comical side to it.*

Reaching the bedroom door, she thought she heard a movement behind it. She tried the knob but the door was locked, unlike the rest of the house. "Is anyone there?" Una called as she leaned against the locked door. She thought she heard another muffled sound, but she wasn't sure. Out of habit, her hand went to her hair – but it was hairpin free. Una held her hair and wondered what she'd been thinking.

Would she really have broken into a friend's house?

Disgusted with herself, Una made her way up to the roof top instead.

The jungle enveloped the house completely; even the narrow path leading to the house was hidden from view. Strangely, at this height, Una felt at peace with the same jungle that had made her feel uneasy just minutes earlier. Closer to the sky, in the middle of the wilderness, Una felt she could breathe for the time since returning from school. She decided she would delay taking the memory card to Sid a little longer.

Carefree, Una made herself comfortable on the narrow, bricked wall of the roof. The view of the formidable purple mountains was spectacular. Cumulus clouds floated below their peaks casting shadows on the hard rock as they gently sailed past. Enraptured, Una lay her head on the narrow wall and, with her index finger, outlined the cloud shapes.

"That one is a car and that one a dog – no a horse. This one is a beautiful wolf." Una twitched. Mentioning the wolf was a mistake. The clouds merged together in the sky to form a large pack of cloud wolves. Terrified, she dropped off the ledge and onto the roof as the wolves raced towards her. She scrambled to her feet and rushed down the hazardous steps as best as she could. The cloud mass darkened and overshadowed her next step. She lost her footing and threw her hands against the wall, grabbing a clump of grass to stop herself from falling further. The large shadow loomed over her. Shutting her eyes tightly, she cowered against the wall. Someone was calling out to her and running up the stairs, hopefully to rescue her. Relieved, she opened her eyes and screamed as the fangs dug into her neck.

✳✳✳

"Wake up, Una, it's just me!" Una prised her eyes open to find Agnes stroking her hair as her head rested on her lap. "Hey, I came looking for you because you were taking so long. I called your name, but you didn't answer so I came running up here and somehow gave you a fright."

Una waited for Agnes to finish her natter before asking, "Where did the wolf go?"

"Wolf?"

"The one that came from the clouds?" said Una.

Agnes smiled as she helped Una up. "Wolves ... you are probably suffering from sun exhaustion. Come, I'll escort you home. Why don't you go down the steps first?"

Una nodded and made her descent.

I believe you are ready, Una?

"Ready for what?" Una uttered.

"I didn't say anything," Agnes replied.

Chapter 32

Dr Verma excused Una from attending the wedding due to her confused state and throbbing migraine. He offered her his usual amber injection, but Una was mindful of the words of the Sharman. If she wanted to escape the jungle she needed to be alert and remember everything. She also wanted to know if those doping her were doing it for her benefit, or for their own sinister reasons. Based on Avi's information, she was sure Gag left Major's house to pick her Dad up with Johnnie Walker. Yet, where was he? It was almost midnight and there was still no sign of him. Una sighed and realised how much she wanted Gag's pick up to be her Dad. She'd hoped leaving with him for Manchester would mean she stayed human. Unfortunately, Avi had been misinformed. Her Dad wasn't coming. Despite her wish to leave, Una puzzled over her urge to enter the jungle, just before the mango rolled to her. Rubbing the back of her head, she whispered to herself, "It's not the jungle I fear. It's more that I fear myself." Whether she liked it or not, the blissful abandonment she'd felt on Sid's roof, with the jungle tree tops below and the mountains above, gave her a sense of peace she hadn't felt, even while her mother was alive. The admission filled Una with guilt. *How could she even think that when her Mum had filled her days with so much love?* Una scrunched her eyes. This self-destructive and selfish side of her could only worsen if left unchecked by human sensibilities, which her mother had tried so hard to instil in her whenever she showed a lack of empathy when others made mistakes, or when she easily disregarded the feelings of others. Girls her age would have rushed over to the jungle to rescue Avi, but it hadn't occurred to her, despite how he made her feel. But, did she like the way he made her feel? Mum called her pragmatic, but she wondered if she was just plain cold. Una cranked her neck. She was tired of living in a smog with wisps of lucidity exposing disjointed memories. She was sure that if she didn't take a stand, she would be torn apart inside out and her soul would perish to nothing, irrespective of being a human, or some other abomination.

Her thoughts and the painful wedding band music – on par with badly played bagpipes – broke the dam holding her tsunami migraine. Darkness was usually the best remedy for a migraine, but it was stifling indoors. Even though it would take her closer to the source of the music, Una left her bed and made her way to the roof.

Major's contacts in the army were working hard. They'd supplied armed guards and HMI lighting equipment to keep the jungle animals away. Major must have known someone in the electricity board, too, because the electricity curfew in the evenings was lifted and the house was lit up like it was Christmas or Diwali.

✳✳✳

Unknown to Una, a male wolf stood in the shadows of the hill just behind Major's house. He noted Una's presence, but focused his attention on Meeru, who was standing on her roof, blowing a silent whistle. He couldn't see her tears, but he felt her distress. Yet, he chose not to help her escape. He knew she wondered why. She believed she had redeemed herself when she'd delivered the kitten to Una. He had convinced her by promising to rescue her from the wedding so they could live together.

✸✸✸

Suddenly, the lights covering Major's stairwell blew out, although the light bulbs draped along the perimeter of the property and all the outbuilding were still twinkling. The music from the bridegroom's brass band briefly halted in surprise. The bridegroom, seated on his horse, along with his dancing guests, lifted their heads in unison to the roof. One of the groundsmen aimed the HMI light beam upwards, until it found the bride's dead body, wrapped in lights, hanging from a hook on the stairwell roof.

On her way down, Una found Meeru's discarded note close to the bag the kitten had arrived in. It read:

Avi's not going to forgive me for what I have done, and will loathe you for what you will become. But what I did, I did for his own sake.

Chapter 33

One month later

The evening light ebbed behind Una's profile. In its yellow metallic hues, Avi could no longer distinguish Una's face. Despite his disapproval, he couldn't help but admire her deliberate stance. She was standing on the water tank, legs apart and a hand on one hip, whilst drinking from a mug. She was taunting him, and anyone else who was watching. She was letting them know she knew she was next. Rather than hide and cower, she was baiting them. He knew the Forced Blessed, lying low in the undergrowth, would admire her bravado – Wolf, more than anyone else. Avi just wished she would leave Khamosh Valley and be safe. As if hearing his sentiments, she replied.

"Avi, I might not be able to see you, but I know you're there. Why won't you face me? Is it because you were wrong about my Dad and you tried to scare me with the Big Bad Wolf routine?"

Avi sighed. If only she knew how he'd shadowed Wolf just to protect her. But, what was the point? He'd only done so for his own selfish reasons. Until her arrival, he had hated himself for being so unlovable, a spare in a large family, despite being the first grandchild. However, perhaps for the first time, he realised there was a part of himself that he liked. It was the part of him that was kinder and tender towards Una. Before she came, he felt nothing, but now he felt too much. Although she now knew she was also changing and was no longer scared of him, he wished he had told her how he felt when they'd spend time together in the jungle. He hadn't trusted his feelings then, mostly because they barely knew each other. Now, it was too late. He just wanted to save her from his destiny. After Meeru's death, Wolf began to camp in the hills behind the two main houses during the curfew period. Almost daily, he tried to access Una's mind, like he'd done when she was at Sid's house. Luckily for Una, Avi began reading her thoughts after he heard her cry out while running down the stairs on the outside of the building. Wolf's words, 'you are ready', alarmed him and, with some reluctance, he informed the Sharman and asked him for help in protecting her. So far, his Nana had succeeded in blocking Wolf from her head by manipulating the enchantments around the property, but he warned they would not work as effectively during the coming monsoon season.

"Avi, I know you are there with some of your buddies, so 'man up' and talk to me. 'Man up' ... Can I still use that phrase with you?"

The B-word sprung to mind, but he restrained himself. God! Una drove him mad, and she knew it. She was trying to rile him again, just like she'd been doing the whole month. Just to prove she knew he was there, she held up her mug and mouthed, "Cheers, Avi!"

Avi winced. She couldn't hear him because of the bubble wall he'd put up. However, he knew she could still sense him, just as he could her before he was Blessed. This precious human connection kept him in the peripheral of the jungle, unsafe, much to the dismay of his nana the Sharman. He couldn't help it. Avi shrugged and perused the area again.

None of the OTHERS, a.k.a. humans, ever noticed Una's presence on the roof during the curfew period. His relatives were locked indoors with curtains drawn to protect themselves, but he knew that, even if they saw her standing on the roof, they would have ignored her, just as her grandad had ignored him in the past. Una's grandparents did care that she stayed safe on the property, but it wasn't out of love. It was for purely monetary gains. Avi was sure they had coaxed their son into not attending Meeru's wedding, or persuaded him not to spend part of the summer break with his daughter, just in case she chose to go back with him. Una's OTHERS were creatures of habit. Every evening, before the forced 'blackout', they sat in their drawing room watching some deadbeat series on television, totally oblivious to everything. As far as they were concerned, the roof was inaccessible to the family since they had heavily bolted the roof door. Seven months ago, Dev found Rosetta's maggot infested snow leopard body on his roof. Petrified, he notified the Sharman to take her carcass. He'd then used the Jungle Rules document to force him to apply enchantments along the roof walls and redo the ones along the perimeter walls. Initially, Dev thought a heavy-duty padlock was sufficient to secure the house. However, the day after Meeru's death, they found the padlock open and the door left ajar. Una's grandmother was convinced the snow leopard, or Meeru's ghost, had something to do with it and insisted the door was bricked that same day. From all accounts, the stairwell was now a storage space crammed with pickle jars and other harvested produce.

Avi turned to his guardian, his Nana, who was crouched in a nearby tree, keeping an eye on the pack of Forced Blesseds, while guarding Una from any possible harm they could wreak. Even in his langur-guise, his tortured lines and suffering eyes were evident. He was broken inside. Avi hated that Nana and the Forced Blessed were akin to rival scavengers, hoping for first dibs when their victim finally gave in. He was the only one who was truly protecting her, but he was insignificant on his own. Nana promised the Blessed would wait for her unless the Forced Blessed made a move, which was within their realm. They'd shown their ruthless arrogance when they killed the snow leopard. They did not care about cursing all the Blessed and Forced Blessed as they had succeeded in defiling Meeru's body by squeezing Rosetta's soul into her. The Forced Blesseds depravity had put the Blesseds on high alert.

"Nana, did you guard me like this, too?"

Without taking his gaze off Una, the Sharman replied, "No,

your mother did that for you. We hadn't experienced the merce-nary attitudes of the Forced Blesseds towards Blesseds until they killed your mother, the leader, and when they tried to kill you, the heir, for their own evil purposes."

Avi watched his nana's furry shoulders tremble before he checked himself. Even in thought talk, his voice sound grainy. "They broke all laws and dishonoured her in the way she died. It is the rule of the jungle that all occupants, Blessed or animal are given clean deaths." The Sharman's tone altered mid conversation to controlled rage. "We will avenge her dishonourable death."

"How?"

"That has been yet to be decided."

Guilt flooded Avi's being. Himself, and many of the Blessed elders, blamed him as much for her death as they did Wolf. If it weren't for him, their leader would have lived in dignity with her people, and perhaps safeguarded them as she would have done more against property development. To protect her son, she had allowed Wolf to kill her, and left them without a leader. Disregarding the River Rule meant the next generation of pure snow leopards did not exist. Avi breathed in deeply and asked what everyone else in the Blessed camp wanted to know.

"I still don't understand why you didn't save Rosetta ..." Nana didn't like it when Avi used his mother's name. "Sorry, I meant Ma ... instead of me? Her life was more valuable than mine and you would still have a leader."

The Sharman plucked a mango from a branch that was obscuring Avi's face.

"If Rosetta had not sent you to the jungle, I could have saved you both. But, when Rosetta sent you off on your own, I had no choice. My daughter would not have forgiven me if she had outlived you. In hindsight, it has proven to be the right choice. You know the ways of the modern Forced Blesseds, and how they think. It also helps that you were all at the same school. It could also be true that I believed Rosetta would outwit the Forced Blesseds and make her way to the temple later. In fact, I could still have saved her if it wasn't for ..."

His guardian fell silent and chose that moment to scoff the mango he'd plucked earlier. Avi knew not to rush him when he paused. After devouring the fruit, with juice dripping down his hairy chin, he continued once more.

"I might still have saved Rosetta if Dev and his wife had let me know several nights earlier that they'd heard relentless mewing coming from their roof. Wretchedly, they only summoned me when they were sure she was dead. I was so shocked; I thought she'd died on the same evening you arrived."

"Why did you think that?" Avi interrupted.

"Wolf told me he had killed her, and I believed him."

The rest Avi knew. Rosetta and Tommy's death, on the same night, had broken the weak truce between the Blessed and the Forced Blessed. Unfortunately, Wolf was poaching the Blessed off-spring before they turned to Blesseds. The Blessed youth believed Rosetta was a weak leader, and Wolf a worthy one to avenge the OTHERS, who had held their leader captive for so long. Avi was accused of lying about the Wolf wanting to trap Rosetta's soul in Meeru. Wolf was therefore hailed a leader by them, simply because he had achieved the impossible task of drawing Dev's granddaughter all the way from England. They thought it was sheer bad luck that the taxi driver they'd chosen to pick up Una and her father from the airport, was an elusive serial killer.

Avi looked over to where Una stood, sipping her tea. Of course, the Wolf's admirers missed the point that, if the Sherman hadn't intervened and stopped the taxi, Una and her father would have been dead by the time the Forced Blesseds had arrived in their police guises. The youth could see no flaws in Wolf, but Avi saw a glaring one: he planned elaborately and manipulated people effectively, but his execution was not perfect.

✳✳✳

Una was bored with the posing, so she sat cross-legged on the water tank and removed the whistle that was digging into her skin from her denim shorts back pocket. It had unexpectedly fallen into her lap during Meeru's funeral. Her funeral had taken place in the early hours of the morning. The timing of the funeral was rather crass, but Major insisted that it went ahead at that time as all the relatives, and the priest, were already there. The summer weather was a deciding factor, too, as was the Hindu ritual of cremating the deceased as soon as possible. Yes, he was pragmatic, but did he realise she was cremated at the exact time she would have been taking seven rounds of the sacred fire to seal her marriage vows? Was it not eerie that the priest who had been preparing for her wedding rites, delivered her soul's passage to the heavens instead? Normally, a police enquiry would follow a suicidal death, but Major used his contacts again. The Deputy Inspector of Police was at the wedding, and swiftly had a coroner and other bureaucratic officials woken up to complete the necessary paper work. Worst of all, Una had to wear Meeru's white kaftan once again because only 'white' could be worn at the funeral. Strangely, though, Meeru's closest friends were not there. The whole of Sid Rao's family was suspiciously absent, despite doing most of the preparations for the wedding. Luckily, Meeru had left a suicide note saying she loved another. During the funeral, Meeru's body was covered by a white sheet and placed in the courtyard, where the men and women sat segregated. The wailing from the women was unbearable. Una wondered, *were they crying for Meeru, or for their own fragile pathetic lives?* Una had been thankful that her Mum was Irish and, instead of the wailing, they had a wake to celebrate her life after the funeral. Cross-legged on the floor, Una's stony gaze had remained fixed on a point just above Meeru's white-shrouded body, until a breeze fluttered the hem of the sheet and exposed her legs. Una's breath hitched in her throat – Meeru was still wearing her wedding outfit. Major covered her up and, with his sons, carried his daughter on a stretcher over their shoulders, ready to leave for the cremation grounds. Una recoiled as Gag carried the marriage ceremony sandalwood for the pyre. Meeru's sisters-in-law increased the intensity of their wailing pitch as her body passed them. Una lowered her eyes instead. Her demure composure faltered when Meeru's lifeless arm slipped out from under her shroud, and dropped a metal object on her lap.

Sitting on the water tank, Una raised the object to her lips and then dramatically dropped it when something heavy landed on her shoulder. *Prrr*

"You've fed yourself, I noticed, Cat," Una said dragging the kitten off her shoulder, only for him to reposition himself on her lap. Una groaned! Why couldn't the thing work out that she found it abhorrent? She preferred dogs, and even if she didn't, after Tommy's brutal death, she didn't want any pets. Not that Tommy had ever been like a pet. Despite its cute efforts, Una refused to take ownership of the kitten and come up with a better name than Cat.

"Just as well you fed your face. It's not like I will be able to feed you once I'm back at school ..." Without thinking, Una examined the muscle under its furry coat. His limbs were far more muscular and much larger than any domestic kitten she had ever seen before.

"Talk about surviving – you're definitely thriving. Look at these muscles!" Cat looked over his shoulder, then rolled onto his back with his legs in the air.

"What are you eating?" Una grimaced when images of rat's tails and dead birds filled her mind. Cat curled his tail around Una's nose in reply.

"Cute!" Una's sarcasm changed to bewilderment as she held its tail. "Cats don't normally have tails longer than their bodies, do they?" Cat didn't care for the examination and playfully pawed her.

"Daft thing." Una raised her hands to tickle him and then stopped, her hand in mid-air.

"You nearly got me." She couldn't afford to weaken for Cat's own sake. He had to find another companion, perhaps someone in Major's family. Someone like ... Avi. Frustrated, Una pushed Cat off her lap and jumped off the tank herself.

"Meowww!"

"Look, Cat, you don't need comfort from me. We are free spirits, you and I. We come and go as we please and we don't need others to protect us. We BELONG to no one."

"Did you hear that, Avi?"

Not a word.

"Just as I thought – Please leave ME ALONE!"

Una watched a bough of a tree bounce upwards, as if a weight had been taken off.

Despite the still evening, an unexpected breeze whipped her face. Una smiled. The presence always reacted when she was rude to Avi. The same presence scared her grandparents out of their wits, resulting in the doorway being bricked, uncannily giving Una a real place of solace. Una knew the presence would prefer her not to acknowledge its existence, but she couldn't help herself. Besides, who'd ever heard of a spirit who wanted to be left alone?

"I like what you have done with the place. I so love the way my body temperature drops instantly, despite the summer heat. It's like walking into an air-conditioned room!"

Another unexpected breeze picked up. This time her hair was tousled and blown in every which way. Una didn't mind and laughed. "Touché!" Una's mood changed to a playful one. Giddy, she jumped off the tank, ran a short distance and leapt up into the air before landing in a squat position against the short wall. Firmly placing her hands on the wall, she lifted herself over. She had learnt this by watching Cat. She then swung over the pipe that jutted out from the tank, just as she used to do in Manchester, but over metal hand rails there. Cat thought it was fun and joined in. Just like on the other days, for almost a month, the two were in sync, executing the same moves. A thought came to Una – *I'm going to wall run*. 'The Cat' executed a perfect wall run, while Una stood, relaxed. She laughed aloud. "I knew, just knew! When you're not involved, the Cat copies my moves after I've done them. When I plan them carefully in my head, Cat is perfectly synchronised. At other times, Cat carries out moves in stages, like he's teaching me."

Una didn't expect a reply, so carried on talking.

"Thanks for the lessons. It helps me relieve my boredom and enables me to see my constricted space in a different light." She paused and noticed Meeru's whistle on the ground. "Oh, this might intrigue you. Besides you and Avi, I've also learnt of another presence – listen."

Una retrieved the whistle and blew it. A wolf howl disrupted the evening as soon as she removed it from her lips.

It's a mystery to me why Meeru wanted to call a wolf? I suppose, roof spirit, you don't have the answer, or do you?

A gust of wind forcibly threw the whistle out of her hand and flung it to the other side of the roof.

"Jealous, are we? Well, you can have it till I come back tomorrow."

Smiling, Una placed her hands wide apart on the roof wall and swung her legs between them. Then, she flung out her arms and leapt on to the boundary wall. From there, she jumped onto the ledge of her bedroom window and swung into the open skylight, landing on her bed. She read while the electricity was available and then waited for a knock. When it came, she shouted, "Good night, Grandad," and fell asleep.

❊❊❊

The Sherman leapt through the trees back to the temple, pondering over Una's feline companion. While his eyes could deceive him, the scent didn't. Yet, if it was true, Gopan would have reported back to him, especially as he was feeding it. Although his daughter had not spoken to him, he knew her spirit form was on the roof. Surely she would have broken her silence if his doubts were true, but then, would she? It was already too late for Avi.

Chapter 34

It was another day, void of activity for Una, until she felt the first drop of the monsoon rains on the back of her hand as she squatted on the carport roof. It was a big drop of rain, thrice the size of the ones that fell in Manchester. "It's true ..." she spoke aloud. "... The smallest things can leave you in awe."

Water slid off her eyelashes as she raised her face upwards. A ponderous cloud, directly over her, opened its mouth wide and soaked her through. The rhythmic clatter of the downpour on the gravel pulsated through her, and the mixed aroma of soil and crushed eucalyptus leaves surged up her nostrils. She clambered down the wall of the veranda and was surprised to find water pooling underfoot, despite the thick inches of gravel. Slowly, she walked up the veranda steps and sat on the top one so she was under cover. With nothing else to do, she focused on her first monsoon deluge.

Flick!

Her vision seemed odd. Suddenly, the landscape turned into a single raindrop. Her eyes magnified and locked on to a minute detail. She tried to pull them away and close her eyelids, but her brain had made up its mind. It focused on a single raindrop as it fell on the marble steps below, forming an air bubble. Hypnotised, she studied the expanding trapped air as it made the drop increase in size until it popped and burst into ripples of water again. Her eyes moved to another raindrop. She began to study its cycle and, when that ended, she went through the cycles of countless other raindrops. It wasn't just her microscopic vision that scared her. Her brain had picked up on the presence of rose petals and dead plants in the raindrops – not just eucalyptus oil and soil. Her human instincts rejected her unwelcome acute sense of smell and sight. She was scaring herself. Had Avi gone through these changes, too? The old questions roamed in her head. Was there more to fear than the jungle? Was she to fear herself? Perhaps the amber teas and injections had been a blessing in the past. She wished she could have some now.

"Everyone, get in the house and close the windows. The weather is making headline news across all stations on the television. Higher in the hills, they had a day's worth of rain in less than an hour. The rain is bringing down the sides of the mountains, as well as swelling the streams into fast moving and widening rivers."

Grandad then shouted at his wife and Johnnie Walker as he rushed to switch off the hoses that fed his orchard in the back. "Has anyone seen the girl?"

"I'm here," Una poked her head around of the side of the building so he could see her.

A sheet of lightening hit close to the house and lit the sky. It threw Grandad's sharp facial angles into focus as he strode in the direction of the mango and lychee orchard. Noticing her, he shouted, "Be useful, bolt the gates. We can't have the jungle tribe or animals swimming over here when their river burst its banks."

How did a bone dry bed turn into a roaring river in just … Una realised she must have spent more than half an hour watching the rain fall. Hurrying to the gate, Una noticed her feet were no longer visible. Water was noisily swishing against the metal. Unable to help herself, rather than bolting the gate, she opened it wide and stepped out. She had to witness the burst river banks for herself. Immediately, fast moving water coursed around her feet and made its way down the valley towards the 'Modern Ruin', submerging the newly gravelled dirt track path as it progressed and blurred the lines of the jungle.

Another sheet of lightening – this time just metres behind her! Una jumped forward, trying to save herself.

For no reason at all, Avi flashed in her mind, which then split into two. Although her feet were firmly placed outside her grandfather's house, she felt like she was chasing a moving object through the jungle on all fours. She tried to refocus to where she stood and physically widened her stance over the shifting gravel. Her toes curled, desperately trying to keep the throng of her rubber flip-flops from moving forward and being swept away. Terrified, Una looked down. Instead of her legs, she saw dark, matted furry ones. She shrieked. The shock propelled her forward through the fur, and flung her into a body of long hair. Her new body was more agile, and had a lower centre of gravity. She was still bounding forward, going a few more metres before her new body panted and came to a halt.

She opened her eyes. Her vision was wider and sharper and she didn't have to shift her gaze. Noticeably, reds and greens were missing altogether. Everything she could see was in shades of pale yellow, blues and grey hues. The shadows ahead were in greater depth, too.

A silky, black butterfly with blue borders and a delicate laced pattern fluttered between the flaps of umbrellas, somehow enabling her to react to the world more quickly than a human. She was freaking out. The detail was overwhelming.

Wait! The oddly placed umbrella stand was familiar. It was the one she'd seen in the 'Modern Ruins'. She was at a door, then inside the room it led to.

A quick surge of energy and she jolted backwards and forwards inside the body she was in. She looked ahead. Agnes and Grace stared back at her. She wasn't looking at them. She was transfixed on the mirror behind them. Instead of her own reflection, she saw Tawny's face. His eyes were flittering about, looking for something. He pushed past the girls to the dresser and tightly grabbed a chain, which he quickly put on as he looked up at his ... his completely naked reflection ... he wore just the chain and a ring. Somewhere in the distance, her human body shuddered and yanked her back to it.

❋❋❋

"This girl is becoming a nuisance!" complained Grandad. "She is never where she should be. Always somewhere she shouldn't be." His voice lowered, "I think the lightening must have fallen quite close. Her eyes are wide open in shock."

Una stirred, and then her feet gave away.

"My days are numbered," Una muttered.

Her Grandad and Johnnie Walker carried her indoors; her remark was lost in the rain.

Chapter 35

For a whole week, Una and her grandparents were cooped together in her room, playing card games with the backdrop of rain relentlessly falling against the windows, gushing down the drains leading off the roof. It was like living in a waterfall.

On the eighth day, Una felt she couldn't take another game and gave her hand of cards to Johnnie Walker to play in her stead. With nothing else to do, she sat on one of the low ledges of the floor-to-ceiling windows and stared out. Una was impressed by the construction of Major's and Grandad's houses; they were built a couple of feet off the ground. Sid Rao's unfinished house was another matter. His half-built 'Modern Ruins' was only a step above ground level.

"Grandad, have you heard from Uncle Sid?"

"No, he and his girls have not come back from Meerut. His mother lives there on her own and she is not very well. Why do you ask?"

Una froze. How could that be? She had seen the girls in their room.

"Are you sure, I thought the girls were back."

"No."

"Do the girls have a brother or a cousin who stays with them?"

Johnnie Walker looked over at her.

Engrossed in his cards, her Grandfather irritably replied. "No ... Sid doesn't have any male relatives – he was an only child and he had two girls. Why all the questions?"

"Their house isn't as high as yours, so the ground floor rooms must be underwater."

Grandad placed a card on the pile in the middle. "Don't worry about Sid's house. It is much further away from the river, and is on a slope. If there were any problems, Gag would have said. He is house-sitting for them, which is a joke. Locking the doors in that house is pointless when half the roof's missing. Major was quite surprised when Gag suggested he would stay ..." But it hadn't been Gag in the mirror, it was Tawny.

"*Burf Bili!*" Grandma interrupted.

"*Mar Chuki Hai* – She has died!" Grandad grunted under his breath, throwing daggers at his wife.

Who has died? Una couldn't ask because that would mean letting on to Grandma and Grandad that she understood and spoke Hindi beyond the basic greetings. What was the word Grandma had used? Burf Bili? Burfi she didn't know, but Bili was cat in Hindi. She'd forgotten about ... Cat.

Una nervously raised her eyes to the ceiling and then hastily looked down again when she realised her grandparents were watching her.

She excused herself and made for the bathroom. Locking the bathroom door, she climbed through the bathroom window and stood on the ledge.

"Una! Don't be stupid! Cat is fine and safe, which is more than I can say for you."

Una tried to look for Avi, but couldn't see a thing in the rain.

"Una look down!"

Squinting, she followed his instruction and saw a large, greenish-scaled snake swim past with its head and forked tongue poking out of the water. It was a King Cobra.

She jumped back through the window, narrowly missing the French-styled sunken squat toilet. She then ran the shower for a few minutes to give her an excuse for her wet hair. Wrapped in her dressing gown, she returned to her room to find that her grandparents and Johnnie Walker had already left.

The phone was ringing from the bureau in the drawing room. *That was weird.* Una tiptoed to the landing and hid herself in the folds of the heavy curtains that framed the adjoining closed door between her Grandad's bedroom and the drawing room. Una could hear what Grandad was saying, despite him whispering into the phone receiver. Some of her changes were useful.

"Are you crazy? Which part of 'I don't have the money to invest in the timber company in Kangra,' do you not understand? I know I promised I'd go in with you, but I've already sunk two-thirds of the money Vivek left for Una's school fees for next term on the other timber stocks you recommended. They haven't grown in value as you said they would."

Una imagined Major trying to sweet talk her grandfather into investing.

"She is not ... for sale ... Major! What do you mean by 'it was my intent to milk the opportunity of her being here?' It was your idea ..." Grandfather mumbled under his breath.

Una's eyes widened. Surely her grandparents weren't looking after her for their own financial gain? Una parted the curtains a little.

"Major, Vivek must have changed his plans ... I will ring him ... tonight, when he is back from work. Of course, he's fine – he just changed his mind. What has his flight cancellation got to do with you negotiating a price for her?"

Una's throat constricted. Perspiration droplets formed on her forehead, causing her body to shiver.

"I know she is a firstborn," remarked Grandad. "In fact, she is the only offspring of that useless son. But ... but, it was agreed she would leave before then. What do you mean you forgot? It was your plan ... Don't you remember persuading me to keep her after I rejected Alice's last wishes? I only agreed because the wretched girl refused to read her mother's letter. Vivek left it for her. Well, I read it and stupidly told you. You don't have to remind me about the note he wrote at the bottom of that letter.

Of course, I remember! Vivek promised Una that he would come back for her in the summer, and that she could decide whether she wanted to stay or go back home with him. So what? He must have changed his mind. She obviously didn't know about his intentions, otherwise she would have asked after him."

Una sank to the ground. Her Dad had meant to come back, just as Avi had said. Questions arose in her head: *How did Avi know about her Dad and why hadn't her Dad come? What did Grandad mean by 'she's not for sale'? What was Major up to?* She wished she hadn't refused to read her mother's letter. Unfortunately, Dad's handwriting on the envelope had misguided her.

"No, Major, she's my granddaughter ... you have no right ... how can you say that ... I'll not go back on my word. Look, I've just thought of something ... I'll just take her out of that hoity-toity school of her mother's choice, and put her in the local school. The local school's fees will be peanuts ... and I can always manipulate the girl into believing her father can't afford it. Listen now, Major! There will be no more talks of negotiations. Good ... okay, that's settled then." With that he banged the receiver down.

Shaking like a leaf, Una returned to her room. Through that one telephone conversation, she'd found out the most treacherous secret, one she would never have suspected. She knew it was crucial that she learnt to understand the depths of wickedness, but her mind buckled. What she'd heard did not make any sense. When she first arrived, Major had been adamant that the property developer's firstborn grandchildren weren't to be given. But now, for a tidy sum of money, he was eager to do an exchange. Her grandparents' indifference made her believe that they were forced to be her guardians but, in truth, she was a cash cow. Yes, Grandad was reluctant to hand her over, but it didn't sound as though Major was convinced. From the conversation, even she believed Grandad could be easily persuaded, if not by words, then something else. It was difficult to forget the evening Major and Avi's uncles surrounded him at gunpoint. Dizzy and short of breath, she dropped backwards onto her bed clutching her heart and inwardly cried, *Dad, what have you done?* No sooner had she thought the words, it hit her. It wasn't her father's fault. It was all her fault. Her truancy and illegal urban exploration forced her father to bring her to India. Between sobs, she realised he had ignored Mum's wishes to send her to Windsor School three years earlier. If she had read the letter that day, she could have contacted him while she was at Windsor school. She could have returned home. Una sat up mid sob, *Wait! She can still contact him.*

When everyone had gone to bed, Una slipped into the drawing room to unlock the bureau with her basic equipment: a piece of wire and a hairpin, but failed. The lock mechanism was too sophisticated. The only way to open the bureau was with the key – the key that hung around Grandad's neck. She would have to try and steal it while he was drunk on rum. In the meantime, she split and bent her hairpin to open the glass cabinet and retrieve her mother's letter, only to find it had been replaced by her school house badge – Flycatchers.

Chapter 36

Over the rim of her coffee cup, Una studied Grandad's slow and deliberate gait as he approached the breakfast table, pretending to clear tears from eyes and his spectacles. Sure of her attention, he dramatically blew his ruddy nose with the same handkerchief, stuffed it in his trousers and drew up a dining chair adjacent to her. If Una didn't know what was coming, she would have been truly taken in.

"Your father hasn't sent next term's money, and because of the rains, I haven't been able to contact him either. Your school has strict rules about payments and will not allow you back until they receive the full term's fees. I wish I could pay them for you, but I don't have monies to cover such expensive school fees. All I can do is withdraw you from Windsor School and inform the principal of our changed circumstances."

Even though Una knew it was coming, it still affected her. "But Grandad, I am in my final A level year. Windsor is the only school where girls can take A levels in this valley. Without them, I can't get into Cambridge University."

Grandad showed concern and empathy. "Look, Una, I know it is hard, and I'm sure Vivek will sort the situation out quickly once I get hold of him." Una flinched when he put an arm around her and said, "*Beti,* in the meantime, as a temporary measure, it's best that you attend a day school so you don't miss out on your studies." Una stared at him blankly as he dropped the sorrow and picked up a piece of toast. The words 'temporary measure' hung in the air between them.

After breakfast, Una returned to her room. From her school attaché, she retrieved an inland letter form, ready-printed with the school's address and postage stamp on it. In its neat folds, she penned a short letter to her school principal, explaining their financial situation. When Johnnie Walker came to dust the room, she deliberately used pigeon Hindi to ask him to post it with her grandfather's letters. Thinking of his stomach, he promised he would deliver it to the principal by hand if she parted with her evening snack of parathas. Una felt sorry that Grandma didn't feed him well, but only agreed to part with the parathas if she got a response from the school in the next few days. Luckily for Johnnie Walker, a letter arrived from the school's principal two days later. Her grandfather's face dropped when Una read the part of the letter where the principal stated that she was happy to postpone the payment of fees, and that she was looking forward to seeing Una on the first day of term. He faked relief when she read the option of allowing her father to pay in instalments when he was able.

At tea time that day, Johnnie Walker served Una warm milk and a plate with two parathas on it. She pushed the plate back towards him after showing him the letter. Beaming, he accepted it. Squatting on his haunches, he leaned against the low wall Una was sitting on and tore a third of his paratha and chucked it on the ground. From nowhere, his pet crow swooped down and picked it up in its beak. Una leaned back to avoid the bird's beak and, in the process, fell off the low wall. She couldn't help but laugh, and set Johnnie Walker off, too. Bewildered, his crow flapped its wings and flew to the water tank.

"*Shukriya,* Johnnie. *Chitthi ko lai janai kai liyai* – Thank you for delivering the letter."

"*Theek Hai* – It's okay," he said, scoffing the last few morsels of paratha in his mouth.

"Your name isn't really Johnnie Walker, is it? Sorry, *aapka asli nam Johnnie Walker tow nahi hai?*" she repeated her question in fluent Hindi. A piece of paratha fell out of his mouth.

"*Aap achii Hindi bol saktai hai? –* You can speak good Hindi? *Itnai kum samah mai kaisai seekha? –* How did you become fluent in such a short time?" he asked incredulously.

Una just shrugged her shoulders. It was too strange to be holding a conversation with him; she'd never seen anyone else talk to him, beyond commands. Forget talking, Una was ashamed to think she hadn't even taken in what he actually looked like. Until now, he had been invisible to her. Rudely staring, she noticed he had a youthful face; embarrassingly, she'd thought he was much older than her. "*Merai height kai ho –* You're the same height as me," she said, putting her hand up in the air to measure him and then froze when he jumped back in shock. "In the valley, girls don't touch men unless they are related, and they definitely don't touch male servants." Johnnie Walker's solemn voice broke into laughter as he pointed to her goldfish impression. "My real name is Gopan, and that crow is called Kawa. And, just like you, I am seventeen." Una gawped some more. She wasn't the only one hiding their fluency in a second language. Una realised she'd given Tommy more attention. In fact, when Tommy was alive, he had a greater profile and place in the house than Gopan. Una blushed ashamedly. She blushed further when she thought of all the times she had spoken in English to herself, or with Avi, about personal matters in Gopan's presence.

Una shifted her gaze to Kawa, hoping to distract her mind from her embarrassment. Kawa was not a common house crow. He was missing a grey ring around his neck. He also had purplish flumes instead of grey. Curious, Una strolled over to Kawa and raised her hand to stroke his plumes.

"Careful, he loves meat and might just think you are offering your fingers up for food."

"Really?" Una retracted her hand and looked back at Gopan. It was strange to see Gopan smiling wryly at her – generally, he showed no emotion.

"What breed is he?"

"He is a Jungle Crow."

Lights appeared in the windows. Kawa flew away, squawking.

"I'd better go," Una said, holding her right hand out to Gopan. Gopan shook his head but smiled.

"If you ever need anything, let me know. But please, be careful, or I will lose my job, or worse. Young girls are not meant to be talking to the help if the help is male and the same age. Memsahib will think we are thinking of eloping!"

"*Hum gupt bhasha mai bol saktai hau* – We could use a code," she said in Hindi.

"Mention Kawa, and I will know you need to talk to me," Gopan replied in English.

Chapter 37

It was the end of Una's holidays. The rain had eased off and the river had receded back to its banks. Una was on the steps of the front veranda reading a book from her A level English Literature summer reading list when Gopan returned from an errand at Major's house. He dropped an envelope on Una's lap.

The colour drained from her face when she pulled out two train tickets from the envelope. They were two outbound tickets, with Grandad's name and hers, reserved for the coming Sunday – the day she was meant to be returning to her boarding school. The tickets were from Dehra Dun to Kangra in Himachal Pradesh. *Wasn't that the same town where the timber company Major wanted Grandad to invest in was?* Fingers shaking, Una returned the tickets to the envelope and proceeded to look at the sky. "There are no Kawas in the sky today."

Gopan answered in deliberate pigeon English, "Kawa, charpoy – string bed – sitting 2 o' clock."

※※※

At 2pm, Grandad and Grandma went to meet the bride-to-be for Major's youngest son, Chaz. Una was taken aback by the notion that the family could even consider another marriage in the family. A month had barely passed since Meeru's death. Disgusted, she shared her sorrowful thoughts with Gopan, who in turn explained that, in her grandparents' and Major's community, there was a shortage of girls of marriageable age. Something like a death was not a good enough reason to miss out on a 'suitable' match. Una found the whole thing barbaric. She furiously paced around Gopan's string bed in the garage.

"What are you doing?" said Gopan in pure bewilderment.

"Pacing, I do that when I need to think."

"Oh! In that case, you need to think about leaving the house immediately, before your grandparents come back."

Una paused and nodded. "But where do I go? School is closed until Sunday. That's three days away."

Gopan beckoned for her to sit down. When she complied, he sat on his haunches on the ground nearby. "Stay with your friend from school, the one who lives in the army cantonment."

Una looked at him suspiciously. "How would you know where my friend lives? *Kya Sabki baat suntai ho?* – Do you eavesdrop on everyone's conversations?"

"I can't help if I hear and notice things such as rare guests. I remember the one occasion your friend came with her father to visit; he was in uniform."

Una felt uncomfortable that he'd paid so much attention to her activities. "Okay, so what should I say to her to convince her to let me stay?"

Gopan puzzled over her problem. "It is simple, just tell the truth."

"The truth ... yes, or some of the truth at least." Una jumped up and began pacing around the *charpoy* again. "I'll tell her the truth, that Grandad is going away on business. As there is no one else in the household who can understand me, my grandfather thinks it would probably be best if I stayed with them until school started on Sunday. The only thing is, how do I ask her without access to a phone."

"Not a problem."

Una was not convinced, until she followed him to the bureau in the house and watched, aghast, when he produced a key that opened it. How and when had he made a copy of the key?

Gopan must have read her mind. "Some time ago, he was in the shower and ran out of hot water, so I was asked to fetch some. I did, after I picked up the key, along with the bucket. While I was heating the water, I made an imprint of the key in soap and had the key made later."

"But why would you want the key ... Oh, it doesn't really matter," Una was too on edge to deal with Gopan's resourcefulness. Nervously, she picked up the receiver of the antique telephone. With great fascination, she put her finger in the first metal circle that represented the first digit of her friend's number.

Her school friend was thrilled to have her 'English' friend over for a few days. Between whoops of excitement, her parents gave permission for Una to stay at their place, and even agreed to take her back to school at the beginning of the term. Luckily, they understood the importance of business trips and her grandmother's inability to drive Una to school. On top of that, they knew her Grandad well and were happy to help him out. Una promised them that her Grandad had asked her to make the phone call on his behalf. The call ended with the decision that her friend's parents would send an army vehicle to pick her up.

As soon as Una put the receiver down, she wrote a note to her Grandad saying she had been invited by her friend and thought he wouldn't mind since she had been so lonely during the holidays. Una knew her Grandad would be upset with her, but her friend's parents were well known in the army circle. He wouldn't want to make a fuss and offend them.

In the meantime, Gopan retrieved her attaché case from under her bed in her room and helped her quickly pack her toiletries and some other clothes. Most of the clothes she'd brought from England had mysteriously disappeared from her cupboard. They were not in the wash, either. She didn't have time to hunt for them in her grandparents' cupboards because her 'ride' was waiting. The car had arrived twenty minutes after her phone call.

Una was expecting an army jeep. Instead, she was faced with an army truck and four soldiers. As it drove out of the gates, something fell on top of its canvas roof. Una smiled to herself in the passenger seat. She knew that something was 'Cat'.

Chapter 38

On a roof ledge, invisible to the naked eye, Wolf stretched languorously in the warmth of the day. His coat of tan and grey camouflaged him as he lay sprawled on the unfinished brick wall. Resting his head on his paws, Wolf couldn't stop smiling. He knew it was impolite to show pleasure at someone else's misfortune, but he couldn't help it. His two-year-long waiting game was finally over – if the note he'd found attached to his late lunch was anything to go by. Wolf licked his lips in satisfaction. Kawa had proved to be a decent meal – not as bony as Wolf had thought he would be.

According to Kawa's note, the army truck was on its way to the bridge from Cantt Road ... in precisely, five minutes. The army worked like clockwork but, just to check and cherish the slow build-up to his victory, he swivelled his ears to scan the expanse for the expected sound, then yawned – this was going to be easy for him. The nearing clamour of the army truck expounded in his ears as it sped through the hairpin turn of the cliff, where many a human body had fallen like flies. A sly smile spread across his face. Wolf's human-like instinct of mourning for humanity had long since left him. "At least they don't have far to go," he muttered to himself. Closing his eyelids, he focused his mind on a point above his nose, then opened his third eye to gaze upon the geography of the hairpin cliff. On the cliff, a saffron flag fluttered as the truck whizzed past it. The ancient temple beneath it, with its shadowed entrance, was ever ready for the arrival of the few who'd chosen salvation and entry to the world of the Gods. Wolf sniggered. Even in death, most human souls were too scared to chance a meeting with the so-called half-human, half-animal Blessed beings.

Something was wrong! The army truck seemed to have lost control as it rounded the treacherous bend. Alarmed, Wolf's eyes flung open. The truck was zig-zagging at full speed towards the bridge that ran over the fast-flowing river. Wolf willed it to stop and thought it was going to when it straightened. Instead, a cloud of dust rose as the truck reared and continued forward at break-neck speed. Wolf howled as the truck took off. It was airborne for a few seconds, then jolted down clumsily on its tyres. He couldn't believe the stupidity of his second-in-command, who'd replaced one of the army personnel. Furious, he watched the unnecessary struggle in the front cabin of the army tank, but was relieved when he saw a body thrown over the side from the cabin.

A smaller body followed!

Mission half accomplished – Wolf searched hard for another airborne body, but there wasn't one. The truck had already moved on. *Without the cub, how would the transformation take place?* Due to his reluctance to join the Blessed, Wolf wasn't aware of all the facts about Blessed initiations. He didn't care about the outcome; Una was now in the jungle. All Wolf had to do was get to her first. He sprung across the wall and with one giant leap, met the jungle floor below.

✳✳✳

Arms and legs flaying, Una screamed soundlessly as she spiralled downwards in mid-air. She frantically opened and closed her fingers, hoping to grab onto anything as the scenery charged past her, but, alas, only thin air passed between them. Trying to save her own life wasn't working for her. The distance between herself and the monsoon swollen river was decreasing. With her end near, Una's voiceless screams turned into her last prayer.

"Glad you ceased whimpering, but you'd better zip the pathetic begging and pay attention," a vaguely familiar voice said. It was neither Avi's, nor the Sharman's.

"You can stop flaying your arms, too. Fold them and bring your knees up." When she didn't react, he commanded, "Do it!"

Once she'd complied, he continued, "Now, do a forward roll and tuck your head in."

She loosened the muscles in her face and arms.

"Slowly loosen your arms and reach out to the front and bend your knees."

She followed his instructions carefully.

"Good, now put your hands out, like a cat," the voice instructed. "No, don't splay them to your sides. Are you imagining a giraffe trying to sit down?"

Flustered, Una brought her arms forward and pointed her fingers downwards, but not before using one to slap the side of her head.

"Stop your wise cracks – I'm concentrating."

"How do you know I'm not your subconscious speaking?"

"Your voice is too deep, and masculine."

"Too deep, hey! Well, I'm not in your head – I'm here."

"Where's here?" Between somersaults she scoured the ground, but found it hard to focus. Her vision was blurred and the colours were all wrong. Everything was blue and green, and barely in focus. Had she knocked her head coming down. Had it impacted her vision? She couldn't make out anybody in the moving fuzziness and gave up. Instead, she instinctively reached out to the approaching branches of the trees that hung over the riverbed below, to break her fall. Immersed in her own thoughts of how to break her fall, she instinctively swung to the widest branch. After a few quick manoeuvres, she managed to use her hands and feet to walk her way down the tree trunk.

"Good landing for a first time," the voice chuckled admiringly.

Una was too unravelled to react to his condescending statement – a first for her. Instead, she asked, "Where are you?"

"Here!"

The voice was very close to her. In fact, it was at waist level – behind her. Slowly and tentatively, Una turned around with baby steps. She was prepared to find a man in his mid-twenties or thirties, but was confounded when she set eyes on a ghostly-looking wolf.

Una's head felt heavy. Her legs collapsed on the spot where she was standing on the river bank. Avi had warned her about a wolf.

"Face me, now!" Wolf bellowed.

Una lifted her fuzzy head and simply uttered, "But your voice is coming from a ..." she swiftly looked around, hoping to see a man hiding in the terrain, just like the Sharman did.

"You really ought to have better manners. LOOK AT ME – CAREFULLY!" His voice shook to match his murderous expression.

Una tried. Although she saw colour, her vision was still distorted. It was like looking through eye drops. "I must be hallucinating because your voice is coming from that wolf, over there." Una's pupils enlarged, and the single wolf became a kaleidoscopic vision of twelve wolves. Transfixed on the voice's source, she watched in horror as the wolves leapt into the sky and towards her, forcing her to lie down. *You're the one I saw before!*

"Yes, the one that found you on the steps. You'd better BELIEVE IT!" Wolf growled.

Gasping from his breath, Una stuttered. "I d-do!"

"You are Meeru's wolf ... the one that howled at curfew," Una said as calmly as she could manage. She only just managed to stop herself from saying, 'Avi warned me about you'. Una had to make her way back to the path. If she could work out where the four boulders were ... before ...

"Oh, I can help you with that, they're causing the rapids over there." Una followed the direction of his paw pointed and was horrified. Even without a clear head, she knew the currents would tear her apart.

"Correct, especially since your unnecessary courage and guts can't keep your Blessed destination from you. It didn't keep me from becoming a Blessed Wolf either."

"Blessed destination ... never, I'd rather risk my skull on those rocks than become a creature like you." She gulped inwardly as saw a log smash and splinter against the boulders.

Wolf snorted. "I hear you. After all, what good is a body without passionate blood swirling in it. You'll make a great addition to my Forced Blessed army."

"Did you not hear me? I'd rather die than become a creature like you." Una swung her head from the swirling torrid to Wolf.

"What kind of creature do you think you are?" Wolf barked walking back to where he had originally stood. He swiftly sat down and made himself comfortable, with his four legs and tail sprawled out.

Una took a good look at the wolf ... The tan and grey coat, the dark face, and the fact that he said he was Blessed. Was this what Avi ...? *Wait, what did the wolf ask ...? Did he just ask what creature am I? Surely that was obvious, I'm a ...*

Girl? Wolf quizzed and then mimicked a quiz buzzer for an incorrect answer. *Wrong answer!*

Una gave him an intent look, before apprehensively letting her gaze slip down her body.

Minutes passed, but for Wolf, it could have been centuries.

Una's eyes widened as she took in the mass of white fur with grey rosettes in place of her human torso. Slowly, she stretched her paws out in front of her and used them to touch her face. She found more fur. Her slumped body was wrapped by the longest possible tail ... Shock and terror registered in her eyes.

Wolf knew exactly how she felt. He remembered the first time it had happened to him, so he bent his head and stared at the ground. Words were meaningless when one was lost in an abyss.

I've become the very thing I was running away from. I should have been at my friend's house, ready to go to school – safe. Somehow, by running away, I've delivered myself to the jungle.

A whole year early!

Una's ears pricked up. She could hear a scuffle, perhaps a deer or something else. Una let out a sob, but a cat sound came out instead. She didn't want to hear the jungle in her head and raised her hand ... paws ... to cover her ears, but couldn't. Her anatomy was completely alien to her. She didn't know how to use it.

How can I live like this ... no, why would I want to live like this? Images of Rosetta and the snow leopard in the outbuilding now made sense. The outbuilding ... if she went back to her Grandad's, would she be locked up like Rosetta? The horrors of living in the jungle, or going back to her Grandad's, let rip in her head. Overcome by the hostility and danger of both, a piercing wail left her body and ricocheted off the surrounding lime cliffs.

Wolf wanted to barricade himself from her thoughts and her reaction to her unexpected morphing, but he didn't. He had to stay in contact with her mind.

First came the waves of fear, then shock, followed by fear again, and finally, her unadulterated anger. Enraged with the injustice, she roared. Instead of a mighty roar, a hiss sounded from her lips. Not only had she lost her world, she had lost her voice. Exhausted and confused, she slipped to the ground. Giant tears filled her almond shaped eyes as she gave in to her desolation.

Silence prevailed between them as the sun set. Not even a curfew howl was made.

✳✳✳

She lay for several hours, curled on the ground. Tears soaked her once soft, pristine white fur until it was matted. Motionless himself, Wolf watched her misery engulf her. But he did nothing. The thought of comforting her did not enter his head. Compassion was a human instinct, surplus to requirements in the jungle world. If nothing else, compassion would only lead to one's own demise.

Wolf's apathy died when Venus winked at him from the open skies. He lifted his head and surveyed the other celestial bodies frosting the night sky.

"It is time – time to guide you through the terrain while the OTHERS sleep. I've given you ample time to wallow, more than I thought I would."

Una didn't move.

"Una, I heard all your nonsense thoughts about the jungle – there are no good or bad animals in the jungle – just the ones that eat, and the ones who are eaten. Luckily for you, you are high up on the food chain. So, you can relax a little ..."

He was interrupted by a stomach rumble of sorts.

"Talking about food, you're famished! The first thing we have to do is make sure you are fed."

On that note, he quickly rose, thinking, *I hope you are a good, quick learner.*

Una used her front limbs to lift herself up, but when she saw paws instead of hands, despair and panic overcame her again. Fear, an unfamiliar emotion, pressed down on her. However, her hunger prevailed. She followed Wolf without a fight this time. She had a single purpose. Her nerves had calmed, and parts of her old fighting-self returned. *I'm still in here, I have to get a grip ...* the Disney image of Pinocchio in a blue whale gave her some comfort, until she realised she'd never seen the clip herself. Old fear penetrated her new body. Somehow, she had to learn to stop Wolf from doing that again, before she completely lost herself. Fear, based on a lack of information was worse than any reality she could face. But, it was time to learn. She was determined to shake off her vulnerability, and quickly, before Wolf used it to his advantage.

Turning to Wolf, she thought it was time she let him into a little secret.

"Luckily for you, Wolf, I am a quick learner."

Wolf stopped dead in his tracks and snapped around to face her. Una turned the tables on him and read all his thoughts: How did she know he was reading her thoughts? More importantly, how could she have possibly learnt to read and talk to him telepathically so soon, and with such ease? It was new to her, surely? Some of his new recruits still couldn't do it, even after nearly a year of training! He, himself, had taken a while to practise his skills to perfection ...

"Didn't you mention eating?"

Her jaw never moved!

Wolf replied out loud, "Yes, I did. Come, let's get some food."

Clumsily, she followed his lead on all fours again.

Una's stomach was empty, but she felt wretched when visions of the food that a leopard would probably eat popped into her head.

"Yeah, no Big Macs here – get used to it," he chuckled. When she inwardly winced, he knew he had the advantage. He wanted her to be vulnerable. "Remember, this is your place now. It's your life." When she stopped on the spot, he nudged her. "We will break you in, slowly." His demeanour softened. "The food you eat today will be edible, I promise."

Una grimaced. She hadn't frozen at the thought of no Big Mac's, it was the fact he'd confirmed that this was her place now. "My place now?" A lump formed in her throat.

They unnecessarily walked through low shrubbery and boulders. Una found it hard to move around on all fours, and use her foggy eyes effectively. Luckily, her paws were fur-padded so she was able to walk more steadily than expected. Her whiskers aided her sense of direction. In the beginning, while trying to catch up with Wolf, she had lost her balance and nearly skidded on some boulders, but her long tail instinctively saved the day and helped her regain her balance. "Thanks, tail," she said, looking over her shoulder.

"Unbelievable! She's talking to her body parts," muttered Wolf.

"They are not my body parts, I am human."

"Una, get this into your head STRAIGHT AWAY – There is no way back. You will never be a whole human, so get used to it."

Una grizzled. "I won't get used to it. This is only temporary, anyway."

"The girl has spirit."

"My name is Una."

"Una, Una," Wolf rolled her name on his tongue, as if he was tasting it. "Too short I think. It doesn't sound like a full name."

"It's an Irish name. It means 'Hunger' or 'Lamb.'"

"Hunger? Oh! You'll feel that enough," Wolf chuckled. "I thought you would be named after Una the 'Faerie Queen', who, I think, was a metaphor for Elizabeth the first? Una, tell me, are you feisty and daring, and a proclaimed virgin?"

Una glared (if snow leopards could).

"Are you stumped because I asked you whether you were a virgin? Or is it because you don't know what I'm talking about, despite coming from England, where the poem originated? Surely, you must know about the longest, original unfinished epic poem written in English."

"No, it wasn't in my curriculum, but answer this, how do you know ...?" Una quizzed in disbelieve, but then stopped midway. It was quite possible.

"How do I know, Una? About the epic 16th century poem by Edmund Spenser? Or, were you trying to ask: 'How is it possible that wolves can read?' Well, it is quite elementary, Watson – I can't be entirely wolf ... I must be JUST like you, but better educated."

First Edmund Spenser, whoever he was, and now Sherlock Holmes! This wolf obviously had an excellent, enriched education – yet no one had mentioned another teenager having disappeared in recent years. He was far too well educated to be a Blessed from the tribesmen.

"Who are you?"

"My name is Wolf."

"Wolf, how original, but what was your name before?" Her question was drowned out by the loud growl erupting from her tight belly.

Wolf guffawed and carried on walking.

Una's stomach continued to growl.

"Come along ... Lamb, I think I like that name the best."

Una would have grumbled, but, for the first time, she understood the true meaning of her name and meekly sped up.

Chapter 39

From a four-legged's point of view, the 'Modern Ruin' was ingeniously deceptive and sophisticated in its provision of access to and from the jungle.

Two months earlier, at the beginning of her summer break, she had tripped on the steps leading to the girls' room and puzzled over the odd and haphazard placement of the steps. Now, it was obvious – they were perfectly adapted to ease Wolf's access to the property, at any point and direction, from the jungle below. The outdoor stairs were a washed-out brick colour, which now looked deliberately weathered by lime wash to help camouflage Wolf. Deliberate crevices were strategically built to allow thick clusters of grass to grow. The hanging vines concealed the hard edges of the steps. Una knew Wolf would be undetectable when the sun and moon were not casting shadows on the walls.

Even now, with the moon shining directly on the wall, he was difficult to spot. Una followed his small shadow, which was darting randomly against the wall. From afar, she imagined they looked like arbitrary shadows, especially when the clouds played peek-a-boo with the moon. Standing face forward, quite close to the climbing wall of sorts, she used his shadows to find him amongst the many lookouts and short perches, but to no avail. Although his profile was hidden, Wolf's presence was strong. She was sure he was moving up and down the steps. Her awareness of him mirrored how she'd felt climbing the steps on her first visit. Just as she formed the link, Wolf came forward from his hiding place on the top-most step level with the roof.

As she went to him, she paused at the umbrella stand. The disturbing memory of being in the room floated through her mind. Despite the warm night and her thick furry coat, shivers ran through her new body. Mind-boggling as it may be, Una was certain she had chased, and then inhabited, Wolf's animal body during the recent monsoon rains, before he turned into a human. Ice wrapped around her lungs and heart. She'd seen Wolf's human face in the mirror. It was Tawny. Wolf was Tawny. She wondered whether the sisters were in their bedroom. Involuntarily, Una placed her paw on the door knob and tried to turn it. Without fingers, she had no grip.

"You remember the time you came here, on Meeru's wedding day, don't you?" queried Wolf.

Una nodded, noting his right eye twitch. Earlier, while immersed in morose thoughts, she had not been entirely idle. She had paid close attention to Wolf's mannerisms and learnt that, like a poker player, Wolf's eye twitched before he read her thoughts. Surprisingly, Wolf hadn't heard the thoughts that had just passed through her mind. Surely, that meant he didn't know about the ... Una blanked her mind.

Wolf's fur bristled. Impatiently, he summoned her to the roof. Moving back, he gave her room to climb the last few steps. Once she was there, he placed his paw on her shoulder and positioned her so that she was staring ahead.

"I think it's time you learnt the truth about our first meeting." Una wasn't sure if she wanted to. "Relax. Just look straight ahead and reflect on the day of the wedding. You will understand the significance of that day," commanded Wolf.

Una nearly jumped out of her new skin. From the space between her eyebrows, she magically projected a magnified image onto an invisible vertical plane several feet away. The weird sensation akin to being an onlooker in a dream overcame her.

The projection began with Una hiding between two trunks. She was staring at Meeru, who was perched on a stool. Agnes, Grace and the makeup artist were 'dolling' her up. Meeru was just a shell of her former self.

"Why is the projection more detailed than my memory?" Una asked in a trance.

"What?" Wolf croaked.

"The detail ..." Una stopped when she noted Wolf's demeanour. *Was he affected by Meeru's listlessness?*

Wolf caught up. "Detail ... yes, of course. You see, you are not projecting a memory. You are projecting everything your eyes and ears captured that day. That consists of more detail than what you consciously paid attention to."

He leaned forward to read the message on the cigarette box in Agnes' hands. She followed suit.

'Bedi substitute, all is forgiven.'

Una knew Meeru was going to mouth the answer and that Agnes' head would get in the way. Perhaps she would find out what Meeru had said that day.

Patiently, from her hiding place, she watched Meeru grab the box back. Shakily, with two fingers, she pulled out a cigarette.

This time, she saw Meeru's lips mouth 'Avi' in the reflection of the makeup artist's cosmetics box.

"What is Avi forgiving her for, I wonder?" Una whispered.

Wolf didn't say a word. She glanced over to him and was taken aback.

Wolf had tears in his eyes. From a distance, he was absent-mindedly stroking Meeru's projected tears away. Una immediately realised that Wolf and Meeru had a more intimate connection. He had to be the wolf she'd called with the whistle. Una turned her head sideways, towards Wolf. This movement instantly severed the projection.

"Look ahead," Wolf growled as he pressed down hard on her shoulder with his resting paw.

"Fine!" Una decided to ask questions later. She returned to her previous stance and projected the day ahead again. Wolf, in turn, reduced the pressure on her shoulder.

Sid Rao entered the room and took many pictures of Meeru's dowry jewellery and her art paraphernalia.

Una looked hard but, despite the extra detail, she still couldn't find her portrait.

Who had she drawn it for?

"Damn, damn, damn. I've filled my memory card, girls, and we haven't even got to the ceremony yet." Sid looked pleadingly at his daughters. "Which one of you will go and fetch my other memory card?"

Una realised how easy it had been to discover her when she'd been crouched between the two trunks, covered with Meeru's trousseau. Her feet were poking out when Sid trained his camera lens in her direction. This time she noticed, with special interest, how the other girls silently protested against his decision. Meeru's protesting intrigued her the most, then, when Sid gave instructions, she watched the others carefully. She hadn't expected Sid to deliver the first shock.

Holding his three middle fingers wide, he used his index finger from the other hand to trace the insides of the trio in a 'W' shape and said, "What nonsense! She just needs to stay on the path until she gets to the house. She can't miss it. Una, just look for an unfinished house."

On the actual day, she thought he had said 'What nonsense' ...

The two sisters made 'oh' faces and Meeru's switched from sadness to dread.

Una gasped in shock.

"I expect you didn't see that on the day?" Wolf spoke softly.

Una nodded her head.

Una watched as Meeru put the hair scarf on her. Meeru was mid-sentence when she paid attention again.

"... Look at how the turquoises and greens in the scarf make your face come alive. You look like a ..."

"Cat," Una uttered.

Wolf was watching Una attentively this time.

"'Cat'... Meeru gave me a gift that day – a kitten!"

"Una, the fact that you are a snow leopard now, suggests your kitten was actually a cub. Gosh! Meeru planted a snow leopard cub in your care?"

Una was flummoxed.

"I heard the tribe had fixed a price for your deliverance. Major is always looking for money to invest. It now makes sense. The only thing I can't believe is that Meeru planted a snow leopard cub in your care ... she was against the tribesmen, but she must have lied. The cub must have scratched you."

"Why do you think 'Cat' scratched me?" Una asked.

"You had to have been scratched. Nothing else entered the jungle with you. You see, there isn't another snow leopard in the jungle that could have helped you with your initiation."

"That can't be right. What about Avi? He must be a snow leopard, too."

"Avi? No one has seen him in his animal guise yet. It's rumoured that his initiation was incomplete."

Una turned a few shades whiter – if that was actually possible for a snow leopard.

Meeru's cryptic note made little sense, except, it suggested Meeru had had a hand in Avi's misfortune. She was confused.

"You are a Blessed, so you must be involved, too. In fact, her whistle only ever reached you. You obviously worked together!"

Wolf's hackles stood up in anger. "Okay, I did care for her. That's why I am shocked. I don't understand why she would go against me. I oppose the Blessed – I'm the leader of the Forced Blessed, who oppose the ritual of making Blesseds from firstborn teenagers. So, no, I wasn't involved," lied Wolf.

"Is that why she didn't want me to come over?"

"Who knows? Personally, I think she didn't want me to see you in those skimpy shorts you were wearing that day." Wolf sniggered. "Little did she know, she made it worse. The kaftan made you far more captivating. Poor Meeru."

Una was appalled by his blatant sexism.

Wolf cocked his head to the side, as if waiting for her to react. She chose not to give him the satisfaction and stared ahead.

She was walking past her grandfather's house.

Both Wolf and Una watched her pick up a mango. This time, Una was in no doubt that the marks read 'NO'.

Wolf twitched when a vision of black fur retrieved the mango.

"Oh!" Una exclaimed.

"So you didn't notice the fur?"

"No," she lied. Of course, she'd noticed. The fur reminded her of when she had fainted in the monsoons and her soul had somehow momentarily inhabited a furry beast, while it was chasing ... Wolf.

"It seems the one and only Blessed bear in this part of the jungle stalked you. That's bad news, Una. You are going to have to be even more careful."

"Why?"

"Because he is less human and more animal. We think he must have been initiated by an old mauler. The bear in question has maimed several of my group."

Una visibly shivered.

"Don't worry, I will protect you. From your vision, you will notice that I kept an eye on you, which is just as well. I have saved you from the clutches of the Blessed tribe. The bastards plotted against you and forced you to become a Blessed snow leopard, even though you are not a permanent resident of Khamosh Valley." He paused. Una looked exhausted and petrified. "Perhaps the projection of how we met can be saved for another day," he finished, removing his paw from her shoulder.

"No! It's fine."

Wolf looked forward and placed his paw on her shoulder again, pleased with her decision.

Together, they watched Una walk up to the 'Modern Ruin's' veranda and admire the pillars poking out towards the skies. They heard her call out for Sid Rao's wife before she entered the premises. Wolf sniggered when he watched her decide to investigate the rest of the house, instead of returning to Major's house with the memory card.

"A modern-day Goldilocks!"

Una smarted under the accusation, but knew it was a true interpretation. She had thought the same on that day.

They watched her sneak into the master bedroom. Una caught sight of the photographs on the wall again. This time she tried to study them. Like before, the human Una was distracted by a noise. She was faced with the kitchen in the projection instead.

"Keep watching," Wolf said impatiently, pressing his claws further into her fur.

Una looked comical as she stared up at the odd steps leading up to the sisters' padlocked bedroom door.

"I'm surprised you didn't try and break the padlock, Goldilocks."

Una was blushing under her fur.

"You guessed right. I read your thoughts on that day, too, which makes me think you had been infected by a scratch. I couldn't have heard your thoughts, unless the Blessed particles were already in your blood system. It only takes a little scratch. When a Blessed germ enters your body, it takes hold of a body cell and injects its genetic coding, thereby altering the cell's coding. At the same time, it uses the cell's enzymes to create more Blessed particles. These then break away from the host cell and use the blood stream to find their own hosts – other cells in the body. It seems Meeru left you a lasting present in that kitten-cub."

Wolf's explanation of the mechanism confused Una. She was already communicating through thought talk before 'Cat' arrived, so something else must have contaminated her. She didn't dwell on the problem in case Wolf picked up on her thoughts. Luckily for her, there were no eye twitches from him. He was concentrating on her projection.

"Oh, do concentrate, we have got to the point where we meet."

Una did as she was told.

Her human body was on the roof, rotating to catch the panoramic view of the wild jungle as it hugged the building from the three sides. She watched her elated human-self climb onto the narrow roof wall and lie down, facing the mountains.

Open-mouthed, Una cringed inwardly as her human-self lazily eyed the scudding clouds and tried to match the cloud shapes to shapes found on earth.

A car, then a horse, a dog, a wolf, another wolf and then another ... and then her younger self sprung up as cloud wolves appeared in all dimensions, in a variety of poses, from the sky.

Blessed Una's heart raced as she watched her human-self scuttle off the wall and make her way down the stairs. She had been right to be scared. This time she could see the wolf clouds were not fuzzy shapes, they were well-defined outlines of wolves – not wolves – they were all the same wolf. Blessed Una recognised WOLF immediately! Shocked, she abruptly turned her furry head to Wolf, but he pressed on her shoulder again. She was forced to turn back to the projection, just in time to witness a detail she'd missed on the day.

Below the house, the jungle foliage parted and Wolf appeared. Unnoticed by her, he sprung up the steps from around the corner, but was stopped in his tracks by her coming down. He bared his teeth and sprung onto a higher step, which led nowhere. In slow motion, her animal-self watched her human form bow her head to avoid eye contact with Wolf. Una walked back up the stairs as his shadow crept towards her. Then she stumbled. Wolf snarled, and the human Una crouched, crossing her wrists in front of her face as she awaited the attack that never happened.

"Just to let you know, I was NOT going to hurt you! I just wanted to see you close up."

She was distracted. Her Blessed self could hear a high-pitched whistle sounding in the projection. Her human-self was cowering and, naturally, missed the whistle. She hadn't realised that Wolf had been distracted. Blessed Una scouted for Agnes and found her on the grounds, hurriedly walking through the rooms and blowing on the silent whistle. The human Una had believed that Agnes had come looking for her and the memory card, but now she knew the truth.

Agnes gave up on the whistle and ran up the steps leading to the roof.

"Una, its okay. It's just ...!"

She fixed her eyes on Wolf, then on Una's cowering body. Wolf leapt out of sight. From the shadows, an arm gripped Una, causing her to fall back and fall unconscious for ten seconds.

Agnes screamed, "Warwick, let go of her ..." while she pushed Wolf away and speedily moved in his place to catch her. Blessed Una was taken aback when Agnes bent down over Una's face and innocently uttered, "Hey, I came looking for you. Dad wondered where you were."

She watched Agnes closely. She didn't flinch as she lied about Una imagining the wolf and fainting.

Disgusted, Blessed Una shifted from under Wolf's paw.

"Was this the first time you saw me?"

"No, I was never too far away. This time, though, Meeru had already told me you had changed."

She believed him. He had answered when she had blown the whistle. So Meeru must have blown it when she had left Meeru's room that day.

"So that's why you got Sid to send me on a pointless errand to your house. I'm confused. Why would Meeru be in cahoots with the Blessed and send me a cub, then let you know I had changed? And then there's the fact that Agnes came looking for me."

"Perhaps Meeru was forced to give you the cub by her father, then evened her bad deed with a good one by letting me know you had changed."

"And Agnes's arrival?"

"Oh! She probably thought I ate you like the big bad wolf in Red Riding Hood. You did look quite delicious in the kaftan."

Laughing, he disappeared down the steps.

Una shuddered, despite her thick mass of fur. She knew he

was joking, but she didn't believe everything he'd told her.

✳✳✳

Too hungry to think and make decisions, Una was happy no one else joined them in the kitchen. It was obvious that someone had been in the kitchen to prepare their dinner. Two oversized platters with lukewarm mince and a bone had been set out on the kitchen floor. Una didn't care if it was a member of Sid's family, she was ravenous. Quickly, she walked to one of the plates and, without much ceremony, fell upon the food. She wasn't sure what to do with the bone. She keenly watched Wolf gnaw at it and tear the flesh off the bone. To Wolf's annoyance, she seemed to be stronger than him and chewed the bone clean much quicker than he did! The meat was cooked, but, in truth, her animal instincts didn't care – she knew she would have eaten it raw.

Once her stomach was sated, her sensitive smelling mechanism kicked in. Without instruction, her mouth moved as if she was tasting air. The smell was revolting.

What's that foul smell?

Humans.

They smell like ... like butter gone off!

Yeah, sometimes they smell like smelly socks and vinegar too!

Una walked out of the building to get away from the rancid smell. Finding a clear spot, she sat down, her tummy full. Soon, she found herself yawning, and almost scared herself. Her jaw kept stretching backwards until she was forced to squeeze her eyes shut. A chilling thought entered her head.

Did the fact that she was yawning mean that she felt secure, and that Una the girl was almost gone, in the space of just hours?

Worried, she suppressed the next yawn.

"Don't hold back your Blessed instincts. You will be miserable in the end if you do. I tried hard to hold back my wolf instincts, but look at me now – it's a losing battle."

Una knew what he meant. She was nearly ready to give up cooked meat.

He continued, "You have to trust me."

Trust him? Of course she didn't trust him, not one iota. She felt an undercurrent emitting from him, which made her fur hackle. She was certain that he was hiding things from her, important things. Una openly assessed him. Although he held her gaze, he quickly looked away when she blinked. She knew it was no coincidence that he happened to be around the bridge when she fell. Una was more than convinced that he was hiding a plethora of other stuff. For instance, why would Sid paint the house so it was the exact shade of his coat? Why would the family harbour him when Sid wasn't publicly keen on the tribesmen and the Blessed?

Una couldn't trust anyone. Her trust in her father, Meeru and her Grandad, had led her to her altered state. Una had no reason to trust Wolf, but then again, he had no reason to help her, did he? Was the undercurrent just natural between leopards and wolves? They were natural enemies and competed for the same prey in the wild.

"All that thinking is not getting you anywhere ... hmm? I'm helping you for an altruistic reason, and you're doing me a disservice. Look, I'm willing to show you around our shared accommodation – the jungle."

Although he had not alleviated her doubts about him, it was paramount that she learnt how to survive. At the moment, he was the only one who could teach her.

"Up you get, lazy bones. We can't stay here. The OTHERS in the house will be awake in a few hours, and you've got heaps to learn. Especially as your coat stands out in this terrain. It doesn't take long for poachers to appear."

Poachers!

Una was scared, but she couldn't show it. "I'm not sulking, but I might not be as hopeless as you think. I'm a leopard and this is meant to be my habitat. I'm sure my instincts will kick in soon enough."

"Instincts ... yeah, they will come slowly, but you aren't a leopard. You're a snow leopard and your habitat is somewhere in a lofty place in snow clad mountains, in high altitudes. I would have thought the fur and grey colouring would have been unbearable for you, especially in this heat."

Una felt stupid. What did she really know? Wolf's support and instruction was necessary. Chastised she might be, but old habits die hard. She purred and said, "*Fine, Warwick, my hero – lead the way.*"

"I wondered when you would bring that up. That isn't my name. The name is WOLF; end of subject."

Something niggled at the back of Una's mind. It was something she had heard or seen during the projection. She couldn't remember, but it was about Wolf.

"Remember, I can hear your thoughts," Wolf thought talked.

"I need to learn how to block you," Una returned waspishly.

"You can't."

"Don't bank on that."

Wolf said nothing. She looked up, but he was gone.

Chapter 40

Panic set in.

Where was Wolf?

Where was she?

Una stilled her body and hoped her sharper ears and night vision would make sense of her location in the jungle. They didn't. She was clueless.

If only she had explored the jungle and the river bed better during her summer break, instead of staying away. She had been so sure of avoiding her Blessed fate that she hadn't even explored the permissible areas. Partly because of the encounter with the Sharman, and partly because of the rule – the River Rule.

She had broken all her grandparents', and the valley's, rules, but not the River Rule. She wasn't sure why, except that the river, when it was dry, gave her the heebie jeebies. She had only walked along the restricted quadrant of the dry river bed when Avi had cajoled her there. Despite her reluctance to head to the river, it was possibly the only geographical part of the jungle she was most familiar with. She really didn't want to, but she knew she had to rely on her memory to avoid possible dangers.

With trepidation, she closed her eyes and began to scroll through her memories. She stopped when she came to the day she'd learnt of the River Rule. Her recollection was faint. It was a memory of her first escorted walk in daylight around the valley, with Avi. Una furrowed her furry brow in concentration, hoping to glean the dangers she'd encountered. Alas! It didn't help. She couldn't remember anything that would have deterred her from exploring the valley on the other side and breaking the River Rule; especially as the river was dry then. Una cursed in her head.

"Una, you've suppressed the memory to survive." Wolf yawned while he thought talked.

"*Why are you in my head again, Wolf?*" Although, she was secretly relieved to hear his voice. She sighed and continued, "*You just can't stay away, can you?*"

"Not if you are projecting your memories into the ether so all can see," Wolf drawled. "You're zapping too fast through the images, and whilst that's frustrating enough, it's even more infuriating that you're wasting your time. Just explore the valley for yourself, rather than waste these dark hours." Wolf ended his thought talk with another yawn.

She listened to Wolf's speech with some interest, but she was distracted by the wonder ahead of her. Her memories were flicking around like cards in a rolodex before her eyes, instead of in her head. She was literally whizzing through them all, from the start to the present, then back to the first day she stepped into the jungle.

"Una, stop. You're making me sick!"

She didn't. Firstly, she didn't know how to stop. Secondly, she didn't trust Wolf, and refused to believe that her memories were irrelevant. She was who she was because of them – even if her bones were now rearranged in a new configuration.

"For a cat, you seem quite dogged in your attempt to recall your useless memories. Tell you what, I'll give you something for nothing. To re-live an event, you don't need your memory – you need a concrete image of something you saw or touched on that date. An approximate date will do."

Una considered his suggestion.

"Una, don't be so stubborn! Put the brakes on your memory bashing, before you pass out!" Wolf's tone was full of doubtful concern.

"*How?*" Una thought talked just as the bile began to rise.

"Taste the air and breathe through your nostrils. Flare them!"

Many deliberate breaths later, the 'rolodex' disappeared.

"Good, you've calmed down." Wolf spoke softly. "Now, listen carefully. A memory becomes tainted and altered by future experiences. Quite simply, over time, your initial memory will change.

"You can't accurately recall the River Rule because of what the event meant to you. Your mental and emotional state at the time impacted you. Una, you didn't recall the River Rule enough to remember it. Only recalled memories stay, the rest eventually fade from your mind."

"Wolf, enough of the 'analysis' – where do I start?"

"From the glimpses I got, you were on a mission to find your dad and leave the valley. Is that right? Your memories are masked by your emotions for the boy, Avi."

Una twitched uncomfortably.

"Seriously – Avi?" Wolf asked

"Do I hear a note of jealousy?" Una retorted.

Piqued, Wolf carried on, "He could be the real reason why you don't remember the sinister nature of your precious River Rule. What can I say about a teen girl's crushes and her hormones?"

"I get the message – my mission and crush have diminished my recollection of the River Rule. Rather than ranting on, tell me how to recall an event without having to rely on my memory," Una sighed.

"It's quite simple. Think of an object or item, one that still exists, from your memories of that day."

Something she might have been wearing? A coat, perhaps? She wasn't sure if she was wearing one that day. Una rummaged through her brains for something she would have passed *en route* to the river and smiled.

The gate's grill pattern was too intricate to visualise, but the half-moon shaped latch was easy. Una chuckled. How appropriate, the stupid thing almost chopped off her hand whenever she tried to open the gate. The date? That was easy – it was the 18th of

December, two days after she'd arrived in India.

No sooner had she remembered the date, sparks began to fly. Glowing atoms emitted from her, and began to expand and bathe the surrounding area in a golden light. Her mind cleared of thought and she relaxed her eye muscles. She focused on the growing vision.

"Just so you know, you created the 'vision cast' last time, too."

"I did? I thought it was you. Didn't you bring it on by pawing my shoulder?"

"No, I focused your mind by keeping you still. Only you can project your own life events. Like you said before – the logistics are not important right now – watch and listen."

Una agreed, but Wolf wasn't finished.

"Whatever you do, don't think of a false memory. Both will stop the vision."

"Okay. Can I watch now?"

"Be my guest."

Una couldn't believe that she'd magically created the scene unfolding in front of her, herself.

Ahead, a patch of the night sky transformed into sunlit ultramarine blue. Una was standing at the gate, poised, holding the latch. Her mouth was not moving, but Una could hear something. They weren't whispers, they were thoughts.

"Switch off the thought processing first, otherwise you will be overloaded. Believe me, people think a great many mundane things. Unless required, don't bother listening to them in the first place."

"How do I do switch off the thoughts?"

"Just concentrating on your physical self in the vision. Listening to your past thoughts and reading past feelings might seem irresistible, but you'll miss relevant details if you get caught up in them. Remember, your eye takes in more than your mind chooses to register."

"Can you hear my thoughts in the vision, too?" Una asked, worried.

"No, because this is not my incident. If I'd been there and projected the same incident, then I could have."

"Why didn't I hear the thoughts when we were on the roof?"

"Because I blocked you."

Their conversation was interrupted by Una's gasp. She'd forgotten about Grandma, her speed and bulk as she tackled Una.

"GET OFF HER!" snow leopard Una screamed into the jungle night.

"Oh, do stop. She can't hear you, Una. Although, I think it's cute how you are referring to yourself as 'her'."

Una chose to ignore Wolf's jibes and focused on Avi instead. It did funny things to her to see him again after such a long time. She'd forgotten how he looked in his usual jeans, t-shirt and hoodie, with his mop of hair falling forward. His physical loss gnawed at her heart. She had heard his voice often, but now she could see him as he was ... then.

Avi was tugging on her hand, leading her out the gate, closing it behind them.

There was something not quite right. Her eyes were glazed. She looked as though she had been drugged ....

She fast forwarded to the exploration of the jungle and passed any conversations beyond those that explained the jungle and its rules. Her eyes furiously darted around to capture as much information of the jungle as she could. She only stopped when she heard Wolf's agitated and almost threatening voice, again.

You wanted to remember the River Rule, but you haven't even got there yet! Remember, Una, you are meant to find me using your instincts, and while it has been quite entertaining, I suggest you stop wasting time. YOU WILL LEARN NOTHING.

He was right. But just then, her earlier self and Avi began walking back on the path and were soon at the cowshed.

She watched Avi roughly wrap a rope around her waist, and then fling her far onto the pebbled river bed. Helplessly she gazed on as she watched herself step out beyond a boulder.

Blessed Una gasped. "How did I forget this?"

Even though she knew she was looking at a past incident, dread and fear of what was to come loosened her guard against Avi's thoughts. His mind was in turmoil.

They are here, he thought. But why are they not attacking?

Why am I doing this ... what if I can't haul her back? Damn Dev and Dada! I've got to stop this ... she doesn't have to be here ... she's an innocent who wasn't even born in India.

His final thought was said with force and indignation. If Uncle Dev wants to teach her the River Rule, then he should do it himself. Coward!

Una was relieved when his spoken voice crowded out his thoughts.

"Forget this ..." Avi exclaimed as he moved towards her.

"Walk back to me, Una, it's not safe!" he yelled – the desperation in his voice was clear and loud.

Una cupped her hand to her right ear and then giggled. "I can't hear you."

"Listen, you silly fool!" Blessed Una shouted.

"Una, stop walking backwards and don't tug the rope!" hollered Avi.

Una dawdled with the rope as he furiously looped the slack in his hand and tugged her back.

She countered him, which he had not expected, by pulling the rope back towards herself and called out, "Jesus, Avi, there's nothing here, so chill ..."

Una shuddered as cold dread slipped down her spine. The blood curdling scream came, drawing a scream from her that sounded like something short of a yowl. It was from this point that she didn't remember anything. Petrified she looked on. The vision cast had somehow become a paranomic view.

Avi was staring at a point behind her. Una stood to the side to see what he was looking at.

Her earlier self was backed against an elastic sphere-shaped object. As soon she was closer to Avi, she was jolted back by a greater force, all the way back.

A ripping noise rasped behind her human form.

The blood in Una's feline body congealed as she watched on. With her guard down again, she experienced the torturous pain, like sharp blade tips running down her human back in the vision cast.

Her human form darted forward but not far enough, making it easy for many arms to grab her and pull her back savagely. Desperate, she took baby steps forward, tilting her torso unnaturally in the same direction, her rear jutting in the opposite direction. The appendages were still gripping her, applying strength with the intention of ripping her arms out of her sockets. She couldn't move fast enough. Despite her valiant efforts, her arms passed through the tear in the bubble.

Her anguished human screams pierced the air as her body flagged. It no longer had the strength to continue moving forward. She twisted her head to look over her shoulder, wanting to face her nemesis.

Nothing was there.

"How do I fight what I can't see?" she cried. The hopelessness of the situation sank her and she no longer provided any resistance. Tears rolled down her cheeks.

Her surrender softened her aggressor's grasp. All arms, except for a single pair, let go of her. With her head flopped forward in a daze, she watched her boot heels drag noisily backwards over the smooth river stones.

Avi had anticipated their move. He waited for the tension in the rope to slacken, then began to pull her back with all his strength. He wound the lax rope around his midriff, whilst stepping backwards towards the cowshed. The cutting rope sliced back and forth between his palms and fingers as the creatures on the other side hauled her back several steps with renewed force. No longer passive, human Una took a few steps forward. Suddenly, the battle of 'tug and war' ended with her being bulleted forward into Avi, almost knocking him down. Luckily, his right foot was anchored strongly on the ground. Victorious, he caught her wrists and, holding her dazed gaze, continued to step back in slow movements.

Nervously, she looked over her shoulder again and let out a short gasp.

"What can you see Una, what is there?" Avi whispered, his breath brushing her right ear.

"Nothing," she said and buried her head into his shoulder. Avi led a zombie-like Una back to the cowshed, where she collapsed. Blessed Una could see something and understood why Wolf wanted her to skip memory lane. She had glimpsed a crowd of holographic images that alternated between human and animal bodies in the slit sphere. Centre stage was a snarling creature with very sharp teeth and tan coloured skin.

Electric shocks sparked in Blessed Una's head. Her eyes rolled back and she fell, bringing the projection to an abrupt end.

She wished she could have blacked out like her human self.

Chapter 41

Una hated to admit it, but Wolf was right about not dwelling on memories. Now she was in a worse state. She felt bad about Avi and the way she'd treated him at the end, especially as he had saved her from a worse transformation than the one she'd just experienced. She was even more unsettled by Wolf, though.

Wary, Una made up her own Valley Rule: Face your fears, or they'll come back to haunt you!

"Add one more to your list: Vision casting is to be done rarely. If done more than once daily, they can knock you out and leave you with headaches for days. Oh, and keep them short." Wolf scribbled his silent words on the evening sky. How was he able to do that?

"Come on, Una, don't get distracted! Find me ... with your natural animalistic instincts."

The words 'natural' and 'animal' instincts should have sent her further adrift, but they didn't. Her ears obediently twitched in the direction his words were coming from and, just like that, her depleted courage went up a notch. Wolf's voice would guide her. In any case, he knew where she was – so she wasn't really lost, or in any danger.

"No way, Una! I'm not your crutch. I intend to block you from my thoughts. This is our last communication until you find me. Oh, and you're right, don't have any foolish notions of friendship between us, or any other jungle creature for that matter. You need to know straight up that I'm not like Avi. I won't come to your aid if another predator thinks you're their next meal. If you were attacked and left injured, I would leave you to die, then possibly come back to eat you myself!"

Una squirmed.

"This is the jungle – not a playground. Survival of the fittest simply means that you learn to eat, or hide before you are eaten. In the jungle, there are only two choices – 'dead' or 'alive'."

Una was still in the same place Wolf had left her. She had no definite references or experiences, and was aware of her abilities, or lack of, in her new guise. When she first came to Khamosh Valley, she'd been in a better place. She understood human nature, and could adapt easily in an alien culture. Now, she knew ... nothing.

"I wish I was a newborn child or cub, who was not aware of the dangers. I would have met the world boldly, without fear." Una lamented. Unfortunately, she was a teenager, and the realisation of how much she didn't know scared her. So much for her new Valley Rule!

Una closed her eyes. Wolf was right – she had to find her own way. Forget the jungle – she had to learn about herself first – what were her limitations? Or, on the positive side, her abilities? Spurred on and curious, Una decided it was time to seek out Wolf.

Just as she was about to set off, something brushed past her in the undergrowth. The sensation of touch didn't come from a limb or the rest of her bulky body. To Una's astonishment, it had come from her whiskers. Her brain independently assimilated the touch and smell and, soon enough, a picture of a wolf formed in her mind. Surprisingly, her instincts told her to walk away! It seemed that this wolf was not Wolf. Worse, her involuntary sniffing told her that this wolf was part of a large hostile pack!

I'm on my way, Wolf!

She had no choice and launched in the direction Wolf's voice had come from. It had to be her starting point. Apprehensively, she began to run through the thicket of the jungle.

Her human eyesight might have been better in the daylight, but in the dark her larger pupils made it easier for her to detect movement. The moonlight helped her see better. Annoyingly, and most inconveniently, she was honing onto useless creatures a little too well. Ugh! She hated the flutter of moth's wings as a human, and that hadn't changed now she could see and hear them better. Unfortunately, her narrower vision, when looking at smaller creatures, seemed to completely absorb her, leaving her oblivious to everything else, which wasn't helpful. She flung her head from side to side, to re-focus. Looking back, her peripheral vision kicked in and she could make out the pack of wolves, stealthily making their way towards her.

"It's not all that bad being a Blessed, is it Una?"

"I thought you were not talking to me, Wolf."

"Yeah, but I thought it only sporting to let you know that I'm not where you're heading."

That was true – his voice was coming from the opposite direction!

How do you do that, she wondered.

Easily! The location of his voice changed again.

Chapter 42

So, he was throwing his voice around to confuse her sense of direction?

I can play games too … Una thought, then stopped when she remembered the teeth and tan coat in the vision cast.

Why did she trust someone at face-value, someone who had plainly watched her since her arrival in the valley? According to the last 'vision cast', he could have hurt her, too.

Slowly, it dawned on Una that Wolf was already dictating her existence in the jungle, and she was letting him. When would she learn to stop succumbing to the choices and plans others made? She felt sick when she thought of how her Mum, Dad and grandparents had drastically impacted her.

She gave herself a 'pep talk':

"I AM IN CHARGE! NO ONE ELSE IS TO BE TRUSTED."

With just those two mantras in her head, she decided to begin the evening's exercise.

"If I'm going to learn my way around the jungle, then I'm going to do it on my terms. I'm certainly not looking for you, Wolf! If I'm going to look for anything, it is a way out!" she thought as she ran ahead.

"Forgetting something, aren't you? I can hear you, and work out where you are. I can outsmart you." Wolf snarled in her head.

Una chose to ignore him. She imagined her human-self smiling, and bet Wolf was livid with himself – he had just given her the chance to get away.

"I underestimated you, my dear. It won't happen again."

She had to cloak her thoughts – but how? She remembered singing sugary 'One Direction' songs when she was with her friends and wanted to mask the painful thoughts after her mother had died. If it could fool them, then there was hope it would fool Wolf, too.

She began to sing the first song that popped in her head – a Florence and the Machine song.

... How big, how blue, how beautiful ...

"How ridiculous you are, Una. I will know what direction you're heading based on the strength of your singing."

She hadn't learnt how to project her voice in different directions yet, but he had, once again, accidentally given her a solution. By whispering the song in her thoughts, then, at other times, singing out loud, she could reduce his advantage over her, and frustrate him. Hopefully, she would be able to mis-direct him with her singing.

She sang the chorus with conviction.

Before he worked out her strategy, she had to move quickly and choose a direction. It was paramount that she left the undergrowth and trees.

"I'm disappointed that you don't trust me. I have only been kind and patient with you. In fact, I will even apologise for expecting too much from you on your first day. Why don't we call an end to tonight's shenanigans?" Wolf spoke in a polite, but curt manner.

She hadn't managed to block him out completely.

She wouldn't find her way without thinking ... she concentrated harder on the singing and made sure she didn't dwell on her thoughts, removing them almost as soon as they popped up in her head.

The rock formations in the forbidden area would give her the added advantage of higher ground. It would also give her a better perspective of where she was in relation to Wolf. Perhaps her thought waves would not overlap with his if he stayed at ground level, due to the height difference. It was worth a try.

The only problem was that the rocks were easier to get to from the river bed, where Avi had taken her. She was still terrified of going there, especially now that she remembered why. Yet, it was her only chance to throw Wolf off. He wouldn't be expecting her to go there.

She continued singing the verses.

Using her fresh recollection from the first 'vision cast', she summoned the panoramic jungle view and easily mapped the river from the position of the house. With her orientation skills, she knew exactly where she was going. Wolf was wrong to think all memories were useless.

She stealthily moved away from the protection of the trees and made her way to the low growing shrubs. Using her common sense and her new sense of smell, she was soon at the wild flowered shrubs edging the river. Taking in a sharp breath, she ran and leapt over small boulders in the flowing river, until she stood upon one of the significant four boulders she'd identified earlier from the visual casting. She hesitantly looked at her paws on the rock and found some sort of marking under one of them. She removed her right front paw. There was another paw print similar to hers.

"Keep looking. I told you to keep the pack close to her. You were too close earlier. She knew you were there, and now you can't keep up with her ..." Wolf fumed, interrupting her investigations. He was thought talking, unshielded, with a pack ... the pack of wolves she had brushed against!

"What do you mean that she's not in the trees or the undergrowth, her singing suggests she's there!"

Una felt light and happily dizzy. Her scam seemed to be working.

"*We lost her because of her pace,*" one of the wolves pathetically whined.

Una smiled at that. Yes, a snow leopard could definitely

outpace a wolf or two. Oh God! It was so good to have the upper hand, even if for a short while.

"Use the renegade Blesseds and look everywhere," Wolf ordered in a clipped voice, no longer thought talking. Instead, he projected his voice so it travelled forcefully past the inner hairs of her ears.

"Damn! Find her before the Sharman finds her and learns of my folly," Wolf voiced in disgust.

"Una, if you are listening, you can't make it out of here. Make it easier for yourself before you unnecessarily exhaust your new body. If you don't, I promise it won't be pleasant when my cohort finds you."

Una shivered, then vigorously shook her body.

They're words, just words to unravel me. I mustn't pay attention, she thought, still shielding her thoughts with song.

Una ramped up the song and trained her mind and ears to access Wolf's thoughts or speech. Wolf's rattled demeanour brought a sense of calm to Una. The power had shifted from him to her. His shield was down, exposing his vulnerability, motives and the scale of potential danger she was in.

Invigorated, she bound forward, still singing the same song, and leapt over the larger boulders in the river. Soon she was at the precipice that shouldered the bridge.

After a lingering gaze at the spot her human form had met its end, she lifted her tail and propelled herself nimbly up the cliffs. She stopped when she reached a thin, rock ledge supporting a pine tree with an overhanging branch. The tree was precariously rooted in a large crevice between the rocks. Its height gave her new hope and the chance to rest.

Much of the night had been spent, yet there was no sign of the cohort. Even if they were behind her, they would be tired. But best of all, she didn't think they could follow her up a tree with no low hanging branches. Eyeing the pine briefly, in a gutsy move, and without a second thought, she removed all stability from under her feet by leaping up the trunk. She spread her powerful, stout front limbs wide on either side of her, then used her hind legs to push up in short bursts. Her tail both balanced and thrust her up the narrow girth of the trunk. Without much effort, she was at the fork where the tree spread its tempting branch across the ledge. Her tail carefully steered her as she attempted to walk on the wider part of the branch, before it tapered off into spiky leaves.

A pine-scented breeze ruffled her fur and tickled her flared nostrils, masking her own scent. She breathed a lung full of the air and momentarily shut her eyes, slowing her heartbeat to a calm pulse. Thrilled, she lowered herself onto the branch and settled in the crook between the trunk and the branch, letting her tail hang above the sheer drop.

Cradled in the tree, she peered out at the long shadows shaped by the moonlight over the valley below. Distant lights on the adjacent mountain twinkled as before. Although, this was the first time she'd witnessed the illuminated blanket of the urban part of the valley, where her school was based.

Something shifted in her. All at once, her awareness expanded beyond her body. She was at one with everything: the moonlight, the moon and even the rugged barren twig. She was truly alive. Eventually, her concentration lapsed. Slowly, her awareness retreated to the confines of her body. Her connection to all things, alive or otherwise, remained. A sigh left her mouth. Even if her transformation was irreversible, she now knew she could cope. Perhaps, in time, she would accept her situation. Strangely, she felt completely in tune and more restful in the jungle than she did anywhere else in the world. She truly belonged here. Saying that, her furry body was like a radiator in the balmy heat. Even if Wolf hadn't informed her about her natural habitat, she would have realised the need for a cooler environment. Her mission to leave the valley was back on. Nightfall was the best time to move on and climb higher.

Spurred on, she gave the valley a last look. It was a mistake. The act of peering down burst her bubble of lightness, and doubts flooded her mind. Her grandparents' compound, where she had been trapped during her holidays, was miniscule, yet she was only free from it while she was in this new guise. In the jungle, she knew Wolf would eventually track her. Worse still, if she wasn't human, would her life hover at the lower rung of existence, trapped high in the mountains, just striving to survive extinction and hunger?

The most important question came to her last – what would happen to her Dad if she didn't return to him?

Chapter 43

"Why is she roaming in higher grounds, when her food is down here?"

A second voice spoke, "She mentioned her Dad, but he's not there, he's ..."

"Idiots! You've given yourselves away!" Wolf's clear voice came from just below her branch.

Una leaned over slightly. Her long gaze was met by many pairs of eyes reflecting the moonlight.

"How did you? ... I thought I blocked you?" Una asked, concerned now.

Shrieks of laughter let rip in the air. Three wolves closed in. A growing crowd of animals, of different species, assembled behind them.

One of the wolves said, "You did, when you were singing. That was clever, and it confused us, especially when you changed the pitch."

Another wolf nodded in agreement. "We all had to coordinate ourselves to track you beyond the river. Wolf told us you would never go near the river. It didn't cross our minds that you'd climb the rocks above the river when the singing tapered off."

The first one spoke again, "Wolf was furious. The singing had stopped and we thought you were out of range. But luckily, after wasting a couple of hours, we heard despondent thoughts booming down to us."

Una realised her folly. The euphoria of climbing up to the ledge, and then the tree, filled her mind and she had stopped singing.

"You couldn't have been more subtle if you had left neon lights on, as they do in Las Vegas!" said the second wolf.

"Sorry, I'll try better next time," she said, insincerely. Too right, she would! The Forced Blesseds gave too much away. Her singing had confused them, but there had been a moment when she was able to block them out completely, and that was when she was ... confident. She'd learnt the secret. Height and distance helped, but resolute confidence formed an impenetrable wall. It was only when Wolf wasn't confident about finding her that she began to hear him.

Laughter burst out in the crowd; someone had said something about her. The crowd was distracted, but Una knew Wolf was listening to her thoughts. Before she drew the iron curtains in her mind, she couldn't help but taunt him a little.

"They have no idea that they have just taught me something."

Anyone standing close to Wolf would have seen him shudder. Luckily for him, no one had picked up on his moment of weakness. Una smiled. In less than fifteen hours, she had him riled. She'd also demonstrated that she could outsmart him when she put her mind to it.

"Enough! Everyone quieten down. The OTHERS will pick on your cackle," Wolf commanded. The jungle went eerily quiet.

"Aren't you sweet, you want my grandparents and Major to sleep well," Una sighed.

"Enough of your sassiness. Come down, now!" he ordered loudly.

If it had just been Wolf, she might have obeyed, but an organised crowd had assembled. The crowd looked hungry the way they had in her 'visual cast', when they wanted to rip her arms off. She wasn't going down to find out if they would succeed in ripping her to pieces this time.

"I'm fine here, Wolf."

"'Una, what do you see beyond the peaks of the mountains to your right?" Wolf said smugly.

"Lights, I imagine," Una retorted, refusing to look.

"No, Una, look! Don't guess," Wolf said gently.

The softness in his voice unnerved her. She raised her gaze to the spot he suggested and noticed the sky between the peaks was a few shades lighter than the rest of the sky.

"Sunrise will arrive in a few hours," explained Wolf.

"So?" Una responded, puzzled.

"When daylight hits, you're not camouflaged in this landscape. You would have been if you were an ordinary leopard, but your white fur makes you a target. In the morning, you can easily be hunted by the OTHERS, or by other predators."

"How will the OTHERS know?"

Wolf just shrugged his shoulders.

Una knew she had little choice. She knew she wouldn't last on her own in daylight. She didn't even know how to kill to eat ...

Wolf's desperate search for her suggested he wasn't likely to kill her yet. Besides, he'd had a good opportunity to do that after she had first transformed. Meat was scarce in a jungle. He most definitely wouldn't feed her, only to kill her for sport later.

"Exactly," Wolf agreed with her thoughts.

Watching the light, Una climbed down from the tree and onto the ledge. Once there, she scanned the crowd below and, after a measured moment, leapt into their midst, extracting a collective gasp from them.

Whilst in the air, she made a decision, she would start afresh. This was a new beginning and she was not going to allow fear into her head. She had absolutely nothing to lose but her life – a life which, as an animal, could be over in sixteen years. With that thought in mind, she forcefully hit the ground, just inches from Wolf's snout. Exhilarated, she bunched her facial muscles and readied her body to pounce and defend. She pulled her ears back, causing her face to contour into deep lines of black and white fur, and made her kohl-outlined green-grey eyes menacing.

For good measure, she scrunched her nozzle with its protruding, straight, long whiskers and bared her canine teeth. Hissing under her breath, she stayed still in her crouching poise as the various forms of Forced Blesseds encircled her with murderous eyes and tongues hanging out.

Wolf moved in closer and whispered, "Good show, but don't forget, a REAL snow leopard would leave its kill if a wolf turned up." Una drew back in surprise. Pleased, Wolf continued, "I just thought I would let you know." Then, in a clear voice, he addressed the mob, "I told you she was plucky. Look how she stands focused, even though she is green, having recently changed. I say we welcome the new Forced Blessed in our usual way."

The jungle resounded with a cacophony of roars, hisses and howls.

Wolf did not join in. Instead, he openly observed the way she ignored the others and remained focused on him. She neither flinched nor changed her stance, which amused and annoyed him in equal measures. He waited for the cheering to die down before he spoke. "We are the Forced Blesseds, and now, you are one, too. The tribe Blesseds are just called Blesseds. The humans on the other side, who are not altered, are called the OTHERS. And then, of course, there are the animals – the usual predators and prey. All in my cohort were human, but we are the Forced Blesseds as none of us chose to be Blessed. We were sold out by the OTHERS. You are welcome here, but if you cross us, you will be ostracised. It won't be long before you are easy prey to the animal predators or the OTHERS. Staying with us means you are part of our core. We work together to fulfil our one purpose."

Una knew she wasn't going to like the answer, but she had to ask, "And what is that?"

Instead of Wolf, the rest of the Forced Blesseds answered in unison.

"To rule the jungle."

Wolf cocked his head even closer to her and muttered in her

ear, "Or change the ones we need into Forced Blesseds – if we are lacking skills."

All cards were on the table. Wolf had just told her he was instrumental in her transformation, and for some reason, he needed her. No wonder he was present when she was pushed off the bridge. She had been right not to trust him.

There was a movement amongst the ranks in the crowd to her left. A chant of "Kill, Kill, Kill ..." filled the silence.

Wolf shouted, "Halt the chants!"

In the abrupt silence, Wolf spoke clearly so the crowd could hear every word he said to Una. "I think I forgot to mention that, for us to allow you to join our little band, we have to trust you," he paused, "and to trust you, and for you to truly be accepted in our core, you must kill the OTHER who made you a Blessed. And that is ..."

Una cried out, "But that was you!"

Wolf spoke close to her ear again, "Yes, but you see, for you, the granddaughter of one of the two most hated OTHERS, your grandfather and Major, they all will make an exception. You must kill the stooge instead."

Wolf was pleased. He had finally got the expected reaction from Una.

The chants of 'kill' began again and the circle became an organised horse shoe. They closed ranks and flanked her, driving her forward. She only just managed to negotiate the stones under the shallow water of the river bed, using her sharp claws. Incensed, she tried to swipe at the Forced Blesseds behind with her heavy tail, but she didn't have enough space to swing it.

Tired of being shunted, she let her limbs relax and fell to the ground where the river had receded. There still wasn't enough space around her. Una barred her incisors and lunged for the neck of one of the wolves. She missed. The rest of the pack made ready to ambush her.

"Halt! What did you expect? Give her some room!" hollered Wolf.

Quickly, she was given a wide berth. Wolf blocked her path to the four rocks that outlined the rectangular area, beyond which, humans, especially teenagers, did not venture. Once all were assembled in a semi-circle around her, stamping and splashing of feet began in time with the drone of the chant, "Kill, kill ..." Finally, two of the wolves ran across the watery quadrant and into the darkness behind the cowshed. She heard screams, and then the two wolves reappeared. One was dragging a man by his leg. The poor man had his hands tied with rope, but he tried to protect his face and neck. Una wondered whether the rope was the same one Avi had used to save her months ago. The wolf dropped the man in a heap at the edge of the quadrant and joined his companion to walk towards her. As they neared, they switched from wolves to tattooed teenage boys.

Wolf strolled into the quadrant and dramatically changed into a human form – the young man from the photographs in the master bedroom on Sid Rao's wall.

He was Tawny, the twenty-year-old who had commanded the urban teenagers when the tribesmen came to her Grandad's house, but, most sinister of all, he was the taxi driver who'd driven her to her Grandfather's house. The same one who'd reluctantly helped her climb the gate. She wasn't sure, but he might have posed as the policeman, too. She vaguely recalled meeting a policeman, but wasn't sure.

Warwick, aka Wolf, picked up the human's arm and dragged him to Una. All the time, he kept his tawny eyes transfixed on hers, until he threw the unfortunate scapegoat at Una's feet. He stepped out of the rectangle, returned to his wolf guise and said, *"I'm Wolf, Warwick the boy is gone, and don't forget it. So, no more tagging me with human names."*

Una snapped her attention away from Wolf and looked down.

Her insides turned over when the bloodied, upturned face pleaded with his eyes.

"Gopan!" she exclaimed.

"Don't be distracted from your task by naming him, Una. He's just an OTHER," said Wolf.

Una, in a quiet controlled voice, said, "Gopan, why have they brought you to me?"

"Stop talking, Una! Deal with the person who altered your destiny, or you will be finished today," warned Wolf.

"I can't take a human life under any circumstances. I have no intention of taking one innocent life to save my own. We both know you are the reason I am a Forced Blessed – not him."

That was the last straw for Wolf.

"It's such a shame to lose a snow leopard from the pack. However, if you can't be controlled, then you are of no use to us."

Someone pushed her closer to Gopan.

Gopan panicked and began to plead loudly in Hindi.

Una's head was close to his mouth.

Gopan squealed and moved backwards. "Please ... please ... forgive me, don't hurt me, I had no choice in either case."

Shocked that he was terrified of her, Una stood tall, turned around and began to move away from Gopan. Several of the Forced Blesseds blocked her path and threatened to kill her.

"Let her walk," barked Wolf. Then, to her, he tersely thought talked.

"You could have been my second-in-command. However, it seems you act irrationally, with too much emotion, and you are unable to follow commands and rules – making you most undesirable. You are no use to me, or even to yourself."

Una stopped and looked over at Wolf. "Well, let's hope this is one of your last speeches. You sound like my Dad. He likes to lay the rules out to no avail. You are a control freak, just like him."

"I agree – I'm finding that, too."

"Wait! What do you mean?"

"Ask the guy you just reprieved. Didn't you hear what he said?"

Una rushed back to Gopan.

She stood over him and whispered close to his ear in Hindi, "Gopan, where is my father?"

Gopan spurted blood as he whispered, "He ... he ... he came to Meeru's wedding ... said he informed you in a letter ... me and Gagan bhai took him. Wolf made us ... he made us take him."

Stunned, Una asked in a quiet and controlled voice, "What did you do?"

"I ... brought him here," Gopan answered as his body shook vigorously.

"... To this place?"

"Yes ..."

"Were the Forced Blessed present here that day, too?"

He nodded.

"Did you watch?"

"Yes – no – I don't know!" Gopan's eyes protruded in fear.

"Were they ... hungry?"

"... save me, Una, madam!"

Una side-stepped Gopan. Wolf had had enough. He raised his paw for the Forced Blesseds to finish Una and Gopan. Before they could react, Una rotated her body and ran past him like the wind, whipping his face with her tail. She soared high as she leapt to a boulder and then somersaulted and landed on the ground, facing forward. In just a few quick paces, she was upon Gopan's neck. With one swift bite, she took his life. Blood trickling between her teeth and fur, she raised her head, walked steadily to Wolf and spat a chunk of flesh out.

A hush fell upon the river bank.

Chapter 44

From a distance, he knew it was a human body. He couldn't tell who it was and wished for a better view, rather than the godforsaken acute sense of smell. The flesh ranked, even though it was lying at a distance. Yet, the stench didn't stop the rumbles in his stomach.

"While there isn't a shortage of food, it's a shame you're human and not a goat or something. I could have really done with some carrion meat today," Avi growled.

"Shame you missed the initiation party – the gift, if you want it, is courtesy of your true love!"

True love?

"Who are you?"

"Wolf, or Tawny – the knife thrower, the killer of your Ma, and now the kidnapper of your girl."

Avi swung his head around madly, but couldn't see anything.

"Thought that would get your attention. You tried so hard, Avi, to keep her away. It is Avi, isn't it?"

"Where are you, coward?" Avi bellowed.

"You don't deny it, so it must be you, Avi." Wolf sniggered, and continued. "I wondered what had become of you. I only found out today, when I saw a sloth bear's paw retrieve a mango with the word 'No' on it. There is only one bear in the jungle, the one that chased me, and now I know why. You have done well to keep low."

After a pause, Wolf spoke again.

"I feel really bad because I have your girl, and she doesn't even know you exist!"

Avi began to make his way to the human body.

"Oh, don't worry – it isn't her. She's fine."

"Wolf, what did Una and I ever do to you?"

"Nothing ... you just helped me accomplish phase one of my mission."

"Phase one?"

"To change the fate of all three: the girl, the boy and the leader – relatives of the hated Major and Dev."

Avi stalled. "Is there a phase two?"

Wolf's laughter faded into the distance.

Avi shuddered. *If this had just been phase one then what lay ahead for the two of them?*

Chapter 45

Jungle howls and roars in the morning?

A cold shiver ran down Dev's back as he waited on the veranda, staring at the gate, hoping the servant Johnnie Walker would return soon with some milk from the cow herder's shed. His wife was waiting on the milk to finish making the tea for the visiting British Embassy representative and local policemen. He was under suspicion because his two 'near and dear' British relatives were listed as 'Missing'.

To be continued in Broken Rule coming in 2018.

Printed in Poland
by Amazon Fulfillment
Poland Sp. z o.o., Wrocław